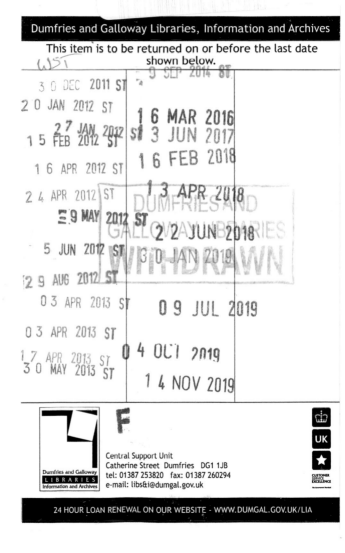

J. A. Jance is a top-ten New York Times bestselling author. Born in South Dakota and brought up in Bisbee, Arizona, Jance lives with her husband in Seattle, Washington, and Tucson, Arizona. Visit www.jajance.com

ALSO BY J. A. JANCE

Trial By Fire
Cruel Intent
Hand of Evil
Web of Evil

J.A. JANCE
FATAL ERROR

SIMON &
SCHUSTER

London · New York · Sydney · Toronto

A CBS COMPANY

First published in the USA by Touchstone, 2011
A division of Simon & Schuster, Inc.
First published in Great Britain by Simon & Schuster UK Ltd, 2011
A CBS Company

1 3 5 7 9 10 8 6 4 2

Simon & Schuster UK Ltd
1st Floor
222 Gray's Inn Road
London
WC1X 8HB

Simon & Schuster Australia
Sydney

www.simonandschuster.co.uk

A CIP catalogue record for this book is available from the British Library

ISBN 978-1-84739-406-4

Printed and bound in Great Britain by CPI Cox&Wyman Ltd, Reading, Berkshire

For Pat S.

FATAL ERROR

1

G et on the ground," Ali Reynolds ordered. "On the ground now!"

"Make me," Jose Reyes said, glaring back at her with a withering sneer. "Try and make me, bitch."

Jose Reyes was a stocky Hispanic guy in his early thirties, tough as nails, with the muscle tone of a serious weight lifter. A guy with attitude, one who could toss out schoolyard taunts and make them sound deadly.

"I gave you an order."

"And I told you to go to hell."

Ali moved in then, grabbing his arm and setting up for the hip toss. Only it didn't work the way it was supposed to. Jose spun out of the way and suddenly Ali was the one flying through the air. She landed hard on the gym mat and with him right on top of her. The blow knocked the wind out of her and left her seeing stars. By the time Ali got her breath back, she was face down on the floor, with her wrists at her back, imprisoned in her own handcuffs. Lying there under Jose's full weight, she felt a rage of impotent fury flood through her. She was still there, helpless but furious, when a pair of highly polished shoes appeared in her line of vision.

"My, my, little lady," Sergeant Bill Pettit said. "I don't believe that's the way takedowns are supposed to work. He's the one who's supposed to be wearing *your* handcuffs."

Ali Reynolds was in week four of a six-week-long course at the Arizona Police Academy. Of all the instructors there, Pettit was her hands-down least favorite. The class had started out on the fourth of August with an enrollment of one hundred seven recruits, five of whom had been women. Now they were down to a total of seventy-nine. Two of the original females had dropped out.

"Uncuff her," Pettit told Jose. "Good job."

The restraints came off. Jose tossed them to her, then he grabbed Ali by the elbow and helped her up.

"No hard feelings, Oma," he said with a sly Cheshire grin that said he was lying. He had done it with malice and had hit her far harder than necessary, to prove a point and because he could.

To begin with, Ali's fellow classmates had called her "Oma" behind her back. Originally the word came from one of the other young recruits, a blond-haired, ruddy-faced guy whose family hailed from South Africa. In Afrikaans *oma* evidently meant something like "old woman" or maybe even "grandma." There it probably had an air of respect about it. Here in the academy, however, most of Ali's classmates were fifteen to twenty years younger than she was. In context, the word was intended as an insult, meant to keep Ali in her place. To her knowledge, this was the first time she had been called that in front of one of the instructors.

"That's why female officers end up having to resort to weapons so often," Pettit said. "They don't know how to use their bodies properly. By the way, what's that he called you?"

Ali's face flushed. "Old Lady," she answered.

"What?"

"Old Lady, sir!" she corrected.

"That's better. Now get your butt over to first aid. You should probably have a Band-Aid on that cut over your eye. And have them give you an ice pack. Looks to me like you're gonna have yourself a real shiner."

It was a long walk through the sweaty, overheated gym. The Phoenix metropolitan area was roasting in triple-digit heat. Although the gym's AC was running at full strength, it couldn't do more than thirty degrees below the outside temp of 116.

Ali's classmates stopped what they were doing and stood on their own mats to watch her walk of shame. Some of them were sympathetic, but more shared Jose's opinion that no self-respecting fortysomething female had any business being there, and they wanted her to quit. Blood dribbled down the side of her cheek and onto the neck of her T-shirt. She made no effort to wipe it away. If her classmates were looking for blood, she'd give it to them.

She stepped out of the gym into glaring sunshine and brutal afternoon heat. The mountains in the distance were obscured by a haze of earth-brown smog. August was supposed to be the rainy season with monsoon rains drenching the thirsty Sonoran Desert, but so far the much-needed rains were absent although the rising humidity was not.

By the time Ali arrived at the administration office, she had made herself a promise: sometime in the next two weeks, Jose Reyes was looking at a takedown of his own.

BettyJo Hamilton, the academy's office manager, was also in charge of first aid. "Oh, my," she said, peering at Ali over a pair of horn-rimmed spectacles. "What do we have here?"

"Just a little bump," Ali said.

After determining that no stitches were required, BettyJo applied a butterfly Band-Aid to the cut and then brought out an ice pack. "If I were you," she said, "I'd take it pretty easy for the rest of the afternoon. Let me know if you feel faint or experience any nausea."

Ali was glad to comply. She wasn't used to losing, and she didn't need to go back to the gym to revisit her ignominious defeat. Instead, she returned to the dorm, shut herself in her room, and lay down on the bed, with the ice pack over her eye.

Most of the academy attendees from the Phoenix area made the nightly trip home. The out-of-towners, recruits who lived too far away for a daily commute, made use of the dorm facilities. The three remaining women had rooms to themselves. Ali was especially grateful for that now. She needed some privacy to lick her wounds.

Months earlier Ali had been serving as an interim media relations consultant for the Yavapai County Sheriff's Department when Sheriff Gordon Maxwell had broached the idea of sending her to the academy. Once a well-known TV news anchor in L.A., Ali had returned to her hometown of Sedona, Arizona, after both her career and marriage came to sudden ends. Paul Grayson, Ali's philandering, late, and very much unlamented second husband, had been murdered the day before their divorce would have been final. As a divorcée, Ali would have been in somewhat straitened financial circumstances. As Paul's widow, however, and through no fault of her own, she was now an extremely wealthy former anchor and aspiring cop.

After her life-changing pair of crises, Ali had spent a year or two back in her hometown, getting used to the idea of being on her own. Her parents, Bob and Edie Larson, owners of the Sugarloaf Café, lived there in Sedona, as did Ali's son, Christopher, and his fairly new and now newly pregnant bride, Athena, both of whom taught at Sedona High School.

For a while it was okay to be Bob and Edie's daughter and Chris's mom, but Ali was used to working, used to being busy. Finding herself bored to distraction, she took on the project of purchasing and remodeling the house on Manzanita Hills Road, which she shared with Leland Brooks. Mr. Brooks was her aging but entirely capable personal assistant or, as she liked to call him, her majordomo, since both he and the word seemed to hail from a more gracious, bygone era. Ali had had a boyfriend, but at her age the word *boyfriend* rankled. She liked to think of B. Simpson as her "lover." When speaking to others, she referred to him as her "significant other."

Ali was lying on the bed, wondering what B. would think about her showing up for Labor Day weekend with a shiner, when her cell phone rang. She checked the caller ID.

"Hi, Mom," Ali said to her mother, Edie Larson. "What's up?"

"One of your friends dropped by the Sugarloaf this afternoon, looking for you."

"Really," Ali said. "Who was it?"

"Dad said her name was Brenda Riley. She used to work with you in L.A."

"Not exactly worked with," Ali replied. "She was the anchor for a sister station in Sacramento when I was in L.A. So we were acquaintances and colleagues rather than friends. She got booted off the air about the same time I did for approximately the same reason. They thought she was too old. I haven't heard from her in years. What did she want?"

"She told Dad that she really needed to see you—that it was urgent. You know your father. He's such a softie, he falls for every sob story on the planet."

"What kind of sob story?"

"Just that she needed to see you—that she was looking for help. From what he said, I wouldn't be surprised if she was really looking for money."

Ali had found that old acquaintances did have a way of doing that, of showing up on her doorstep and asking for a loan or an outright handout. They seemed to think that since she had money and they didn't, she was obligated to give them some of hers.

"Did Dad give her my number?"

"I chewed him out for it, but yes, he did. Worse than that, he also told her where you were and what you were doing. He said she seemed shocked that you were in the process of becoming a police officer."

Ali ran a finger over her rapidly swelling eye. "I'm shocked by that myself sometimes," she said with a laugh.

"Anyway," Edie Larson continued. "From what he said, she may very well be on her way down to Phoenix to see you right now."

Ali suppressed a groan. Brenda Riley was pretty much the last person she needed to see right now—especially with a cut on her eyebrow and with a black eye coming on. Brenda had been one of those irksome women who never went anywhere without being perfectly put together—hair, makeup, and clothing. She had been almost as tall as Ali—five ten or so—but as far as Ali was concerned, Brenda was better-looking in every way.

"Thanks for the heads-up, Mom," Ali said. "Tell Dad not to worry about it. Whatever Brenda wants, I'm sure I can handle it."

"Are you coming home for the weekend?" Edie asked.

Ali knew that B. Simpson was flying in from his most recent business trip and was due to arrive at Sky Harbor late the next morning. Ali had been looking forward to going home for the long Labor Day weekend and escaping the August heat in the Valley of the Sun. There would be socializing and barbecues galore, but knowing she'd be showing up with a black eye made Ali think twice.

Small towns were small towns, and Sedona was no exception. If Ali appeared in public with B. Simpson and a black eye, tongues were bound to wag. She could try explaining that her injury was a result of her police academy training, but she doubted anyone would listen. In fact, the more she protested, the more they would talk behind her back.

"I'm still planning on being home," Ali said, finally, "but I've got a whole lot of studying to do this weekend. I may have to bail on the barbecue end of things."

"I hope you don't dodge out on everything," Edie said. "Chris and Athena would be so disappointed. I know they're planning on having everyone over on Sunday afternoon."

"We'll see," Ali said.

The call waiting signal buzzed in Ali's ear. The number was one she recognized as having a Sacramento area code.

"Gotta go now, Mom," Ali said. "I have another call."

"Ali?" a woman said when Ali switched over. "Is that you?"

"Yes, Brenda," Ali said. She might not have recognized the voice without the benefit of her mother's advance warning. "How are you doing? My parents said you might call. Where are you?"

"I'm in a place called Black Canyon City, although it doesn't look like much of a city to me."

"Coming from California, it wouldn't."

"Could we get together for a while tonight? Is there someplace where we could meet near where you are, like a bar or something?"

"There's a joint called the Rimrock Inn," Ali said. "It's off Grand Avenue here in Peoria. If you're on the 101, exit to the right and turn right. That's only a couple of miles from here. I've heard some of the guys here at the academy talking about it. According to them, the Rimrock has great burgers."

Ali had also heard that the Rimrock was something of a dive—cheap and relatively dingy. Maybe in the dim light Ali's bruised and swollen eye wouldn't show up quite so much.

"How long will it take me to get there?" Brenda asked.

"Probably forty-five minutes." Ali glanced at her watch. "It's coming up on rush hour. So maybe a little longer than that."

"Okay," Brenda said. "See you there."

Ali got off the bed, stripped off her bloodied T-shirt and shorts and made her way into the bathroom. She was grateful she didn't have to share the bath with anyone else. The half-inch cut over her eye was no longer bleeding, so she peeled off the Band-Aid before she got in the shower. After blow-drying her hair, she used makeup to repair as much of the damage as possible. It wasn't great, but it was better than nothing. By the time she left the dorm, classes were getting out for the day. She managed to dodge her returning classmates as she headed for her car.

She had no intention of running into Jose Reyes and giving him a chance to rub her nose in it.

2

Peoria, Arizona

It was a little more than an hour later when Ali pulled into the lot at the Rimrock Inn. She'd expected to arrive before Brenda, but what looked like Brenda's signature vehicle, a BMW with California plates, was parked just to the right of the front door.

Ali remembered that Brenda had always taken great pride in her vehicles. This one was shabby and more than a little the worse for wear. For one thing, it was covered with grime and a film of reddish road dust. The rear bumper and trunk were both dented in as though they'd made contact with something substantial, like a bollard. There were smaller dents in the side panels too, and some of the chrome trim had disappeared. The window in the rear driver's side door was missing, and the empty space had been covered over with a combination of clear plastic and duct tape.

As Ali walked past the car, she glanced inside. The Beamer looked lived in. It was full of trash—empty food containers, soda cans, and more than a few empty booze bottles as well. None of this fit with the Brenda Riley Ali knew.

Things went downhill from there. Ali stepped inside and looked around. It was late afternoon, so there were plenty of men lounging around the long bar—plenty of men and only one woman. At first Ali didn't believe it was Brenda. Even in the tavern's dim lights it was possible to see that Brenda's trademark long, straight blond locks were gone. The hair was still there, but it stood out around her head like a fright wig. She had evidently tried a do-it-yourself dye job/permanent kit, and it hadn't worked out very well. Most of her hair was a very convincing shade of pink, fluffed atop an inch of brown roots. Cotton candy immediately came to mind.

As Ali walked up to the bar, Brenda was chatting with the guy next to her, joking and laughing. Only when Ali was a few steps away did she see the set of three shot glasses sitting in front of Brenda. There was also a plate of lime sections and a salt shaker, so Brenda Riley was doing shots of tequila at four thirty in the afternoon.

"Hello, Brenda," Ali said. "How's it going?"

Brenda spun around and studied her. "Ali?" she asked. "You look like hell. What did you do to your eye?"

"Ran into a door," Ali said.

As if Brenda had any room to talk. Ali could have asked her the same question, because Brenda Riley really did look like hell. The perky smile that had greeted Sacramento viewers for more than a decade was long gone. Brenda looked haggard and careworn. She wore no makeup of any kind. None. There were dark circles under her red-rimmed eyes. She appeared to be years older than Ali knew her to be. Her clothing was grimy and wrinkled and looked as though it had been slept in. And she had put on weight—forty pounds at least, more weight than even her relatively tall frame could handle.

The guy on the stool next to Brenda's moved away, clearing a place for Ali to sit. The bartender came forward. "What can I get you?" he asked.

"Do you have any coffee?" Ali asked.

Making a face, Brenda salted the side of her fist, licked off the salt, downed one of the shots of tequila, and then sucked on a lime wedge as she pushed the shot glass back across the bar. There wasn't anything about this that was genteel cocktail-hour-type sipping, and Ali recognized it for what it was—serious drinking.

The bartender nodded in Ali's direction. "Give me a few minutes," he said. "I'll make a new pot."

"And maybe a menu," Ali said. "We should probably have something to eat."

The bartender picked up the empty shot glass. "Got it," he said. "Coming right up."

Brenda gave Ali a sly, squint-eyed look. "Are you really a cop?" she asked.

"Not yet," Ali said. "But I'm going to be. What about you? My dad said something about your needing my help."

Brenda nodded. "I do need your help," she said, slurring her words ever so slightly. "It's a long story, a very, very long story. I was engaged to a guy named Richard, Richard Lattimer. He dumped me."

Which meant it was also an old story. As Brenda began to recount her tale of woe, some of Ali's classmates from the academy, including Jose Reyes, wandered into the bar. Wanting to avoid them if at all possible, Ali steered Brenda and her latest shot glass into a sheltering booth in the back corner of the room, beyond the bank of pool tables. Once in that airless section of the room, Ali realized how much Brenda reeked of booze—not just what she was drinking now but what she had most likely been imbibing for the past weeks and months. This was way more than recreational drinking.

"What happened?" Ali asked, trying to seem interested but not intrusive.

"Richard was working down in San Diego. Things just seemed funny, out of sorts. I thought we needed to see each other face-to-face to get things sorted out. So I drove all the way down there to see him, and he was gone. I went by the place where he supposedly lived, but they had never heard of him. The same thing happened when I went by the place where he told me he worked. They said they had another man named Richard who worked for them once, but his last name wasn't Lattimer. I was just frantic. I didn't know what to think."

Unlike Brenda, Ali had a pretty definite idea of what to think. In her current guise, Brenda Riley was clearly a very troubled person. Under those circumstances it made perfect sense that most right-thinking men would have done the same thing Richard Lattimer had done—run like hell in the opposite direction.

Their food came, along with another cup of coffee for Ali. She was starved and lit into her burger. Brenda picked at her fries and ordered another shot of tequila. Keeping count, Ali was astonished at her capacity.

"So anyway," Brenda continued. "Like I said, he'd been acting all weird for weeks—sort of distant, like something was bothering him. That's why I went down to see him—to surprise him. When I got back from San Diego, I called Richard and told him I knew he had left San Diego and that I knew he had lied to me."

"What happened then?"

"He hung up on me. I tried sending him text messages and e-mails, but he blocked them. I haven't heard from him since. That's why I'm here. I need you to help me find him," Brenda said miserably. "Even if he doesn't love me anymore, even if he lied to me, I still love him. I need to be sure he's okay. Finding him should be easy, right? I mean, especially now that you're a cop."

That was when Ali finally understood what Brenda wanted and why she was here. Ali also knew the ramifications. Using law enforcement tools and sources to track down personal information on someone who was not a suspect in a specific crime is illegal. Yes, cops did that kind of thing occasionally, but it was also grounds for instant dismissal if the snooping was discovered.

"Tell me about him," Ali said.

The floodgates opened. "Like I said, his name is Richard," Brenda said. "Richard Lattimer. He grew up in Grass Valley, California. We met in an Internet chat room, a support group for abandoned spouses. My husband had left me and his wife had left him. Once we met, we just clicked. I know it sounds trite, but it seemed like we had always been meant to be together. For one thing, we had so much in common. We both had cheating spouses in our backgrounds. Our fathers died at an early age when we were both in high school. His father committed suicide. Mine had a heart attack and died.

"Richard and I talked about everything, and he was always there for me. When the station fired me, he was the only one who stood by me. We spent hours on the phone, talking, texting, e-mailing. Whenever I felt like I was falling apart, he was there to bolster me up and help me get a grip. At least he was for a while. Once I wasn't working any longer, there was no reason I couldn't drive down to see him on occasion, but every time I made plans to go, something seemed to come up at the last minute. Once his daughter, Suzanne, was sick; once he got called out of town on a job-related problem; once he got called in to work on some kind of emergency and was there for five solid days, fixing some problem or another."

"What does he do?" Ali asked.

"He's an electronics engineer," Brenda said. "He said he did highly classified work for a small defense contractor down in

Southern California. He told me they really counted on him. He was always on call, even on the weekends. He had to have a suitcase packed and ready to go in case he had to take off at a moment's notice."

"So he was part of an AOG team?" Ali asked.

Brenda gave her a mystified look. "A what?"

"The way my ex explained it to me, it's a term used by airplane companies, and it means 'aircraft on the ground.' Team members have to be ready to go wherever that broken plane is, repair the problem, and get it back in the air. Paul Grayson always had his own AOG bag packed. It took me a long time to realize that when he took off at a moment's notice, it turned out he wasn't fixing problems; he was making them."

Brenda nodded, but she was so caught up in her tale of woe, Ali doubted if what she said had penetrated.

"I didn't mind him being on call like that," she said. "I know what it's like to have a demanding job. I didn't worry about it. I was patient. I didn't want to rush him. We were supposed to get engaged on my birthday in May. He sent me links to a couple of jewelry websites. He showed me three different rings and asked me to choose which one I wanted. I did, and I didn't even choose the most expensive one, but when he went to order it, that one was already sold out. We talked about what kind of wedding we'd have, where we'd go on our honeymoon, the kind of apartment we'd have . . ."

Brenda's voice drifted away into silence.

"But you didn't get a ring," Ali supplied.

"No, I didn't," Brenda said sadly. "I had made the mistake of telling my mother and my sister that I thought a ring was coming. They haven't given me a moment's peace about it since, especially my sister. She said I had to be out of my mind to get engaged to someone I had never met. That's why I finally decided

I had to go see him no matter what. I drove to San Diego without letting him know I was coming, and that's when I found out he was gone.

"You have to believe me, Ali, this is all so out of character," Brenda continued, barely pausing for breath. "Richard would never do something like this—especially like cutting me off without any reason. Something must be terribly wrong. I'm sure of it. What if he has cancer or something? What if he's dying? What if he has only a few months to live and doesn't want to drag me through it with him?"

"Wait a minute," Ali said in dismay as something Brenda had said earlier finally penetrated. "You're saying you were practically engaged to a man you'd actually never met?"

"You don't have to be standing next to somebody to know him," Brenda said. "We talked on the phone for hours almost every day. Now that I can't talk to him anymore, I miss him so much. I just need to know he's all right—that he's not sick or dying."

For a time Ali was stunned into silence. Brenda was a well-educated professional woman. How was it possible that she could fall in love and be virtually engaged to someone she had never met? Clearly *virtually* was the operant word. The man Brenda Riley supposedly loved wasn't a person at all. What she knew about Richard Lattimer was what he had told her in a stream of words typed on a computer screen, endearments uttered over a cell phone. The whole idea was beyond bizarre. It made no sense.

Ali found herself in full agreement with Brenda's mother and sister. Richard whoever-he-might-be was a lying son of a bitch, and he most definitely had been stringing Brenda along.

"Have you ever thought about running a background check on him?" Ali asked.

Brenda frowned. "You mean the kind of thing employers do when they're getting ready to hire someone?"

Ali nodded.

"It sounds expensive," Brenda said. "I probably couldn't afford . . ."

"The people who handle my computer security issues do background checks all the time," Ali said. "I'm sure they'd be happy to look into it for you."

"Really?" Brenda grasped at this slender thread of hope with heartbreaking eagerness.

"Really."

"All I want is to know that Richard is okay. If he doesn't want me in his life, that's fine, but I need to know for sure that he's not sick or dying."

"I understand."

"What do you need?"

"Just his e-mail address." Ali knew that once the people at B. Simpson's High Noon Enterprises had Richard Lattimer's IP address, they could go from there and find all kinds of things Richard might prefer to leave unfound.

Brenda's sad face was suddenly radiant with hope. She reached into her purse and dug around for a piece of paper and a pen. While doing so, she placed her car keys on the table. Ali quietly slipped them into her pocket, although what she was going to do from there was anyone's guess.

Brenda was still scribbling down Richard's e-mail address when a broad shadow loomed over their table. Ali looked up and was astonished to see Jose Reyes standing there. In one hand he held a cup of coffee. In the other another shot. "This is for you," he said, setting the coffee cup in front of Ali. "And this is for your friend." He handed the shot glass to Brenda.

"Peace offering," he said to Ali. "Thanks for not raising hell about today," he said. "You could have. I was out of line."

Brenda downed the drink and then gave Jose a bleary-eyed smile.

"I'm willing to let bygones be bygones," Ali said, "on one condition."

"What's that?" Jose said.

"I need some help. My friend here is drunk out of her gourd and is in no condition to drive. There's a motel next door. Would you please help me get her there?"

"How much has she had?" Jose asked.

"Too much," Ali said.

Jose nodded. "Sure," he said, then he held out his hand to Brenda.

"What's going on?" Brenda asked.

"We're moving the party," he said.

"Really? What fun."

Jose guided Brenda across the two adjoining parking lots while Ali hurried on ahead. Fortunately the VACANCY sign was still lit. Inside the office, Ali rented a room and told the clerk, "My friend's had a little too much to drink. I'm keeping her car keys. Tell her to call me in the morning."

When she went back outside, Ali discovered that Brenda was violently sick. If Jose hadn't been holding her up, she might have fallen in her own mess. Ali opened the door to the room. After the spasm passed, Jose picked Brenda up and carried her into the room.

"On the bed?" Ali asked.

Jose shook his head. "She'll be better off on the floor in the bathroom."

He propped Brenda against the wall beside the toilet. Ali threw a couple of bath towels in her direction. On the way out she turned the wall AC unit on high.

Jose was waiting for her out in the parking lot. "Thanks," she said. "I appreciate the help."

"You're welcome."

They shook hands. As they did so, it occurred to Ali that she might pull off a hip toss right now. Jose wasn't expecting it, but he also didn't deserve it. She had needed his help with Brenda. She couldn't have gotten the almost comatose woman out of the bar, across the parking lot, and into the room by herself.

"See you tomorrow," she told him and walked away.

Ali took herself back to her dorm room at the academy and climbed into bed. The fall she had taken had hurt more than her ego and her eye. Her whole body ached, and the several cups of coffee she had drunk in the bar earlier in the evening kept her from going to sleep at a reasonable hour that night. Instead, she lay awake and thought about Brenda Riley, about what she had been once, and what she was now.

The difference between the two was nothing short of astonishing.

3

Grass Valley, California
August

By 4:30 a.m. Richard Lowensdale was up, had made his first pot of coffee, and was at his computer. It was ironic that he worked harder now than when he had been working and that he put in far longer hours. Thank God he had cut back to just two fiancées at the moment. Trying to juggle three of them had been a killer. If it hadn't been for his storyboard file, he never would have managed.

There had been a time in Richard's life when he had thought about being a writer. He had even gone so far as to take a correspondence course taught by Gavin Marcus Hornsby, a once-published but relatively obscure novelist who, in his old age, supported himself by teaching his "craft" to flocks of deluded wannabe authors. Richard figured it must have been as easy as taking candy from a baby. No doubt Hornsby had kept his "students" on the string for years, assuring them that they were each writing and rewriting the great American novel.

That's what the writing instructor had told Richard about his first paltry attempt, that it had the potential of being "great litera-ture." Since Richard was an expert at dishing out BS, he recognized that comment for what it was. He deleted his novel file and never sent another rewrite, but what he had learned in that creative writing class hadn't been a total loss. Richard had hung around long enough to learn about storyboards. Gavin Marcus Hornsby was a big believer in storyboards. After that Richard had never again tried his hand at fiction, other than what he did each time he re-created his own next persona, but the storyboard suggestion had appealed to him. Over time he had made good use of it.

He located Lynn Martinson's storyboard. Forty-one years old. PhD in secondary education. Divorced for three years. Super-intendent of schools in Iowa City, Iowa. Richard liked targeting high-profile women. They often didn't want to spill their guts or their troubles too close to home. When they needed to vent, they needed to do so with someone far away, someone who didn't know where all their personal bodies were buried. After his troublesome breakup with Brenda, being from out of state was first and foremost on Richard's list of requirements. The women in his life all had to be from out of state.

When Richard was working in San Diego and had been in-volved with someone else, having Brenda Riley as a side dish safely stowed in Sacramento had been ideal. For a long time the distance thing had worked in his favor, right up until Brenda lost her own job. After that, she had started harping about coming down to visit and spending some time together. Richard knew that wouldn't do. He had spun some wild stories about who he was and what he did, and he didn't need Brenda Riley showing up at his office and blowing the whistle on him.

With that in mind, Richard kept stalling with one excuse after another. It worked for a while, but then Richard's own carefully constructed real world imploded. Mark and Mina Blaylock gave him his walking papers. They said it was all about losing the defense department contract and the economy and all that other crap, but Richard didn't believe that was all there was to it. He suspected that Mark Blaylock had finally wised up to the fact that maybe his sweet little wife liked some of their employees—and Richard in particular—just a little more than she should have.

But the point was, Richard was out of a job. He needed a place to stay—a cheap place to stay. He had always despised Grass Valley and had sworn he would never go back there. When his mother and stepfather died and he had inherited their house, he had rented it out, furnished. Now though, even though Grass Valley was alarmingly close to Brenda's Sacramento home, Richard wasn't stupid enough to walk away from a free house. The renters weren't happy about leaving, and the eviction process had taken time. But while Richard was getting rid of the renters, he was also getting rid of Brenda.

At that point he was still under the impression that breaking up was hard to do. Now that he'd had some practice, he realized it wasn't difficult at all and that he could have dumped Brenda much faster. That's what he did these days, but back then, during his first time out, he had enjoyed playing her and watching her squirm. Faced with losing him, she had exhibited the whole entertaining gamut of reactions from anger to despair, from raging to resigned, from hopeful to devastated. She had begged him not to leave her and pleaded with him to take her back. The more she groveled, the more he liked it.

Brenda Riley had willingly given him a kind of control over her life that he had never experienced before. She had been putty in Richard's hands, and he had loved every minute of it. Wielding that power had hit his system like some incredibly addictive drug. Once he started on that path, he couldn't let go. He had strung Brenda along for months, making promises he never intended to keep because it was fun to put her through her emotional paces.

Richard Lowensdale was almost fifty years old. He was out of a job, living off the insurance settlement that had come to him after the drunk-driving incident that had claimed the lives of his mother and stepfather. He understood that much of the rest of the world might look at him and see a loser, but not Brenda Riley and not the women who had followed her either. To them, Richard was the ultimate prize—the most wonderful man in the world.

In a strange way, he owed much of his newfound happiness to two very different women—Mina Blaylock, who appeared to know more about sex and how to use it than anyone Richard had ever met, and Brenda Riley, who taught him exactly how stupid women could be, stupid and pitiful.

So back to Lynn Martinson. Her sixteen-year-old son, Lucas, had just gotten sent to juvie for drug dealing. How embarrassing it must be for her to be the top educator in her small town while at the same time having a kid who was totally out of control. No doubt every parent who had a child in that district was looking to Lynn to lead by example when it came to parenting skills, yet here was her son, totally off the charts and into drugs in a big way. That was where Richard had met Lynn in the first place, in a chat room for parents dealing with out-of-control kids and trying to survive the hell of tough love.

Richard—Richard Lewis in this case—understood every nuance of how that kind of family disaster felt. He had told Lynn how his own life had devolved, with an ex who married a drug dealer after their divorce and who took his kids along for the ride. For a moment, Richard had to go back to his storyboard file to verify the exes' names and details. Lynn's former husband's name was John. Rather than working as an electronics engineer as he had in San Diego, the newly minted Richard Lewis was a well-respected executive with a Silicon Valley software company. His former wife's name was Andrea and the teenaged daughter who had just gotten out of rehab was Nicole. Happily for Richard Lewis's fictional existence, seventeen-year-old Nicole had managed to make a seamless transition from being a druggie to being clean and sober, thank you very much.

Over time Richard had learned that it was easy to keep his own background story hazy and out of focus. After all, these desperately needy women weren't really interested in him. They were totally self-absorbed. What they really wanted was someone to listen to them while they bared their souls.

Richard was always glad to oblige in that regard, but only up to the point when he was ready to stop being glad to do it. Once that happened, he sent his poor ladyloves packing. He thought of it as a kind of "catch and release." Or else maybe "shock and awe," depending on his mood at the time. First he went to the trouble of reeling them in, then he let them go. Not kindly. Not gently. No, he took pains to tell the losers they were losers and that they needed to do the world and him a favor and get lost.

He was getting close to doing that with Lynn. She was starting to bore him. She was so focused on that damn prick of a kid of hers that she just wasn't fun anymore. Phone sex didn't count for much when one of the partners was totally preoccupied.

Richard had asked Lynn his customary trick question by sending her to the links with diamond engagement rings. He told her he had a ring in mind for her, but he didn't tell her which one he preferred. If she lucked out and picked that one—the one he regarded as the right one—then he'd let her hang around for a while longer. If she picked the other one, the wrong one? Too bad. It was time for a quick dose of "So long, babe. Have a nice life."

So far, with the notable exception of Brenda Riley, there hadn't been any blowback from any of his breakups. Why would there be? What could the women do about it? They couldn't very well go around crying on the shoulders of their friends and relations because they had been dumped by a fiancé they had never met. Telling that story was bound to be a winner. People would laugh their heads off.

And what other recourse did Richard's lovelorn victims have? They couldn't go to the cops either, because Richard Lowensdale had committed no crime. Unlike breaking into somebody's house and stealing someone's stuff, breaking somebody's heart wasn't against the law. As far as Richard was concerned, this whole thing was like playing a very complicated video game, only better because he got to do it with real people.

"Morning, sweetie," he said cheerfully to Lynn Martinson over his VoIP connection when she picked up the bedside telephone receiver at her home in Iowa City. Richard sometimes teased her about still clinging to her guns and religion as well as to her landline. He was firmly entrenched in the camp of Voice over Internet Protocol users. For someone with his particular brand of hobby, not having to pay long distance charges was a major money-saving consideration.

"I didn't wake you, did I?" he asked. "How are things? I wanted to hear the sound of your voice and wish you good morning before you have to go off to work."

4

Peoria, Arizona

When Ali's phone rang at six the next morning, she assumed it was B. calling her. He was spending a lot of time doing consulting work in Japan these days. The sixteen-hour time difference meant that early mornings for Ali and just before B. went to sleep were the best times for them to talk on the phone. At other times they made do with text messages and e-mail. The phone was still ringing by the time Ali realized that he was probably on a plane somewhere over the Pacific. When Ali finally answered, Brenda Riley was on the phone and she was outraged.

"What the hell do you mean stowing me in this fleabag hotel and taking my car keys?" she demanded.

No good deed goes unpunished, Ali thought.

"You were drunk," she said calmly. "You were in no condition to drive. Would you like me to bring your keys?"

"You're damned right I want you to bring me my keys."

"I have to be in class by eight, but between now and then, I'll treat you to breakfast. There's a Denny's just up the street."

Brenda started to say something else and then stifled. "All right," she said grudgingly. "I'll meet you there."

By the time Ali got out of the shower, she saw the text message from B. that she had missed earlier when the phone rang.

Bordng now. CU at home. Dinner? LV. B.

By the time Ali reached the restaurant, Brenda, dressed in an oversized man's shirt and a pair of ragged jeans, was already seated in a booth, drinking coffee and sulking. She had evidently showered in the motel room. Her hair was still damp and smelled of shampoo, but a cloud that reeked of tequila still lingered around her.

Ali remembered a friend of hers who had gone into AA after he got tired of what he called "drinking and stinking." Ali wondered if Brenda was there yet. If she wasn't, she ought to be.

Ali put the car keys down on the table and then slid them across to Brenda. "I couldn't let you drive," Ali explained. "You were an accident waiting to happen, a danger to yourself and others. What if you'd had a wreck? What if you had ended up in a hospital or if you had killed someone else?"

Brenda closed her fist around the key fob. "Thank you, I guess," she muttered, but she sounded mutinous rather than grateful.

Ali slid into the booth and picked up her menu. The waitress was there with a coffeepot before Ali found the breakfast pages.

"Coffee?"

Ali nodded. The waitress slapped a mug on the table, filled the mug with coffee, and then took off. Efficient? Yes. Personable? No. The service made Ali long for the down-home comfort of her parents' Sugarloaf Café.

"So," she said, for openers and hoping to break the ice. "Last night you told me about your boyfriend, Richard Lattimer, and your difficulties with him. Do you still want me to have someone run a background check on him for you?"

Brenda looked surprised. "You'd still do that? Even after . . . well . . . you know."

"You mean after you made a complete fool of yourself?"

Brenda made a face and nodded. "Yes," she said meekly. "I guess I just got carried away."

To Ali's relief it sounded as though Brenda was genuinely sorry.

"So yes, I'll still do it because I told you I would," Ali said. "I'll need an address so I can send you the report."

"But . . ." Brenda began, then she stopped. "I don't have an address right now," she admitted. "I don't have a computer either. I guess you can send it to my mom's house."

Ali located the piece of paper Brenda had used the night before to jot down her missing fiancé's e-mail address. "Use this," Ali said. "That way I'll have all the information in one place."

Brenda scribbled an address on the paper. The waitress came, took their order, and disappeared again.

"I don't have much money," Brenda said, as she handed the paper back to Ali. "How can I possibly pay for a background check?"

As a customer of High Noon Enterprises, Ali knew she could ask for a routine background check with no charge, but Brenda didn't need to know that.

"I'll tell you how you can pay for it," Ali said.

On the way to the restaurant, Ali had decided that she wasn't going to pull any punches. "You're a mess right now, Brenda—a wholesale mess. Yes, your fiancé dumped you, but considering the way you look and act right now, I'm not surprised. If you don't believe me, you might take a gander at yourself in a mirror."

Two bright angry splotches appeared on the surface of

Brenda's once-narrow cheekbones. "How can you talk to me like that?" Brenda demanded, as tears of self-pity welled in her eyes. "I thought you were my friend!"

Ali didn't relent. "I am your friend," she declared. "And that's the very reason I'm telling you this. Your broken-down wreck of a BMW is parked outside. It looks like you're living in it."

At least Brenda had the good grace to look embarrassed. "I lost my apartment," she said. "Living in my car beats living on the street. What was I supposed to do?"

"You're supposed to pull yourself together," Ali told her. "Find a job, any kind of job. You say you don't have money, but you had enough money to buy tequila last night."

"My mother gives me an allowance," Brenda said.

"That allowance isn't helping you, Brenda. It's enabling you," Ali said. "Stop using your mother and stop using whatever else you're on. I don't know if it's just booze or if it's something more than that. You told me Richard dropped you. I don't blame him. He probably didn't want to be involved with an addict. He's not the one who's sick or dying. You are. The amount of tequila you put away just last night should have been enough to kill you."

Brenda stared into her coffee cup and said nothing.

"If booze is all you're on, go to AA," Ali continued. "If you're on drugs, go to Narcotics Anonymous. Put yourself in a treatment center if you have to. Get your life back on track. Once you're clean and sober, if Richard Lattimer is the kind of empathetic guy you seem to think he is, maybe he'll take you back."

Their order came. Instead of touching it, Brenda shoved the plate across the table. Then she stood up and stormed out of the restaurant without touching a bite.

The waitress came back over. "Something the matter with the food?" she asked, picking up Brenda's abandoned plate.

"No," Ali said. "Something's the matter with her."

The waitress shook her head. "Some people don't have a lick of sense."

A few minutes later, when the waitress brought Ali the bill, the charge for Brenda's food had been removed. Ali left enough cash on the counter to cover Brenda's breakfast along with a generous tip. Outside in the parking lot, Brenda's BMW was long gone.

At least I tried, Ali told herself. *It was the best I could do.*

5

Peoria, Arizona

Ali headed back to the academy. She was there in plenty of time to get into her uniform for the early morning session. Some of the swelling had gone down, but the bruise on her cheek was still purple. Ali thought about trying to cover it with makeup but decided against it. She had earned it the hard way; she might as well show it off.

Cell phones were forbidden during class. The last thing before she went out the door, she turned on her cell phone and called B.'s number. "You're still in the air," she said. "I won't have access to my phone again until after four. You had said something about going out for dinner. I'm ready to stay home. I'm going to call Leland and ask him to pull together a light dinner for tonight. Hope you don't mind."

Then she called Leland and asked him to do just that. "Very good, madam," he said. "I think a nice chilled fusilli pesto salad would fill the bill. Sam will be glad to have you home. I think she much prefers your company to mine."

Sam was Ali's aging cat, a one-eyed, one-eared, sixteen-pound tabby who had come to Ali on a supposedly temporary basis, which was now comfortably permanent for all concerned.

"I miss her too," Ali said with a laugh.

Off the phone, Ali hurried to the parade ground, where she was dismayed to find Jose Reyes waiting for her.

"Morning, Oma," he said with a cheerful grin. "How's it going today?"

Jose's friendly overture, made in public, sent a clear message to those around them that whatever problem he'd had with Ali before was over—at least on his part. She understood that he was enough of a ringleader that if he buried the hatchet, the others would follow suit.

But that didn't mean it was completely over. That day, when they went to the shooting range, Ali made sure she had the slot next to Jose's. When target practice was over, she had beaten him six ways to Sunday. She knew it. He knew it. Neither said a word. They signed off on their respective targets and handed them over to the range instructor.

On her way to the next class, Ali wondered if the antagonism between them had really been put to rest.

All things considered, Ali thought, *it doesn't seem likely.*

Barstow, California

In an unreasoning rage, Brenda Riley slammed out of the Denny's parking lot with her tires squealing. Her speeding BMW left behind a rooster tail of gravel as she roared into traffic. She missed the entrance to the 101 and decided to stick it out on surface roads rather than taking a freeway. Somewhere along Grand Avenue she finally caught sight of a drive-in liquor store. She stopped at the drive-up window and filled her purse with a collection of three-ounce bottles of tequila—a little hair of the dog.

Ali Reynolds wanted Brenda to stop drinking? Big deal. Who had appointed Ali Reynolds as the ruler of the universe? What business was it of hers? What right did she have to go around pointing fingers? Brenda Riley would stop drinking when she got around to it—and only when she was good and ready.

Then since her mother's credit card was still working, Brenda decided to take the scenic road back home. She stopped for lunch in Wickenburg and ended up having to spend the night when an alert bartender in the Hassayampa River Inn took away her car keys. For Brenda, having her car keys confiscated twice in as many days was something of a record.

On Saturday morning, Brenda was up bright and early—well, ten o'clock, which was bright and early for her. She ate half a bagel and some cream cheese from the breakfast buffet at the hotel and was on the road as soon as she got her car keys back. She was doing just fine until she made pit stops in Kingman and again in Needles. By the time she was outside Barstow, she was feeling no pain. That was when she drifted off the highway. Without even noticing the rumble strips, she slammed into a bridge abutment and rolled over several times into a dry riverbed.

Brenda was knocked unconscious. Her seat belt kept her from being ejected from the vehicle, but the sudden force exerted by the belt broke her collarbone in two places. By the time rescuers reached her, she had regained consciousness and was screaming at the top of her lungs. Her nose was broken, as was a bone in her right wrist. There were several cuts on her body as well, some from flying debris from the windshield but others from glass from numerous broken booze bottles, most of them empty, that had gone flying around the passenger compartment of the battered BMW as it finally rolled to a stop.

One of the early first responders was a San Bernardino deputy sheriff who noticed the all-pervading odor of tequila and took charge. He summoned an ambulance. Once Brenda was loaded into it, he followed the ambulance to Barstow Community Hospital, where he saw to it that the doctors caring for the patient also administered a blood alcohol test, which came back at more than three times the legal limit. That was enough to maintain the deputy's interest and make his paperwork easier. It was also enough for the alert ER doc to admit her to the hospital for treatment of her injuries as well as medically supervised detox.

Afterward, Brenda Riley would recall little about her three-day bout with DTs. The acronym DT stands for "delirium tremens," and Brenda was delirious most of the time. Even with IV drips of medication and fluids, the nightmares were horrendous. When the lights in the room were on, they hurt her eyes, but when she turned them off, invisible bugs scrambled all over her body. And she shook constantly. She trembled, as though in the grip of a terrible chill.

During her stay at Barstow Community Hospital, Brenda Riley wasn't under arrest; she was under sedation. She wasn't held incommunicado, but there was no phone in her room. Besides, when she finally started coming back to her senses, she had no idea who she should call. She sure as hell wasn't going to call her mother or Ali Reynolds.

Finally, on day four, the doctor came around and pronounced her fit enough to sign release forms. Once he did so, however, there was a deputy waiting outside her room with an arrest warrant in hand along with a pair of handcuffs. Brenda left the hospital in the back of a squad car, once again dressed in what was left of the still-bloodied clothing she'd been wearing when she was taken from her wrecked BMW—her totaled BMW, her former BMW.

It didn't matter how the press found out about any of it, but they did. There were reporters stationed outside the sally port to the jail, snapping photos of her as the patrol car with her inside it drove into the jail complex.

Sometime during that hot, uncomfortable ride from the hospital to the county jail with her hands cuffed firmly behind her back Brenda Riley finally figured out that maybe Ali Reynolds was right after all. Maybe she really did need to do something about her drinking.

First the cops booked her. They took her mug shot. They took her fingerprints. They dressed her in orange jail coveralls and hauled her before a judge, where her bail was set at five thousand dollars. That was when they took her into a room and told her she could make one phone call. It was the worst phone call of Brenda's life. She had to call her mother, collect, and ask to be bailed out of jail.

Yes, it was high time she, Brenda Riley, did something about her drinking.

Peoria, Arizona

Back in Peoria that Friday, Ali Reynolds knew nothing of Brenda's misadventures in going home. At noon Ali went back to her dorm room to check her cell for messages. Ali understood that the major purpose of academy training was to give recruits the tools they would need to use once they were sworn officers operating out on the street. Weapons training and physical training were necessary, life-and-death components of that process. The rules of evidence and suspect handling procedures would mean the difference between a conviction or a miscarriage of justice.

Drills on the parade ground were designed to instill discipline and a sense of professional pride. That sense of professionalism was, in a very real sense, the foundation of the thin blue line. Still, some of the rules rankled. There was a blanket prohibition against carrying cell phones during academy classes, to say nothing of using them. In the first three weeks, instructors had confiscated two telephones and kept them for several days as punishment and also as an object lesson for other members of the class.

Ali had definitely gotten the message. She had taken to returning to her room for a few minutes at lunchtime to make and take calls. That Friday, there was only one text message awaiting her. B. said that he had landed in Phoenix, picked up his vehicle, was on his way to Sedona, and would see her at dinner. That was all Ali really wanted to know.

On her way back to class, Ali encountered one of her fellow recruits, Donnatelle Craig, out in the hallway. Donnatelle was an African American woman, a single mother, who hailed from Yuma. She was standing in front of the door to her room, weeping, and struggling through her tears to insert her room key into the lock.

Ali stopped behind her. "Donnatelle, is something wrong?"

"I flunked the evidence handling test," she said. "Sergeant Pettit just told me if I screw up again, I'm out. I can't lose this chance," she sobbed. "I can't."

When she finally managed to push open the door to her room, Ali followed her inside uninvited. Donnatelle heaved herself down on the bed, still weeping. Looking around, Ali noticed that, unlike the comfortable messiness of her own room, this one was eerily neat. Nothing was out of place. The only personalization consisted of a framed photo on the small study desk—a picture of Donnatelle flanked by three smiling youngsters, two boys and a girl. The girl, clearly the youngest, was missing her two front teeth.

"Are these your kids?" Ali asked.

Donnatelle nodded but didn't answer.

"Who takes care of them while you're here?"

"My mom," Donnatelle said.

Ali didn't ask about the children's father. He wasn't in the photo, and he probably wasn't in the picture anywhere else either.

"What did you do before you came to the academy?" Ali asked.

Sniffling, Donnatelle sat up. "I was a maid, in a hotel," she said. "But I wanted to do more. I wanted to do something that would make my kids proud of me—something besides making other people's beds. So I went back to school and got my GED. The sheriff said he'd give me a chance, but I'm not good at taking tests, I'm scared of guns, and Sergeant Pettit has it in for me."

School had always been easy for Ali. She aced written exams at the academy in the same way she had aced exams in high school and college. And she had come here with a more than nodding acquaintance with her own handgun and how to use it. Her notable failure with Jose Reyes was the first real black mark on her academy record.

Donnatelle, on the other hand, had come to the academy with a school record that was less than exemplary, but Ali found her determination to improve herself for the sake of her children nothing short of inspiring.

"That may be true," Ali said ruefully, "but I seem to remember you were fine in the hip toss. You threw your guy down and you don't have a black eye either. Besides I think Sergeant Pettit has a problem with women—any women."

Donnatelle sat up and gave Ali a halfhearted smile. "But my guy wasn't as big or as tough as yours was."

"Are you going home this weekend?" Ali asked.

Donnatelle shook her head. "It's too far. I'm going to stay here and work on the evidence handling material. They're going to let me retake the exam next week. As for the gun thing?" She shrugged hopelessly. "I don't know what to do about that."

"Had you ever handled a gun before you got here?"

Donnatelle shook her head. "No," she said. "Not ever."

"You need to practice," Ali said. "Spend as much time on the range this weekend as you can."

"I was going to, but now I can't," Donnatelle said. "They told me the range here is going to be closed because it's a holiday."

"Use a private one then," Ali said. "Go practice somewhere else."

"But where?"

"Just a minute," Ali said. She returned to her room and woke up her iPhone. She returned to Donnatelle's room a few minutes later with a list of five shooting ranges in the nearby area.

"Try one of these," she said. "And next week, when I get back, maybe I can help you with some of the written material."

"You'd do that?" Donnatelle asked.

"Absolutely," Ali told her with a smile. "After all, the girls on the thin blue line have to stick together, don't we?"

Rising from the bed, Donnatelle went into the bathroom and washed her face. Then rushing to keep from being late, they hurried to their next class. When the recruits were finally dismissed at four o'clock on that scorching Friday afternoon, Ali joined what seemed like most of Peoria in migrating north on I-17 in hopes of escaping the valley's crushing heat. On the way Ali speed-dialed High Noon Enterprises and spoke to Stuart Ramey, B.'s second in command about doing a background check on Richard Lattimer, originally from Grass Valley, California. Ali could have gone directly to B. with her request for information, but she had grown accustomed to dealing with Stuart during B.'s many absences. Besides, Ali assumed B. was probably dealing with a killer case of jet lag and there was a very good chance he was napping. She gave Stuart all the information she could remember from what Brenda had told her. She even dragged out the scrap of paper with the addresses on it and gave that information to Stuart as well.

"You want me to mail this to that address in Sacramento?" Stuart confirmed. "Do you want a copy too?"

"Why not?" Ali said. "I'm a little curious about this guy. The idea that he could get a fairly intelligent, accomplished woman to fall for him sight unseen is a little over the top." Of course, Ali realized that Brenda had severe "issues," but she was nonetheless baffled. Brenda had, after all, worked as a journalist, albeit the eye candy variety.

Stuart laughed aloud. "You'd be surprised," he said. "And you'd also be surprised at the number of requests we get these days that are just like this—somebody checking out the real deal of the new person who's supposed to be the love of his or her life."

"How long does it take?" Ali asked.

"The background check? Not long," Stuart said. "A couple of days at most, but this is a three-day weekend, so some of my sources may not be back online until Tuesday."

"That's all right," Ali said. "No rush."

As far as she was concerned, there was no big hurry. Yes, she had agreed to order the background check on Brenda's behalf, and she was doing so because Ali Reynolds was a woman of her word. But Ali could see that Brenda's problems went far beyond her simply being dumped by a boyfriend. Somehow, in the last few years of troubles, Brenda Riley had lost herself.

That could have been me, Ali thought. *If it hadn't been for the people around me, I might have gone down the tubes the same way.*

6

Sedona, Arizona

One of the people who had helped keep Ali on track was B. Simpson and his considerable charms. Ali and Bartholomew Quentin Simpson had both been born and raised in Sedona, but Ali was enough older than he was that they hadn't been friends or even acquaintances during grade school and high school. They weren't formally introduced until years later, when as adults and in the aftermath of failed marriages, they had both returned to their mutual hometown to recover their equilibrium.

Due to unmerciful teasing from his classmates, B. had shed his first name in junior high. The other kids had ragged on him constantly about that "other" Bart Simpson until he had abandoned his given name entirely. B.'s nerdy interest in computer science may have made him the butt of jokes in small-town Arizona, but it had translated into two successful careers—the first one in the computer gaming industry and his current gig as an internationally recognized computer security guru.

After a rancorous divorce, B. had returned to Sedona as a

reluctant bachelor with no particular interest in cooking. For months he had survived by eating two meals a day at the Sugarloaf Café. Over time he had struck up a friendship with Ali's father. It was Bob Larson who had suggested to Ali that she might want to turn to B.'s start-up computer security company, High Noon Enterprises, to safeguard her computers.

From shortly after they met, B. had made it clear that he was interested in more than a client-only relationship, and the man should have qualified as a good catch. He was an eligible bachelor with plenty of money and a beautiful custom-built home. He was tall, good-looking, and had a pair of gray-green eyes that seemed to send female hearts into spasms. He functioned well under difficult circumstances. He wasn't needy. He didn't whine.

But even with all those things going for him, Ali had been immune to his entreaties for several reasons, one of which was their similarly checkered marital pasts. Ali had lost her first husband to cancer. Her second husband, Paul Grayson, who had cheated on her repeatedly, had been a terrible mistake. B.'s wife had divorced him and was already remarried to someone B. had once regarded as a good friend. In other words, they'd both been burned on the happily-ever-after score, and that meant that more than a bit of wariness was well in order.

For Ali, though, the biggest stumbling block had been and continued to be B.'s age. It didn't help that there was now a specific epithet—"cougar"—for a woman in her situation, an older woman involved with a younger man. It was worrisome to Ali that B. was fifteen years younger than she was. She didn't like thinking about the fact that B. was closer in age to Chris and Athena and to most of Ali's police academy classmates than he was to Ali herself.

In a weak moment, she had finally let down her defenses enough to succumb to his charms, and now she was glad she had. She enjoyed spending time with him. They were having fun; they were devoted to one another, but they also weren't in any hurry to take the relationship to another level. On the other hand, Ali was occasionally troubled by the questioning looks that were leveled at them when they were out together in public.

Ali drove up the driveway from Manzanita Hills Road to her remodeled house. By the time she finished parking in the garage, Leland Brooks appeared in the kitchen doorway to collect her luggage.

"Oh, my," he said, peering at her face. "It looks like you ended up in a pub fight and lost."

"You're right," Ali said. "I did lose, but it happened in the academy gym, not in a bar."

"If you say so, madam," he said. "And, if you don't mind my asking, how does the other fellow look?"

"I'm sorry to say he's fine," Ali said.

"So most likely you'll be dining at home this weekend?"

Leland's question made Ali smile. It was a very nice way of saying she looked like crap. It also meant that he was back to his old mind-reading tricks.

"Yes, please," she said.

"I'll probably need to go out and find some more food, then," he said. "I was under the impression that you and Mr. Simpson would be going out a good deal of the time, but apparently that's not in anyone's best interest."

"Thank you, Leland," Ali said. "I don't know what I'd do without you."

Initially Ali had wondered about the advisability of keeping Leland around after the demise of his previous employer, who had also been the previous owner of Ali's home. He was a godsend.

B arrived in time for dinner at eight. Afterward, they sat outside on the patio and watched as a late-summer thunderstorm rumbled away off in the west without ever dropping any rain on

Sedona proper. They talked about lots of things including Brenda Riley's visit and Ali's encounter with Jose Reyes.

"So nobody at the academy is giving you a free ride," B. said. "Have your parents seen your shiner yet?"

Ali shook her head.

"No guts, no glory," he said. "We'd better go have breakfast at the Sugarloaf tomorrow morning and give your mother a shot at you. Otherwise you're never going to hear the end of it, and neither will I. Now what say we go to bed?"

They went to bed early but not necessarily to sleep. When Ali woke up the next morning, B. was sitting in the love seat, shuffling through a set of papers. A tray with a pot of coffee and two cups sat on the side table.

Ali scrambled out of bed, pulled on a robe, and poured herself a cup of coffee. She would have sat down on the love seat, but the spot next to B. was already occupied by Sam. Rather than move Samantha, Ali went back and perched on the end of the bed.

"What's that?" she asked.

"The background check you ordered," B. replied.

"It's already here?"

"Stu's been a busy little bee. And he gets things done. He must have dropped it off last night. Leland found it just inside the gate when he went down this morning to collect the newspaper. From the looks of this, your friend's ex-boyfriend is a pretty interesting character."

With that, B. handed Ali the first of several pages.

"But wait," Ali said as soon as she read the top line of the header. "This is about somebody named Richard Lowensdale. I'm sure Brenda told me Richard's last name was Lattimer."

"That may be what he *told* her," B. corrected, "but if you keep reading, you'll learn that Richard Lattimer is a figment of someone's imagination. Richard Lowensdale is the guy who was raised in Grass Valley, California, and worked for Rutherford International in San Diego. As far as Stu can discover, Richard Lattimer doesn't exist."

Continuing to read the report, Ali was appalled. "It looks like everything Richard Lowensdale told Brenda is a lie."

"Pretty much," B. agreed.

Yes, Richard had worked for a defense contractor, but as a minor player, not a big one. It turned out that Rutherford International was a small, minority-owned company with a niche market that supplied drone controllers. Lowensdale had a degree in electrical engineering from UCLA, but his career wasn't exactly stellar. For one thing, he had spent time bouncing from one employer to another. For another, Stuart Ramey's search of various databases revealed no patents issued in his name and no scientific papers listing him as author. His only listed hobby included a lifelong interest in model airplanes—remote-control model airplanes.

"Model planes," B commented. "That fits."

"What fits?" asked Ali.

"He's worked on drones, UAVs. Unmanned aerial vehicles—like the ones our troops are using in the Middle East."

"Aren't those a lot bigger?" Ali asked. "Like Piper Cubs?"

"Some are," B. agreed. "The ones they're using in Afghanistan, the Predators that fire the big missiles, are about that big, but the ones Rutherford was working on are much smaller. The most they could possibly carry would be a forty-pound payload, and some not even that much."

"So what's the big deal then?" Ali asked.

"There's an even smaller variety that's about the size of those remote-control helicopters that were such a hit at Christmas a couple of years ago. They can look in a window of a building and take out a single target sitting in the room without damaging anyone else."

"So there's less chance of collateral damage," Ali said.

"Exactly," B. agreed. "They cost a lot less because of size. They can go places where it would be too dangerous to have a piloted aircraft. Regardless of size, drones are relatively silent. They fly low enough to avoid radar detection. They can do precision targeting, and if you release enough of them at once, you can create a swarm.

"Think about it. If you have a single offensive weapon flying at any given target, chances are you've got a missile defense of some sort that has a good chance of taking that one missile transport device down. If you've got several hundred tiny drones heading in all at the same time, defenders can probably take out some, but not all of them."

"Like trying to chase off a swarm of killer bees with a fly swatter."

"Exactly."

"So Lowensdale worked for Rutherford and then he stopped," Ali said. "How come?"

"Because the bottom dropped out of the drone market," B. explained. "For a long time it looked like Rutherford was going to snag one of the big cushy military contracts. When that didn't happen, when those opportunities went away, so did most of Rutherford's employees, including Richard. The only people left working there are the owner and her husband, Ermina and Mark Blaylock and maybe a secretary. Definitely a skeleton crew."

"Richard Lattimer or Lowensdale or whoever he is told Brenda that he was an integral part of the design team. Was he?"

"I think it's more likely that he was just a cog in the wheel. When the layoffs hit, Lowensdale was let go right along with everyone else."

Ali studied a line in the report. "It says here that he was laid off in February of last year."

"That's right."

"But that's over a year before Brenda had any inkling he was no longer working in San Diego. Every time she made plans to go down there to see him, he came up with some phony excuse or another as to why she shouldn't come to visit. They were in this supposedly serious relationship without ever laying eyes on one another. How on earth could he deceive her like that for so long?"

"You tell me," B. said with a smile. "On paper, at least, he's nothing special. He has two degrees to his credit—a BS from UCLA and an MBA from Phoenix University. He also routinely signed documents with the PE designation, even though there's no record of his ever having earned it."

"Physical education?" Ali asked.

"Professional engineer. Requirements vary from state to state, but you have to take and pass exams that demonstrate an understanding of all kinds of engineering principles with an emphasis on your own specialty. I suspect he's an adequate kind of guy."

"Adequate but not brilliant," Ali said.

"And with a real tendency to inflate his accomplishments. I'm thinking his BS was totally appropriate."

Ali agreed and went back to reading. After being laid off in San Diego, Lowensdale had moved back to Grass Valley. His parents—his mother and stepfather—had died in a car crash more than two years earlier, leaving Richard as their sole heir. For a while he had renters living in the house, but after he lost his job and needed a less expensive place to live, he got rid of the renters—evicted them, actually—and then had moved back to Grass Valley in July.

"What a creep," Ali said. "He's spent the past year living forty miles or so from Brenda, all the while claiming he was still in San Diego."

"Right. Since he was no longer there, no wonder he needed to find one excuse after another to explain why Brenda shouldn't go to San Diego to visit him."

"What's this house in Grass Valley like?" Ali asked.

After shuffling through some extra papers, B. plucked a single sheet out of the bunch.

"According to his Zillow report, Lowensdale's place on Jan Road is valued at two hundred eighty-five thousand."

"That's pretty reasonable," Ali said. "Especially for California real estate. Must be fairly modest, but still, if he hasn't worked in more than a year, what does he do for money?"

"He doesn't appear to need much," B. said. "He was on unemployment for a while, but there was also some kind of insurance settlement—with an undisclosed amount—that came as a result of the drunk-driving incident that killed his mother and stepfather. His ride is a ten-year-old Cadillac, which, like the house, he inherited from his mother. He apparently orders online and has everything delivered—food, clothing, books, electronics, you name it. His medications come from an online pharmacy in Canada. Oh, and as far as Stu can tell, he doesn't have garbage service, or at least he doesn't pay for it."

"What about his father?" Ali asked.

B. gave Ali a puzzled look. "Did his father have garbage service?"

"No," she said with a laugh. "Richard told Brenda that his father committed suicide. Did he?"

"That part was true. His father blew his brains out in his office at the Grass Valley Group/Tektronix plant while Richard was a junior in high school. His mother remarried two days after her first husband's funeral. She married a guy who was supposedly one of the father's best friends, which sounds all too familiar to me," B. added.

"If the wife was screwing around behind his back, that might account for the father's suicide," Ali offered. "And look here. It says Richard has never been married and has no kids, but I distinctly remember Brenda saying that one time when she was planning on going to visit him, he told her she couldn't come because his daughter was sick. His nonexistent daughter."

"There you go," B. said. "So yes, we know that he lied about that—or at least, according to Brenda he lied about it—but he has no criminal record, no pending lawsuits, and no bankruptcies. He's coming through this downturn with an excellent credit rating. On paper the guy looks solid."

"Which is how he must have looked to Brenda too," Ali said. "What happens now?"

"You told Stuart to mail the report to her," B. said. "I'm sure he will, but it probably won't go out until Tuesday."

Ali emptied her coffee cup. "That'll be plenty of time," she said. "He's kept the wool pulled over Brenda's eyes for this long. I'm sure an extra day or two isn't going to matter. Let's go have breakfast and show my parents what having a daughter in a police academy really means."

When the long weekend was over, Ali gave B. a ride to Sky Harbor to catch a plane for D.C. after which would be another trip back to Taiwan. From the airport, she headed back to the academy.

For the next two weeks, Ali Reynolds threw herself headlong into the program and worked her butt off. In a way she hadn't anticipated, helping Brenda had inarguably helped her. The antagonism from Jose Reyes and some of his cronies that had been the bane of her existence during the earlier weeks faded into the background, sort of like the bruising and swelling around her eye.

Donnatelle had taken Ali's advice and had spent much of the weekend on the practice range and hitting the books. By the middle of the week, she had managed to retake and pass the evidence handling test and had eked out a qualifying score on the target range as well. Each evening that week, there were impromptu study sessions in the common room of the women's dormitory, with Jose and some of his pals in attendance.

There were no e-mails from Brenda Riley and no calls either. Ali took that to mean that her well-intended advice about seeking treatment had come to nothing. The same thing must have been true about the background check. Richard Lattimer/Lowensdale may have turned out to be a liar and a cheat, but Ali resigned herself to the idea that Brenda would do what Brenda would do regardless.

On the last Friday afternoon just before graduation, Sergeant Pettit once again paired Ali and Jose for what would be her final attempt at a hip toss try with a wily adversary. Ali figured the instructor was looking for a repeat of their previous performance. What the instructor didn't see as Ali approached Jose was the wink he sent in her direction.

When the confrontation started, instead of the expected hip toss, Ali surprised both Jose and Pettit by taking him down with a simple leg sweep. Once Jose was on the ground, she cuffed him and it was over. The fact that he had put up zero resistance made Ali feel like she was cheating the system, but when Sergeant Pettit came over to slap her on the back and tell her "Good job," she didn't tell the instructor otherwise. She just reached down and helped Jose up.

"We're even now?" Jose asked her with a grin.

She nodded and smiled back. "Even," she said.

When she removed the cuffs and shook hands with Jose, Ali knew it really was over. She was ready to go home and be a police officer, and so was he.

7

On Friday afternoon, Mark Blaylock made his way through the deserted administrative offices of Rutherford International. They had finally let Mina's secretary go, so now it was just the two of them. They'd hung on to the office space in hopes that things would turn around, but that wasn't happening. They had gotten a hell of a deal by paying the lease in advance, but time was up. The landlord had someone who was interested in moving in.

Renters for the warehouse/manufacturing spaces in the office park complex were few and far between at the moment, so he was letting them hang on to their storage space at a greatly reduced rent. That gave Mark and Mina a place to store the office equipment and furniture they had been unable to unload. How much longer they'd be able to manage even that paltry amount of space was a question for which Mark had no easy answer.

Mark slammed open the door to his wife's office, then he went inside and collapsed into the nearest chair.

"How'd it go?" Mina asked.

Mark shook his head. "I don't know," he said. "There's something wrong with the controls. The drone flew fine for a while, like there was nothing at all the matter with it. I was putting it through its paces and it was perfect, but when I tried to land it, everything went to hell."

"It crashed?" Mina asked.

"I'll say," Mark said with a nod. "And I don't know why—no idea."

"What about the wreckage?" she asked.

"Don't worry," Mark said. "That's the only good thing about all this. It went into the water. No one will ever find it."

The water in this instance was the Salton Sea, near Mark's rustic cabin. It was possible that someday if the lake dried up, someone might find the wreckage, but it wouldn't happen anytime soon.

"Good," Mina said.

That was all she said. She could have said a lot more. When Mark had insisted on doing the test run himself, she had worried about how capable he was, but right then there really wasn't anyone else to do the critical flight. They'd let everyone go, and Mina sure as hell couldn't fly one of the damned things herself. When Mark said he could do it—that it was "dead simple"—she had believed him. Evidently she'd been wrong about that, but playing the blame game wasn't going to serve any purpose. Ermina Blaylock was nothing if not absolutely practical.

"What can we do to fix this?"

"I'm no engineer," Mark said, shaking his head. "And I don't have the technical skills to sort it out. We need help, Mina, and we need it fast. If we're going to make this deal work, we're going to have to bring back someone from engineering."

That was a risk and they both knew it. When the military contract went away, they had bought up an entire warehouse of UAVs as scrap and for pennies on the dollar with the understanding that the UAVs would all be destroyed. Rutherford International had been paid a princely sum to make sure they were. The powers that be were concerned that if one of the UAVs happened to fall into the wrong hands, people unfriendly to the United States might manage to reverse engineer the product and come up with a workable drone design of their own.

Together Mark and Mina had falsified records showing the scrapped UAVs had all been destroyed and a helpful inspector had signed off on the paperwork. Now after months of putting out discreet feelers, Mina had finally stumbled across a potential customer, one Enrique Gallegos, who wanted to buy several working UAVs, for which he was prepared to pay an astonishing amount of money into a numbered account in the Cayman Islands. Before anything could happen, however, Mark and Mina needed to put on a successful demo flight. Mina was grateful that Enrique Gallegos hadn't been on hand to witness this afternoon's show-and-tell disaster.

It was easy to see that once they made the sale to Gallegos, they'd be financially whole again, but all of that depended on their having a working product. Right now they didn't.

"We need it to work," Mark said desperately, giving voice to what Mina herself already knew to be true. "We're going down for the third time."

Mina couldn't help feeling a little sorry for the man. She slept easily each night while he lay awake trying to find a way around their disastrous cash flow problems. Gallegos had been very specific in his request. He needed his UAVs capable of making an hourlong flight. He also wanted them equipped with some kind of self-destruct application.

Mina was good at playing stupid, but she wasn't stupid. She

understood that Gallegos's principals intended to use the UAVs to smuggle illicit cargo—drugs most likely—from somewhere in northern Mexico to predetermined landing areas in the United States well north of the last Border Patrol checkpoints. If each drone was capable of carrying a valuable ten-kilogram payload, she was a little puzzled by the need for a self-destruct mechanism, but she had agreed that any UAVs they sold would be so equipped.

"What about Richard Lowensdale?" Mina asked Mark casually. "Maybe we could bring him in on a consulting basis."

Mark let his breath out. "I never liked Richard," he said. "I'm not sure he can be trusted."

"Yes, but he's a good engineer, and he knows the product," Mina said.

"But how the hell are we going to pay him?"

"Let me see what I can do," Mina said. "Maybe I can get him to defer payment until after he gets us up and running. To bring him on board, though, I'll have to go see him. We can't risk sending him an e-mail about any of this. I don't want to put anything in writing."

"Yes, definitely," Mark agreed. "Nothing in writing."

He stood up and stretched. "I'm going to go home and shower. It was hot as hell out there today, but by now the ATVers are all showing up for their long weekend. I was glad to come back to town."

Once Mark left, a worried Mina paced the small confines of her office. If the feds could pull a wrecked 747 out of the ocean and reassemble it, they could do the same thing to a drone that had gone down in the Salton Sea. All the parts, even the smallest integrated circuits, had source codes that would come straight back to Rutherford and to her. There were laws, federal laws, against selling supposedly scrapped equipment to unauthorized purchasers. Enrique Gallegos was definitely not authorized.

Mina wanted to be rich again—she liked being rich—but she most definitely didn't want to go to jail.

Two nights later, she sat in a darkened bar in the Morongo Casino outside Palm Springs. She sipped a tonic with lime and waited for Enrique to pull himself away from the baccarat table. The casino was far enough out of the way for Mina to meet him there without raising any San Diego eyebrows.

"Is there a problem?" he asked.

She nodded. "My husband is hung up on the idea of blowing up the hardware," she said. "It's possible, of course, but in order to make sure it works, we'd have to take another drone out of our inventory. And there's always the very real danger of an event like that leaving a debris trail. We'll need to do a test run."

"What are you saying?"

"If you want us to use two UAVs—one for us to blow up and the other for you to own—then you'll need to pay us in advance for two UAVs."

Enrique lifted his glass to his lips. "Sounds expensive," he said. "I don't know if I can make that work."

"We're the ones taking all the risks," Mina said. "If we get caught, Mark and I could end up in jail for a very long time."

That's what Mina said, even though she had already decided that she would disappear long before any possible fallout hit. She'd be gone; the money would be gone; and Mark—poor old Mark—would be the one left holding the bag.

Without another word, Gallegos stood up and walked away. He didn't say he'd be back, but Mina was sure he would be, and she was right. He returned twenty minutes later.

"All right," he said. "We'll buy two of them up front."

Mina was impressed. Twenty minutes wasn't very long to get the go-ahead on that kind of expenditure. Whoever was behind this was someone with very deep pockets.

"We've already paid a quarter of that amount as an advance on the other drone, with another quarter due after a successful demo and the remainder on delivery," Gallegos continued. "We'll buy the second one at half price on the same terms—a quarter now and the rest on completion of a successful demonstration."

All of which means they really *want this,* Mina told herself.

"Seventy-five percent, not fifty," Mina said. "And I'm going to need that first quarter up front in cash. I need operating capital."

And running money.

8

Barstow, California

Valerie Gastellum Sandoz, Brenda's older sister, was the member of the family drafted by their mother to make the seven-and-a-half-hour, almost four-hundred-mile trip from San Francisco to Barstow in order to bail Brenda out of jail. She'd had to use one of her precious vacation days. So when it came time to sign Brenda out of the jail, Valerie was not a happy camper.

She and Brenda were sisters; they had never been pals. Brenda had been the golden child, from grade school on. She had been an exemplary student, a cheerleader, a star, while Valerie merely plugged along in the background. Val had been a late bloomer who married for the first time at age thirty-seven. While her younger sibling had embarked on her high-flying broadcasting career, Valerie had labored away in school, changing majors several times before finally settling in to become an architect. She had worked her way up from several lowly drafting positions until she landed herself a decent position in a commercial architectural firm in the Bay Area.

Now that their situations were reversed, with Valerie in the catbird seat and Brenda on her uppers, Valerie was not amused by her younger sister's plight, and she wasn't very sympathetic either.

"What the hell were you thinking?" Valerie demanded as they headed west on California Highway 58. "Mom's been frantic. Where the hell have you been all this time?"

"I went to Sedona," Brenda answered. "I went to see a friend from L.A., Ali Reynolds. I thought she might help me, but she didn't. She's becoming a cop."

"Too bad she didn't arrest you before you wrecked your damned car. Did you talk to the insurance adjuster?"

Brenda shook her head. She didn't want to say there was no insurance adjuster. Her auto insurance had been canceled two months ago, after her second DUI. Not canceled really, but they had raised the premium so much that she couldn't afford the payments. Her insurance stopped when the premiums stopped. The remains of her wrecked car had been towed to the impound lot and they were going to stay there.

"Thank you for coming to get me," Brenda said contritely sometime later.

"If it had been up to me, I would have left you to rot in jail or else walk home," Valerie continued. "Mom has been beyond upset. You were gone for a week and a half. Did it ever cross your mind that she was worried? Would it have killed you to take out your cell phone and call her?"

There was nothing Brenda could say in response to Val's tirade. Before the wreck she hadn't wanted to call and hadn't answered her mother's calls. Since the wreck her phone had been MIA and was probably even now toasting its circuit boards in the impound lot. As for her other reason for not calling? Telling Val that she'd been hospitalized for four days with DTs didn't seem

•

to strike just the right note. Besides, Val was on a roll. She wasn't interested in any response.

"The only reason I agreed to come get you is that I was afraid Mom would try to do it on her own. She can't drive anymore. At least, with her macular degeneration, she *shouldn't* drive anymore. But she still does. And since you're her favorite, she would've tried to come riding to your rescue herself if I hadn't told her I'd do it."

Brenda said nothing. Had she been drinking, she would have fought back. But if being sober meant sitting there and having to take this kind of bitching out, she didn't think it was worth it.

"With three DUIs, you are *not* under any circumstances to drive Mom's car, understand?" Valerie added.

Brenda nodded. That pretty much went without saying. Besides, the cops had just confiscated her driver's license.

"I won't," she said. "Just take me to Mom's."

"What about your apartment?"

Brenda didn't want to admit to her sister that three weeks ago she'd been evicted from her apartment because she hadn't paid the rent. For months. That was one of the reasons she'd hit the road. She'd been living out of her car, but she was still afraid that someone might see her and recognize her.

Was that what hitting bottom really meant—living out of your car or not caring if people knew you were living out of your car? Which was worse? And did it really matter? Whatever possessions she'd had left had been in the car with her. Now the car was gone and so was everything else.

She tried to lighten the somber mood. "It's like they say in that old song: 'I figure whenever you're down and out, the only way is up.'"

"Don't even start," Valerie said. "Give me a break."

After that they pretty much stopped talking. By the time Valerie stopped in front of their mother's faux Victorian house on P Street in Sacramento, it was well after dark. A single lamp was lit in the living room, and Brenda caught sight of her mother sitting in the halo of light. She was just sitting there, waiting. There was no television set glowing in the background. There was no book on her lap. She was simply waiting.

Brenda looked at her sister. "Are you coming in?"

"I guess," Valerie said. "But only for a minute. If I stay any longer than that, I might say something I'd regret."

"Thank you for the ride."

"You're welcome," Valerie replied. She didn't say the rest of it, but she was sure Brenda got the message—just don't let it happen again.

Palm Springs, California

One week later, again on a Friday afternoon, Mina made another trip to the casino, where she found Enrique Gallegos waiting for her in the bar. He sat in a corner booth with an athletic bag on the banquette between them. After a brief chat, Gallegos walked away, leaving the bag behind.

As Mina drove out of the parking lot, she called Mark. "Did they spring with the cash?" he asked.

"Some," she said. "Not as much as I wanted but enough to bring Richard Lowensdale on board." The truth was they had given her exactly what she'd asked for in terms of the cash advance, but she wasn't going to tell Mark the whole truth about that. He'd find a way to fritter away the money on things he felt were essential— like bringing their mortgage payments up to date.

Mark sighed with relief. "So you're off to see Richard?" It had taken some talking, but she had finally convinced Mark that

Richard was their only hope of resolving their technical problems without bringing in a lot more people.

Mina glanced at her watch. "Yes," she said. "I'm on my way to the airport. If I can get a flight to Sacramento tonight, I'll go see Richard in the morning. The sooner we get him started working on this, the sooner we get the rest of our money."

She couldn't help feeling just a little sorry for Mark. The man was incredibly transparent. He was afraid of losing what they had, and by most standards, they had a lot. Generally speaking, having was better than not having, but Mina wasn't nearly as hung up on that prospect as Mark was.

Losing possessions held no particular terror for Ermina Vlasic Blaylock. She'd already been through that once. She'd lost everything and everyone she'd held dear as a thirteen-year-old child during the Bosnian war. A Croat by birth, she had hidden in a barn while her entire family was slaughtered—her parents, her grandparents, her brothers and sisters. Of all those people, she was the only one to survive. More than survive, she had thrived. She had been adopted by an older couple from America, Sam and Lola Cunningham. Lola had wanted a daughter. Sam had wanted something else, but that had been her ticket to the American dream, one she had made her own.

She had been working as a minimum wage server for a caterer at what turned out to be the memorial reception for Mark Blaylock's first wife, Christine. Mina had seen Mark looking brokenhearted and handsome and needy—to say nothing of rich—and had sought him out like a heat-seeking missile. She had managed to put herself in his way, and he had taken the bait. They had been married now for seven years.

Somewhere along the line Mark had been given what was supposedly an inside track on getting a military contract for guidance systems on a particular class of UAVs. It had the potential of turning into a financial gold mine. Mark had mortgaged everything they owned to buy Rutherford International. They had put Mina at the helm of the new entity so it would qualify as a woman-owned company in terms of government contracts. Had they managed to get the drone contract, they would have been millionaires several times over, but the drone contract had gone away completely, and now they were broke.

One thing was certain, however. Ermina Vlasic Cunningham Blaylock was nothing if not resourceful. She was pretty sure she'd be able to bring Richard Lowensdale to heel just as she had Mark Blaylock and Enrique Gallegos. Instead of heading directly to the airport, she drove east past the Palm Springs exits, toward Indio. With the bag of money safely in her trunk, she turned south on California 86.

She had changed clothes at the office, slipping out of her work clothes and into a golf shirt, jeans, and sandals. Dressed like any other weekender, she drove to Mark's cabin. She was glad to be coming from the north. That meant she could turn off toward the cabin miles before the Border Patrol checkpoint. The cash was most likely in unmarked hundred-dollar bills. She knew, however, that far too many of those bills might have come into contact with the drug trade in one guise or another. She didn't need a drug-sniffing dog to point out the cash.

The property on the outskirts of Salton City had been in Mark's family for generations. The cabin was a stout clapboard affair that decades after being built still somehow managed to hold together and remain upright in the face of howling desert winds and scorching dust. Nothing if not austere, it included a single multipurpose room that was kitchen, dining room, and living room combined, a tiny bedroom with a minuscule closet, and a bathroom that was functional but definitely not deluxe. When the AC was on, the place was comfortable enough. There was running water, but the brownish stuff that came out of the taps tasted and smelled like dirt—salty dirt. There was no real furniture, only a collection of odd mismatched outdoor chairs and lounges that were stored inside and then dragged outside and to the sandy beach as needed.

Mina knew how much Mark had appreciated the fact that she understood his need to hang on to the derelict old wreck. It had escaped being mortgaged along with everything else, because the lending officer from the bank had claimed it was essentially worthless.

Sometime earlier—during that terrible year the fish in the Salton Sea all died for no apparent reason—there had been a period of months when almost no one had been able to use their cabins owing to the fierce odor of dead fish. While the owners were mostly absent, someone had broken into Mark's cabin and most of the others and vandalized them all. As a consequence and at great expense, Mark had insisted on installing a system of roll-down metal shutters that covered the cabin's windows and doors.

It had been an expensive process, not unlike putting lipstick on a pig, but the shutters made the cabin, humble as it was, impervious to intrusion. Once the shutters were in place, Mina had made her own contribution. She had hired a workman to install a fireproof safe concealed behind what appeared to be an electrical box in the cabin's only closet. The safe made a perfect hidey-hole for Mina's private hoard of cash, not just Gallegos's cash but other monies she had accumulated over the years by skimming funds off the top and hiding them without Mark's ever being the wiser.

Mark Blaylock was under the impression they were going broke. Mina knew that wasn't entirely true. Mark would be broke; Mina would be fine. She would see to it.

Driving to the Salton City cabin early that evening, Mina

threaded her way through various campsites with their outdoor bonfires and their amazing collections of ATV rolling stock parked outside massive motor homes and fifth-wheel campers. Using her remote control, Mina opened only the shutter that covered the front door, then she let herself inside with a key. Without the AC on, the place was like an oven. She held back only as much cash as she thought Richard might demand. She stuffed that into her Gucci bag and then put the remainder in the safe.

She was in the cabin for only a matter of minutes, but by the time she left, she was dripping with sweat. She paused outside long enough to relock the front door and close the shutter. With the now-empty athletic bag safely stowed in the trunk of her car, she headed for the airport.

Mina knew that she was cutting it close, but she didn't need to check any luggage. Besides, with this new influx of cash, she was once again flying first-class. That meant security wouldn't be a problem. She'd be there in plenty of time to board her plane.

9

Grass Valley, California
September

Richard Lowensdale was busy chatting with Lynn Martinson that Saturday morning, trying to prop her up in the face of that day's so-called family meeting, which was part of her son Lucas's incarceration process. Lynn, her ex-husband, the ex's new wife, the druggie sixteen-year-old, Lucas's court-appointed attorney, and his counselor would all be in attendance. Lynn was expecting the session to be one of blame-game finger-pointing, and Lynn's devoted listener, Richard Lewis, allowed as how that would probably be true.

He read Lynn's messages and sent back what he hoped sounded like sympathetic one-word comments—encouraging words, as it were. The truth is, committee meetings of any kind bored the hell out of him, so listening to Lynn going on and on about a meeting that was going to take place half a continent away was not high on Richard's agenda. The more she blathered on about her problems, the more he knew it was time to take her off his list. She just wasn't fun anymore, and any woman who wasn't fun wasn't worth having around.

So when there was an early-morning doorbell ring at his front door—a totally unexpected doorbell ring—Richard was grateful for the interruption and was glad to tell Lynn someone was there, that he had to go to the door.

Richard was smart enough about home security to have a CCTV camera on his front porch, one with a video feed that went directly into his computer. Before leaving his desk, he switched over to that screen and was pleased to see Mina Blaylock—the beautiful Mina—waiting there for him to open the door. He wasn't surprised to see her. He knew exactly why she had come and what she would need. The only thing that did surprise him was how long it had taken for her to show up on his doorstep.

As he started toward the door, however, he looked around the room and had a glimpse of how bad it was. The house was a mess. When his mother and Ron had lived here, you could have eaten off the floor. Now you couldn't eat off the dining room table. For one thing, Richard had turned that into his primary assembly station for model airplanes. His own collection, layered with dust, covered the bookshelves where his mother had once kept her collection of murder mysteries. Those had been banished to the trash heap at the bottom of the basement stairs.

There were plenty of people who wanted to fly model airplanes but didn't have brains enough to put them together properly. In addition to building his own planes, he made several hundred bucks a month on the side by doing the assembly work for those dunderheads. They sent him their kits and their money; he sent them their planes.

Doing that, however, meant he needed packing material. That was also in the dining room. The packing station was his mother's old buffet, where instead of good china, packing boxes and tape and shipping labels held sway. To the side of the buffet, on the floor, a huge plastic bag spilled a scatter of foam peanuts in every direction.

Richard spent most of his waking hours either working at the dining room table or at his computer at the far end of the small living room. Over time, there had come to be trails from the computer station and the dining room table that led through the debris field to other rooms in the house—the bathroom, bedroom, and kitchen. Most of the time he didn't worry about any of this.

The string of women he romanced over his VoIP connection had no idea how dirty his house was or how long it had been since he'd had a haircut—or a shower. The delivery guys who handed him packages or dropped them on the front porch or picked up the outgoing ones didn't mind how Richard or his house looked. It wasn't their business, and it wasn't their problem.

Now, though, with Mina standing out on the front porch, Richard realized how the house would look through her eyes—how he would look—and he was embarrassed. He spent a few minutes clearing a spot on the couch so she'd have a place to sit down. Finally, when she rang the doorbell again, Richard made his way to the door.

"Hey," he said. "What's up?"

"Hello, Richard," Mina said. "Can I come in?"

"Sure," he said. "What brings you to these parts?"

He pushed open the screen door. Mina looked great, but then she always looked great. He often wondered why she put up with Mark. He seemed so . . . well . . . ordinary. Boring and old. Mark had to be pushing sixty, probably twice Mina's age.

Richard led her through the entry and into the living room. He gestured her to a place on the couch while he resumed his place on the chair in front of the computer. On the screen, Lynn

Martinson was leaving him a long text message. More whining, no doubt.

"I need some help," Mina said, then she corrected that statement. "We need some help."

Clearing a path through the mess on the floor, Richard rolled his desk chair closer to the couch. "With what?" he asked.

That was disingenuous. Richard knew exactly what Mina needed help with—a problem with the drone guidance system. The reason Richard knew all about that problem and how to fix it was that the problem was his own creation. One of his last acts when leaving Rutherford International was a bit of "gotcha" sabotage. He had inserted the problem, a single set of rogue commands, buried deep in the thousands of commands it took to run the supposedly scrapped drone and make it work on GPS coordinates.

Richard knew that a sharp programmer might be able to locate and fix the problem, but a search like that would take time and money—lots of money. He also understood why it had taken so long for the problem to come to light. That had to do with the fact that no one had bothered to do a drone test flight for well over a year. No test flights meant that RI had no customers.

If Mark and Mina knew about the problem now, that meant they had needed and tested a working model—for someone. A customer of some kind must have come out of the woodwork. Richard knew it sure as hell wasn't the military, because as far as they knew the drones were history. Besides, if it had been someone on the up-and-up, Mina wouldn't have come skulking up here unannounced to ask Richard for help.

As far as Richard was concerned, a customer who was interested in staying under the radar was very good news. It meant money was in play—lots of money, for the Blaylocks and, if Richard played his cards right, for him as well.

"What do you think is the problem?" he asked.

Mina shrugged. "I have no idea," she said. "Neither does Mark. We need someone who can troubleshoot for us. We're not in any condition to start bringing people back on a permanent basis," she added, "but since you're so familiar with the project, we were hoping you'd agree to come on board on a consulting basis."

"What happened?" Richard asked.

"We put a drone up in the air, or rather, Mark put it up in the air. He's flown them before with no trouble, but this time it crashed and burned."

Which, Richard thought, *is exactly what I programmed it to do: take off, fly flawlessly for a while, and then drop out of the sky for no apparent reason.*

Richard let the silence between them stretch for some time before he shook his head. "I just don't see how I can do it, Mina," he said reluctantly. "Not after what I hoped would happen between us. There's too much history. Just seeing you again is enough to break my heart."

Lying to someone's face was a lot more difficult than telling lies over the phone, but between the last time Richard had seen Mina and now, he'd had a whole lot more practice in the art of prevarication. And he had to admit that she was a pretty capable liar herself. Ignoring the mess around her, she watched him with a kind of almost breathless, bright-eyed attention. That was how she made men sit up and take notice.

"I'm so sorry, Richard," she said. "Please understand. I had to let you go along with everyone else. Otherwise Mark would have figured it out."

For months after Richard went to work at Rutherford, Mina had flirted with him shamelessly and hinted that she was interested in having a little fling with him. That was all that happened in the end—flirting. In actual fact, he'd hardly ever gotten to first base with any real women. They scared the hell out of him. Richard talked a good game, but when it was time to deliver the goods, he always came up short.

He had hoped things would be different with Mina, but the flirting had come to naught. Later, when he'd been given his pink slip, rather than facing up to his own shortcomings, Richard had convinced himself that was why he'd been let go—because Mark had somehow caught on to what Mina was thinking. That was the real reason Richard had dropped that little programming bomb into the Rutherford works. It was the best way for him to even the score. And now, months later, when they finally knew they had a problem, not only did they not know he was responsible for their difficulty, they had come to him to fix it. How wonderful was that?

Richard wanted to leap off the couch and dance a little jig. Instead, he sighed and shook his head as though he were allowing himself to be persuaded entirely against his will.

"All right," he said resignedly. "What do you need and when?"

"I need to fly a ten-kilo payload, one hundred or so miles, to predetermined coordinates."

Richard had been wondering about the end user. Mina's statement provided the answer. After all, this was California. Other businesses might be struggling to survive, but the illegal drug industry was still booming. Richard wanted Mina to verify it, though. He wanted her to understand he wasn't as dumb as she thought he was.

"I suppose that means we're dealing with one of the drug cartels," Richard said.

Mina looked him square in the eye and didn't deny it, and she didn't object to his use of the word *we* either. In fact, she used the same word herself.

"We'll make a lot of money," she said.

"Who's we?"

"All of us—you, me, Mark. How long do you think it'll take to troubleshoot the problem?"

The real answer was about two minutes, but he didn't tell her that. She wouldn't pay for two minutes.

"I don't know how you expect me to do that," he said. "I don't have any of the code, and even if I did, finding something like this won't be easy."

Mina reached into her purse and pulled out a thumb drive, which she handed over to him. "I brought the latest version of the programming with me. Here it is," she said. "Everything you need should be on that."

The fact that Mark and Mina still had drones and were getting ready to sell working models meant that the Blaylocks had gone over to the dark side. From Richard's point of view there was a definite upside to working the dark side—lots of money.

"It'll take me at least six months, but that's not a guarantee," he said. "Fifty thou total. All communications are to be done this way, in person and eyeball to eyeball. No e-mails back and forth; no telephone communications; all payments to be made in cash. Half down; half on delivery."

"Five months, not six," Mina countered. "I need to be able to do the test flight before the end of January. I'm offering twenty thousand down, and ten a month until the job is completed. Plus, I'll give you a twenty-five-thousand-dollar bonus in January after a successful test flight."

Once again Mina reached into her oversized purse. This time she plucked out a packet of cash and handed that to him as well. "Count it if you want."

Richard didn't have to count it. He knew it was all there. He couldn't help but be a little disappointed. He'd had no idea that she knew him so well. The fact that she was offering more than he'd asked was surprising.

"Oh," Mina added. "There is one more thing. We'll need the ability to remotely detonate this thing."

"As in blow it up?"

"Yes," she said. "Blow it to pieces."

"That's a little more complicated," Richard said with a laugh. "But I get it," he added. "It's like the beginning of one of those old *Mission: Impossible* stories on TV where they say, 'This tape will self-destruct in thirty seconds.'"

Mina frowned. "I don't think I ever saw that movie."

"It wasn't a movie," Richard said. "It was an old TV series. From the sixties."

"I never saw that either," Mina said.

But Richard had seen those shows, countless times. Ron Mills, Richard's stepfather, had loved *Mission: Impossible,* especially Cinnamon. He had owned DVD versions of all three seasons. Richard had found those DVDs in the same box in the basement where he had found his mother's prized boxed sets of *Murder, She Wrote* VCR tapes.

"Too bad," he said. "You're missing out on an essential piece of Americana."

Mina stood up and gathered her purse. Richard didn't bother getting up to show her out. He looked at the money—money he had never expected to see. Without having to pay taxes and at his current rate of expenditure, that much money and the rest Mina had promised him would last for a very long time.

Richard felt an immense sense of satisfaction. He had Mina Blaylock just where he wanted her. Richard knew that if there was that much money lying around just for the asking, then there was obviously far more where that came from.

Sacramento, California

Brenda's enforced jail-based sobriety didn't exactly take. It lasted long enough for Valerie to drive her home to Sacramento from Barstow. It lasted long enough for Brenda to be far too sober during the name-calling blowup between her sister and her mother, Camilla, when Valerie dropped Brenda off at their mother's P Street home.

"Here's your jailbird," Valerie had said, opening the door so Brenda could make her way inside. "I brought her home to roost."

Camilla heaved herself up out of the chair and hurried to meet them. "I'm so glad you're safe," she said, hugging Brenda close. "When I didn't hear from you, I was worried sick."

"She's a drunk, Mom," Valerie said. "She wrecked her car and she damned near killed herself. She probably would have done us all a favor if she had."

"Valerie," Camilla said, "you mustn't talk like that."

"Why not? You don't think she's learned her lesson, do you? Just wait. She'll be drinking again the minute your back is turned."

"Valerie . . ."

"Save your breath, Mom. I don't want to hear it, and the next time she gets in hot water, don't bother calling me. I did this once. I won't do it again."

Valerie had slammed out the door on that note and hadn't been heard from again. She hadn't phoned. Camilla called and left messages. Valerie didn't call back.

As for Brenda? Unfortunately, Valerie's assessment proved to be correct. Brenda was all right for a couple of days, but then she got around to opening the mail, including the background check on Richard—Lowensdale, it turned out, not Lattimer. Reading through the material and uncovering the fabric of lies behind everything he had told Brenda was enough to push her off the deep end once more.

That night, after her mother was asleep, she let herself out of the house, walked six blocks to the nearest liquor store, and bought a supply of booze that she smuggled back into the house and upstairs to her room. One of the pieces of furniture in the room was her mother's old hope chest. From Brenda's point of view, the best thing about it was the fact that it came with a lock and key. Brenda deposited her booze purchases in among mother's extra sheets and pillowcases, then she turned the old-fashioned key in the lock and hid the key in her purse, concealed in her hard plastic tampon holder.

She drank the rest of the night, reading and rereading the background check and fanning her anger to a fever pitch. She was furious to think that while she had been sick with worry about Richard's health, he had been fit as a fiddle and only an hour or so away. She thought about calling him, but then she realized that wouldn't work. He had stopped taking her calls, and once he recognized her new cell phone number, he wouldn't take calls from that device either. No, what was called for was a visit—a personal visit, one where Brenda would have the opportunity to let Richard have it. She wanted to talk to him face-to-face and tell him how contemptible he was.

She fell asleep around four a.m. and woke up at eleven. She had breakfast in the kitchen while her mother was having lunch. Camilla greeted her daughter with a smile. "Good morning, sleepyhead," she said. "You're keeping the same kind of hours you did in junior high."

"I couldn't sleep," Brenda said.

"Is there anything I can do to help?" Camilla asked.

Yes, Brenda thought. *Leave me alone.* "Can I borrow your car for a while this afternoon?"

"Well, of course," Camilla said. "When do you expect to get your own car back?"

The answer to that was never. Valerie would have spilled the truth about that in a minute. Fortunately for Brenda, Valerie hadn't hung around long enough to do a huge amount of damage.

"They're getting the parts in," Brenda lied. "It's going to be a while."

On that sunny afternoon in early October, Brenda stocked her purse with enough booze to tide her over, then she borrowed her mother's car keys and took off for Grass Valley in Camilla's twenty-year-old Taurus. All the way there, Brenda rehearsed exactly what she would say to Richard Lattimer Lowensdale. By the time she reached the house on Jan Road, she was only partially drunk, but she had worked herself into a seething rage.

Ready for war, she marched up to his door, stomped across the front porch, and gave the doorbell button a furious punch. But nothing happened. Richard didn't come to the door. The house was totally silent. Convinced he had recognized her and was simply hiding from her, she wandered around to the side of the house, where she found a second door. This one didn't have a doorbell, but it did have a series of glass panes.

Without giving any thought to the consequences, Brenda picked up a rock and smashed one of the lower panes. Then she unlocked the door and let herself inside. Entering through a utility room, she found herself choking on the terrible odor. It made her throat hurt and her eyes itch. The kitchen was fine, but the mess in the remainder of the house was appalling.

Richard had passed himself off as an urbane, witty, neat guy, yet here he lived in a squalid hovel. Brenda wandered through the filthy house, letting the scales fall from her eyes. Richard had lied about far more than his name and his place of employment. Everything about him was false.

With Richard not there, Brenda was ready to vandalize the place. Standing in the living room, surveying the mess, she caught sight of the most logical target. Richard's command central, his computer desk, stood at the far end of the room.

Brenda remembered Richard's telling her that he never turned off his computer. *Maybe I'll turn it off for him,* she thought. *Permanently.*

She looked around for a suitable weapon and settled on a sooty fireplace poker. She carried it over there and was ready to smash the CRT when she saw there was an open file showing on the screen. The file name was Martinson in a folder called Storyboards.

Scanning through the open file, Brenda learned far more than she wanted to about Lynn Martinson's sad life—her drug-addicted son, her difficult ex-husband, her complicated job, and her loving relationship with someone named Richard Lewis who had a troublesome ex-wife named Andrea and a teenaged daughter, Nicole, who was also involved with drugs. Lynn's social security number was there. Her preferred nicknames and suitable terms of endearment were duly noted. There was also a log of calls and e-mail conversations that included transcripts of what Richard had said to her and what Lynn had answered in return. Glancing at the contents of the storyboard was like eavesdropping on a two-way conversation.

Suddenly a light went on in Brenda's head. Making a mental note of Lynn Martinson's name, Brenda hit the open file command. When a list of fifty-seven items appeared, Brenda scrolled through it. She found her own name, Brenda Riley, three-quarters of the way down the list.

She could have opened her file just then, but she didn't dare take the time. She wanted the contents of this folder—all the contents. Fortunately Brenda was conversant with the Mac operating system. She went back to the Storyboards folder and hit command P to activate the printer. As pages spun out of the printer, one after another, Brenda scanned one or two, realizing as she did so that she was far from alone in being victimized by Richard Lowensdale and his various aliases.

It took precious minutes and more than a hundred pages to print the storyboard folder. At one point, the printer ran out of paper and Brenda had to look around to find paper to load into it. As soon as the printing job was finished, Brenda reopened the Lynn Martinson file, leaving the computer much as it had been when she found it.

Then she picked up the printed material and fled. Back at her mother's home on P Street in Sacramento, Brenda locked herself in her room and read through what she had printed, studying every single page and drinking as she read.

By the time she finished reading and passed out again—at five o'clock the next morning—Brenda Riley had given herself a new purpose in life: one way or another she would find a way to take Richard Lowensdale down if it was the last thing she ever did.

10

F our months after graduating from the Arizona Police
Academy, Ali Reynolds was doing something she had
never expected to do again—manning her mother's lunch
counter in the Sugarloaf Café.

"Order."

Summoned to the serving window by the café's substitute short-
order cook, Ali Reynolds picked up two platters of ham and eggs
and delivered them to the two customers seated at her station.

This Friday morning in January the restaurant had been
slammed from the moment Ali opened the doors at six a.m. until
only a few minutes ago. Once the pace slowed slightly, Ali leaned
her hip against the counter and gave herself permission to sip a
cup of coffee.

Six days down, one to go, Ali told herself.

Ali's parents, Bob and Edie Larson, were on the next-to-last
day of their seven-day Caribbean cruise. Ali was on the next-to-
last day of filling in for them.

After nearly a week of working her mother's early morning shift, Ali had a renewed respect for the jobs her parents had done in running their Sedona area diner for all those years. She also had a renewed respect for her mother's killer schedule. Edie Larson came in to the restaurant at four a.m. every day to bake the restaurant's signature sweet rolls as well as that day's supply of biscuits.

Ali's one attempt at duplicating her mother's sweet roll recipe had been nothing short of disastrous. Fortunately, Leland Brooks had come to her rescue. For the remainder of the week Edie and Bob Larson were gone, Leland had agreed to come in each day to handle the baking. Leland went back home each morning about the time Ali and the substitute short-order cook turned up to take over.

When Ali had first broached the topic of a Caribbean cruise as that year's Christmas present to her parents, they had turned the idea down cold. Both of them had insisted that they couldn't possibly be away from the restaurant for that long. Ali, however, had refused to take no for an answer. She had found a substitute cook and had sorted out a passport renewal for her mother and a new passport for her father. But it was only when she agreed to come in to the restaurant herself every day to keep an eye on things that Bob and Edie finally acquiesced.

To Ali's knowledge, this was the first long vacation her parents had ever taken together. From the tenor of the short e-mail updates Edie sent home on a daily basis, it seemed they were having the time of their lives. Ali was not having the time of her life. She was tired. Her feet hurt. Her back hurt. She put on her smile every morning when she put on her uniform—a freshly laundered Sugarloaf Café sweatshirt and a pair of jeans. She did her best to be cheerful and pleasant as she served coffee and wiped up spills, but the truth was Ali Reynolds was still annoyed. She was also bored.

This wasn't the way her life was supposed to be right now. She loved her parents and was glad to help with giving them a break, but the truth was she shouldn't have been available to work for a week as a substitute server in the Sugarloaf Café. The way she had seen her future, she should have been working as the media relations officer for the Yavapai County Sheriff's Department. The problem was, she wasn't.

The previous September, Ali Reynolds had graduated third in her class at the Arizona Police Academy in Peoria. For someone who was the oldest member of her class and a female besides, that had been a big accomplishment. She had been tossed into a class filled with much younger recruits, and she had made the grade.

Her parents, her son and daughter-in-law, and B. Simpson, her significant other, all of them beaming with pride, had shown up for her graduation. They had congratulated her and told her what a great job she had done. And she had shaken hands with all her fellow graduates, who, like her, were going back to towns all over the state of Arizona to begin their law enforcement duties. The whole experience had been an incredible high.

As a result, nothing could have prepared her for what happened to her the following Monday morning. Dressed in a perfectly creased uniform, she drove to Prescott fully expecting to resume her media relations duties. Before the scheduled preshift roll call meeting at nine, however, Sheriff Gordon Maxwell called her into his office, sat her down opposite his desk, and gave her the bad news.

"I'm sorry to do this, Ali, but I'm going to have to furlough you."

At first Ali didn't think she'd heard him right. "Furlough?" she repeated. "As in let me go?"

He nodded.

"Are you kidding? I just busted my butt for six weeks getting through the academy."

"I understand," he said. "And no, I'm not kidding. Believe me, I'm very, very sorry. The county budget-cutting axe fell on every aspect of county government about three weeks ago. I knew then this was going to happen. I didn't tell you, because I didn't want you to drop out without finishing the course. And you did great, by the way."

"Right," Ali replied sarcastically. "I did so well that now I'm being fired."

"Furloughed, not fired," Maxwell insisted. "Once the fiscal situation straightens out, I fully expect to bring you back as a sworn officer, but right this minute my hands are tied. Last in, first out, and all that jazz. Hell, Ali, it was either you or Jimmy. He's got a couple of kids and really needs this job."

Deputy Jimmy Potter happened to be a recent hire as well. He and Ali shared office space in the Village of Oak Creek Substation. He was a nice guy with a wife and a pair of preschool-aged children. Ali could see that Sheriff Maxwell had a point. Ali had no dependents. Her financial situation made work an option for her rather than a necessity, but she really wanted this job. She loved it. She was good at it.

"So that makes me expendable?" Ali asked.

"Not expendable, not at all."

Despite what he said, it turned out Ali Reynolds was indeed expendable. Without ever attending that morning's roll call, she turned in her laptop, her cell phone, her weapons, and her badge and went home. She wasn't in disgrace, but it certainly felt like it.

In a way, losing the media relations job was somehow worse than losing her newscasting job in California years earlier. Her response to that had been to pack up and go home to Sedona. This time she was already *in* Sedona. That left her nowhere else to run. L.A. was big enough to allow for a certain amount of anonymity. Sedona was another proposition entirely. Everyone seemed to know she'd been laid off. Even though most of the comments came in the inoffensive guise of harmless well-wishing, the lack of privacy in both her love life and job situation bothered her.

She had been forced to sit on the sidelines licking her wounds and watching while the media storm over the "sweat lodge wars" once again catapulted the Yavapai County Sheriff's Department to national prominence. And who was doing the media relations work for the department in the midst of that maelstrom? The guy with his face on TV and voice on the radio was Mike Sawyer, a twenty-two-year-old college kid Ali had brought on board as an unpaid summer intern while she was down in Phoenix at the academy. Instead of returning to school to work on his master's degree in the fall, he had stayed on.

It irked Ali that Sheriff Maxwell couldn't scrape up enough money to pay her but had managed to find enough funds in the budget to pay Mike. It probably wasn't a living wage, because Mike was living with his parents, but still . . .

One of the customers at the counter held up his coffee mug and caught Ali's attention. "Can I have a refill?"

"Sure."

Ali poured coffee, dropped off a check, picked up some menus, and put them back in the holder over by the cash register.

So what had Ali done since that day of her surprising "furlough"? She'd read books, dozens of them. She was just now working her way through *The Count of Monte Cristo*. It was a book Mr. Gabrielson, her English teacher at Mingus Mountain High, had recommended to her years ago. With nothing else pressing, Ali had decided this forced hiatus was a perfect opportunity to read all those books she had said she would get around to reading someday when she had time. At the moment finding time for reading was not a problem.

Reading aside, Ali Reynolds was bored. She was beyond bored. When she'd been working for the department, she'd enjoyed everything about her job including the hour-and-a-half commute on those days when she'd drive from Sedona to the county seat in Prescott. Yes, she hadn't been well accepted by some of the old-timers there, but she'd been working on getting along with them and she was surprised to discover that, once she was sent packing, she missed everything about her work for the Yavapai County Sheriff's Department, including some of the prickly clerks in the front office.

Ali's mother had suggested that Ali give the garden club a try, but Ali's lack of anything resembling a green thumb precluded that. She had zero artistic skill, so taking up drawing or painting wasn't an option. She didn't play golf or tennis. She didn't ride horses. She wasn't into hot-air ballooning.

When B. was in town, the two of them had fun hiking in Sedona's red-rock wilderness, but these days B. was out of town as much or more than he was home. Most of the time her parents were bound up with the Sugarloaf Café and their own peculiar squabbles. Chris and Athena were building their own lives together and getting ready for the birth of their twins.

Ali had Leland Brooks to fall back on, of course. He kept her house running in tip-top shape. Theirs was a pleasant, untroubled relationship with each respecting the other's privacy, but Leland wasn't someone she could talk to, not really talk.

What Ali missed more than anything was having friends, close friends. Her best pal from high school, Reenie Bernard, had been dead for years. Dave Holman was still working for the sheriff's department as their lead homicide investigator. Dave and Ali were friends, but when Dave wasn't at work, he was preoccupied with raising his two teenaged daughters.

Ali had one new friend, a seventysomething nun named Sister

Anselm. They had met in the course of caring for a badly injured burn victim and had bonded after surviving a shootout with a suicidal ecoterrorist. Sister Anselm lived at Saint Bernadette's, a Sisters of Providence convent in Jerome that specialized in treating troubled nuns. Unlike Ali, Sister Anselm was fully employed, either at the convent itself or traveling all over Arizona as a patient advocate for severely injured and mostly indigent patients.

Had anyone asked Bob and Edie Larson about their religion, they would both have claimed to be Lutheran. Because Sunday mornings were big business at the Sugarloaf, other than attending occasional weddings and funerals, they'd barely stepped inside a church of any kind for years. Having grown up as a relatively unchurched child, Ali had remained so as an adult and had raised Chris without regular church attendance. In advance of the twins' birth, Athena and Chris had joined the congregation of Red Rock Lutheran.

All that background made the growing friendship between Ali and Sister Anselm seem unlikely, but the two women managed to get together once a week or so for a quick dinner or for one of Leland Brooks's sumptuous English teas. Sister Anselm was a trained psychologist, and it sometimes occurred to Ali that their visits turned into informal counseling sessions in which Ali ended up grumbling about being let out to pasture.

It was at Sister Anselm's gentle urging that Ali had broached the idea of sending Bob and Edie away on a January cruise. January, of course, was the best time for them to go since it was still far too chilly in Sedona for a full snowbird onslaught. That would come later in the spring.

The front door opened. Ali was pulled from her reverie by a group of eight people who piled into the room, bringing with them a gust of cold air and a buzz of conversation. Jan Howard, the Sugarloaf's longtime waitress, had been outside on a break, puffing on one of her unfiltered Camels. She hurried inside as well. She grabbed up a handful of menus and helped the new arrivals sort themselves into three groups. A four-top and a two-top went to booths in Jan Howard's station. The other two made for Ali's counter. As they sat down to study the menus, Ali went to make a new pot of coffee.

For the next two hours she worked nonstop. When they finally closed the Sugarloaf's front door on the last lunchtime customer at two thirty in the afternoon, Ali was beyond tired, and that was before they finished doing the cleanup work necessary to have the place ready to open the next morning.

When it was finally time to head home, she could hardly wait. She was ready to shower, take a nap, and sit with her feet up.

She had earned it.

11

Sacramento, California

I n terms of getting sober, Brenda's breaking and entering arrest the previous October had proved to be pivotal. That humiliation was the last straw, the one that had finally convinced her to crack open the door to her very first AA meeting. Since then, she'd been fighting for sobriety on a daily basis and was halfway through those first critical ninety meetings in ninety days.

Just past noon on a Friday in late January, Brenda Riley's cell phone vibrated inside her pocket just as the AA meeting moderator was leading the Serenity Prayer. Her mother, Camilla Gastellum, hadn't been feeling well that morning as Brenda left for the meeting. Concerned about her, Brenda hurried out of the church basement and answered the phone without bothering to check caller ID.

"Hi, Mom," Brenda said. "Are you okay?"

"Someone just called here looking for you," Camilla said. "At first I thought she might be another bill collector, and I wasn't going to give her your number. It turns out, though, that she's calling about your book. She says you've contacted her before and wanted to interview her."

Of the fifty-seven names listed in Richard Lowensdale's Storyboards folder, Brenda had spoken or attempted to speak with all of them. Some of them had refused to speak to her outright or had accused Brenda of lying about their particular iteration of Richard. Others had been happy to have the mask ripped from the face of their present or former "cyber-lover" so they could begin to come to grips with the emotional damage he had done in their lives. Embarrassed by their own gullibility, some of those spoke to Brenda only on condition of anonymity.

Brenda was a trained journalist. She knew how to follow stories, and she had done so. Using the storyboard data as a starting point, she had tracked down one woman after another. What she found most disturbing in all this was that the details she discovered about the women's lives appeared to coincide with the information gleaned from Richard's files. Each of them had willingly revealed her innermost life to a man who had given her nothing but empty lies in return. From what Brenda's mother was saying, it appeared that one of the reluctant interviewees was now ready to come forward.

"Did she leave her name?" Brenda asked.

"No, but I did give her this number. I hope that's okay. She said she was going to call."

"Sure, Mom," Brenda said. "That's fine. Are you okay?"

"I'm still feeling a little puny. I think I'm going to go lie down for a while."

"Turn off the phone then so you can get some rest." Brenda's phone alerted a new incoming call from a number unavailable phone. "I'm sure that's her calling now. I have to go."

"Is this Brenda Riley?"

"Yes," Brenda said. "Who is this?"

"My name is Ermina Blaylock, but everyone calls me Mina," the woman said. Her English was precise, but there was more than a hint of an eastern European accent. "Your mother gave me your number. I believe you attempted to contact me a few months ago about a book you're writing about Richard Lowensdale. At the time I wasn't interested."

Ermina Blaylock's Storyboard file was the only one that had contained no information other than her name, date of birth, and social security number. There were none of the phone or e-mail exchanges that had been part of the other women's files, so there had been no details for Brenda to check on either. The lack of information had intrigued her. If there had been no correspondence between them, why was Ermina's name in Richard's list in the first place? Was she someone Richard had targeted who had been smart enough to turn him down?

Even Richard couldn't have had a one hundred percent success rate, and Brenda suspected that the names of the women who didn't make that initial cut never hit the Storyboard folder. Brenda had attempted to do some fact checking on her own, but as far as Ermina Blaylock was concerned, she could locate nothing about the woman prior to her marriage to widower Mark Blaylock in 2002.

"Are you interested now?" Brenda asked.

"Yes," Ermina said. "If you still want to speak to me, that is."

"You're aware that Richard was involved with any number of women?"

"Yes," Ermina said. "In your book, will you be naming names?"

"Only with permission," Brenda said. "Some of the women who spoke to me insisted on anonymity."

"Sounds good," Ermina said. "I'd probably want that too."

"When do you want to get together?" Brenda asked.

"It happens I'm in Sacramento today, and I believe you are

too. I know it's late, but what about lunch? We could meet some-where, or I could stop by and pick you up."

After receiving yet another ticket for driving with a revoked li-cense, Brenda had given up "borrowing" her mother's car. These days when she went someplace, she took a cab or a bus or she walked.

Brenda glanced at her watch. She had already missed most of the meeting. She was wearing a pair of sweats, which meant she wasn't dressed to go anywhere decent for lunch. It would take her half an hour to walk home and change clothes. If her mother was taking a nap, maybe she could get in and out of the house without waking her.

"If you wouldn't mind, how about picking me up in about an hour?" Brenda gave Ermina the exact address and then set off at a brisk walk. One of the things she had done was use other sources to verify what the women in Richard's life had told her about their lives. As far as Ermina was concerned, there was no information available. By the time Brenda reached the house on P Street she had come up with a plan.

She entered the quiet house and hurried to her upstairs bed-room. Brenda changed into more appropriate clothing, wishing she had footwear that weren't tennis shoes. She took another crack at fixing her hair and makeup and went downstairs. The dining room often doubled as Brenda's home office. She kept a printer and an elderly laptop on top of the wooden hope chest she had moved from her bedroom to her make-do headquarters.

With the printer and the computer out of the way, Brenda used the key from her purse to unlock the chest. The booze bottles she had once concealed inside it when it had been what she called her "hopeless chest" were long gone. Some of the liquor had been drunk, but when she finally got serious about getting sober, she had emptied the others down the drain in her bathroom. Now the locked chest held hope once more. It was where Brenda filed everything about her book project, including her copies of the contract she had signed. It was where she kept the passbook to her newly established bank account, printed accounts of her interviews with Richard's various victims, as well as the printouts she had made from Richard's Storyboard folder.

At very the bottom of the heap, she found the file that contained the original background check High Noon Enterprises had done on Richard, the one Ali Reynolds had ordered for her. There was a phone number at the top of the page. She dialed the number and then disconnected the call while the phone on the other end was ringing.

Instead, after returning all the paperwork to the chest, locking it, and then stowing the key in her purse, she opened her laptop, booted it up, and jotted off a quick e-mail.

> Dear Ali,
>
> You'll be glad to know that I'm finally getting my head screwed on straight, and yes, I am in treatment. Finally. I'm working on a book about Richard Lowensdale and all the women's lives he has adversely impacted through his cyberstalking.
>
> I'm having trouble locating information on one of the women on his list, Ermina Vlasic Cunningham Blaylock, who is either Richard's former employer or the wife of his former employer. I'm guessing the company was in her name in order to latch on to the women-owned business gravy train in government contracts.
>
> I started to call the company you had do the background check on Richard last summer. Then I decided that they might take the request more seriously if it came from you instead of from me. If there's any charge, you'll be relieved to know that I'm now in a position to pay for it myself even if I haven't earned back the right to have my own credit card.

I'm attaching everything I know about Ermina below. Thanks in advance for your help. I expect I'll be talking to her today and tomorrow, so the sooner I can have the info the better.

Brenda R.

After pressing send, Brenda closed the laptop and put it away. Then she hurried downstairs. Her mother's worsening vision problems made leaving Camilla a note impossible.

I'll call her later, Brenda thought.

She stepped out on the front porch just as an older-model silver Lincoln Town Car pulled to a stop in front of the house. As Brenda hurried forward, the passenger window rolled down. A well-dressed woman was at the wheel.

"Brenda?" she asked.

"Yes," Brenda answered.

"I'm Ermina," the woman said. "Get in."

Ermina Blaylock was lovely. Her auburn hair glowed in the cold winter sunlight that came in through the sunroof. She had a flawless complexion and fine features.

"Thank you for picking me up, Ermina," Brenda said. "I don't have a car right now, and that makes getting around tough."

"No problem," the woman said. "But call me Mina. Everybody does."

12

Grass Valley, California

Waiting to see if Mina would show that Friday, Richard had a tough time concentrating. He was distracted enough that he didn't dare do any of his usual Internet correspondence. It was important to keep all his stories straight, and he didn't want to end up saying the wrong thing to the wrong person.

He had delivered his completed programming fix to Mina the week before. He knew the test flight had been scheduled for Wednesday. He and Mina were still operating under his eyeball-to-eyeball protocol, so she didn't send him an e-mail. She didn't call.

She had told him that if the test flight was successful, she would bring him his bonus on Friday, so Richard waited on tenterhooks. Earlier in the morning he had briefly considered cleaning house in advance of her visit, but he had eventually decided against that. He was sitting at his desk watching for her through the living room window when she arrived, apparently on foot. She pushed open the lopsided gate and walked up the weed-littered sidewalk.

When Richard had first returned to Grass Valley, his neighbors had been incredibly curious about him. He wasn't a very personable guy, and he'd been firm in rejecting their overtures of friendship. Over time they had adjusted to the fact that he was reclusive. If they wondered about why he ordered anything and everything online, they didn't discuss any of that with him.

Because the neighbors were used to a steady stream of delivery folks who left their vehicles on the street below and trooped up and down the sidewalk leading to Richard's house, he and Mina had hit upon her masquerading as a delivery person whenever she came to see him.

Today, as usual, Mina arrived on his doorstep using a faux UPS driver uniform with brown khaki trousers and a brown jacket. And as she had done on previous occasions, she carried a stack of boxes to lend credence to the disguise.

Richard didn't want to appear overeager. Nonetheless, he hurried to the door to meet her. "It's about time you got here," he said. "How did it go?"

"How do you think it went?" Mina asked with a smile as she set down her boxes. "I'm here bearing gifts, aren't I?"

"Great." Richard could barely contain his relief. "Come on in."

He led the way into the living room. He was halfway back to his desk when a powerful blow hit him squarely on the back of the head. Down he went.

By the time Richard struggled back to woozy consciousness, she had secured him to one of the dining room chairs with packing tape—probably his own packing tape from the dining room—and there was tape over his mouth as well. He was in a sitting position, but the chair had tipped over onto its side.

The room was surprisingly dark, as though night had fallen while he was unconscious. Mina was seated at the desk in front of his computer, her face eerily aglow in the lamplight. She was dressed in clothing that was different than he remembered. The brown uniform was gone. Her shoes were covered with something that looked like surgical booties; she wore gloves.

Struggling to loosen the bonds, Richard tried to speak. He meant to say, "What are you doing?" but his words came out in an incomprehensible mumble.

"Quiet," she ordered. "Be still!"

She left the computer and came back over to where he lay on his side on the floor. Picking up the hammer, she waved it in front of his face. "Do not make a sound," she said.

Richard understood that the hammer was a very real threat. He fell silent.

"Where's the money I gave you?" Mina said. "I want it. I also want my thumb drive."

Richard tried to make sense of this. She was robbing him of the money she had paid him? Worried about the possibility of some drug-crazed addict breaking into his house, Richard had hidden the money, and he had hidden it well, but it had never occurred to him that Mina might be the one trying to take it away.

But it was *his* money. He had worked for it. She owed him for getting her damned UAVs back in the air, and he *would not* give her back that money, not in a thousand years. The same thing with the thumb drive. He looked at her and shook his head.

That seemed to throw Mina into a fit of rage. She ran back to the dining room and cleared his mother's curio shelves of Richard's entire model airplane collection, knocking them to the floor, where she stepped on them and ground them to pieces.

"Tell me," she said.

With his mouth taped shut, he couldn't have told her if he had wanted. But it was a grudge match now. He wouldn't tell her no matter what. He shook his head. Emphatically.

She disappeared from view for a time. When she returned,

she was carrying his mother's old kitchen shears. At first he thought she was going to cut through the tape and free him. Instead, she walked behind him. The pain when it came was astonishing. Even with the tape over his mouth, he howled in agony.

When he could breathe again, tears were streaming down his face. She came around and dangled the remains of one of his fingers in his face.

"Tell me," she said.

He knew then that he was going to die, and the only satisfaction he could have was to deny this woman what she wanted. Twice more she went behind him. Twice more Richard's world exploded in absolute agony. He passed out then. When he came to sometime later, he was aware of a peculiar racket, and the air around him was filled with the stale odor he always connected with his mother's old vacuum cleaner.

Why is that running now?

Then she appeared again, bringing with her another of the dining room chairs. She set the chair close to his head and then sat on it.

"Tell me," she said again.

"No," he managed. Even with the tape over his mouth, it sounded like what he meant to say, *"N-O!"*

Suddenly, out of nowhere a plastic bag appeared. With a single deft movement, she pulled the cloudy plastic down over his head.

"Tell me and I'll let you live."

Richard was an experienced liar. So was Mina Blaylock. He knew that, no matter what, she going to kill him anyway. So since it would make no difference, Richard would not give her his money. No matter what.

He heard her tear loose a swath of transparent packing tape. He felt it tighten around his neck. For a few moments—a minute or so—there was enough air to breathe inside the bag. As the plastic went in and out with each breath, he could see her sitting there, watching and waiting, hoping he would give in.

He didn't. Instead, he closed his eyes so he didn't have to see her. Soon he felt himself struggling for breath as the oxygen inside the bag became depleted.

"Tell me," he heard her say from very far away.

He shook his head once more, and had a fleeting moment of victory. He knew he was dying, but he also knew he had won and Mina Blaylock had lost.

13

Sedona, Arizona

Ali's phone rang as she pulled out of the Sugarloaf parking lot. "Hey, Ali," her very pregnant daughter-in-law said. "Are you busy?"

Knowing a little of Athena's background, Ali did her best to tread lightly in the mother-in-law department. There was enough bad blood between Athena and her own parents that Athena's folks hadn't been invited to Chris and Athena's wedding. The only family member who had broken ranks with everyone else and attended the wedding was Athena's paternal grandmother, Betsy Peterson.

The rift with Chris's in-laws was something Ali couldn't understand. As far as she could see, Athena was a remarkable young woman. She had served in the Iraq War with the Minnesota National Guard and had returned home as a wounded warrior. She was a double amputee, minus her right arm from above the elbow and her right leg from below the knee. When her first husband divorced her—while she was still recovering from her injuries in Walter Reed—Athena's parents for some unaccountable reason stuck with their former son-in-law and his new wife. The previous summer Chris and Athena had made the trek to Minnesota in hopes of normalizing relations, but nothing had changed. The ex-son-in-law was still more acceptable to Athena's parents than their own daughter.

Chris and Athena had met while they were both working at Sedona High School, where Chris taught American history and welding technology and Athena taught math. Athena was fiercely independent, and Ali admired both her spirit and her spunk. Athena had taught herself to do most things, including playing basketball, with her left hand, although she now had a realistic-looking prosthesis in place of her right arm. Getting pregnant, and especially getting pregnant with twins, had set her back some in the self-confidence department. And having two babies this early in their marriage wasn't something that had been in Chris and Athena's game plan either.

As far as Ali was concerned, the appearance of twins was no surprise. After all, Chris's grandmother was a twin, so the tendency was right there in his DNA. Athena's ob-gyn, Dr. Dixon, had allayed many of Athena's worries by telling her that people who can *get* pregnant usually can *be* pregnant. She had also said that studies with pregnant women who had been born missing whole or parts of limbs due to the drug thalidomide had been able to carry babies successfully. Their only major difficulty had been maintaining balance late in their term.

A counselor from the VA had put Athena in touch with another young woman who was also an amputee and a new mother—although she was only a single amputee with a single baby. It helped Athena to know that she wasn't alone, that there was someone else out there with similar problems and dilemmas.

"Just on my way home from the Sugarloaf. Why, is there something you need?"

Athena sighed. She sounded upset. "Yes. I could really use your help. I'd appreciate it if you could come by for a little while."

"Of course," Ali said. "I'll be right there."

"Just let yourself in when you get here," Athena said. "I'm supposed to be on full bed rest."

Ali glanced at her watch. At 2:45 Chris was probably still at school. Then instead of heading home, she drove up to her old place on Andante Drive, where Chris and Athena now lived. Ali had inherited the place from her aunt Evie, her mother's twin, and had sold it to Chris and Athena when she moved on to Manzanita Hills Drive.

The house was actually a "manufactured home," a nonmobile mobile that had been permanently attached to a set of footings and a concrete slab built into the steep hillside, an unusual set of construction circumstances that allowed for an actual basement, which Chris used as a studio for his metal artwork.

As soon as Ali opened the front door, she caught a whiff of fresh paint. With the twins, Colin and Colleen, due within the next three weeks, Ali knew that Chris had been intent on pulling the nursery together. Athena was lying on the living room couch with one of Edie Larson's colorful quilts pulled up over her baby mound.

"How's it going?" Ali asked, closing the door behind her.

"After I took that little tumble last week, Chris made me promise that I'd stay put while he was gone."

Some of Athena's fellow teachers had thrown a shower on Athena's behalf. On the way back to the house, loaded down with gifts and determined to carry them herself, Athena had tripped and fallen. She had scraped both knees and her one elbow but had suffered no major damage. Chris, however, had been beyond upset.

"So what's going on?" Ali asked. "Are you okay?"

"The twins obviously aren't on the same schedule," Athena said with a wan smile. "When one of them is asleep, the other one is wide awake and kicking like crazy. So I'm not getting much sleep, and neither is Chris."

Ali smiled. "That's going to get a lot worse for both of you before it gets better. Is there something I can do to help?"

"It's about the nursery," Athena said.

"What about it?"

"We had a big fight about it before he left for school this morning."

"What about?" Ali asked.

To Ali's amazement, Athena burst into tears. Since Athena was one tough cookie, Ali figured it was either something terribly serious or else it was about nothing more than a storm of late-pregnancy rampaging hormones.

"Chris is determined to have the nursery completely finished before your parents come home tomorrow, so he's been working like crazy, painting until all hours. Last night he managed to get all the furniture put together too—the changing tables and the chests of drawers and the cribs."

"That doesn't sound so bad," Ali ventured.

Athena nodded and blew her nose. "We managed to get all the clothes washed and dried, but when he started to sort them, it turns out he's completely hopeless. I ended up dumping everything back out into one of the cribs. I could sort them myself, but I'm not supposed to be on my feet that long."

"I suspect you both have a bad case of impending parenthood nerves," Ali said. "And I'm happy to do it. Thrilled, even. Now let me at 'em."

Athena offered a thin smile and then allowed Ali to help her off the sofa. She led Ali to the nursery that had once been Chris's room. The room smelled of freshly applied paint. Two walls were pink; two were blue. The changing tables, dressers, and cribs were white. In one crib was a mountain of baby gear—some of it new and some of it secondhand. With Athena sitting in the rocker supervising the process, Ali commenced folding all the incredibly tiny outfits and separating them first by sort (blankets, shirts, nightgowns, and snuggle outfits) and second by colors (blues and greens, pinks and yellows). The blues and greens were destined for Colin's drawers while the pinks and yellows would go to Colleen's.

As Ali did the sorting and folding, she also listened. In the process she couldn't help but think about and be grateful for how different Chris and Athena's situation was from what hers had been when Chris was born. His father, Dean, had died of a glioblastoma weeks before Chris appeared on the scene. Ali had been a single mother from day one—from before day one, actually.

Chris and Athena were in this together. They expected that Athena would be going back to work as soon as possible after the babies were born. The school district had accepted Chris's request to stay home on parental leave. Ali knew he was hoping that he'd be able to look after the twins and still do some metal sculpture work in his basement studio. Ali had sincere doubts about his ability to carry that one off, but she was careful not to mention her motherly case of skepticism. Experience had taught her that looking after two babies would make welding metal art-work pieces an impossible pipe dream.

"You know," Ali said, casually, "I don't mind doing this, but even if he doesn't do it quite the way you want it done, shouldn't Chris be in on this? Once the babies get here, you'll be lucky to get the clothes out of the dryer and into the basket, to say nothing of drawers, but if he's going to be the one staying home, it seems to me he should be in charge of putting all this stuff away."

Athena shook her head. "You don't know, do you?"

"Know what?" Ali asked, although something in Athena's tone suggested that whatever it was, Ali might not want to know about it.

Athena sighed. "I hate to be the one to break this to you, but your son is color-blind. Not completely. Primary colors he can do. Reds and greens at stoplights he can do. Pastels? Not so much. According to him, all these clothes are gray." She waved her one good hand in the direction of the stacks of clothing, now properly sorted by color.

Ali was thunderstruck. "Are you kidding? You're telling me my own son is color-blind?"

The news came as a complete surprise. Eventually, though, Ali dissolved in a hopeless case of giggles. Before long Athena was laughing too.

"I never knew," Ali gasped at last. "I had no idea. From the time he was little he gravitated to blues and reds. I thought he just liked them."

"No," Athena said, sobering. "Those are the only colors he could see. So tell me, how long will it be before the twins can choose their own clothes?"

"They probably start doing that when they're three or four."

"I hope they hurry," Athena said. "Between now and then, with their father dressing them, it's not going to be pretty."

By the time Ali had the last of the clothing put away, Chris turned up with a bouquet of store-bought flowers and a sweet thinking-of-you card. The guy may have been color-blind, but he knew when it was time to turn up with a fistful of flowers.

Ali left Chris and Athena's house still feeling bemused. She and Chris had always been close, and she was incredibly proud of him, but as it turned out, Ali Reynolds didn't know her own son nearly as well as she thought she did.

San Diego, California

Mark Blaylock set off for San Diego that Friday morning tired and hungover but elated. After months of watching their financial situation deteriorate and then more months of worrying about the programming, he had cause to feel happy. It seemed to him that they were about to see some light at the end of the tunnel.

Wednesday's flawless early morning test flight had put his programming worries to rest once and for all. Both reprogrammed UAVs had flown properly. Both had taken off as expected and had followed their prescribed flight plans. The first one had landed exactly as the flight plan dictated, while an operator-issued command had blown the second drone to smithereens.

That night he and Mina had driven into Palm Springs for a celebratory dinner. The next morning Mina had set off for Grass Valley in her older-model Lincoln. She had flown up to meet with Richard that first time, but since then, not wanting to deal with TSA scrutiny or to leave much of a paper trail, she had driven back and forth. The trip usually took a couple of days. Knowing how much Mina despised living in the cramped cabin in Salton City, Mark tried not to begrudge her her periodic absences.

Mark had especially made it a point not to think about her monthly trips to see Richard Lowensdale, give him his partial payment, and check on his progress. If sex with Mina was part of what was keeping Richard on the job, Mark was prepared to overlook it. After all, he had his own occasional dalliances, and he wasn't enough of a hypocrite to begrudge Mina hers. Besides, this was the end of it. Once the program fixes had been installed in the rest of the UAVs, they wouldn't need Richard Lowensdale anymore.

"See you on Sunday," she said, when he kissed her goodbye.

"Stay safe," he told her.

Knowing he'd need to spend a couple of days in San Diego, Mina had left him a fistful of welcome cash to cover food and lodging. Much as he tried not to, Mark couldn't help regarding it as being given an allowance. To regain a little self-respect, he spent most of the day on Thursday drinking and gambling at his favorite hangout, the Red Earth Casino. With some luck and what he liked to regard as skill, he managed to add to that initial sum. On Friday morning, with a smile on his face and money in his pocket, he finally set off for San Diego to fulfill his part of the bargain and install Richard's programming fix in each of their remaining UAVs.

He didn't rush. He stopped off for a beer here and there along the way. One thing he really missed on the drive was the Sirius radio he used to have in his Mercedes. That was one of the problems with being kicked downstairs. Now, tooling along in a secondhand Honda, instead of being able to hum along with the country-western tunes he preferred on the Roadhouse or Willie's Place, he had to search through what was available—mostly Spanish-speaking stations or blabbing news.

So losing the Mercedes was a noticeable blow that was both economic and emotional. When he reached the industrial park complex that had once been home to Rutherford International, he took another hit as he drove past what had once been their official headquarters. There was a new name on the sign above the door, and Mark couldn't help but take the change personally. Rutherford's failure was Mark's failure, and he was grateful that Mina had found a way to breathe some life into the smoldering ashes of their financial catastrophe.

He drove through the familiar maze of light industrial and warehouse streets. When they had been looking for a location, having their office address on Opportunity Road had seemed exactly right. And having their warehouse/manufacturing facility on Engineer Road had seemed perfect as well, especially considering the proximity of Montgomery Field, where they had expected to do their test flights.

Whether based on hubris or unbounded optimism, their assumption that they would actually win the much sought-after drone contract had been naive. Mark's contacts had led them to believe that they had an "inside track" and that it was a "done deal." They had leveraged everything they owned to grab the opportunity, and when the contract went elsewhere, they lost big and were still left holding leases they could no longer afford.

Unfortunately their misfortunes coincided with what was going on in the general economy. As they were taking their financial hits, so was everyone else. California commercial real estate went into a downward spiral right along with the residential market, and that was as true for this office park as it was for similar projects throughout the country. Buildings that had once been fully occupied and busy now stood empty and forlorn, their entrances weedy, their walls covered with gang-related tags. Mark was relieved when he saw that no new tags were in evidence on the part of the one building that still had Rutherford International stenciled on the doors.

For a time their company had occupied office space in a building on one street and in two adjacent sections in one of the nearby buildings that had been designated for light industry. One space, equipped with rolling garage-type doors, had been used primarily for shipping and receiving. In the other, and at great expense in tenant improvements, Rutherford had constructed a clean room, which they planned on using as an assembly facility.

When it was clear Rutherford was going down the drain, the

landlord had been lucky enough to find someone who was willing to take over the office part of their lease. Because the property manager wanted to maintain a minimum level of occupancy, he had offered Mark and Mina a huge break on the lease for warehouse space. In other words, Mark was glad they still had a place to store their stock of illegal UAVs, even though he sometimes worried about how Mina was managing to pay the rent, even with the steep discount.

Mark used a clicker to let himself into the shipping/receiving bay, then he used a connecting door between the two to gain access to the assembly area. After turning off the alarm and switching on the lights, he set to work.

The UAVs were stored in the cage—a locked interior chainlink structure that had been been constructed in the assembly area. Originally it had been intended to hold their inventory of needed parts. Now there was no assembly operation and no need for parts either.

One by one he removed the UAVs from the cage and deposited them on the remaining assembly tables. Installation of the programming upgrade took approximately fifteen minutes per drone. Once each one was finished, Mark loaded it into a specially designed cardboard shipping box. After cushioning the UAV with a collection of air-filled plastic bags, he then closed the box, taped it shut, and slapped on a suitable collection of labels. If anyone asked, these were model airplanes. Large model airplanes. Specially ordered model airplanes, manufactured in China and shipped to dealers in the United States.

As each box was loaded, closed, taped, and labeled, Mark carried them back to the cage and stacked them one on top of another. There was no particular hurry. The timetable Mina had given him said that she would return to the cabin sometime on Sunday and that they would deliver the finished UAVs to

Enrique on Tuesday. By Wednesday morning, Mark and Mina would be new people. Armed with new names and matching IDs, they would head off into their new lives.

Mark was excited by the prospect. He was ready for new faces and new places. He was still hurt and disappointed by the number of people he had thought of as friends who had simply turned their backs on Mark and Mina once they fell on hard times. Mark was ready to be someone else entirely. He wanted to go live on a tropical island somewhere with no worries except maybe what kind of fish to catch for dinner. He had tried running the show with Rutherford, and that hadn't worked out very well for either of them. Now Mark was content to step back and let Mina do the running.

That wasn't to say he wasn't grateful, because he was. It was Mina's wheeling and dealing that had made this deal possible. Mark's part of the bargain was to be the on-site tech guy and have the UAVs properly reprogrammed, packed up, and ready for delivery. Ten hours later, right around midnight, Mark stacked the last box in the cage. After locking the door behind him, he put his tools away, turned off the lights, and set the alarm.

Leaving the warehouse, Mark decided he would reward a job well done by having some fun before leaving for home. Retracing his route back through the office park and back out onto Clairemont Mesa Boulevard, he pulled into the familiar parking lot of the Demon Sports Bar. When he had worked in the neighborhood, Mark had been a regular here. When he walked into the place just prior to last call, he was shocked by how much it had changed.

In the time Mark had been away, the Demon had apparently undergone a remarkable transformation. There was a redesigned menu. Flat-screen TVs had replaced the old rear-projection models. Settling onto a barstool, Mark looked around in search of a familiar face, but a whole new crop of female bartenders and cock-tail waitresses had replaced the ones he had known previously.

"What'll you have?" the bartender asked. She was red-haired, good-looking, and maybe five years younger than Mina, which made her much younger than Mark.

"A draft beer and a burger," he said with a wink, "with maybe a little salsa on the side."

She gave him a look that said she got the message. "Coming right up," she said.

So there's been some turnover since I was here last, Mark thought as he sipped that first beer. *No problem. If you're a good enough tipper, it's easy to win friends and influence people.*

14

Sedona, Arizona

When Ali let herself into the house well after four on Friday afternoon, the aroma of baking scones reminded her that this was Friday, and Sister Anselm was expected around five for what Leland liked to call his Cornish cream tea.

"I forgot," she said.

"No worries," Leland said. "Sister Anselm called a little while ago and said she was running late too."

Realizing that a nap was out of the question, Ali hustled out of her Sugarloaf Café duds and took a quick shower. Then she settled down on the love seat to let her hair air dry for a few minutes. Within seconds, Samantha appeared at Ali's feet and then scrambled up on the love seat next to her.

Sam had arrived in Ali's life in what was supposedly a temporary fostering situation with no official papers of origin. Ali hadn't particularly liked cats in the beginning, but Sam had grown on her. Their temporary situation had now stretched into years. Sam's vet estimated her to be somewhere in her early teens, which meant she was verging on feline elderly. Her sixteen-pound body could no longer deliver the graceful leaps that had once carried her to the top of the running clothes dryer, her favorite snoozing perch during the day.

Leland Brooks's concession to Sam's diminished mobility was a kitchen step stool he placed next to the dryer, an aid which she deigned to use on occasion, but only when no one was looking. Ali had done her bit to solve Sam's mobility difficulties by placing a set of pet steps next to the bed in her bedroom. That way Sam could make it on and off her favorite spot on the bed without having to suffer the indignity of being lifted up and down.

With Sam purring contentedly at her side, Ali checked her e-mail. There were more than a dozen lined up and waiting, but she chose to open only four.

The first one came from her mother:

> Your father is acting like a kid. He bounces out of bed at the crack of dawn and doesn't go to sleep until all hours. I can't believe he's the same man I've been married to for all these years.
>
> I think he's sad that today is our last full day on the ship. So am I, but I'm like an old dray horse, and I'm ready to get back in harness. See you tomorrow. There's a chance we may be able to switch our reservation to an earlier flight.

Next up was an e-mail from someone named Robert Dahlgood with a subject line that said, "Velma Trimble."

Years earlier when Ali had retreated to Sedona in the aftermath of the end of her marriage and the loss of her job, she had started a blog called cutlooseblog.com. Velma Trimble had been one of her blog's most ardent fans. During the dark time Ali had been dealing with Paul Grayson's death, Velma had taken a cab from her home in Laguna Beach and had come all the way across Los Angeles to Ali's hotel in Westwood in hopes of offering her assistance.

As a result of that selfless action despite the age difference between them, Ali and Velma had become good friends in a way that was not unlike Ali's friendship with Sister Anselm. When Velma had been diagnosed with breast cancer at age eighty-eight, her son had opposed her seeking treatment. Ali had encouraged it, and the treatment had worked. In the intervening years, Velma had managed to take a round-the-world first-class private jet tour with another new friend, Maddy Watkins.

Now, though, Velma's cancer had returned. Expecting bad news, Ali opened the e-mail from Velma's nephew with a sense of dread.

> Dear Ms. Reynolds,
> Robert Dahlgood here. I'm not sure if you remember me, but my aunt, Velma Trimble, asked me to be in touch with you.
> I regret to inform you that her situation is deteriorating rapidly and she is now receiving hospice care at her home in Laguna Beach. The nurses are able to manage her pain, which is a real blessing.
> I'm helping her put her affairs in order, and she is most interested in meeting with you and would like very much to do so in person. I know that a request of this kind is a major inconvenience, but as you know, once Velma sets her mind to something, she is not easily dissuaded.
> If you could see your way clear to come see her any time in the next few days—time is of the essence—I would be eternally grateful. If it's not possible, I certainly understand

and will be glad to pass along that information in hopes I can
convince her to settle for some other arrangement.

Sincerely,

Robert Dahlgood

Considering what Velma had done on Ali's behalf years earlier,
Ali could hardly ignore this very real plea for help. She wrote
back immediately:

Dear Robert,

I'm so sorry to hear this. I have a prior commitment that
will keep me stuck here in Sedona until tomorrow at the earli-
est. I may be able to fly over tomorrow evening or Sunday morning. I'll let you know.

Please tell Velma that I'm thinking about her and that I'll
be there as soon as I can.

Ali

Next Ali opened the e-mail from Brenda Riley. What she
read there left her feeling both relieved and anxious. On the
one hand she was delighted that Brenda was evidently working
at putting her life back together. That was a good thing, but
the idea that she was writing a book about Richard Lowensdale
was worrisome.

Ali was well aware that without the information contained in
the High Noon background check, Brenda wouldn't have known
the man's real name, to say nothing of the names of his former
employers. If Brenda was writing a book about her experience
with him as well as that of "other women" in his life, there was
a chance that B.'s company might well be pulled into some kind

of unsavory drama. On the other hand, doing background checks was part of High Noon's bread-and-butter business.

In the end, Ali simply forwarded Brenda's request to B. with a subject line that said, "What do you think?"

The last e-mail she opened was one from B., written to her during a lunch break at his conference in D.C. Ali scanned it quickly and then marked it unread because by then it was past time to be dressed and ready for tea.

Sister Anselm was already seated by the gas log fireplace when Ali entered the library a few minutes later. A driver from the Phoenix archdiocese had dropped her off for tea on the condition that Leland Brooks agree to take her the rest of the way back to Jerome once the visit was over.

They passed a pleasant hour together in front of the fire, sipping English breakfast tea, nibbling on Leland Brook's tiny egg salad and cucumber sandwiches, and downing still-warm scones slathered with clotted cream.

In the course of their conversation, Ali mentioned her dying friend's request that Ali come visit her. "You're the one with the Angel of Death moniker," Ali said to Sister Anselm. "I know you deal with ill and dying people all the time, but how do you handle it? How do you know what to do or say? I know Velma has a son. Why is she asking for me to be there instead of him?"

Sister Anselm's blue eyes sparkled cheerfully behind her gold-framed glasses as she answered Ali's question.

"You don't know that," Sister Anselm said. "The son may very well be at her side when the time comes. When someone in a family is dead or dying, it's been my experience that one of two things may happen. Occasionally, long-standing quarrels and fissures in families are suddenly and inexplicably healed. In other families, relationships that may have seemed untroubled in the past sometimes splinter completely due to some invisible fracture that has long lain hidden beneath an otherwise placid surface. When I'm summoned in this fashion, I always set off on the journey trusting that I've been called there for a reason and that I'll be able to offer comfort to those in need."

"But going there at a time like this feels like an intrusion somehow," Ali objected.

"The nephew indicated that your friend wants you there, right?"

Ali nodded. "She specifically requested that I come. I told the nephew that I'd fly over to California either tomorrow or the next day."

"Go as soon as you can," Sister Anselm advised. "A lot of the time, loved ones are in denial and think they have more time than they actually have. Whenever you go, Ali, do so in the knowledge that what you're doing places you in your perfect place to do the perfect thing, whatever that may be."

Ali smiled at her friend. "You really believe that, don't you?"

"Yes," Sister Anselm said forcefully. "I certainly do."

When Leland left to take Sister Anselm home, Ali retreated to her bedroom once more.

An instant message from B. told her he was off to a conference banquet and wouldn't be available until much later. He also told her he had alerted Stuart Ramey about Brenda's request for a background check and that Stuart would be working on the problem.

Ali knew that her parents were due to be back home on Saturday afternoon and that they would be on duty at the Sugarloaf bright and early on Sunday morning. With that in mind, Ali made arrangements to fly out of Phoenix to LAX Saturday night. After her conversation with Sister Anselm, leaving sooner rather than later seemed like the right thing to do.

Once all the travel arrangements were in hand, Ali tried calling B. His phone was still off, so she sent him an e-mail bringing him up to date on Velma Trimble's situation as well as her travel plans. After that, Ali took to her bed in the company of the Count of Monte Cristo. Within minutes, the book was facedown on Ali's bed covers, and she was sound asleep.

15

B renda Riley awakened confused and frightened in a terrible moving darkness. Somewhere nearby her cell phone was ringing, but she couldn't reach it, couldn't answer. Her hands were bound behind her. Her feet were bound too. There was a strip of something fastened to her face, and she was desperately cold.

She realized she had to be in the trunk—the large trunk—of a moving vehicle. She could hear the rush and scrape of pavement under the tires, but she had no idea where she was, where she was going, or how she came to be there.

Her memory was fuzzy. Foggy. She vaguely remembered being at home in the morning. After that she had gone to her meeting, her usual Friday noon meeting. And then she was supposed to meet someone for lunch, but right that minute, Brenda couldn't recall the woman's name. She had no idea of what had happened to her or how much time had elapsed. What she did know for sure was that she needed to pee desperately.

Brenda tried moving her legs and managed to make a few

feeble thumps with her feet. It didn't do any good. The car kept on moving and her sudden movement, compounded by the cold, made her need to urinate that much more critical. If the person driving the vehicle heard the racket from the trunk, it made no difference, at least not at first, but then the car seemed to hesitate. It turned off the pavement onto a rough gravel track of some kind.

As the vehicle came to a stop, Brenda's heart filled with dread. Moments later, the engine died. With a thump, the trunk release was engaged and the lid opened automatically. For a moment she was astonished by how bright the night sky was overhead. After the impenetrable darkness, the stars above were more brilliant than she had ever seen.

She heard the crunch of footsteps on gravel. A moment later a woman's face appeared in the starlit night. In that moment of clarity, Brenda recognized her. Mina Blaylock, the mystery woman on Richard's list.

Brenda struggled against her bonds, tried to say something. "Please, let me out. I need to use the bathroom."

For an answer, Mina reached inside. Brenda saw the hypodermic in her hand. She tried to dodge out of the way, but she couldn't. The needle plunged deep into the muscle of her upper arm. That was one of the reasons Brenda was so cold. Her arms were bare. Where was her coat? Where was her blouse? Brenda tried to struggle, but she couldn't escape the woman's fierce gloved grip. At last Brenda lay still.

"Good," Mina said. "That's better."

She reached inside the trunk again. As Brenda watched, Mina took Brenda's purse out of the trunk. With the purse gone, so was Brenda's cell phone and so was any hope of summoning help. Next Mina wrenched off Brenda's shoes.

"Where you're going, you won't be needing your purse anymore, and you won't need shoes either."

Dimly, Brenda heard a sound from somewhere nearby. Mina heard it too. She looked over her shoulder, then slammed the trunk lid shut. There were more footsteps, hurried ones this time, then the engine turned over, and the car moved. As darkness enveloped her again, Brenda realized that her prison was now lit with an eerie reddish glow leaking into the trunk from the taillights outside the car. She wondered how much time had passed, enough to turn day into night.

Brenda considered briefly about the kind of substance that had been in the hypodermic. Moments later, however, she felt her heartbeat speed up. For a time she had difficulty catching her breath. Then, gradually, the drug overwhelmed her and she drifted into unconsciousness once again, unaware and unembarrassed that when she lost control of her mind, she also lost control of her bladder.

16

San Diego, California

The trip from the Scotts Flat Reservoir to San Diego took more than ten hours. Mina stopped for gas only once, in Bakersfield. She worried that Brenda might awaken when the vehicle came to a stop and start bumping and thumping around in the trunk. Fortunately that didn't happen.

Maybe she's dead, Mina thought. Considering how much Versed Mina had plugged into Brenda's system, death by overdose would have been a likely outcome. Parking at the pumps, Mina stood for a moment listening. When there was no sound from the trunk, she hurried into the gas station, where she used the restroom and paid cash for her fuel as well as for bottled water and a collection of energy bars.

Back outside, there was still no sound from the trunk as Mina filled the gas tank and drove away. Once she was on I-5 heading south, Mina kept herself awake by thinking about Richard Lowensdale.

When Mina waved the hammer in front of Richard's face, he must have known that it wasn't an empty threat. He had fallen still and silent just as Mina had known he would. That was what most people did when they were faced with an unanticipated threat: they complied.

That was exactly what Mina's family had done all those years earlier when a gang of marauding Serbs had invaded their home in Bosnia. In hopes of surviving, they too had done exactly what they'd been told. Not imagining that people who had once been their neighbors would turn against them, Ermina's family had allowed themselves to be herded into the living room, where a gang of armed thugs had opened fire and gunned them down.

That was the first defining moment of thirteen-year-old Ermina Vlasic's life. Hidden in the stone cellar under the barn with her flickering candle and her precious books, she had heard the arriving vehicles first and then the shouting and finally the gunfire. Staying hidden was the only thing that saved her life that day. And only later, long after silence returned and as the sun set, she finally crept out of the cellar and went in search of her family.

She had found them, slaughtered in a bloody heap in the darkened living room, all of them riddled with bullets. Crumpled and dead, they had been left where they'd fallen to send a message to other Croats in the neighborhood—leave or die. It was a scene that was forever indelibly inked in her consciousness, and standing there in the carnage she had made the first decision of her new life: she decided to leave.

Leaving her loved ones where they lay, Mina went to her room, packed a bag with a few clothes and as many books as she could carry, and went in search of help. It was a group of Bosnian Serbs who had murdered her family. Ironically, it was another group of Serbs, a family whose farm was just down the country road, who took her in, cared for her, and who finally took her to the orphanage that had eventually led her to her adoptive home in Jefferson City, Missouri.

Mina had always supposed that was the difference between her and people like Richard Lowensdale and Mark Blaylock. She was tough. But for the first time in as long as Mina had known Richard, he had surprised her. He had stood up to her. She had thought he would cave, but he hadn't. In the grand scheme of things, the fifty thousand dollars she had paid Richard was chump change, but it was Mina's chump change.

Had she been able to keep on looking, Mina probably could have found Richard's stash, but by then Mina's other guest, treated with a hefty dose of Versed and bound with the same transparent packing tape she had used on Richard, had been left alone in the trunk of her parked Lincoln on a city street for far longer than she should have been. Still Mina waited until it was over, until Richard's pitiful struggles ceased completely, before she rose from the chair and walked away.

And even though she walked away without her money, Ermina Blaylock had left Grass Valley with something unexpected—a grudging respect for Richard Lowensdale.

There was very little traffic as she made her way up and over the Grapevine, but by the time she hit L.A., rush hour was starting. Just past eight o'clock in the morning, Mina pulled into the shipping/receiving bay of Rutherford International in Clairemont Mesa Business Park and closed the rolling garage door behind her.

She had given Mark a strict set of instructions. Once he finished installing the programming fix, she had told him to pack the UAVs in shipping containers and put them in the shipping/receiving bay. When they weren't there, Mina's heart went to her throat.

What if Mark had betrayed her? What if he had unloaded the UAVs to someone else?

Then she turned on the lights in the assembly area. Much

to Mina's relief, the UAVs were there, locked in the parts cage. They appeared to be properly boxed and labeled, so maybe moving them to the shipping bay was the only part of Mark's to-do list that he had ignored.

Luckily Mina had her own cage key on her key ring. It was inconvenient for her to have to do all the moving and lifting herself, but she finally managed to lug all the boxed UAVs into the shipping bay. When she popped open the trunk of the Lincoln, a cloud of urine-permeated air rose up out of the trunk. It struck her as funny that she had cut off Richard's fingers without a qualm but the smell of Brenda's having wet herself made Mina want to gag.

Brenda was still asleep. After donning her gloves, Mina used a box cutter to slice through the tape imprisoning Brenda's ankles, although she left her wrists firmly bound. Then, after removing the tape from Brenda's mouth, Mina shook the unconscious woman's shoulder.

"Wake up!" Mina ordered. "We need to get you out of there."

Brenda's eyes popped open. She looked around fearfully. "Where am I?" she rasped. "What's happening?"

"I need you to walk with me," Mina said. "It's not far. Let me help you."

She reached into the trunk, grabbed Brenda's shoulder and wrestled her into a semi-sitting position.

"Please," Brenda begged. "Not so fast. I'm dizzy."

The slight pause seemed to bring more clarity to her thought processes. "Wait. I remember now. We went to lunch. That's the last thing I remember. What are you doing?"

"Tying up a loose end is all," Mina said. "Now come on."

Eventually she was able to lever Brenda up and onto the edge of the trunk. Leaving Brenda's arms taped behind her, Mina walked her prisoner from shipping/receiving into the assembly room, where she shoved her into an old desk chair they hadn't managed to unload with the rest of the furniture. Mina used that to wheel Brenda the rest of the way into the cage.

"Let me go," Brenda said.

"No. That's not possible."

"I'll scream."

"Go right ahead," Mina said. "Be my guest. No one will hear you."

She turned and walked away. Brenda was screaming after her as she left, but Mina paid no attention. After locking the cage, she set the alarm, turned off the lights, and let herself out. She was weary, almost to the point of exhaustion, but she didn't linger. Instead, she headed for the cabin in Salton City with every intention of giving Mark Blaylock a piece of her mind.

17

Sedona, Arizona

On Saturday morning, the Sugarloaf Café was an absolute zoo. By eight a.m. there were people standing outside in the cold because there was no room to wait for a table inside. By ten o'clock they were on the last tray of that morning's sweet rolls, and Ali's feet were killing her. Things had lightened up a little and she was finally grabbing a cup of coffee when her cell phone rang.

Hoping it might be B. cut loose from his morning conference sessions, she answered without glancing at the caller ID.

"Is this Ali Reynolds?"

She didn't recognize the man's voice and she wondered how he'd gained access to her cell phone number. "Yes, it is," Ali said. "Who's calling, please, and who gave you this number?"

"My name is Camilla Gastellum. I'm Brenda Riley's mother. Have you seen her or heard from her?"

Obviously the gravelly voice that sounded like a man's wasn't.

"No," Ali said. "The last time I saw Brenda in person or spoke to her was months ago, right at the end of August."

"Yes," Camilla said. "She was on her way home from seeing you when she wrecked her car. She landed in jail in Barstow charged with driving under the influence."

"I'm sorry," Ali said. "I had no idea."

"She's taken off again," Camilla said. "She left home Friday morning and hasn't been back."

"I had an e-mail from her on Friday," Ali said. "She said she was doing well and that she was working on a book about her former fiancé."

"She may have been doing well then, but she probably isn't now," Camilla said disparagingly. "This is what always used to happen to her. She'd do all right for a while, then she'd fall off the wagon, go off on a binge, and disappear for weeks at a time."

"But I still don't understand why you're calling me," Ali said. "And how did you get my number?"

"I have macular degeneration," Camilla explained. "I had a neighbor come over today to help go through my phone records, which are also Brenda's since I pay the bill for her cell phone. She read off the numbers from last summer's bill. I guessed that this one might be yours and here I am. And the reason I called you is you're where she went for help the last time this happened. I was hoping lightning might strike twice in the same place."

"She sent me an e-mail," Ali said. "But she didn't hint that anything was amiss."

"When?"

"I'm not sure exactly what time. Sometime in the late morning or early afternoon. I could check my e-mail account and call you back with the time it was sent."

"And what did she want?"

"From me? She wanted one of my friends to do a background check on Richard Lowensdale's former employers, Mark and Ermina Blaylock."

"Did she say why?"

"Something about meeting with Ermina sometime soon, but she didn't give me a lot of detail about why she needed the information. Tell me about this book. What's it about?"

"I tried to tell Brenda that Lowensdale was trouble, but she wasn't interested. It seems he had any number of women hanging around and I suppose Ermina was one of them. When Brenda finally wised up about him, she decided to track down all his women friends. I believe what she said he was doing was cyberstalking."

"And now she's missing," Ali said. "Since when?"

"Since she left to go to an AA meeting yesterday morning. I tried talking to our local police department. At first the guy was really sympathetic, but then he was off the line for a while. I suppose he was checking her record. When he came back on the line, he pretty much told me to go jump in the lake."

Ali waited while Camilla took a ragged breath. "You see, I don't care if Brenda's drinking again. I just need to know that she's okay. That she isn't lying dead in a ditch somewhere."

"Was she driving?" Ali asked.

"No. She lost her license. I used to let her drive my car, but not anymore. If she had an accident, my insurance wouldn't cover it."

"So she left your house on foot?"

"Yes. She walked from here to her meeting. At least I assume she went to her meeting. That's where she told me she was going."

"Couldn't you ask some of the people who were at the meeting?"

"I don't know their names," Camilla said. "They're anonymous. That's the whole point, you see. I was hoping I could talk you into coming here to help me with this situation. You've been a police officer. That guy at Missing Persons would probably listen to you, even if he won't listen to me."

"Don't count on it," Ali said with a self-deprecating laugh. "Professional courtesy isn't always offered to visiting cops. I suggest you keep right on calling until you get someone who's willing to take a report."

"What if she doesn't come back?" Camilla asked. "What if we never find her?"

"Don't think like that," Ali said. "You're probably one hundred percent right. She's off on a toot somewhere. Eventually she'll sober up and come home."

"But would it be possible for you to be here?" Camilla insisted. "Just in case?"

Ali seemed to remember there was another daughter. "What about Brenda's sister?" Ali asked. "Can't she help out?"

There was a pause before Camilla said, "I'm afraid Valerie and I are estranged at the moment. She's made it perfectly clear that if it's something involving Brenda, she won't lift a finger to help. If she were here, all she'd do is say she told me so."

"I'm sorry to hear that," Ali said sincerely. "And I'm also sorry that I can't come help out right now. I have another obligation that's taking me to L.A. for the next day or two. If I can clear that up in a timely fashion, I might be able to come by Sacramento while I'm still in California, but I can't promise."

Two of Ali's counter customers had walked over to the cash wrap, where they were waiting patiently for her to deliver their check and take their money as two more customers settled onto the recently vacated stools.

"I'm so sorry, Mrs. Gastellum," Ali said. "I'm really busy right now. I'll have to get off the line. Keep this number handy so you can give me a call the moment Brenda shows up."

"I will," Camilla said. "I surely will."

Ali closed her phone, grabbed her order tablet out of her pocket, and added up the checks for the two waiting customers.

By the time she did that, several more people had filtered into the restaurant and the rush was back on in earnest.

Ali glanced up at the clock. Eleven thirty. Three more hours to go, then Edie and Bob would resume command.

If I live that long, Ali thought. *And if my feet don't give out completely*.

18

Brenda's prison was completely dark and silent. Not so much as a crack of light appeared under either of the doorways she knew to be off toward her right, across the part of the room that wasn't enclosed in the chain-link fence. Occasionally overhead she heard the sound of what seemed like military aircraft. They were certainly noisy enough to be military aircraft, but that was the only sound she heard. There were no traffic sounds, no sirens, no trucks.

After Mina went away and left Brenda alone, she had tried screaming, but no one responded. Finally, falling silent, she had drifted into despair. For a long time, she simply sat and sobbed until she realized that at least she was sitting in a chair. It could have been worse. She could have been thrown down and left on the cold hard floor. With her hands taped—she assumed they were taped—behind her, they soon fell asleep. She finally managed to shift to a partially sideways position in the chair. That at least allowed circulation to return to her hands.

For the first time she was aware of how thirsty she was and

how hungry. How long had it been since that last meal and her last drink? That had to have been sometime on Friday, but she had no idea what day it was now or what time of day. And she had no idea if anyone would ever come here again. What if Mina Blaylock had simply walked away and left her? Would the next person who walked through one of the doors find only her dead and stinking corpse?

How long did it take to die of thirst and starvation? It had taken a surprisingly long time—several days—for her grand-mother to die, even after the hospital disengaged her feeding tube and stopped giving her IV fluids. But Grammy had been old and ready to die. Brenda wasn't ready to give up. She still wanted to live.

Finally, she drifted into an uneasy sleep.

Salton City, California

Mark Blaylock was astonished when he pulled into the driveway late on Saturday afternoon and found Mina's Lincoln parked in the carport. She wasn't supposed to be home until Sunday. Obviously there had been a change of plans. It was possible she had tried to call and let him know, but he had left his phone turned off. He was having fun with Denise, the bartender, and he hadn't wanted anything or anyone—including his wife—to infringe on that.

He let himself into the house. The AC was on. That was the funny thing about this part of the desert. Overnight you'd need to turn on the heat. During the late afternoon, you'd have to turn on the AC.

But if Mina was behind that closed bedroom door, Mark didn't want to disturb her. There would be questions—a real grilling—

about where he'd been, who he had been with, and what he had been doing. No, better to let sleeping dogs lie.

Mark was still about half drunk. He grabbed one more bottle of beer out of the fridge, kicked off his shoes, and then lay down on the couch. Fortunately it was long enough for him to stretch out full length. In no time at all, he was fast asleep.

19

Sedona, Arizona

We did it, Ali told herself when two thirty finally rolled around that Saturday afternoon and she was able to lock the restaurant's front door.

She and Jan Howard met in the middle of the dining room to give one another high-fives, then they both turned their attention to the cleaning, sweeping, and mopping necessary for the Sugarloaf to be ready to open the next morning when Bob and Edie Larson returned. There had been some question about their possibly returning on an earlier flight. That wasn't Ali's concern. All she wanted to know was that they would be in charge come Sunday morning and that she wouldn't.

The substitute cook finished cleaning up the kitchen and left for the day. Jan and Ali were within minutes of leaving themselves when the door opened and in walked Bob and Edie.

"We're home!" Bob announced, beaming proudly. He was as tanned as Ali remembered ever seeing him. "That cruise was just what the doctor ordered and it doesn't look like you managed to burn the place down while we were gone."

Ali put down her broom and let herself be engulfed in one of her father's bear hugs, then she went on to hug her mother.

"I take it you caught the earlier flight," Ali observed.

"You know your father. Once we got off the boat, he was hot to trot to get home. He wanted to get here in time to make sure everything was shipshape for tomorrow."

As Bob drifted away to inspect the status of his kitchen, Edie sank into one of the booths.

"How was it?" Ali asked.

"Glorious," Edie replied. "I've never had so much fun in my life, not even when you and your aunt Evie and I went to England. Your father was like a kid again. You should have seen him on the dance floor."

Ali was taken aback at her mother's effusiveness, and the idea of her father on a dance floor was beyond belief. "Dad can dance?"

"Yes, he can," Edie said. "We have the photos to prove it. The fridge at home is empty, of course. I was going to run to the store before dinner, but we called Athena and Chris while we were riding up from Phoenix in the shuttle. They invited us to come to dinner—all of us, you included. Athena said they have the nursery pulled together. They want to show it to us."

Suddenly Athena's urgency to have the nursery completely finished on Friday made a lot more sense. If the sorting and folding was all done before Bob and Edie got home, there would be no need for Edie Larson to do it.

"You're sure they won't mind if I tag along?" Ali asked.

"Scout's honor," Edie said with a smile. "What about B.?"

"He's in D.C. this week," Ali said. "A conference this weekend and meetings next week."

"Too bad," Edie said. "We'll miss him."

I do too, Ali thought.

Once Ali was in the car, she dialed Chris's number. "Mom and

Dad told me I was invited to dinner," Ali said. "But I'm checking with you all the same."

"It's fine. Athena wants to show off the nursery," Chris said. "I'm barbecuing."

The thermometer on the Cayenne's dashboard indicated the outside temperature was in the low forties.

"Isn't it a little cold for barbecuing?" Ali asked.

"Believe me, Mom," Chris said, "right this minute, freezing my butt off over an outdoor grill is preferable to making any kind of a mess in the kitchen. Athena would have a fit."

"She's into nesting?" Ali asked.

"I'll say," Chris replied. "In a big way."

"It's a good thing you got that nursery situation handled," Ali said. "I don't care what Dr. Dixon says about the official due date. If the nesting instinct has come into play, the twins are liable to turn up any day now. What time is dinner?"

"Grandpa and Grandma are operating on East Coast time. They asked to eat early. I told them to come around five or so."

"Great," Ali said. "I'm catching a plane for L.A. at ten o'clock tonight, but if I leave Sedona by six, that should give me plenty of time to eat and run."

"You're going to California?" Chris asked. "Now? How come?"

Ali explained about what was going on with Velma, who had actually been among the out-of-town guests at Athena and Chris's wedding.

"Don't worry, though," Ali said. "If those babies of yours decide to make an early appearance, I'll be able to get myself home in a hurry."

Back at the house, Ali retreated to her room, where she showered and dressed. Then, after packing a single suitcase, she was on her way out the door for dinner when B. called. He was back in his hotel room for a few minutes before a dinner meeting.

"Your week at the Sugarloaf is over," he said. "Did you live?"

"I'm not sure my feet did," Ali answered with a laugh. "And I'm not sure how my parents do this day after day, week after week, and year after year, but they do. They're back, though. Had a great time. We're all meeting up at Chris and Athena's for dinner. The nursery is twin-ready, and they want to show it off. After that I have a plane to catch."

"A plane? Where are you going?"

Over the next few minutes, she brought B. up to date about her e-mail from Velma and the troubling phone call from Camilla Gastellum. She explained that after seeing Velma, if Brenda still hadn't turned up, Ali planned to make a quick dash up to Sacramento to see if she could be of help to Camilla.

"Let me get this straight," B. said thoughtfully. "Brenda went missing right after she asked you for that background check?"

"That's how it seems," Ali said.

"So the two things could be connected."

"Brenda's mother seems to think she just fell off the wagon, but it's possible," Ali agreed.

"What time are you heading for the airport?"

"My L.A.-bound flight leaves Sky Harbor ten p.m. I'll come back home right after dinner, then Leland will drive me down to Phoenix and drop me off."

"I'll give Stuart a call and see what, if anything, he's come up with on the background check. I'll ask him to swing by with whatever he has before then so you'll be able to take it with you."

When Ali reached Chris and Athena's place, her parents were already there. Chris, wearing a jacket, was out on the deck overseeing the grill. Bob and Edie had come equipped with a stack of cruise photos and were inflicting on their granddaughter-in-law their tandem cruise travelogue.

"And here's the girl who made it happen," Bob said heartily

when Ali joined them. "Cruises are great. I can hardly wait to go on another one, maybe an Alaskan cruise next summer, if we can talk you into looking after the Sugarloaf again. Everything is clean as a whistle. You did a great job."

"Now look what you've done," Edie said, smiling at Ali. "You've turned your father into a cruise-loving monster. Who would have thought it?"

Certainly not Ali.

"Now sit," her father ordered. "Let me show you the pictures. Edie already managed to download and print most of them."

There were candid shots as well as a collection of standard cruise ship photos. One showed Bob and Edie coming on board and standing at the top of the gangplank. Another showed them dressed in formal attire. It was only the second time in her life that Ali had seen her father in a tux. A third showed them standing together on a sandy beach.

From the wide grins on their faces in the various photos, it was clear that Bob and Edie had been having a great time. They had some videos as well. Chris came in long enough to download those onto his iMac for all to see. Ali deemed the one of Bob attempting to dance the limbo and coming to grief in the sand as worthy of either YouTube or America's Funniest Videos.

By the time Ali finally left Chris and Athena's, it was later than it should have been. There was enough time to make the plane, but just barely.

Back at the house she found Leland pacing in the kitchen and checking his watch. Ali's packed suitcase sat on the floor next to the door into the garage. "We don't have much time," he said, "but don't forget. Both your Taser and your Glock need to be in your checked luggage."

"Thanks," Ali said. Without his timely reminder, she might well have forgotten.

When she had finished stowing both of those, Leland handed her a thick manila envelope. "Stuart Ramey from High Noon dropped this off a little while ago. I'm assuming you want to take it along as well."

"Thanks," Ali said, stuffing it in her purse. "Something to read along the way."

But reading it along the way didn't happen. She was beyond tired. The week's hard work had taken a physical and mental toll. With Leland behind the wheel, she fell asleep almost as soon as she got in the car. She made it to Sky Harbor with just enough time to clear security before boarding her plane. Once the flight was airborne, she fell asleep again.

What Ali really wanted to do was collapse into her very own bed and sleep for twenty-four hours straight, but that wasn't in the cards. She had told Velma Trimble and Camilla Gastellum that she was coming to see them, and she was. What kind of condition she'd be in by the time she got there was anybody's guess.

Ali had made arrangements for a rental car to be waiting at LAX. Knowing she'd be arriving in the middle of the night, she had made a hotel reservation at the airport Hilton. By the time she collected her luggage and her car and staggered up to the hotel registration desk, she was just barely upright.

Ali fell into her unfamiliar hotel bed. Lying awake for a few short minutes, she was grateful that it was her mother who would be in charge of the Sugarloaf Café in a few short hours. Walking in Edie's very capable shoes for just one week had left Ali exhausted.

She fell into a deep sleep. There may have been countless airplanes passing overhead and traffic streaming by outside, but Ali didn't hear any of it. She was far too tired.

20

A t precisely 3:28 a.m. on Sunday morning, Florence Haywood smelled smoke. Flossie's maternal grandmother had been a smoker, and she had died a gruesome death when she fell asleep while smoking in bed. Florence had been only six at the time, but that event had a lasting influence on her life. She was scared to death of house fires. Her husband, Jimmy, assured her that their motor home was completely safe, but Flossie remained unconvinced. She insisted that he replace the batteries in their smoke alarm every six months rather than once a year, just to be on the safe side.

For the past ten years, starting in November, she and Jim had driven their aging Pontiac down from Bismarck, North Dakota, so they could spend the worst five months of winter in their motor home near the Salton Sea. Their "affordable" RV lot was part of a mostly failed residential subdivision called Heron Ridge, where they had an electrical hookup, a concrete slab, and nothing else. Once a week they had to drive into town to empty the RV's holding tanks.

The beach cabin closest to them belonged to Mark Blaylock. For several years, Mark had been the cabin's sole sometime occupant. Up until a few months ago, Flossie and Jimmy had assumed he was single. In the past two months, however, his witch of a wife, a woman named Mina, had shown up. She had been living at the cabin more or less on a full time basis ever since.

Flossie believed in being neighborly, and she had done her best, but Mina had rebuffed all of Flossie's best efforts. She had taken over a plateful of freshly baked cookies. She had given cookies to Mark Blaylock on occasion, and she knew chocolate chip cookies were his particular favorite. Mina had accepted the plate but hadn't bothered to invite Flossie inside.

Fine, Flossie told herself. *Be that way.*

She continued to be on good terms with Mark, but she had nothing further to do with his standoffish wife.

That Sunday morning, after pulling on her robe and ascertaining that there was no sign of fire inside their RV, Flossie went from window to window. Flossie's recent cataract surgery had left her with something she had never had before—perfect 20/20 vision. Once she located the source of the flames, she could see quite clearly that Mina Blaylock was standing outside, wrapped in a coat, and tossing items into the already roaring fire burning in her husband's trusty Weber grill.

Yes, there was definitely some wood smoke thrown into the mix. Mark Blaylock usually ordered a cord of mesquite each fall that was delivered to the far end of his lot. This year he hadn't ordered new wood. Last year's load was dwindling, but there was definitely a hint of mesquite in the smoke Flossie smelled.

But there was something else too. Flossie was old enough to remember how back in the old days before there were plastic trash containers at the end of every dirt road in America, people had been responsible for their own garbage. Many people, especially people living out of town, had maintained their own personal burning barrels. That's exactly what this smoke smelled like—burning garbage.

The whole thing seemed odd. Flossie was tempted to go outside and ask Mina if everything was all right, just to see what she'd say, but then Jimmy woke up.

"Floss," he called from the bedroom. "Are you coming back to bed or not?"

"Coming," Flossie said. "I'll be right there."

21

Grass Valley, California

The call came into the Nevada County Emergency Communications Center at ten past eight on a cold but quiet Sunday morning. It was January in the foothills of the Sierras, but it was also unseasonably warm. It wasn't snowing or raining, and the roads were relatively clear. The Saturday night drunks had all managed to make it home without killing themselves or anyone else.

Phyllis Williams was one of only three emergency operators working that shift, and she was the one who took the call. The enhanced caller ID system listed an out-of-state telephone number. There was no way for Phyllis to tell if the call was coming from a cell phone or a landline.

"Nine-one-one," she said. "What are you reporting?"

The caller paused for a moment, as if uncertain what she should say. "It's about my fiancé," she said finally. "He lives there in Grass Valley. I'm worried about him. I'm afraid something may have happened to him. He always calls me on Saturday night, but last night he didn't. I've been calling and calling ever since last night. He doesn't answer. He may be sick or hurt."

This was going to end up being a judgment call on Phyllis's part. If the woman was talking about somebody who was elderly and frail or if it was a kid, it was a different story, but at first blush this sounded like this guy had missed making a phone call by a little over twelve hours. Something that trivial was hardly the end of the world. Twelve hours wasn't nearly long enough for most police departments to be willing to take a missing persons report, but maybe a routine "welfare check" was in order.

"What's his name?" Phyllis asked. "Where does your fiancé live?"

The woman blurted out the name Richard Lydecker and a street address on Jan Road in Grass Valley.

"Your name?" Phyllis asked.

"My name is Janet," the woman said. "Janet Silvie."

"And where are you located?"

"I'm at home," Janet said. "In Buffalo. Buffalo, New York. I don't know what I'll do if something has happened to him. What if Richard's dead? I know he has an ex-girlfriend who's been stalking him. She's evidently dangerous and very unstable. What if she did something to him?"

Janet Silvie's voice was rising in volume. Phyllis could tell the woman was close to losing it. A lot of callers did that. They worked themselves into such a frenzy before making the first call that they fell apart on the phone. Often it was virtually impossible to retrieve any usable information from someone who was hysterical. Still, the idea that a threat had been made upped the ante and Phyllis needed to learn what she could.

"Please calm down," Phyllis said. "You'll be better able to help us help Mr. Lydecker if you stay calm. Does this woman who threatened him have a name?"

"Brenda something," Janet said. "Something Irish, maybe. O'Reilly or maybe just plain Riley. I don't remember her name.

She even called me once, trying to feed me some line about Richard cheating on me. When I told Richard about it, that's when he warned me that she's some kind of nut, like on drugs or something. I don't blame him for being scared of her."

"You actually spoke to this woman?"

"There was no speaking. It was more like she was talking—yelling really—and all I could do was listen."

"Does she live at the address you gave me?"

"No. They're not married. I already told you Richard is *my* fiancé. We're going to get married next summer. Sometime in June. We haven't set an exact date."

Phyllis tried not to roll her eyes. TMI—too much information—and none of it was the information she actually needed. In the meantime, Phyllis did a quick check of the records available to her. According to the county assessor's office, the property on Jan Road belonged to Richard Stephen Lowensdale. There was no Grass Valley listing of any kind for someone named Richard Lydecker.

"Tell me about Brenda. Do you know if she's armed?" Phyllis asked her questions calmly. That was the secret to working as a 911 operator. You had to remain calm no matter what. "Is she dangerous?"

"Maybe she is or maybe she isn't," Janet replied. "How would I know? I've never met the woman. I've never even seen her. After all, I'm a whole continent away. You're right there in Grass Valley. Isn't there something you can do?"

Phyllis's desk in the Nevada County Communications Center was actually located in Nevada City rather than Grass Valley, but she didn't quibble.

"Yes, ma'am," Phyllis told her caller. "I'm dispatching officers right now to do a welfare check."

"And you'll get back to me if you find out that something's wrong?" Janet Silvie asked.

"I'm only an emergency operator," Phyllis told her. "I won't be the one getting back to you. The address you gave me is inside the Grass Valley city limits. Once I pass this information on to them, the Grass Valley Police Department will be handling the response. Maybe one of their uniformed officers will call you back. Or else Mr. Lydecker himself. I'm sure the officers on the scene will let him know that you're concerned."

"Thank you," Janet Silvie said gratefully, then she blew her nose loudly into the mouthpiece.

Phyllis Williams wasn't offended. She was used to it. In her line of work, nose blowing was actually a good sign. It beat hyperventilating. Or screaming. Or the devastating sound of gunshots when a simple domestic violence call suddenly spiraled out of control and into a homicide situation.

That had happened to Phyllis on more than one occasion. Once she heard the sound of gunfire, she knew there was nothing to be done. Nothing at all. It was over. People were already dead or dying. All Phyllis could do then was send officers to the scene even though she knew their arrival would be too little, too late.

Nose blowing, on the other hand, meant that the people on the other side of the telephone conversation were still alive. They were trying to pull themselves together and regain control. Their grip on self-control might be tenuous but it counted big in Phyllis's book.

"Try not to worry," Phyllis said reassuringly. "As I said, officers are currently on their way to that address."

That was a small white lie because the officers weren't on their way right that very minute. They wouldn't get word until Phyllis notified Dispatch at the Grass Valley Police Department. Phyllis did that immediately, but she still felt that there was no real urgency to the matter. After all, it was a simple welfare check. No big hurry. No need for lights or sirens. The officers would get there when they got there, probably after taking their morning coffee break rather than before.

Phyllis then glanced at the clock on the wall across the room. It was almost time for her coffee break. Wanda Harkness, the operator at the next desk, had just come back from her break, and she was now involved in taking a call that sounded no more critical than the one Phyllis had just handled.

For the remainder of that Sunday morning, Phyllis and Wanda handled calls most of which shouldn't have been 911 calls in the first place. One woman was frantic because her declawed house cat had escaped through an open door and taken off for parts unknown. What if a coyote caught it and ate it? Couldn't they please do something to help? Someone else had crashed into an empty plastic garbage can hard enough to split it wide open. The car was most likely damaged, but apparently no people were. And one woman, an almost weekly caller, begged them to do something about the noise of those church bells. did they have to ring that loud every single Sunday morning?

Time dragged. Between calls, Phyllis sipped her coffee, worked the *New York Times* Sunday crossword, and kept an eye on the clock.

At eleven thirty-eight, Phyllis's phone lit up. "Nine-one-one," she said. "What are you reporting?"

"I want to report a missing person," a woman said, sounding reasonably controlled. This one wasn't panicky. She wasn't yelling.

Caller ID said that the call had originated in area code 541. Phyllis recognized that as being somewhere in Oregon. Phyllis's sister and brother-in-law lived in Roseburg.

"Is the missing person a child or an adult?" Phyllis asked.

"An adult. He's fifty-three."

"He's a relative of yours?"

"Well, sort of. We're engaged. At least we're going to be. We had this little disagreement on Thursday. He sent me a link to an engagement ring he was thinking about getting me for Valentine's Day. The problem is, I didn't like the one he picked out, and I told him so, but I can't imagine he's still mad about that. We talked briefly on Friday morning. He was still upset, but he thought we'd be alright."

"All right, then," Phyllis said. "Let me get some information. What's your name?"

"Dawn," the woman said. "Dawn Carras from Eugene, Oregon."

"And your missing fiancé's name?"

"Richard," Dawn said. "Richard Loomis."

"Do you have an address?"

"Yes. It's nine sixteen Jan Road."

Whoa! Phyllis thought. *Another man named Richard AWOL from the same address? How interesting.*

Phyllis managed to keep her voice even and businesslike as she checked Grass Valley records for any listing for Richard Loomis. She found nothing, just as earlier she had found no listing for Janet Silvie's Richard Lydecker.

This seemed like more than a mere coincidence. Two women had called from opposite ends of the country on the same morning to report two missing fiancés both of whom were named Richard and who evidently shared a residence with yet a third person, also named Richard. Once you added a psychotic ex-girlfriend into the mix, Phyllis's Sunday morning shift at the com center was suddenly a whole lot more interesting than it had been earlier.

Dutifully she took down all of Dawn Carras's information, but the moment Phyllis was off the phone, she called Grass Valley PD and spoke to Sandy in Dispatch.

"About that welfare check I called in earlier—"

"I forgot to get back to you," Sandy said. "It's turned out to be a whole lot more serious than a welfare check. Responding officers found a body. If this is Mr. Lydecker, the guy's dead and has been for some time—a couple of days at least. The ME is on his way there right now. The cops on the scene said someone trussed him up with packing tape, put a plastic bag over his head, and taped that shut as well. Can you give me any additional details?"

"No," Phyllis said. "I already gave you everything I had on that one, but it turns out I do have one more piece of the puzzle. I just had some other woman, one from Oregon this time, who called in a missing person report on her fiancé. This guy is named Richard Loomis. He happens to live at the same address on Jan Road that Janet Silvie gave me for Richard Lydecker.

"The second caller is a woman named Dawn Carras who lives in Eugene, Oregon. According to her, she and Richard Loomis had a lover's spat the other night because she wasn't wild about the engagement ring he had chosen for her. They had words over it on Thursday evening. He was still upset when she spoke to him on Friday morning, but she expected that all would have blown over in time for their regular Saturday date-night phone call, but he never called."

"So we've got three guys named Richard, one dead guy, and two missing fiancés," Sandy said. "What does it sound like to you?"

"Sounds like our little Richard was playing with fire and got burned. He must be one good-looking dude. Or else he's loaded. Think about how ugly Aristotle Onassis was."

"Who?" Sandy asked.

Phyllis Williams, Phyllis James back then, had been a freshman in high school on that day in November when President Kennedy was gunned down by Lee Harvey Oswald. Years later, she had been appalled when his widow and Phyllis's own personal idol, Jackie Kennedy, had taken up with billionaire Aristotle Onassis. It seemed impossible to Phyllis that Sandy had no idea who Aristotle Onassis was, but then again, Sandy might be so young that she didn't know who Jackie Kennedy was either.

This wasn't the first time in Phyllis's many years at the Nevada County Com Center that she had run headlong into a generation gap with her younger counterparts, and it wouldn't be the last.

"Never mind," she said. "It doesn't matter."

But if Richard Lowensdale, Richard Lydecker, and Richard Loomis were all one and the same, Phyllis wondered what exactly the guy had going for him. Whatever it was, it had obviously been good enough to attract women like flies to honey.

Too bad it wasn't enough to save his life.

22

Los Angeles, California

Ali Reynolds didn't awaken in her Los Angeles hotel room until after ten the next morning. As soon as she heard the rumble of planes overhead, she was surprised that she had been able to sleep through the racket. She ordered coffee and breakfast from room service. Knowing she needed to check on Velma before showing up at her home, Ali dialed Velma's phone number in Laguna Beach and then waited for someone—a hospice worker, most likely—to answer.

What if I waited too long? Ali wondered.

"Velma Trimble's residence."

The voice on the other end of the line was brisk and business-like.

"My name is Ali Reynolds," she began. "I was told Velma wanted to see me—"

"Ali? It's Maddy—Velma's friend, Maddy Watkins. I'm so glad you called."

When Velma had defied her cancer diagnosis by signing up for that round-the-world private jet cruise, she had been assigned a stranger, Maddy Watkins, as roommate by the travel agency. By the end of the trip, Maddy and Velma had become fast friends. Maddy, a wealthy widow from Washington State, was an aging dynamo who traveled everywhere by car in the company of her two golden retrievers, Aggie and Daphne. When she and Velma had been invited to attend Chris and Athena's wedding, the two dogs had come along to Sedona.

"How are your kids?" Maddy asked. "Aren't those twins due most any day now?"

"Soon," Ali said. "But how's Velma?"

"The dogs and I drove down and have been here for the past three days. Aggie and Daphne weren't trained to be service dogs, but try to tell them that. Aggie has barely left Velma's bedside. By rights her son should be the one who's here supervising the hospice workers, but he's not. If you don't mind my saying so, Carson is a real piece of work. If I didn't know better, I'd think he and my own son were twins. Anyway, I believe Carson is a little afraid of me, and rightly so. He was ready to pull the plug on his mother four years ago when she first got her cancer diagnosis. And I don't blame her at all for wanting people with her right now who don't have a big vested interest in what's going on."

"What is going on?" Ali asked.

"She's dying, of course," Maddy said brusquely. "But she's interested in tying up a few loose ends before that happens, you being a case in point."

"I flew into L.A. last night," Ali said. "If it's convenient, I could come by later this morning. It'll take an hour or so for me to drive there, depending on traffic."

"Midafternoon is a good time," Maddy said. "She takes a nap after lunch. If you could be here about three, it would be great."

"Three it is," Ali said. There was a knock on the door.

"Room service."

"My breakfast is here, Maddy. See you in a few hours."

Ali let the server into the room. Over coffee, orange juice, and a basket of breakfast breads, Ali opened the High Noon envelope, pulled out a wad of papers, and began to read.

23

Grass Valley, California

Detective Gilbert Morris of the Grass Valley Police Department wasn't having an especially good weekend. Once upon a time, when Gil first hired on with the department, being promoted to the Investigations Unit was more of an honor than anything else. Sure you had a few car thefts and break-ins to investigate from time to time, but not many murders. Maybe one every two to three years. At that point, the Investigations Unit would get called out to do their homicide investigation dance. That, of course, was back before the meth industry came to town and set up shop.

People had started killing one another with wild abandon about the time Gil got promoted to the I.U., and there didn't seem to be any sign of the homicide count letting up. That didn't mean, however, that the city fathers had seen fit to adjust the budget enough to allow for any more than four detectives. In the short term that had been good for Gil's overtime pay, but long-term it had been bad for his marriage. This week had been especially tough. Dan Cassidy, the lieutenant in charge, was out for knee surgery, Joe Moreno was off on his honeymoon, and Kenny Mosier's father was taking his own sweet time dying in a hospital somewhere in Ohio. That meant Gil was the only Investigations guy in town, and this was fast turning into a very crowded week.

Friday was a good case in point. That night, two brothers, some of Grass Valley's less exemplary citizens, had gone to war with each other and had both ended up dead. George and Bobby Herrera were a pair of homegrown thugs who had graduated from small-town thievery to running a meth lab out of their rundown apartment on the outskirts of town. Both had been pumped up on a combination of booze and meth. What started out as a verbal confrontation had escalated to physical violence when they took their furious sibling rivalry into the unpaved parking lot outside their apartment.

When weapons appeared, fellow residents ducked for cover and called the cops. By the time officers arrived on the scene, both brothers were on the ground. Bobby had died instantly George died while en route to the hospital. Gil arrived at the crime scene to find both brothers were deceased, leaving in their wake a mountain of evidence and a daunting amount of paperwork.

Gil had spent all day Saturday working the crime scene. It wasn't a matter of solving the crime, because the double homicide pretty well solved itself. Several witnesses came forward to claim that they had seen everything that had happened in the weed-strewn parking lot. A hazmat team came by to dismantle the meth lab George and Bobby had been running in their cockroach-infested one-bedroom apartment.

"It's a good thing they're both dead," the hazmat guy told Gil. "If they had started a fire in their meth lab kitchen, the place would have gone up like so much dried tinder and the other people who lived here might not have been able to get out."

Gil took one statement after another. The witnesses' stories were all slightly different, but the general outlines were all the same. When the brothers were sober, they were fine. When they were drunk or high, look out. Bobby and George had been pleasant enough earlier that Friday morning, but by the middle of the afternoon they were screaming at one another and, as one young mother of a three-year-old reported, using some very inappropriate language.

Bobby, the younger of the two, had come running out of their downstairs apartment carrying a rifle of some kind and wearing nothing but a pair of boxers. Gil Morris had to admit, going barefoot in Grass Valley in January was something of a feat. Friday had been clear but very cold. Obviously Bobby was feeling no pain.

Bobby stood there holding the gun pointed at the door and yelling at his brother to man up and come outside. Otherwise he was a lily-livered something or other—several expletives deleted. At that point several of the neighbors, crouched behind furniture, saw the weapon, picked up their phones, and dialed 911. Unfortunately, before officers could get there, George emerged from the apartment. He was fully dressed and carrying a firearm of his own.

According to witnesses, both men stopped screaming for a moment. They seemed to be listening to the sound of approaching sirens before Bobby resumed his rant.

"You stupid son of a bitch!" he screamed. "You had to go call the cops, didn't you."

Just like that, as though they were on the same wavelength, they both pulled their respective triggers. George was evidently the better shot of the two. His bullet removed most of his brother's head. Bobby was dead the instant he was hit. Bobby's shot went low and tore through George's femoral artery. By the time the EMTs were able to get to him, he had lost too much blood and couldn't be stabilized.

As a police officer, Gil found himself being grateful that those two dodos had killed each other without damaging someone else. Then, late Saturday evening as he was about to call it a day, he found himself face-to-face with Sylvia Herrera, Bobby and George's grieving but furious mother.

"Why?" she wailed at him. "Why are my boys dead, my poor innocent babies?"

Bobby and George had been twenty-six and twenty-nine respectively. As far as Gil was concerned, they were a long way from babies. And they were a long way from innocent too. They were a pair of drug-stupefied losers, but Gil couldn't say that to their mother, and Sylvia Herrera was inconsolable.

Finally, when she quieted enough for him to get a word in edgewise, Gil said, "I'm so sorry for your loss, Mrs. Herrera. It's the drugs, you know."

"Drugs?" she screeched back at him. "You say it's the drugs?"

He nodded. She reached out a hand and waggled a finger at him, thumping him on the chest as she spoke, like a mother remonstrating with a difficult child.

"Don't you know drugs are illegal?" she demanded. "You're the police. You should stop them."

"Yes, ma'am," he agreed. "We certainly should."

On Saturday night it wasn't necessary for him to call Linda in advance and tell her he was going to be late. Months earlier his wife of twenty some years had given up on being married to a policeman. She had taken the kids and the dog and the cat and had gone home to live with her folks in Mt. Shasta City. It was too bad, "a crying shame," as some of the guys at work had put it. The truth is Gil had done his share of crying about it, although he'd never tell his buddies at the department a word about that. Instead, he kept a stiff upper lip and motored along from case to case.

He was sorry about losing his family, but there didn't seem to be a damned thing he could do to fix it any more than he could stop the overwhelming flood of drugs that had taken the lives of Sylvia Herrera's sons.

So Detective Morris dragged his weary body home to his empty house that was furnished with whatever leavings Linda's father hadn't been able to cram in the U-Haul. Linda had left him one plate, one bowl, one glass, one coffee cup, and one set of silverware. That simplified Gil's meal planning, and it simplified clean up too. He washed every dish he owned after every meal. He thought about microwaving one of those Healthy Choice dinners, but he didn't bother. They tasted like crap, and anyway he was too tired to eat. Or even drink. He stripped off his clothes, fell crosswise on the bed, and fell asleep.

The next morning Gil was still in his shorts, eating the crummy dregs from the bottom of a nearly empty box of Honey Nut Cheerios, drinking instant coffee, and wishing he had a toaster so he could have an English muffin, when the phone rang.

"Uniformed officers are reporting what appears to be a homicide at the top of Jan Road," the dispatch officer for Grass Valley PD told him. And so, at eleven forty-five on a chill Sunday morning in January, Gil Morris found himself summoned to his third homicide case in as many days.

Yes, it's a good thing Linda is gone, Gil told himself as he hurried into the bedroom to get dressed. *Otherwise she'd be pitching a royal fit.*

24

Grass Valley, California

Gil got dressed and drove straight to 916 Jan Road. The front yard was unkempt and weedy. There were dilapidated remnants of what might have been flower beds long ago, but no one had planted anything in them for a very long time. The front gate on the ornamental iron fence hung ajar on a single bent hinge. Two uniformed officers, Dodd and Masters, waited for Gil on the front porch.

"What have we got?" Gil asked.

"It's pretty ugly in there," Dodd said. "One victim, but he's been dead for a while and the thermostat is set somewhere in the upper eighties."

With no explanation needed, Dodd handed Gil an open jar of Vicks VapoRub. Nodding his thanks, he slathered some of the reeking salve just under his nostrils. It stank to high heaven, but it would help beat back the pungent odors that were no doubt waiting for him inside the house.

"Cigar?" Dale Masters asked, offering one of those as well.

Linda had put a permanent embargo on Gil's having the occasional cigar. With her gone, it was time that prohibition was lifted.

"Thanks," Gil said. He took the proffered smoke and stuck it in his jacket pocket. "If you don't mind, I'll save it for later."

"Be my guest," Masters told him. "You're going to need it."

"What happened here, forced entry?"

"Not that we can see," Masters replied. "There's a deadbolt on the front door, but it wasn't engaged."

That means the victim probably knew his killer, Gil thought. *At least he let the bad guy into the house.*

"But we might get lucky," Officer Dodd said.

"How so?" Gil asked.

Dodd gestured to the upper corner of the front porch to where a CCTV security camera had been mounted on the wooden siding.

"The only way that'll help us is if it's turned on," Gil said. "Now what about the coroner?"

"Fred's on his way," Dodd said. "He should be here any minute."

Without waiting for the arrival of the coroner, Fred Millhouse, Gil slipped on a pair of crime scene booties and a pair of latex gloves. "Do we have a name?"

"Several actually," Officer Dodd said. "We were originally sent here to do a welfare check on a guy named Richard Lydecker whose fiancée called nine-one-one to report him missing. Later another woman called looking for her missing fiancé. She gave the nine-one-one operator the same address, only she says her guy's name is Richard Loomis."

"Curiouser and curiouser," Gil said.

Dodd nodded. "County tax records say the residence is owned by someone else named Richard, only his last name is Lowens-dale. So I'm guessing the dead guy is one of those three or maybe he's all of them. According to them, Lowensdale is age fifty-three. Looks like he lives alone."

My age, Gil thought.

"Were the lights on or off when you got here?" he asked.

"The overhead fixture in the living room was off. The desk lamp is on in the corner, but the blinds were closed in both the living room and dining room. The only way to see inside was through the window in the front door. That allows a view of the entryway only, not the actual crime scene, which is in the living room."

"So no one could see what was happening from the outside."

"I don't think so. I suspect this all went down sometime in the course of the afternoon on Friday or maybe even Thursday. The porch light was off, and we found a UPS package here by the front door, so it was probably delivered on Friday afternoon at the latest. UPS doesn't deliver on weekends."

Gil paused long enough to look down at the label. Zappos. From information on the label and from the shape of the box, Gil figured the package probably contained a pair of shoes. The victim may have needed new shoes and he may have ordered new shoes, but he was never going to wear them.

"So the UPS guy may have some information for us," Gil said. "Any idea who he is?"

"The local driver is named Ted Frost," Dodd said. "I went to high school with him. He's a good guy."

Gil nodded. "See if you can get him on the horn."

While Officer Dodd set off to do Gil's bidding, the detective geared himself up for the task at hand. As he stepped on the grimy hardwood-floored entryway, Gil Morris encountered the appalling stench that immediately overpowered the puny efforts of his Vick's Vaporub.

That one sickening whiff was enough to tell him that he was also stepping into a nightmare.

For a moment, after he crossed the threshold, Gil stood still, trying to get the lay of the land and assimilate what he was see-ing and feeling. As expected, the house was unbearably hot. If he had been able to see a thermostat, he would have turned it down. The overheated air reeked with an ugly combination of odors. Fighting his own gag reflex, Gil catalogued the unwelcome but familiar smells—both the putrid odor of decaying flesh and the lingering coppery scent of dried and rotting blood. Beyond those two, however, was something else besides, something obnoxious that Gil couldn't quite place.

As he stepped into the room, a small coat closet was to his immediate left. The door had been left ajar and the coats, jackets, and sweaters on the pole inside had all been pushed to one side in order to leave enough room for an old-fashioned Kirby vacuum cleaner that had been stowed in one corner of the closet.

For some strange reason that tickled Gil's funny bone. Where was it written that vacuum cleaners always had to be stored in entryway closets? That was where Linda had kept her Bissell and where his mother had kept her Hoover. At that moment, Gil was without a vacuum cleaner and without much hope of ever having one either.

But if I get one, he told himself, *I'm not keeping it in the entry-way closet.*

The overhang of the porch and the closed blinds along the front of the house left the entryway shrouded in shadow. Making a note of how he had found the light switch, Gil used a pencil to turn on the overhead lights. Immediately he saw evidence of tracked blood, coming and going through the entryway, but the patterns were smeared and indistinct. Gil knew what that meant. Whoever had tramped through the blood had been wearing booties.

Gil turned back to the door. "Hey, Officer Masters," he called. "Did you or Dodd leave these tracks in here?"

"No, sir," Masters returned. "We saw the tracks. We walked around them."

Nodding, Gil dropped a numbered marker onto the floor next to each of three prints. Then, using a small digital camera, he took several photographs of the area indicated by the marker. Each time he snapped a photo, he paused long enough to make a corresponding note on three-by-five cards that he carried in a leather-bound wallet. That way, later, he'd be able to use the notes to explain what was in the photos and he'd use the photos to help decipher his sometimes illegible notes.

Gil knew that the corpse was in the living room. Instead of going directly there, he turned instead toward a room that had originally been intended as a dining room. Shelves that had prob- ably once held knickknacks of some kind had been installed high on the dining room walls, but they were empty. An oak pedestal table stood in the middle of the room. There was only one chair at the table. Two others sat off to the side, just under the win- dow. A buffet that matched the table was the only other piece of furniture. The top of the buffet was covered with packing boxes, tape dispensers, and blank shipping labels, while the top of the table was littered with tubes of epoxy and paint and brushes.

On the floor, scattered in among a snowdrift of foam packing peanuts, lay the smashed remains of what must have once been on the now-denuded bookshelves—dozens and dozens of model airplanes, all of them wrecked, ground to pieces on the floor. They had been stepped on . . . no, stomped on, in what Gil read as deliberate, thorough, and wanton destruction.

Okay, Gil told himself. *Kirby vacuum or not, if this is where the victim built his models, that means the guy definitely isn't married. And he isn't living with his mother either. No woman in her right mind lets a guy build model airplanes in the middle of her dining room table or spill packing peanuts all over the house.*

Gil stayed where he was, in the dining room doorway. If he tried stepping into the dining room, he knew that no matter how carefully he walked, he wouldn't be able to keep from crunching larger pieces of wings and propellers and fuselages into smaller bits of plastic, balsa wood, and dust.

At last, turning toward the living room, Gil was appalled by the mess. Except for the wrecked model planes on the floor, the dining room had been relatively neat and orderly. The living room looked like a trash heap, a lived-in trash heap that consisted of discarded magazines, packets of coupons, grocery bags, empty cans of chili, shipping boxes, and dead pizza containers, with little cleared paths like game trails leading through the mess from one place to another. It was possible someone could find out how long the debris had been there by shoveling through it like an archeological dig, but that wasn't Gil's job.

The small desk lamp on the far table did little to illuminate the rest of the room. Once again Gil tracked down a wall switch. Turning on the overhead fixture in the living room immediately revealed the same kind of fuzzy footprints he had seen in the entryway. They meandered in and out of the mess, sometimes following the trails sometimes stepping on or over the trash.

In the lamplight, the victim's body hadn't been immediately visible. Now it was. Just beyond the far end of the couch, a single sock-clad foot hung at an ungainly angle in midair. Only when Gil rounded the couch did he see that a large male was strapped to a fallen dining room chair by layers and layers of clear packing tape. His legs were fastened to the front legs of the chair while his arms and wrists, out of sight, were most likely similarly bound behind his back.

At first glance there was no evidence of any kind of bullet or stab wound that would account for the presence of all the blood that had been trod through the house. Instead, the man's head was encased in a clear plastic bag, the kind that customers in grocery stores peel off conveniently located rolls to carry home their freshly chosen vegetables—heads of broccoli, lettuce, or cauliflower—but the plastic was heavy, not likely to be easily chewed through. Underneath the bag, Gil caught sight of another piece of packing tape that had been plastered to the man's mouth to function as a gag. More tape had been used to fasten the open end of the bag tightly around the victim's bulging neck.

Asphyxiation then, Gil thought. *So why do I see so much blood?*

Stepping to the far side of the corpse, Gil found the answer to that question. The tips of several of the dead man's fingers—four in all—had been hacked off by poultry scissors that still lay where it had been dropped. Beside the shears were the blackened hunks of fingertips, although Gil counted only three, not four. It was likely the missing one had been covered by the man's falling body when the chair had tipped onto its side. And the amount of blood on the floor told Gil what he didn't want to know—that the victim had been alive when the fingers were hacked off one by one.

The gruesome savagery of that was enough to make even an experienced homicide cop want to toss his morning's batch of Honey Nut Cheerios. The other thing contributing to his gag reflex had to do with teeming hordes of insect vermin that were visible both inside and on the body. Since the house itself was a gigantic trash heap, that came as no surprise. The good news about that was that flesh-eating maggots would provide a fool-proof way for the coroner to establish the victim's time of death with a good deal of accuracy.

Needing to step away for a moment, Gil turned toward the wooden desk. It was stacked high with a complicated collection of electronics—several printers as well as a single computer. A single glance was enough to tell Gil that this was high-end, top-of-the-line Mac equipment, and that struck him as odd. In the course of a normal home invasion, the electronics wouldn't have been there. They'd have been among the first items stolen or else they would have been smashed to pieces like the model airplanes in the other room.

Gil made his way around the living room, laying down more evidence markers and taking photos as he went. Finally, returning to the corpse, Gil stepped closer to the body and squatted down next to it. Only then did Gil catch sight of a tiny set of white wires. They came from what Gil assumed to be an iPod in the pocket of the dead man's sweatshirt. They threaded their way under the tape that was attached to his throat. With the victim lying on his side, Gil could only see the left side of the man's head, but he could also see that one of the earbuds was still stuck in the dead man's ear.

"So what went on here, big fella?" Gilbert asked aloud.

He often addressed questions to the corpses at crime scenes during those intimate moments when he was alone with murder victims. They never answered, but Gil's one-sided conversations usually helped him make sense of what he was seeing.

"You were listening to your tunes, and then something happened. What was it?"

It was as Gil rose from his crouch and readied his camera once more that he noticed the presence of an extra dining room chair. He had seen it before, but this was the first time it actually registered. Before that Gil had been too focused on the body itself to realize that a second chair had been brought into the living room and positioned in a spot that was close to the dead man's head.

It took a moment for Gil to grasp what he was seeing. Two dining room chairs had been brought into the living room, one to confine the victim and one to be used as an observation post. Murder was murder, and the bloody mutilations were nothing short of appalling, but the idea of sitting and watching while your victim struggled to take his last breaths moved what had happened in this room to a whole new level.

25

Grass Valley, California

Gil was still struggling with that reality when the Nevada County coroner, Fred Millhouse, arrived on the scene.

"Hey, Detective Morris," Fred said. "We've gotta stop meeting like this. Three in one week is more than I bargained for. Is it all right if I move this chair out of the way?"

"Just a moment," Gil said, laying down another marker. "Let me get a photo first."

While Fred went to work doing what he needed to do, Gil walked through the house. He was looking for evidence, yes, but he was also trying to get the feel of what he was seeing.

A good deal of the mess in the room was trash that had been there for a long time, but the wanton destruction of the model planes was recent. It had taken time to smash them one by one. If the plane smasher and the killer were one and the same, that meant that the culprit had been in the victim's house for an extended period of time. This wasn't a quick in and out. The killer had come here looking for something. The question was, had he found it and taken it?

Gil glanced again at the collection of electronics on the desk in the corner. Gil Morris was no geek, but he knew enough about computers to realize that the computer was a potential source of all kinds of useful information, including the names and e-mail addresses of the people the victim had corresponded with in the last days of his life. It would also tell investigators what, if anything, Richard Lowensdale had been working on at the time of his death. Gil looked around for a cell phone or a landline. At first glance, neither was visible. And if there were some way to view any of the footage from the security camera over the front door, that wasn't readily apparent either.

Not wanting to observe Millhouse at his grim work and not wanting to be in the way, Gil let himself out of the overheated, dimly lit house into bright sunlight and a welcome January chill. He paused on the front porch long enough to search for evidence that the bloodied footsteps had exited this way. There was nothing visible to the naked eye, but luminol might reveal the microscopic presence of blood evidence. A more likely scenario told him that the perpetrator had walked around in the house long enough for the blood on the bottom of his feet to dry.

Gil stood on the porch's top step and breathed in a lung-ful of fresh air. Even with the Vicks right there beneath his nostrils, some of the terrible odors of death still lingered. Gil walked down the cracked sidewalk and let himself out through the crooked gate. A patrol car was parked on the far side of the street. Officer Masters was inside and appeared to be talking on the radio.

Gil pulled the cigar out of his shirt pocket and mimed his need of a light to Masters.

When Dale Masters joined him at the rear of the black-and-white, he brought a second cigar for himself and a lighter, as well as a small metal container which, with the lid removed, served admirably as a makeshift ashtray. Leaving ashes of any kind near a crime scene was a bad idea. The black-and-white had a perfectly functioning ashtray in the front seat, but smoking in city-owned vehicles was not entirely verboten.

Once they both lit up, Gil was pleased to discover that the cigars were impressively obnoxious—the kind Linda had always regarded as "pure evil"—but the smoke helped displace the last of the noxious odors.

"Thanks," Gil said, holding up his cigar.

"You're welcome," Dale said. "You lasted a whole lot longer inside there than I did. By the way, I just got off the phone with Irene in Records. She said there was a B and E at this address on the twentieth of September of this past year. According to the report, an ex-girlfriend allegedly broke into the house in broad daylight while Lowensdale was off getting his Cadillac serviced."

"New Cadillac?"

"Old," Masters said. "The way I understand it, it used to belong to Lowensdale's mother."

Gil pulled out a new three-by-five card. "Name?"

"Mother's name?"

"No. The B and E suspect."

"Her name's Brenda Riley. She used to be Lowensdale's girlfriend."

"They caught her in the act?"

"Not exactly. Lowensdale came home, saw a broken window, and realized someone had been inside his place. Even though nothing of value had been stolen, he raised enough of a stink that the chief finally agreed to have our guys come by to do a crime scene investigation. Her prints were found everywhere. No effort to cover them up whatsoever."

"She's in the system?" Gil asked.

Masters nodded. "She's been booked for a number of moving violations, DUIs as well as driving without a license, and so forth. Once we told him who the perp was, Lowensdale declined to press charges. Said it was the aftermath of a bad breakup and since nothing was taken, he was prepared to let it go."

"Brenda Riley?" Gil asked with his pen poised to write.

"Brenda Arlene Riley," Masters confirmed. "She lives in Sacramento. Irene in Records can give you the exact address, but you may want to check. I believe there was something in that original nine-one-one call this morning about an ex being involved in all this one way or the other."

"Thanks," Gil said. "I'll look into it."

When Masters was called back to the radio, Gil stood there with a cloud of smoke circling his head while he studied his surroundings and the cracked and peeling exterior of Richard Lowensdale's house.

Jan Road was steep. The house was built into the flank of the hill, but the sidewalk leading up to the house was level. A cracked concrete walkway went from the front porch to a small detached garage and from the garage to a side door near the back of the house. Looking at the elevations, Gil realized that meant there was probably a basement under the house and maybe under the garage as well.

Ready to resume his examination of the house, Gil followed the walkway door to door to door. There were no visible footprints anywhere.

He went back to the small garage and opened the side door wide enough so he could peek inside. There was definitely no basement in the garage. The hard-packed dirt floor reeked of decades of old grease and oil. Above the workbench, the wall was lined with a collection of antique tools. The smell and tools hinted that the garage had long been used by a homegrown, do-it-yourself mechanic. What looked like most of a case of motor oil stood inside the remains of a cut-down cardboard box on a shelf above the work bench.

Clearly the garage had been built at a time when vehicles were smaller. Lowensdale's ten-year-old black Cadillac Catera barely fit inside the four walls. If this had been a standard robbery, most likely the car would have been taken along with the electronics. No, this was definitely something else.

Leaving the garage, Gil went to what he assumed to be the back door of the house. The first room inside was a small utility room that held a washer and dryer, an older model top-loading set. The utility room opened into an old-fashioned kitchen complete with a single-bowl porcelain sink and knotty pine cabinets, as well as an avocado-colored fridge and matching stove that had to date from sometime in the seventies. There was no dishwasher. There was a small white microwave on the counter and the freezer was packed full of Nutrisystem food. Obviously Richard wasn't much of a cook.

Considering the condition of the rest of the house, Gil fully expected the kitchen to be filthy. It was not. There was no junk on the floor and no dirty dishes in the sink. The counter was clean and the microwave wasn't greasy. There was a dish drainer with a few clean dishes sitting in it—a single plate, a single glass, a single set of eating utensils. It reminded Gil of his own kitchen. Yes, this guy definitely lived alone.

The kitchen was far enough from the living room that the odor of putrid flesh didn't penetrate. But the other smell, the one Gil had noticed earlier, was much stronger in this part of the house than it had been in the living room. Just outside the kitchen door in a hallway that evidently led to the bedrooms, he found a closed door that he assumed to be a possible broom closet.

When he opened the door, the stench was almost overpowering. Covering his mouth and nose, Gil groped for the light switch using his pen. When the light came on, he found he was standing at the top of a set of planked wooden stairs that led down into a true garbage dump. In the living room, the trash made a layer on the floor that was walkable. Here the heap was tall enough to come halfway up the steps, tall enough to reach Gil's shoulders if not his head. And on the steps were the faint fuzzy footprints he had seen before. The blood must have been nearly dry when the transfer was made. The prints ventured down only three steps then they turned and returned the way they had come. Whoever it was had considered wading into the garbage in search of whatever it was they wanted. But they hadn't wanted it badly enough to go digging through the garbage. No doubt the stench had proved to be too much for the killer just as it did for Gil.

Stepping back, he switched the light back off and then slammed the door shut behind him. Shutting the door didn't fix the problem. Even with it closed, the smell was still overpowering. It was almost as though the smell had leached into the wallboard and wooden trim. Gil wished fervently that Masters had offered him more than just that one cigar.

Unfortunately, at this particular crime scene, cigars were limited, only one to a customer.

26

Los Angeles, California

li left the hotel to drive to Laguna Beach as mad at B. Simpson as she had ever been.

When she started reading the High Noon material, the item on top had been a copy of the e-mail Brenda had sent to her on Friday that she had in turn passed along to B. She read through that. There was nothing at all that indicated anything out of the ordinary. It was lucid. There were none of the self-justifying excuses that are often employed by someone intent on doing something stupid. In fact, the message was exactly the opposite of that—purposeful, organized, and with no senseless meanderings that would indicate a drunken rant. Yes, Camilla Gastellum believed her daughter had gone off on a bender. If so, the decision to do that had come after she sent the e-mail rather than before.

Next up was the Richard Lowensdale background check—the same material that had been sent to Brenda almost five months previously. A copy of that had been sent to Ali as well. It contained nothing new, nothing unforeseen.

Ermina's background check came next, and it contained only

the bare bones of the story. She had been born in Croatia. There was nothing that explained how she had been orphaned. The story picked up again once she was adopted by a family in Missouri as a teenager. The adoptive mother died of heart disease a couple of years later, and the father committed suicide. Ermina moved to California and was doing minimum wage catering jobs when she hooked up with a widower named Mark Blaylock.

So far so good, Ali thought. *Sounds like it was time for her to have some good luck.*

But clearly the luck had recently turned bad once more. Their business, Rutherford International, had gone bust. In the documents section of the report, Ali found information about the Blaylocks' bankruptcy proceedings, foreclosure proceedings on their home in La Jolla, property tax information on a home in Salton City, California, as well as a puzzling document certifying Rutherford's contractual dismantling of forty-six UAVs, which was evidently shorthand for *unmanned aerial vehicles,* otherwise known as drones, as the form helpfully explained for the uninitiated.

Since Richard Lowensdale had previously worked for Rutherford and, as a consequence, the Blaylocks, there was nothing at all in Ermina's background report that gave any hint about why Brenda had been seeking the information or if her inquiry about Ermina Blaylock had in any way contributed to Brenda's sudden disappearance. There was a puzzling notation at the end of the report that said Stuart Ramey was awaiting more information from Missouri and would be sending that along as soon as it was available. Did Ali want him to fax it to her, or would it be all right for him to forward it to her cell?

She sent him an e-mail saying to send the information to her iPhone.

But then she hit the bottom set of papers, and that's when it all went bad. Those sheets were evidently additions to the original background check—they carried the same date stamp—but the material recounted there contained information Ali had never seen before. Apparently Richard had been "cyberdating" any number of women at the time he was involved with Brenda. Stuart Ramey was a skilled hacker who had managed to gain access to both Richard's numerous e-mail accounts as well as his computer.

The Storyboard material Ali read there was nothing short of stunning. It included transcripts of supposedly private e-mails and instant messages that Richard had added to the files as they came in. In each case Richard was Richard, but the last names varied. All of the last names started with an *L*, and Ali was certain those were simply convenient aliases.

Ali remembered clearly how dismayed she had been when she learned Brenda Riley had been engaged to a man she had never met, but Brenda was certainly not alone. By Ali's count there were over fifty women listed in the Storyboard file. A quick survey through the collected correspondence showed that most of the women involved were under the impression that Richard Whatever was their heaven-sent soul mate. More than once Ali saw discussions of possible ring purchases with Internet links leading to possible candidates.

Not surprisingly, Ali found Ermina Blaylock's name listed in the Storyboard index, but when she checked the file, it contained little information other than Ermina's name, her date of birth, and social security number, which Richard Lowensdale probably shouldn't have had.

On the one hand it was infuriating that Richard Lowensdale had preyed on needy women by exploiting them through their various weaknesses. No wonder Brenda had wanted to expose him. No wonder she was writing a book on cyberstalking. Why wouldn't she? But that still didn't explain why she had gone missing. Maybe Richard had learned what she was doing. If he had threatened her somehow, maybe Brenda wasn't out drinking. Maybe she was in hiding.

But what really got to Ali and what sent her temper boiling was the fact that this extra material had been available for months. Ali hadn't seen it, and most likely Brenda hadn't seen it either. Ali had requested that original background check, but what she and Brenda had been given was a severely edited version, a redacted version.

Seeing red, Ali picked up her phone and dialed B.'s cell phone. She was prepared to leave him an irate message. She wasn't prepared for him to answer the phone.

"Hey," he said. "I'm on a break. I was just getting ready to call you."

"You'll be sorry," Ali said. "You're in deep doo-doo at the moment."

"Me? What have I done?"

"It's not what you did; it's what you didn't do. I believe this is called a sin of omission."

"What are we talking about?"

"Richard Lowensdale's background check, both of them. There's the part you gave me and passed along to Brenda, and there's the part you left out. Why?"

There was a pause and a sigh. "It was a judgment call," B. said at last. "My judgment call."

"Why?"

"The material in the background check Brenda got was from readily available sources—sources that are open to most anyone with access to a computer. The other stuff Stuart dug up was a little dicier."

"You mean the stuff Stuart hacked."

"Yes," B. said. "The stuff he hacked. As I remember, he found evidence of a number of girlfriends Brenda probably didn't know about. From what you had told me about her mental state right then, I didn't think she could handle it. I was afraid learning about all that would push her over the edge. I'm the one who told Stuart to send out the ordinary background check material and leave out the rest."

"Why didn't you tell me any of this at the time?" Ali asked.

"Because right then it looked as though you were on your way to becoming a sworn police officer—an officer of the court. If you were in possession of possibly ill-gotten material, that would have been bad for you, bad for Stuart, and most likely bad for me too."

"In other words, CYA."

"Pretty much," B. said. He sounded genuinely contrite, but Ali wasn't buying it.

There must have been something in her voice that told B. the conversation was headed in a bad direction. When the call waiting sound clicked, he sounded downright relieved.

"Sorry," he said. "I've got another call. Do you mind if I take it?"

"Under the circumstances," she said, "that's probably an excellent idea."

Ali was still mad as hell as she showered, dressed, checked out of the hotel, and headed for Laguna Beach. She had no idea where she would spend the night, but she could probably find a decent spot somewhere near Velma.

That, however, wasn't what was on her mind as she drove south. It seemed to her that any decision about how to proceed with Richard Lowensdale's background check should have been hers to make and not B. Simpson's.

27

Grass Valley, California

Trying to put some distance between his nose and the smelly basement, Gil hurried down the hall. Halfway to the end he found a small bedroom stacked floor to ceiling with what appeared to be unopened moving boxes, as though the guy had recently moved in and hadn't quite gotten around to unpacking. The killer had clearly been searching for something, but Gil could imagine the perp looking at that massive wall of boxes and deciding not to bother searching there. Trying to hide something in among all those boxes would have been too much trouble.

There was a powder room off the hallway next to that first bedroom. The surprising cleanliness Gil had found in the kitchen didn't extend all the way to the bathrooms. This one was filthy. Both the sink and toilet bowl were permanently stained black with grime.

What was apparently the master bedroom was situated at the end of the hall. Next to it was a built-in linen closet. The contents of that—sheets, pillowcases, extra blankets, a quilt or two, towels, washcloths, bars of soap, and spare rolls of toilet paper—had been spilled onto the hallway floor.

Stepping around that, Gil went into the master bedroom, which was small in comparison to its counterparts in new construction. An unmade king-sized bed with a tangled mound of covers and grimy sheets occupied most of the floor space. The dresser at the foot of the bed sat against the wall with a small television set and DVD player perched on top of it.

Once again, Gil found the presence of the electronic equipment surprising. Like that in the living room, these devices—valuable electronic devices—had been left untouched. They hadn't been stolen or broken. Next to the bed was a solo bedside table. If there had been two of them at one time, its mate was missing, but every drawer in the room had been upturned and emptied, with its contents spilled out onto the floor or bed. On the table, however, along with an old-fashioned reading lamp, Gil saw a television remote, a set of car keys, and a worn leather wallet.

Picking up the wallet, Gil opened it and counted through a dozen hundred-dollar bills. He slipped the wallet into an evidence bag. Once again, this was no ordinary robbery. The wallet and car keys had been right there in plain sight.

Why not take them? Gil wondered.

The bathroom off the master bedroom was in slightly better shape than the one down the hall, but the presence of one towel bar and only one disgustingly dirty towel testified to Richard Lowensdale's solitary and unwashed existence.

The sound of voices from the front of the house told Gil that the crime scene team had arrived. By the time he returned to the living room, both the plastic bag from the victim's head and the tape gag had been removed and placed in separate evidence bags.

"Some sign of blunt force trauma here on the head," Fred Millhouse said as he dictated his initial findings while, at the same time, wielding a small handheld video recorder. "Enough to knock him out, but most likely not enough to be fatal."

While the coroner continued taping, Gil removed the wallet from the evidence bag and looked through it until he located a driver's license in a clear plastic sleeve. From the photo it looked to Gil as through the victim was definitely Richard Lowensdale, although that comparison wouldn't be enough to constitute a positive ID.

Gil closed the wallet, returned it to his evidence bag, and then added it to the growing collection of evidence being placed in a Bankers Box. He had just made a notation on the inventory sheet when he noticed that one of the CSI techs, Cindra Halliday, was about to remove the victim's iPod.

To Gil's way of thinking, Cindra looked far too young for the job, like she should have been enrolled in a high school biology class rather than being out in the field doing crime scene investigation.

"Is there any way to tell what he was listening to?" Gil asked.

The young woman shrugged. Instead of putting the device into its designated evidence bag, Cindra took it over to the table, examined a collection of power cords, chose one, and plugged in the device. A moment later, the tiny screen lit up. She shook her head. "It's called 'To All the Girls I've Loved Before' by some guy named Willie Nelson. Never heard of him. What do you think that means?"

What Cindra's question really meant was that Detective Gilbert Morris was old. Ancient, really, and out of touch. How could she *not* know Willie Nelson? How young was she?

"Beats me," Gil said wearily. "You guys do your stuff. I'm going to go talk to some of the neighbors and see if any of them noticed something out of the ordinary."

Once again grateful to leave the stink of the living room behind him, Gil had walked only as far as the front porch when Officer Dodd came through the crooked gate and started up the walkway.

"I've got the info you needed," he said, handing Gil a Post-it note. "The stuff about Ted Frost—his phone number and address."

At that point most cops would have reached for a notebook. Not Gil Morris. He took the Post-it note and stuck it to one of the cards in a leather wallet that carried not only his supply of extra three-by-five cards but a fountain pen too. Gil had inherited the pen, a Cross, from his father. The wallet had been a Father's Day present from Linda and the kids before it all went bad. Fortunately for Gil, the wallet and pen had both been in his shirt pocket the day Linda's father had shown up—unannounced as far as Gil was concerned—to move them out.

Gil liked starting his day by sitting at the kitchen counter—both the kitchen table and his rolltop desk had gone north in Linda's U-haul—and going through the ritual of filling his gold pen with that day's worth of ink. He liked taking careful notes on the blank cards. He felt that set him apart from the beat cops. Unlike Allen Dodd, Gil wouldn't have been caught dead passing out Post-it notes.

"Thanks, Allen," Gil said. "I'll give him a call."

But not right away. Gil had studied the street while he'd been standing smoking the cigar. Now he did so again, going inch by inch over the street that bordered Richard Lowensdale's fenced yard. Brittle dry grass took root at the edge of the pavement, so there was no dirt that held the possibility of finding either tire tracks from a vehicle parked in front of the house or of footprints going to or from it. There was no way to tell if the killer had parked there, coming and going in plain view of the neighbors, or if the perpetrator had parked some distance away and arrived at the victim's doorstep on foot.

Gil had directed Cindra and the rest of the CSI team to dust the gate and the doorbell as well as the front door assembly for prints, but he wasn't especially hopeful. This was a killer who had gone to a good deal of trouble to make sure there were no identifiable footprints left behind. Gil had a feeling that he would have exercised just as much care about leaving behind any latent fingerprints.

The killer had clearly spent a considerable period of time inside Richard Lowensdale's home. Either he had known his presence there was unlikely to be challenged, or he had an entirely believable reason for being there.

Gil didn't have much in common with Monk, the neurotic detective in the TV series. For one thing, as far as Gil knew, he didn't suffer from any obsessive compulsive disorders, but when it came to crime scenes, he trusted his instincts. This one struck him as exceptionally cold-blooded.

It was one thing for the Herrera brothers to get all drunked up together, shoot the shit out of one another, and, as a consequence, break their poor mother's heart. Had either of them lived long enough to be put on trial, it seemed to Gil that the charges against them would have tended more to voluntary homicide than to murder.

Richard Lowensdale's murder was on another scale entirely. What Fred Millhouse had referred to as blunt force trauma probably had been delivered for one purpose only—to disable the victim long enough for the killer to use the tape to bind him to the chair. Then, after disabling the guy, the killer had set the iPod ear buds in the guy's ears and had queued up Willie Nelson to sing the same song over and over until the device finally ran out of juice. "To All the Girls I've Loved Before."

You didn't need to be a rocket scientist (which Gil Morris wasn't) or an experienced homicide cop (which he actually was) to figure out that the killer was broadcasting a message with the choice of that particular piece of music, but what message was it? Was it from a rival or maybe a disgruntled lover?

The most chilling aspect of the whole scene had been the presence of that single out-of-place dining room chair in Richard Lowensdale's living room. Gil knew as sure as he was born that the killer had sat on that chair, waiting and watching, while Richard Lowensdale struggled for air inside the taped plastic bag. It seemed likely that he or she had stayed there until Richard gave up trying for a last gasping breath.

Murder as a spectator sport, Gil thought once more. The idea of someone doing that seemed astonishingly heartless. The house had been thoroughly searched for something, but nothing had been taken—at least not as far as Gil could tell. The model airplanes had been smashed to pieces, but the wallet and car keys were there. The electronic equipment was there.

In Richard Lowensdale's case, killing him was the main point, maybe even the only point. And the killer had gone to great lengths to make sure that the victim was helpless, that he couldn't fight back.

For the first time Gilbert Morris was forced to confront the idea that the killer might be female. Unless Richard turned out to be gay or a switch-hitter, it was likely he had been taken out by a woman, one with a very serious grudge.

Richard Lowensdale's house was the last one on the street. Just above the house was a small paved turnaround. Beyond that stood a piece of property covered with second-growth forest. Determined to learn something, Gil set off down the hill. The neighbors would have noticed the police activity around the house and he expected they would be eager to speak to him. That's how things usually worked in small towns. Most of the time witnesses were glad to come forward and help out.

Unfortunately most of the residents of Jan Road had been at work or at school on Friday afternoon. The only exception was Lowensdale's next-door neighbor, a gray-haired retiree named Harry Fulbright, who had spent part of the day out in his yard trimming an overgrown laurel hedge.

"Sure," he said. "I remember seeing the UPS driver go past here right around two thirty. Not the regular UPS guy," he added. "Ted must have been sick that day, 'cause it was earlier in the day than he usually shows up. But it was definitely UPS. Woman in a brown uniform and a brown leather jacket."

"A woman," Gil repeated. "Walking or riding?"

"Walking. The turnaround at the top of this here street is too damned small for them big trucks. Ted never drives up there, and he probably warned his substitute not to try it either."

"Can you tell me anything at all about her?"

"Not really. She was about average. Not fat, not skinny. Fairly long hair."

"What color?"

"Reddish maybe?"

"Did you see anyone else around that day?"

"Actually, now that you mention it, I think there was a second delivery later on. So maybe they made two drops at Richard's house that day."

As far as Gil was concerned, this information was all a step in the right direction.

Excusing himself to Harry, Gil went back out to the street and dialed Ted Frost's number.

"Allen Dodd told me what happened to Richard and that you might be calling," Ted said as soon as Gil introduced himself. "I'm sorry to hear it. Richard was a nice enough guy and he ordered lots of stuff. I stopped off at his house almost every day, and he's one that always gave out little presents when Christmas came around. Do you need me to come down to the station and give a statement?"

"I'll probably need you to do that eventually," Gil said. "Right now I'm just looking for a time line. What time was it when you dropped off that box from Zappos?"

"Right at the end of my shift. Around four thirty or so."

"Is there another driver who might have dropped something off earlier?"

"Not with UPS. This is my territory. As for what time I delivered it? I have a computerized log. I have to enter where and when I drop off anything. I'm definitely sure of when I made Richard's delivery."

"Why did you leave the package on the porch? Was there anyone home?"

"There was somebody inside the house. I heard a vacuum cleaner running. It was noisy. She probably didn't hear the bell."

"She?" Gil asked eagerly. "A woman? Did you see her?"

"The blinds were closed. All I could see was the entryway. I just assumed that Richard had finally gotten around to hiring himself a cleaning lady. I guess it didn't have to be a woman, though, huh? Anyway, I figured he'd got some kind of help. He sure needed it. He wasn't the best housekeeper in the world."

That, Gil thought, *is an outrageous understatement!*

"Thanks, Mr. Frost," he said aloud. "You've been most helpful."

Gil closed his phone, marched back into the house. He stopped by the entryway closet and opened the door. Inside was the old Kirby vacuum cleaner. He left the door open and walked into the living room. By then the body had been zipped into a body bag. Once the body was gone, Gil stopped to chat with the CSI techs who were busily collecting and cataloging computer equipment.

"Found several fingerprints for you," Cindra said. "Including a real clear one on the tape on the victim's mouth. Could be the victim's, could be the killer's. We'll run them through AFIS as soon as we can."

"Good," Gil said. "The sooner the better. While you're at it, be sure to pick up the vacuum cleaner in the entryway closet. Maybe we'll get lucky and find something useful inside the bag, like a missing finger, for instance. Oh, and dust it for fingerprints as well."

28

Salton City, California

Lola Cunningham had been a good cook, an excellent cook, actually, and she had been thrilled to pass those skills along to her adopted daughter. And in an effort to make Mina feel at home, Lola had tracked down a traditional Croatian recipe for *punjene paprike*, stuffed green peppers, and made it her own.

There was a lot about her adopted family and being in the Cunningham house that was repugnant for Mina, but she had loved being in the kitchen with Mama Lola, as her mother liked to be called. They would stand in the kitchen together, side by side, talking and laughing as they diced and sliced, chopped and cooked. Had Lola not died of an undiagnosed heart attack the year Mina turned sixteen, everything might have been different. Mina might have been different, but Lola's unexpected death had changed everything.

Today though, once Mark finished burying the ashes from the Weber grill, he'd probably return to the couch. Morosely silent, he'd sit there, drinking and watching some inconsequential golf tournament while Mina bustled around the kitchen. She prepared the stuffed peppers the same way Mama Lola had done—well, almost the same way—making two separate batches, one for Mark and one for Mina.

Working in the kitchen always made Mina happy. She hummed a little tune as she ground up the necessary ingredients—the beef and the pork and the onions—that would go into the green peppers she had brought home with her from San Diego for this very purpose. Finding decent green peppers or decent anything else in the godforsaken little grocery store in Salton City was pretty much impossible. She estimated that the extra doses of seasonings she added to the mix should be enough to conceal a few other things.

As she hacked the tops off peppers, Mina found herself thinking fondly of Richard. He had surprised her and proved to be far more of a man than she ever would have expected. She was sorry not to have the money back, but even so, Richard had won a measure of respect from his killer that he probably would have appreciated if he had lived long enough to know about it.

As for Mark? He was useless, spineless, and boring. His money had been a major part of his appeal. Now that the money was gone, so was the attraction. She enjoyed the prospect of torturing him with the idea that she expected him to take care of Brenda single-handedly and that she wanted him to do it tonight. It would be immensely entertaining to see him sitting there stone-faced while he struggled to come to terms with the very idea. She didn't doubt that he'd need to fill himself with some kind of liquid courage—gin most likely, gin on the rocks with a twist of lime.

Just to keep him off balance, she would pretend that everything was fine and that she believed that he'd do what she wanted. Wasn't that why she was hustling around in this grim little kitchen fixing him a sumptuous dinner?

Whenever Mina noticed that Mark's drink needed refilling, she would pick up his glass without being asked. And later, along with the brimming glasses, she would hand him one of his little blue pills. After all, Mark was an older man with a drinking problem and a much younger wife. In the shorthand of their marriage, the proffered drink was a peace offering. The little blue pill would be a bribe.

San Diego, California

Brenda awakened in the dark. She was stiff, hungry, and agonizingly thirsty. While she had been asleep, she had evidently shifted positions. The weight of her body had been resting on her imprisoned hands. As circulation returned to her hands and fingers, so did a storm of needles and pins.

"I'm going to die," she said aloud. Her voice was an unnatural croak. "I'm going to die here and alone and in the dark."

She would have wept then, but she didn't want to risk losing whatever moisture might be in her tears.

Her aching shoulder reminded her of her uncle Joe. She hadn't thought about her father's brother in years. Uncle Joe had come home after five years of being a POW of the Vietcong. His teeth were gone—broken out—and his broken limbs never healed properly. He had ended up in a wheelchair, but he had never complained. Brenda had asked him about his experiences once when she'd been putting together a Veteran's Day piece for the news.

"Yes, it was hard," he said, "but all I had to do each day was choose to live."

Returning to the States, he had refused to accept the idea that his life was over. He had gone back to school and married his high school sweetheart. He had gone on to become a teacher and a winning football coach who had taken his team to championship games year after year. He had also been the kindest and most amazingly positive man Brenda had ever met. Could she be like him?

Lying there alone, Brenda couldn't help thinking about how far she had fallen short in that regard, and she had no one to blame but herself. Losing her job and her marriage and being betrayed by Richard Lowensdale were nothing when compared to what Uncle Joe and his fellow wartime captives had endured. Unlike Uncle Joe, Brenda had capitulated. And now, when she was finally sober and getting back on her feet, this happened.

But what is this? she wondered.

Did it have something to do with Richard or with the book she was writing about him? The days before waking up in this place seemed shrouded in fog. Maybe one of the women she had interviewed had gone back to Richard and told him about *Too Good to Be True*, the book Brenda was writing. But this wasn't Richard's house. It couldn't be. This cold, hard floor was too clean.

Thinking about the unfinished book brought Brenda back to her mother. Even if she didn't let on to her sister, Brenda knew that she should have told her mother about the sale. It had been easier to keep quiet. She had kept everything about the book— her research materials, the signed contract for *Too Good to Be True*, and her laptop under lock and key in what had once been her mother's hope chest. She had carried the key with her, in her purse, because she had worried that someone—one of her mother's caregivers or even her sister—might go prying. But now her purse was gone and the key was gone. The only way anyone would be able to gain access to the chest would be to break the lock.

Brenda understood the huge debt she owed to her mother— financially and emotionally—and she fully intended to pay it all back. But not just yet. Brenda had known instinctively that with her still very fragile hold on sobriety, living on her own might well have been too much.

And so for whatever reason—whatever excuse—Brenda had kept a lid on news about the sale. Now, though, since she was probably going to sit in this chair until she died, that didn't seem like such a bad idea.

After all, Brenda had disappointed her mother more times than she could count. If Camilla didn't know about the book, she wouldn't have any unreasonable expectations. It was a blessing for Brenda to know that her mother wouldn't be disappointed.

Again.

In the darkness, Brenda drifted into something that wasn't exactly sleeping or waking. She was a girl again, maybe ten or eleven. It was a Sunday afternoon. She and her older sister were out in the driveway of her parents' house on P Street, shooting hoops at the basket that hung over the garage door.

Aunt Amy and Uncle Joe had come for dinner. As they were getting ready to go home, Uncle Joe had challenged Brenda's father to a two-on-two scrimmage, Uncle Joe in his wheelchair and Brenda against Dad and Valerie.

As Brenda fell back asleep—or into something that resembled sleep—she and Uncle Joe were winning.

29

Laguna Beach, California

By the time Ali fought her way through Sunday afternoon traffic from LAX to Laguna Beach, she'd had almost two hours to give further consideration to her conversation with B. She wasn't over it enough to call him back, but she'd come to realize that he might have had a point. Being found to be in possession of illegally hacked material probably wouldn't have been a good idea for someone who was a newly appointed officer in Sheriff Gordon Maxwell's Yavapai County Sheriff's Department. And it probably would have been a black mark against High Noon's reputation as a high-profile Internet security entity.

But still . . .

Ali's appreciated having a working GPS in her rental car. As she followed the turn-by-turn directions through very upscale neighborhoods, then onto Cliff Drive, and finally onto Lower Cliff Drive, Ali had to laugh at herself. When Velma Trimble had first appeared in the lobby of Ali's hotel years earlier, she had come in a cab and had sported a patriotic walker. The tennis balls on the legs of her walker were red, white, and blue, and a tiny American flag had been affixed to the handlebar.

Since she had arrived by cab, Ali had assumed she didn't have a car and was probably too old to drive. Looking up at Velma's multistoried, controlled-access condo with designated guest parking and spectacular ocean views, Ali could tell right off that Velma T. was anything but impoverished. Even in a down market, a condo that was within walking distance of the beach meant money—plenty of money.

Ali arrived at the gate a few minutes before three, the appointed hour. Once she punched the apartment number and the open code into a keypad, the gate swung open. Off to her left was a path that led to what looked like a covered picnic shelter on the curve of a steep bluff above the cliffs that gave the street its name. In front of her was a lobby complete with a uniformed doorman who called upstairs to announce that "Ms. Reynolds has arrived."

No, Velma T. might be dying, but she sure as hell wasn't poor.

Once on the penthouse level on the sixth floor, Ali found there were only two doors—600 and 602. Those two apartments, each with a panoramic ocean view, evidently accounted for the total number of penthouse units. Ali rang the bell on the one marked 602. The ringing bell set off an answering bark from what sounded like at least three canine residents—two large ones and at least one small noisy one.

"Quiet, everyone," Maddy Watkins ordered sternly. "Get on your rug."

Silence descended at once. Through the closed door Ali could hear the scrabbling of several sets of doggy paws on parquet floors as the dogs hurried to obey. Moments later, Maddy opened the door.

"Why, hello there," she said. "If you aren't a sight for sore eyes." Then, turning back toward the room, she said, "Velma, you're not going to believe it. Ali Reynolds has arrived in the flesh."

Maddy took Ali's arm and led her into what had once been a gracious living room but was now a hospice ward. There was a hospital bed with a rolling hydraulic lifter to aid in getting in and out of bed. There was a hospital-style IV tree and an assortment of other equipment including an oxygen concentrator and a PCA for pain relief. Next to the bed was Velma's walker with its signature patriotic decor.

The whole west-facing wall was nothing but windows that overlooked a panorama of limitless blue water, and the hospital bed had been placed in a position so that when Velma was in the bed, she could gaze out at that million-dollar view. One of the sliders had been left slightly open, allowing an ocean-scented breeze to blow into the room. Velma sat in a wheelchair that had been parked directly in front of the window. A red, white, and blue afghan covered her legs and helped fend off the draft. She looked gaunt—little more than skin on bones—and the skin that was visible was an alarming shade of yellow that Ali knew indicated the beginnings of kidney and liver failure.

"Oh, good," Velma said. Her face brightened as she turned from the window to greet Ali. "I'm so glad you're here. We were about to have our midafternoon round of Maddiccinos."

"Of what?" Ali asked.

"Frappuccinos made with lots of Bailey's," Velma said with a tired smile. "Maddy downloaded the recipe from the Internet, but we can only have those when the nurses are between shifts. They disapprove of my having liquor or coffee, although I can't see what difference it makes."

"Coming right up," Maddy said. She headed for what Ali assumed to be the kitchen. "Come," she added, speaking to the three dogs who were still on their rug command. They rose as one, Maddy's now somewhat white-faced, leggy goldens and some tiny ball of fuzz whose canine origins Ali could only guess.

"They do really well together," Velma said. "Candy is mine. She was a little upset when Maddy's interlopers first showed up, but now they're the best of friends."

Looking around the room, Ali had an instant understanding of why hospice home care was preferable to hospice care anywhere else. Velma was at home in her familiar surroundings. Her dog was here. Her stuff was here. Her view was here, and so was her good friend Maddy and her two dogs. What could be better?

From the kitchen, Ali heard the squawk of a blender as Maddy Watkins mixed the unauthorized treat. Ali moved aside a scatter of Sunday newspapers that littered half a nearby couch and took a seat.

"I'm so sorry . . . ," she began lamely, but Velma waved the comment aside.

"Nothing to be sorry about," she said. "I've had a good run. They're doing a good job of pain management. That was what scared me most—that I'd be in a lot of pain, but I'm not, and I'm reasonably lucid most of the time."

Maddy emerged from the kitchen carrying a tray filled with three rocks glasses filled with generous helpings of mocha-colored drinks. The dogs, having recovered from the arrival of a newcomer, followed docilely at her heels and arranged themselves around the room. Candy scrambled up into Velma's lap, Aggie settled comfortably near the wheel of Velma's chair, while Daphne shadowed Maddy as she bustled around the room delivering drinks.

"Make that lucid *some* of the time," Maddy corrected with a smile as she settled on the far end of the couch. "But when she sets her mind to it, she can still beat the socks off me at Scrabble." She held up her glass. "Cheers."

Ali raised her glass along with the others and tried not to notice the visible tremor in Velma's hand as she lifted her drink to her lips and took a tiny sip. Then she set the glass down on a nearby tray and smiled. Ali tried her drink. It tasted of coffee and chocolate and maybe a hint of whiskey, but not much more than that. Ali suspected that there was probably a thimbleful of booze in the whole blender pitcher.

"The nurses really do disapprove," Velma said. "They think Maddy is a bad influence."

Maddy raised her glass in another toast. "I am a bad influence," she agreed. "And the nurses are unanimous in their belief that a sickroom is no place for dogs, but isn't that what friends are for—to cause trouble whenever possible?"

Both women laughed at that, comfortably, the way only old friends can laugh, although Velma's laughter ended in a fit of coughing. When the spasm passed, she picked up an envelope from the same table where she had placed her glass.

"Here," Velma said, holding it in Ali's direction. "This is for you."

As Ali stood up to take the proffered envelope, her silenced iPhone vibrated in her pocket, but she ignored it. The envelope was made from thick linen-based paper and had Velma's name elegantly embossed on the flap. Ali's name was on the front, written in spidery, old fashioned handwriting—Spencerian script.

"What's this?" Ali asked.

"Go ahead. Open it," Velma urged.

Inside Ali found a single piece of papers—a printed cashier's check in the amount of $250,000 made out to the Amelia Dougherty Askins Scholarship Fund. The scholarship program, established in honor of the mother of one of Sedona's movers and shakers, was designed to help young women from Arizona's Verde Valley go on to college. As a high school senior, Ali had gone to school on an Askins scholarship. Now, in adulthood, she administered the scholarship that had once benefited her.

Ali looked at Velma in surprise. "Thank you," she said, "but this is a lot of money. Are you sure you want to do this?"

"Absolutely," Velma confirmed with a nod. She took another sip of her drink, and it seemed as though she was somehow reenergized, more vital.

"I can say with a good deal of confidence that my son won't like it. As far as he's concerned, everything I have should come to him. Everything else will go to him, but I've noticed over the years that Carson is far more interested in accumulating than he is in doing—like a kid who collects marbles but never plays with them. Carson had the misfortune of being born with a silver spoon in his mouth, and I'm afraid he's never gotten over it. You, my dear Ali, come from humble stock. I know the kind of impact receiving that scholarship had on your life and on the lives of countless other deserving young people. I don't want that well to run dry."

The long speech seemed to have drained her. Closing her eyes, she leaned back in her chair to rest and gave the morphine pump button a discreet punch.

"That's one of the reasons Velma asked me to come down to help out," Maddy explained. "She was going to do this as an addendum to her will, but her nephew—I believe you may have met her nephew—was afraid that if she did that, Carson would hold things up in probate for as long as possible. I was able to do the legwork for her, and now she gets to have the pleasure of giving the check to you herself. But if I were you, I'd deposit that check immediately. Monday's a bank holiday, but I'd do it on Tuesday for sure."

Ali had to think for a minute before she realized that Monday was Martin Luther King Day.

"You think her son might try to make trouble?" Ali asked.

Maddy laughed. "Oh, yeah," she said with a knowing grin. "Carson is what my husband used to call a piece of work. He's going to have a conniption fit when he finds out about it, but he won't have a leg to stand on. He's a signer on all her other accounts, but she left him off one. Velma called that account her 'mad money.' It's empty now—empty and closed."

Next to the window, Velma's breathing slowed and steadied as she slipped into a morphine-induced doze. Maddy got up and shut the door. Without the breeze, Ali noticed for the first time the pervasive sickroom odors that the fragrant ocean air had kept at bay.

"How long does she have?" Ali asked.

Maddy shook her head. "No way to tell. It's already longer than Carson expected or wanted to pay for. He's the one who hired the nurses, and he's made it quite clear that they answer to him rather than her. Generally speaking, hospice is a pretty short ride, but Velma was determined to do this—to get you the money. Now she may be willing to let go."

Ali looked down at the check. The scholarship fund's investments had taken a big financial hit during the economic downturn. This unexpected infusion of cash from Velma was going to make a big difference in the program's long-term sustainability.

She slipped the envelope into her purse while, in her pocket, the silenced cell phone buzzed again. For the third time. Ali took another sip of her drink. It was delicious, if not powerful.

She set the glass down. "I should probably go," she said.

"Where are you staying?" Maddy asked.

"I'm not sure. I'm sure I'll be able to find a room somewhere."

"This is a beach town on a three-day weekend," Maddy said. "Velma was worried you wouldn't find a suitable place. There's a two-bedroom guest unit in the building. As soon as we knew you were coming, we took the liberty of reserving it for you just in case. You could stay here, of course. There's plenty of room, but with all the comings and goings overnight, I'm afraid it's not very restful."

Right that minute, the idea of not having to go look for a hotel room was appealing.

"Thank you," Ali said. "That's very generous."

Maddy got up and collected the glasses. Velma had taken only a few tiny sips from hers.

"I'll just wash up," Maddy said. "The night nurse comes on duty at four. We wouldn't want her to catch us with our Bailey's showing, although what Velma thinks is full-bore Bailey's is a very low-octane substitute. After all the excitement, she'll probably sleep for the next couple of hours. A little later, perhaps you'd like to join the dogs and me for a walk on the beach. I can manage two dogs by myself. Three is more problematic. After that you can join us for a late supper."

"A walk sounds good," Ali said, "and so does dinner."

"It won't be anything fancy," Maddy warned. "Cheese, toast, some fresh fruit. Just go downstairs and let the doorman know that you've decided to stay over. He'll give you a key and show you to the unit."

30

Grass Valley, California

It was late in the afternoon before Gil Morris finally headed back to the department. Sometime in the course of the evening, he would need to consult with the coroner's office to figure out who would be doing Richard Lowensdale's next-of-kin notifications. The problem with that was that Richard's driver's license still listed his mother, Doris Mills, as his next of kin, and Gil was pretty sure Doris was deceased.

Now that he had finally left the crime scene behind, Gil's first consideration was food. He hadn't eaten since breakfast, and he was starving, so he picked up a Subway sandwich, and on the way to his cubicle, he stopped off in the break room to grab a cup of coffee.

Rachel Hamilton from Dispatch was there ahead of him. "How's it going with lover-boy?" she asked.

He gave her a quizzical look. "Who?"

"You mean nobody's told you yet? I talked to Allen Dodd about it but then he got pulled off your case to answer another call. It turns out that dead guy of yours has two fiancées. Two! One lives somewhere in New York and the other one is from somewhere up in Oregon. What happens if they both turn up at the same time? That could turn into some kind of catfight. If you want somebody to sell tickets, here I am!"

Gil stared at Rachel in amazement. From Richard Lowensdale's driver's license photo, he had appeared to be a pretty average-looking guy, but an average-looking guy with at least two different aliases. He also lived like a hermit in a filthy garbage dump masquerading as a house. How was it possible for someone like that to have not just one but two women on the string?

Obviously I'm missing something, Gil told himself. *I've been out of the dating game way too long.*

Since Rachel seemed to have no intention of leaving the break room, Gil didn't leave either. He poured his coffee. He could tell from the acrid smell that it was old coffee—this morning's coffee. On Sundays there weren't nearly enough coffee drinkers around the department to keep the pot fresh, but Gil was desperate.

Taking a seat across from Rachel, Gil unwrapped his sandwich.

"Where'd you hear all that?" he asked. "About Richard having two fiancées?"

"From Phyllis," Rachel said. "Phyllis Williams at the Nevada County Com Center. She took both missing persons calls. The first one was earlier this morning. That's when Phyllis asked Sandy to have officers do a welfare check. The second one came in closer to noon. Phyllis says that as far as she knows, two fiancées is some kind of record."

Rachel was eating a Twinkie. Gil wished they had Twinkies in the vending machine, but they didn't.

"It's a record all right," Gil said. "Is Phyllis still on duty?"

"Nope. Her shift ended at two."

Gil munched his sandwich and made a mental note to track Phyllis down as soon as he got back to his desk. If a pair of feuding fiancées showed up when he and the coroner had yet to have an official next-of-kin positive ID, Gil's life would be infinitely more complicated and so would Fred Millhouse's.

Not only that, the Willie Nelson component in the homicide told Gil that Lowensdale's murder might well be a love affair gone awry. The fact that the two fiancées claimed they were elsewhere at the time of Richard's death didn't count for much. Gil would need to look into both women's backgrounds to see if one or the other of them had the kind of connections that might make it plausible for a pissed-off fiancée to hire a hit man. As far as he knew, that hadn't ever happened in Grass Valley, but there was always a first time.

Once his sandwich was gone, Gil dumped out the dregs of his coffee in the kitchen sink and headed for his cubicle, where he turned on his computer. While he waited through the interminable boot-up function, Gil picked up a well-thumbed hard copy of the Nevada County Employee's directory, where he located Phyllis Williams's home phone number.

When Gil dialed, a male answered the phone. "Hey, Phyl," he called. "It's for you."

"Who is it?" Her voice came from somewhere in the noisy distance, as if the house was full of noisy kids and probably grandkids.

"Work," Gil told him. "Tell her I'm calling from work."

Phyllis came on the line soon after that. She was glad to give Gil the details she could remember from the 911 calls. He'd be listening to the tapes himself in a matter of minutes, but he knew that Phyllis was a longtime emergency operator. He wanted to hear her impressions in case she had picked up vibes from either of the women that someone less experienced might have missed.

"They both sounded like nice women," Phyllis told him. "Worried. Upset. Concerned. Too bad they were both hooked up with a lying, two-timing bastard."

Phyllis Williams also had no strong opinions.

While Gil was talking to her, the department's ponderous computer system finally managed to finish the prolonged boot-up cycle. He typed in the name Richard Stephen Lowensdale and the birth date he had jotted down after looking at the victim's driver's license. There were no citations on his record—not even so much as a parking enforcement listing.

Typing in the address on Jan Road came back with the same information he had heard from Dale Masters concerning the B & E case from early October. Once the investigation had zeroed in on a named suspect, Richard Lowensdale had declined to press charges against the woman he referred to as his troubled former fiancée. He had been advised to swear out a restraining order, but he had declined to do that.

Looks to me like you should have, Gil thought.

The next name Gil typed into the computer was Brenda Arlene Riley, and he hit a gold mine. In addition to the arrest on suspicion of breaking and entering, there were multiple moving violations, including DUIs and driving on a suspended license. Court documents listed her address as an apartment in one of the scuzzier neighborhoods in Sacramento.

"Bingo. Not two fiancées," he muttered to himself. "The count just went up to three."

Gil spent the next hour or so doing a detailed study of Brenda Riley and her arrest record. He spent a long time studying the cavalcade of mug shots. For some reason Gil couldn't quite fathom, the woman looked familiar, as though she were someone he should know. It was only when he made it back to the very first DUI arrest that he made the connection and put the name and features together. That Brenda Riley! The news babe Brenda Riley. How could someone like her be hooked up with someone like Richard Lowensdale?

Scrolling back through the mug shots in reverse order was like looking at time-lapse photographs of meth users. Each photo showed her a little more bedraggled, a little more ill-used. She had put on weight. When she had been queen of the news desk in Sacramento, Brenda Riley had been known for her perfectly blunt-cut blond hair. Now, though, the chic haircuts were clearly a thing of the past as were the blonde dye job touchups and the careful application of flaw-concealing makeup. The last piece of information Gil gleaned in his cursory overview of Brenda Riley's unhappy and swift decline was an eviction order from that scuzzy apartment.

As far as Brenda Riley was concerned, this was all very bad news, but from Gil Morris's point of view, it was terrific. He had a suspect—a real suspect, a suspect with a name. A few hours into his third homicide investigation in three days, Detective Morris felt he was on the way to solving it. All he had to do to clear his case was to track down Brenda Riley and talk to her.

Gil had a feeling that, once the guys in the lab made their way into Richard Lowensdale's computer, he'd have a way to find her. In the meantime, her old driver's license information listed her mother's address on P Street in Sacramento. That was the place to start.

Before leaving, though, he did one more pass through the computer. This time he was looking for information on Richard Lydecker, Janet Silvie's missing fiancé, and the man in Dawn Carras's life, Richard Loomis. As far as Gil could find, there was no record of either one of them, not in Grass Valley and not anywhere in California either. Both men seemed to be figments of their respective fiancées' vivid imaginings.

Finally, shutting off his computer, Gil picked up his car keys and hurried out to the parking lot. When the motor of his Crown Vic turned over, Gil checked the gas gauge. It wasn't quite on empty, but the needle showed there wasn't enough gas for him to go to Sacramento and back. Rather than leaving right away, he stopped by the motor pool long enough to fill up. He'd be better off doing that than trying to be reimbursed for a credit card charge later on.

In Randy Jackman's nickel-diming department, credit card charges—even justifiable credit card charges—had a way of being disallowed.

Same way with overtime, Gil thought grimly.

By the time this long weekend was over, he was sure to have a coming-to-God session with Chief Jackman. With any kind of luck, he'd be able to mark Richard Lowensdale's murder closed before that happened.

San Diego, California

A distant rumble awakened Brenda from a restless, dream-ridden slumber. She had been caught in a nightmare, buried alive in horrible darkness, trapped under the rubble of some catastrophic earthquake. The waking darkness was even more complete than that in her dream. The rumble, she realized, wasn't the arrival of another aftershock but the distant roar of an airplane.

Once she was fully awake, she realized that she needed to relieve herself. Desperately. Even though she'd had nothing to drink—even though she was thirsty beyond any hope of quenching—her kidneys were still trying to function. But there was no way to stand up. Her feet were still bound together. If she once left the rolling desk chair, she might never get back into it. Sitting in the chair was preferable to lying on the cold, hard floor.

Shameful as it was, she had no choice but to relieve herself. Right there. In the chair. As the pungent odor of urine filled the air, Brenda let out a strangled sob. But she didn't let herself cry for long. She couldn't afford to squander the tears.

31

Laguna Beach, California

The doorman from the lobby let Ali into a unit on the second floor. It was neat and clean, modestly furnished, and about a quarter of the size of Velma's penthouse suite. The kitchen contained a coffeepot, toaster, and microwave. There were dishes, glassware, and silverware in the kitchen cupboards as well as clean linens on the bed and in the linen closet. Ali was standing by the westward-looking windows enjoying the view when a doorbell rang, startling her.

It was the doorman again, bearing a paper grocery bag. "Mrs. Trimble's friend asked me to bring this down to you."

Taking possession of the bag, Ali looked inside it, where she found a bag of English muffins, a stick of butter, a collection of nondairy coffee creamers, and some ground coffee.

"And if you want to go for a walk on the beach," the doorman added, "Mrs. Watkins says that she and the dogs will be heading out about an hour from now. You can meet up with her down in the lobby."

"Thanks," Ali said. "I will."

Once she had stowed her groceries, Ali went out onto the deck. The setting sun warmed it enough that it was pleasant to sit there to listen to messages and answer phone calls. The first message was from her mother. Everything at home was fine. No need to call back. No news in the baby department.

Ali erased that one. Second was a contrite call from B. saying he hoped he had been forgiven. Things were better on that score. She called him back. They were evidently doomed to playing phone tag for the duration, because B. didn't answer. She left him a message telling him about Velma's situation and the amazing donation the dying woman had made to the Askins Scholarship Fund.

The third message was from Stuart Ramey. "Call me," he said.

Ali did so, immediately. "What's up?" she asked when Stu came on the line.

"Have you had a chance to look at the material I dropped off?"

Evidently B. hadn't mentioned to his second in command that there had been a big blowup between Ali and B. as a result of that so-called material.

"I skimmed through most of it," Ali said. "Why?"

"I just got off the phone with a retired homicide detective named Jim Laughlin in Jefferson City, Missouri," Stuart said. "I don't know if this has anything to do with what your friend was looking for, but I thought it was intriguing. I mentioned in the background check that Ermina's adopted parents, Sam and Lola Cunningham, died about three years after the adoption was finalized. Lola died of a heart attack. The father's death is a lot more problematic."

"What do you mean?" Ali asked.

"His cause of death was officially listed as suicide. Detective Laughlin doesn't buy that. He thinks Ermina was responsible for the father's death, but there was never enough evidence to charge her."

"What else did he say?"

"When he found out I was just looking for background information, he clammed up. I told him you were an independent investigator who was looking into the matter. He said you should give him a call."

Ali laughed aloud at that. "I'm independent, all right," she said. "Give me his number."

A few minutes later, she was talking on the phone with Detective Laughlin.

"Oh," he said, when she said her name. "You're the private investigator Mr. Ramey was telling me about."

"Yes," she said, letting his misconceptions rule the day. "I'm the one looking into Ermina Cunningham Blaylock's background."

"Some teenagers are gawky," Detective Laughlin said. "Not Ermina. She was a looker and cool as can be—cool and calculating. When people hear about someone's death, there's a right way to react and a wrong way. She got it wrong, but I could never prove it."

"The father's death was ruled a suicide. Did he leave a note?" Ali asked.

"No note. According to his friends, he was despondent after his wife's death."

"How did he die?"

"Got himself good and drunk, then he put a plastic bag over his head. It happened on a Sunday night. Ermina was evidently home at the time. She got up the next morning and went to school. When Sam didn't show up for work at his office that day and when he didn't answer the phone, his secretary stopped by to check. She's the one who found him.

"I personally went to the high school to let Ermina know what had happened. Called her out of her English class and took her to the guidance counselor's office to give her the bad news. 'Oh,' she says just as calm as can be when I told her. 'If he's dead, what's going to happen to me?' Her reaction was totally out of kilter—as though I'd just given her a weather report for the next week."

"What did happen to her?" Ali asked.

"Social services put her in a foster home for a while, but she ran away. As far as I know, she was her parents' only heir. I know she received some money from their estates when she reached her majority, but I don't know how much it was. Sam Cunningham was a well-respected attorney in town here. I suspect she picked up a fair piece of change."

"I take it Stuart Ramey had to do some digging to come up with this," Ali said.

"Ermina was never officially charged in relation to Cunningham's death," Laughlin said. "It happened a long time ago, but there are still enough people in town who are upset about what happened to him. One of them called to let me know that High Noon was making inquiries about Ermina Cunningham. I took it upon myself to call him back. Can you tell me what this is all about?"

"On Friday a friend named Brenda Riley sent me an e-mail asking me for help doing a background check on Ermina Cunningham Blaylock. Brenda disappeared shortly after sending that e-mail and she hasn't been heard from since."

"If your friend got crosswise with Ermina Cunningham," Jim Laughlin said, "you have good reason to be worried. And if there's anything I can do to help, let me know. I still have a score to settle with that girl."

Ali was still thinking about that disturbing phone call a few minutes later when her phone rang again.

"The dogs and I are downstairs waiting," Maddy Watkins said. "Care to join us?"

"Yes," Ali said. "A brisk walk on the beach is just what the doctor ordered."

32

Sacramento, California

When Gil parked in front of Camilla Gastellum's house on P Street in the early evening, it looked as though he had made the trip for nothing. The house was dark. There was no flickering glow from a television set. Having come this far, however, he refused to give up without at least ringing the doorbell.

Once on the porch, though, he thought he heard the sound of classical music coming from somewhere inside the house. He found the doorbell and rang it. Moments later he heard a faint shuffle of footsteps approaching the front door. Two lights snapped on—one in the entryway and one on the porch. The door cracked open as far as the end of a brass security chain.

As far as Gil was concerned, those security chains were worse than useless. They gave the homeowner a false sense of security. If a bad guy wanted to get inside, he would.

"Who's there?" a woman asked.

"My name is Detective Gilbert Morris," he said, holding his

ID wallet up to what he assumed was eye level. "I'm looking for Camilla Gastellum. It's about her daughter."

The security chain was disengaged with a snap, the door thrown open. A gray-haired woman, dressed in a robe and nightgown, stood exposed in the doorway. The way Camilla Gastellum squinted as she looked up at him made him think she couldn't see very well.

"Don't tell me!" she exclaimed. "Have you found Brenda? Is she all right? Come in. Please."

She stepped back and motioned Gil into the house. "Are you saying your daughter is missing?"

"Well, of course she's missing. She left on Friday morning and never came back. I've been trying since Friday night to get someone to take a missing persons report. The last person I talked to told me that since Brenda's an adult, she doesn't have to tell me where she's going. I thought that was why you were here—that you had found her. Where did you say you're from again?"

The fact that Brenda had disappeared the morning of Richard Lowensdale's murder caused a rush of excitement to course through Gil's veins, but he didn't let on.

"Grass Valley," Gil said noncommittally. "I'm with the Investigations Unit of the Grass Valley Police Department."

"Oh, no," Camilla said with a sigh. "Not again."

Using both hands, she reattached the security chain, then she led the way into the house, turning on lights as she went. In a room that seemed more like a parlor than a real living room, she motioned him onto an old-fashioned and exceedingly uncomfortable horsehair couch while she settled in an wooden-armed easy chair. The source of the music was a CD player, which she muted by clicking a remote.

"When I'm here by myself, I generally sit in the dark and listen to music," she explained. "I have macular degeneration. Sitting in the dark helps keep me from thinking about how much I can't see. So tell me," she added, sounding resigned, "what kind of trouble is Brenda in this time?"

"What can you tell me about Richard Lowensdale, Mrs. Gastellum?" Gil asked.

"Please," she said, "call me Camilla. Richard and Brenda were supposedly engaged for a time, but he never actually gave her a ring. It turned out that he had other girlfriends—several other girlfriends. She found that out this past October."

"That would be when she allegedly broke into his house?" Gil asked.

"She didn't 'allegedly' break into his house," Camilla said. "She really broke into his house. She started working on her book right after that—a book about something called cyberstalking. I don't know much about it, but she claims that's what Richard has been doing. And what he did to her personally really hurt her," Camilla added. "She sort of went off the deep end for a while, but I thought she was finally pulling out of it. You know, that she was starting to recover. At least that's what I was hoping. But you still haven't told me what this is all about, Mr. . . ."

"Morris," he supplied. "Detective Gilbert Morris." He removed a business card from his wallet, placed it in her hand, and closed her fingers around it. "That has all my contact information on it."

"But why are you here?"

He didn't want to lower this boom on Camilla Gastellum. She was truly an innocent bystander. Still, he had no choice.

"I need to speak to your daughter," he said. "I need to speak to Brenda."

"Why?"

"A man was murdered in Grass Valley sometime over the weekend, possibly on Friday afternoon. When I left to come here, we still hadn't established a positive ID, but indications are that our victim is Richard Lowensdale. Someone put a plastic bag over his head and taped it shut. He died of asphyxiation."

"Oh," she said. And then a moment later she added, "No, that's not possible. My daughter could never do something like that. Ever."

"Even so," Gil began, "you can see why we're interested in speaking to your daughter. She may know something."

Camilla Gastellum stood up abruptly. "You aren't here to talk to Brenda. You're here to arrest her. You think she did it."

"Mrs. Gastellum, please—"

"You need to go now," she insisted. "You're no longer welcome in this house. And the next time you come back, it had better be with a search warrant."

Camilla escorted him back to the front door. He heard the security chain lock into place as the door closed behind him. Gil headed back to Grass Valley feeling like he was making real progress. He had a suspect. True, Brenda Riley might be among the missing. He didn't for even a moment consider that Camilla Gastellum knew her daughter's whereabouts, but someone did, and Gil was determined to find that person.

In his experience, most people didn't disappear without a trace. Somewhere in Brenda's mother's house on P Street he would find a clue—an e-mail to a friend, a plane or hotel reservation—that would tell him what he needed to know. But in order to find that information and have it admissible in court, he would have to come back with a properly drawn search warrant. To get a warrant, Gil would need to have enough pieces of the puzzle in place to convince a judge that he had probable cause. Probable cause took work, sometimes a whole lot of work.

33

Grass Valley, California

On his way back to Grass Valley Gil called Fred Millhouse. "How are you doing on next of kin?" Gil asked.

"I'm getting nowhere fast," Fred said. "As far as I can tell, Lowensdale is an only child. Both of his parents are deceased, which leaves me at a bit of a loss about what to do about getting a positive ID."

"Maybe one of the neighbors will give us a hand." Stopped briefly at a stoplight, Gil shuffled through his stack of three-by-five cards. "Try getting ahold of Harry Fulbright. He's one of Lowensdale's neighbors. He's a grizzled old Vietnam War vet who clued us in on the presence of that second UPS delivery person. I'm about half an hour out," Gil added. "I'll meet you at the morgue."

Harry Fulbright and Fred Millhouse were waiting in Fred's office when Gil arrived. Once the formality of the positive ID was out of the way, Gil returned to his office and tackled the unpleasant duty of notifying both of Richard Lowensdale's fiancées that the man they knew by another last name had been murdered. Passing along that kind of news to grieving friends and relations was always difficult. In this case it was even more complicated since, in the process, he would also be revealing the fact that their supposed loved one was also a cheat.

Gil dialed the East Coast number first. It was already the middle of the night in New York, but it had to be done. He tried to be kind, but ultimately there was no way to soften the blow.

Janet Silvie listened to what he said with utter mystification. "I don't understand what you're saying," she said. "Is Richard dead or isn't he?"

"That's what I'm trying to explain," Gil said patiently. "Officers went to the address you gave the nine-one-one operator, the house on Jan Road, to do a welfare check. Once they, they discovered the body of a man who has since been positively identified as Richard Lowensdale. We can find no record of anyone named Lydecker living there. Our assumption is that Richard Lowensdale and Richard Lydecker are one and the same."

"You're wrong," Janet declared. "That's just not possible."

"If you happened to have a photo of Mr. Lydecker," Gil suggested, "perhaps you could fax it to me."

"I don't have any photos of him," Janet replied. "None at all. He's so self-conscious about the scar."

"What scar?" Gil asked.

"Richard was in a terrible car wreck when he was sixteen, just after he got his license. He was driving. His best friend was killed in the accident, and Richard was left with a terrible scar on his right cheek. He's spent his whole adult life looking at his face in the mirror every morning, seeing the scar, and remembering what he did to his friend."

"Then most likely the dead man isn't Mr. Lydecker," Gil said. "I was there at the morgue for the positive identification. There was definitely no scar visible."

"Thank God," Janet Silvie said. "I'm incredibly relieved, but if Richard—my Richard—isn't dead, where is he? If you thought you'd found him and you were wrong, does that mean no one is looking for him?"

The truth was, Gil had been looking for Richard Lydecker with all the tools at his disposal, and he had come up empty.

"You should probably call in an official missing persons report."

"But I already did that."

"No," Gil corrected. "The call you placed to the com center turned into a welfare check. I don't think it was ever passed along as a missing persons report."

"Can't you do that much at least?" Janet demanded. She sounded angry.

"Ms. Silvie," Gil explained patiently. "I'm a homicide investigator. That's what I'm doing—investigating a homicide that may or may not be related to your Mr. Lydecker. Since I know nothing about him, however, I can't do the missing persons report. I suggest you call this number tomorrow—"

"Like hell," Janet responded coldly. "Richard is my fiancé. You expect me to just sit here and do nothing? That is so not going to happen. I already called my boss and told him I'm taking a few days of personal leave. I'll be in California as soon as I can possibly make it. I'll be on the first plane out of Buffalo tomorrow morning. I'll call you back after I make the reservation and let you know what time I'll be there."

The idea that Janet Silvie was coming to Grass Valley complicated Gil's life, but it would make it far easier to interview her.

"Good," he said. "Will you want to be picked up at the airport?"

"No. I'll rent a car. If no one else is going to lift a hand looking for Richard, I need to have my own wheels so I can do it myself. My guess is that once you find that crazy woman, that Brenda, the one who was always making up terrible stories about Richard and threatening him, you'll find Richard too. They were engaged once. When Richard broke it off, she went crazy."

Gil didn't let on that Brenda Riley was among the missing, and he wasn't at all sure who was crazy and who wasn't, but he didn't argue the point. "Let me give you my phone numbers," he said. "That way you can get in touch as soon as you get to town."

After putting down the phone, he sat and stared at it for a while. He'd never had a next-of-kin notification go quite so haywire. He personally was convinced that, scar or no scar, Richard Lowensdale and Richard Lydecker were one and the same. Gil was convinced; Janet Silvie wasn't.

Shaking his head, he picked up the receiver and dialed the number for Dawn Carras in Eugene, Oregon. Once again he gave a recitation of who he was and what had happened—that the body of a murder victim, presumably Richard Lowensdale, had been found and that his investigation into the matter indicated that Lowensdale was in fact Richard Loomis, the man Dawn had reported missing earlier in the day.

Dawn heard him out in such aching silence that for a while Gil wondered if the connection had been broken.

"Did you say Lowensdale?" Dawn asked finally.

"Yes. Richard Lowensdale."

"That sounds like it could be the name she told me," Dawn said, her voice suddenly hollow and devoid of any inflection. "But if Richard had to go by another name, he probably had a very good reason."

Yes, Gil thought, *because he's a lying creep.*

"She who?" Gil asked. "Who was it who gave you that other name?"

"Brenda. Richard's ex-fiancée. Somehow she gained access to his computer, and she started calling all of Richard's friends and trying to tell us what a terrible person he was. That his name wasn't really Richard Loomis, that it was Richard Lowensdale, that he was a liar and a cheat."

Which seems to be absolutely true, Gil thought.

"How did she get inside his computer?" he asked.

"I have no idea, but I'm sure Brenda is behind whatever has happened."

Gil thought it interesting that both Janet and Dawn seemed to know about the alleged stalker, Brenda, who probably really was a stalker. It seemed unlikely, however, that Janet knew about Dawn and vice versa.

"Do you have a photo of Mr. Loomis?"

"No," she said. "Richard doesn't allow any photographs of himself."

Right, Gil thought. *The car wreck.*

"He was terribly disfigured by a campfire accident when he was younger," Dawn said. "You can imagine how painful it must be to live with that kind of disfigurement." She paused and then added, "Do you think there's a chance my Richard is still alive?"

Richard, Richard, Richard, Gil thought. *You lying turd!*

"No," Gil said. "I don't think so." It was a brutally honest answer.

"What should I do now?" Dawn said. "If I come down there, do you think I could help find him?"

With Janet Silvie already planning on flying in from Buffalo, the last thing Gil needed was for Dawn to show up as well. His investigation was already complicated enough without having two feuding fiancées land in the middle of it. He remembered what Rachel had said about selling tickets to the catfight.

"It might be best if you didn't do anything right now," he said. "If I find anything out, I'll be sure to be in touch with you."

"All right," she said quietly. Dawn sounded strangely subdued. "Thank you for calling me. I appreciate it."

Gil gave her his cell phone number in case something came

up, not that he thought anything would. He was dead tired. He was sitting there wondering if he should give up for the night and go home when Janet Silvie called back.

"Getting from here to Sacramento is going to take all day," she said. "Even if I leave here at seven-oh-five a.m., I won't be there until after six tomorrow night. That's the best I can do."

Gil was relieved to hear it. He wasn't thrilled that Janet was coming, but he hoped he had managed to deflect Dawn Carras. He stayed at the office for a while longer but not much. He was verging on putting in another twelve-hour overtime day. When Chief Jackman found out about that, he would not be thrilled.

Gil went back to his house. Opening the door, he stopped in the doorway and surveyed his desolate surroundings. There were only three pieces of furniture in the living room and that was it. Linda had left him the low-profile Ekornes recliner that she had always hated because it was so hard to get in and out of it. Truth be known, Gil loved it, but every time he settled into it and tried to relax, the phone rang. Still it was better than having no chair at all. Linda had also left Gil a single television set, his son's cast-off nineteen-inch. It was old-fashioned, definitely not high-def. It was also dying. On the right-hand side of the screen was a black border almost two inches wide. The television sat on top of the chipped brass and glass coffee table that had been deemed unworthy of moving.

That was the living room. In the kitchen he had no table, just a single stool parked by the kitchen counter. His cooking equipment included a coffeepot and his place-setting-for-one set of dishes. The only reason he still had a microwave was that it was a built-in. He had no pots and pans. No extra glasses. For bedroom furniture, he had the AeroBed that he and Linda had once used for out-of-town guests. Oh, and a pair of suitcases. When Linda removed the dresser and the chest of drawers in the bedroom, she had dumped Gil's clothes out of his drawers and into a pair of open suitcases on the bedroom floor. She had taken the washer and dryer too.

That was it. Linda had been gone for two months now. She had told him it was all about the job, but when he had driven up to Mt. Shasta to see the kids, they had told him about the new man in her life—someone she had hooked up with at last year's all-class reunion, one she had attended solo because, surprise, surprise, Gil had been working.

So here he was, living in an almost empty house on Rattlesnake Road. When he and Linda bought the house, they had gotten a great deal on it because the couple who lived there before were going through a nasty divorce. Gil probably should have thought about that and realized that a street address with the word *rattlesnake* in it was most likely a bad omen—that things probably wouldn't turn out well if they tried living there. And they hadn't.

Difficult as it was to fathom, he had fewer possessions now than he'd had in college. He had spent those two months going to work, doing his job, and feeling like a human train wreck. But today he had seen a real human train wreck, the bodily remains of Richard Lowensdale.

After spending so much time at the crime scene, Gil was appalled to see the resemblance between his place and Lowensdale's house on Jan Road. His house didn't stink like that—he still took the garbage out to the street every week—and it wasn't overheated. All the same, it looked forlorn and empty and uncared for, and there were several discarded newspapers on the floor next to his chair.

Someday soon he was going to have to do something about that. But right now he needed sleep, and having an AeroBed in the bedroom beat the hell out of sleeping on the floor.

34

San Diego, California

When Brenda awakened once more, enough time had passed that her clothing was no longer damp. She had no idea what time it was or if it was day or night. She wondered if she was still wearing her watch, but with her arms fastened behind her, there was no way to tell if it was on her wrist or if it had been taken from her somewhere along the way. And even if she had been able to hold it up to her face, she wouldn't have been able to see it. There was no light. Only the occasional rumble of an airplane passing overhead told her she wasn't marooned in outer space.

She tried not to think about how thirsty she was, but her mind tricked her into remembering all the words to an old country/western song that her father used to sing:

> *All day I've faced the barren waste*
> *Without a taste of water— cool, clear water.*

Even when she concentrated on something else, the unwelcome words continued to echo inside her head.

Keep a'movin', Dan.
Don't cha listen to him, Dan.
He's a devil not a man
And he spreads the burning sand with water.

How long will I last without food or water? Brenda wondered. *Six or seven days? Longer? And how long have I been here already?*

Then, just when she was ready to give up, when she was ready to pray to God and ask that in his mercy he take her, Brenda heard Uncle Joe's voice, speaking to her from across the years, his voice low and filled with quiet dignity. "All I had to do each day was choose to live."

Yes, Brenda thought as she drifted back into a feverish sleep. *That's what I choose too.*

35

Scotts Flat Reservoir, California

Grass Valley High School was generally thought to be divided into three separate but relatively equal groups—the jocks, the nerds, and the druggies. The jocks were somewhat smart and drank beer; the brainy nerds were incredibly smart. They were also geeky and drank whatever; the druggies were habitual underachievers who spent lots of time smoking grass, some of which they managed to grow themselves in out-of-the-way places.

John Connor, whose parents were big *Terminator* fans, didn't quite fit in any of the molds. He was a genuine jock—varsity football, basketball, and track. That should have put him firmly in the beer-drinking camp except for the fact that he was a born-again Christian who didn't drink anything, including coffee or tea or even soda. And although he was smart and could have been a nerd, the coffee, tea, and soda prohibitions counted against him.

John may have been "born again," but he wasn't a fanatic about it and didn't much believe in turning the other cheek, which meant that he had knocked the crap out of several guys on the JV football team before they gave up and decided they could just as well be friends. Now, as seniors with their final football season behind them and with basketball season in full swing, John and his best pals, Pete Bishop, Tony Alvarez, and Jack Whitney, were spending Sunday of their long MLK weekend celebrating Saturday night's basketball win and enjoying the fact that there was no school on Monday.

Tony's cousin worked in a liquor store. As usual, Tony had provided the single case of beer and, as usual, John was the designated driver. Pete's dad worked for Nevada County Irrigation, and Pete had grown up trailing his dad around the Scotts Flat Reservoir. On Sunday the boys followed Scotts Flat Dam Road across the dam and off into the woods to a secluded clearing where local teenagers did their illegal drinking.

Now, at eleven o'clock at night and with all the beer gone, they were heading back to town. Just east of the earthen dam, the drinkers started whining about needing a pee stop. John pulled off into a tiny parking area near the dam. While his friends went off into the woods to relieve themselves, John sauntered over to the edge of the lake. He and his father came here fishing sometimes in the summer, but now with a fringe of ice still clinging to the edge of the shoreline, fishing season seemed a long way off.

He stood there on the edge of the lake, watching a sliver of moon make a slender golden splash in the choppy water, and wondered what would happen to him; what did the future hold? John was still hoping for an appointment to West Point, but that was probably a pipe dream. Yes, John was smart and his GPA was outstanding, but his parents weren't well connected, and there were always political ramifications to consider.

So he looked at the cold water and wondered what would happen if he didn't get the appointment. Would he go on to college? He'd had a couple of scholarship offers but not enough to cover the full freight, and his folks couldn't really afford to pay his way. He could maybe try going the ROTC route or perhaps he would end up doing what his father had done and volunteer.

The water wasn't giving him much of an answer. The chill wind sliced through his letterman's jacket and made him shiver.

"Hey, John," Jack yelled at him. "We're done here. Are you coming or are you going to stand around gawking all night?"

Turning away from the water, John tripped over something soft. His eyes had adjusted to the dark enough that when he righted himself he could see the object that had tripped him was made out of leather and was most likely a purse. He looked around. There was no one in sight, no one to connect to this lost property, but then he caught a glimpse of something else—a pair of white tennis shoes, gleaming in the pale moonlight, parked at the edge of the frigid water.

For a moment John stood staring at the empty shoes. There was no other sign of life in this desolate place and no sign of a struggle either. John knew at once that if someone had gone into the water there, they had done so under their own power. They had gone in, and they hadn't come back out.

Of the four buddies in the car, John was the only one who understood the implications of suicide, from the inside out. His grandfather, his mother's father, had taken that road when he was diagnosed with terminal cancer. Gramps had left a note saying he wouldn't put his family through the pain of watching him die, so he had handled it himself. With pills. And the pain of all that—of Gramps's suicide and what had come after it—was one of the reasons the Connor tribe, previously a devout Catholic family, had abandoned Holy Mother Church and become devout Protestants.

Standing there in the moon-softened darkness, John saw the

purse and the shoes and made several calculations. If someone had committed suicide here, he should probably call the cops. With three not exactly sober eighteen-year-olds in his car—*his car*—John couldn't bring himself to do that. There would be questions: What were you doing out there in the woods in the middle of a cold January night? Who was with you? Why were you there? What did you see? All of which meant that if John did the right thing, it would be the wrong thing. He would be in trouble even though he hadn't been drinking and his friends would be in even more trouble because they had been.

But he couldn't just walk away either. That wasn't an option. Gramps had done the same thing this person had done: he had gone off into the forest by himself and taken his pills, washed down with plenty of Irish whiskey. It had taken a week to find the body—a week in the heat of summer.

John remembered vividly the terrible sense of unknowing that his whole family had lived through back then, between the time Gramps went missing and the time someone finally found him. And he remembered his grandmother sitting there in her living room, rocking back and forth and saying that she would never forgive him for going off and leaving her alone like that without even letting her say goodbye. And he remembered his mother's grief when the priest told them that since Gramps had taken his own life, there would be no mass.

John had been twelve at the time. He had been struck by the fact that the people who should have been there to help his grieving family—the cops and the priest—had made things that much worse.

John knew that somewhere nearby was a worried family waiting for answers. He also understood how much having those answers would hurt, but he knew from his own experience that knowing hurt less than not knowing. And so, without really thinking it through and without saying anything to the friends who were still waiting in the car, John reached down and grabbed up the purse and the shoes. On his way back to the driver's seat, he popped open the trunk and dropped the three items inside.

"What was that?" Jack asked.

"Nothing," John answered. "Just some trash someone left on the beach."

"That's John for you," Pete said. "Eagle Scout all the way."

Back in Grass Valley, John drove them to Pete's house, where they all went inside, watched some DVDs and hung out. The other guys finally crashed, but John didn't even try to sleep. A little past midnight he let himself out of the house. Instead of going home, he drove to the local Safeway. There, parked under one of the halogen lights at the far end of the lot, he got out the purse and brought it to the hood of his car.

It was large and made of some kind of soft leather. Intending to dump the contents out onto the hood, John was about to unzip the purse when a cell phone rang inside it. The noise startled him enough that he almost dropped the purse. Once he unzipped it, though, a foul odor spilled out of it, filling the air around him with an awful stench that was all too familiar. John had no choice but to step away from the vehicle. For the next few minutes he stood doubled over in the corner of the lot, retching onto the pavement.

He recognized the odor—the odor of death—because it was the same one that had lingered in his grandfather's old Suburban no matter what remedies his father used to get rid of it. Ultimately they'd had to total the SUV even though it ran perfectly and didn't have a scratch on it.

Finally the spasm of nausea ended. The odor was still there, slightly dissipated in the cold wind blowing down from the mountains. If there was something dead inside the purse, then maybe John was wrong about what had happened at the reservoir. Maybe the shoes by the lake didn't mean that someone had committed suicide. Yes, that was the point when John Connor definitely should have called the cops and reported what he had found, but he didn't do that. He couldn't.

There would be too many questions, ones that couldn't be answered without jeopardizing his future and his friends' futures too. But he couldn't just leave it alone either. Someone had been calling on the telephone inside the purse, looking for whoever owned the purse, and John Connor—this John Connor, not the teenager from the movies or the old TV series—was the only one who could answer that call.

Covering his mouth and nose with his shoulder, John returned to the purse and dug around inside it. Peering inside, he saw something that looked like a twig. When he pulled it out, he saw what it really was—a severed finger with a bloodied nail that gleamed in the yellowish light.

When John saw that, it was time for him to barf again.

This was far worse than he could have thought possible. With his eyes still watering, he forced himself back to searching the purse until he found the phone, an old flip Motorola. When he opened it, the message light lit up—fourteen missed calls, all of them listed as "Mom." A check of the battery life showed that it was down to a single bar.

With his hands shaking, John checked the details screen and copied the phone number into his own phone. Then, stowing the nearly dead Motorola in his shirt pocket, he zipped up the purse, locking in the odor, and returned it to the trunk. Then he punched send on his phone.

"Hello."

John breathed a sigh of relief when the man answered the phone after only one ring. He wanted to talk to a man, not a woman. It would be easier.

"Hello," the man said again. "Is anyone there?"

John cleared his throat. "I'm here," he said. "My name is John Connor. Who's this?"

"My name is Camilla Gastellum."

A woman, John thought. *A woman with a very deep voice.*

"I live up in Grass Valley," he said hurriedly. "I heard this phone ringing a little while ago. It was inside a purse I found."

"Inside a purse?" the woman asked. "A yellow leather purse?"

"Yes."

"The purse probably belongs to my daughter, Brenda. Where did you find it? And where is she?"

Those were questions John Connor didn't want to answer. "I found the purse by a lake, ma'am, a lake outside of town here. The purse was there along with a pair of tennis shoes."

There was a long pause before "They were all by themselves?"

"Yes," John said, "there was no one around at all."

"I'm down in Sacramento, and I don't drive. Could you maybe bring them to me?"

Remembering what was inside the purse, John knew he couldn't inflict that on anyone else.

"No," he said. "That won't work. I can't do that."

There was another long silence on the end of the phone. For a moment John was afraid the person had hung up, but then the silence was followed by a deep sigh.

"I'm sorry to hear that you're involved in all this, young man, but you need to do the right thing. I understand there's been a homicide in Grass Valley. The dead man's name is Richard Lowensdale. He and my daughter were involved at one time. A detective came to talk to me about this tonight. I believe his name is Morris—Detective Gilbert Morris. As much as I hate to say it, you'll need to take that purse to the police department there in Grass Valley. Talk to Detective Morris. Tell him exactly what you told me. Let him know what you found and where you found it."

John really wanted to say, "No. I can't possibly." Instead he mumbled, "Yes, ma'am. I will."

After Camilla Gastellum hung up, John stood there for a while longer, still holding his own phone and crying. He was crying because he wished he had never picked up the purse in the first place. Now, because he had made that stupid phone call on his own phone, the cops would be able to trace it back to him. Even though he hadn't done anything wrong, he'd be drawn into it. He and Pete and Tony and Jack would all end up being kicked off the basketball team. He would never go to West Point.

"Oh well," he told himself finally, "I can still enlist."

He knew where the Grass Valley Police Department was on Auburn Street, but he didn't want to go there by himself. Instead, he put the purse back in the trunk, then he went home and woke up his parents. He told them the truth, all of it.

"It's okay, son," Will Connor said, crawling out of bed and reaching for his clothes. "You did the right thing. Let me get dressed and we'll go see the cops."

36

Grass Valley, California

Detective Gil Morris had been asleep for just two hours when the phone rang at a little past one.

"What now?"

"You're needed," said Frieda Lawson, Grass Valley's night watch desk sergeant. Regardless of rank, nobody argued with Sergeant Lawson. It simply wasn't done.

"Great," Gil muttered. "Is somebody else dead?"

"That remains to be seen," Frieda said. "I've got somebody here who's asking to speak to the detective in charge of the Lowensdale case."

"That would be me, then," Gil said. "I'll be right there."

Despite the seeming urgency, he needed to clear his head. He took the time to grab a shower, wishing that he had more than just one ragged towel. He would have to do something about that very soon. He either had to buy more towels or go to the laundromat, one or the other.

He stopped off in the kitchen long enough to reload ink into his pen and to grab an additional supply of three-by-five cards.

Then he drove back to the department, watching for black ice as he went.

In the waiting room, Sergeant Lawson sat at her desk behind a glass partition. Two people rose from chairs as Gil walked into the room. Gil recognized the older man as Will Connor, the foreman at the local Discount Tire franchise. Beside him, looking miserable, stood a young man Gil also recognized. John Connor, Will's son, had been a tight end on the Grass Valley High football team and was currently a point guard on the varsity basketball team.

Will Connor stepped over to Gil and greeted him with a firm handshake. "Sorry to drag you out of bed like this," he said, "but I didn't think it should wait until morning. This is my son, John."

John stepped forward too. He held out his hand, but he averted his eyes. On the floor next to the boy's feet sat a purse, a big yellow leather purse. On the chair beside him was a paper bag.

"Do you want to come on back?" Gil asked, thinking he'd talk to them in one of the interview rooms and gesturing toward the security door that opened into the rest of the department.

"I think we'd better off doing this outside," Will Connor said.

"Why?" Gil asked. "What's going on?"

"My son found this purse earlier tonight up near the Scotts Flat Reservoir," Will said. "The purse and the shoes. I haven't looked inside the purse, but he tells me there's a finger inside there—a bloody finger. It's pretty rank."

"Crap," Gil said, reaching for his latex gloves. "Let's go outside and take a look."

Once outside, Gil offered Will and John Connor some Vicks VapoRub to put under their noses and gave himself a dose of it as well. Then he opened the purse and spilled the stinking contents into a Bankers Box he had brought outside for the purpose. He used a hemostat to gather up the bloodied finger and dropped it into an evidence bag, which he quickly closed, but isolating the finger did little to diminish the odor. It had bonded onto the leather itself, leaving the gagging stench to cloud the air. Gil zipped the purse closed. That helped some too.

At that point, John reached into his pocket and extracted a cell phone. "This was in the purse," he said. "I heard it ringing. When I tried to answer it, I found . . . that . . ." He nodded in the direction of the evidence bag.

"I called the number later on my own phone and talked to an old woman named Camilla Gastellum who lives in Sacramento. She said the purse probably belonged to her daughter and that I should bring it here and talk to you. She said her daughter's name was Brenda. Brenda Riley."

When it comes to solving homicides, Gil told himself, *I'm three for three.*

He put the lid on the Bankers Box. He would inventory all this later and then he would send it to the crime lab.

"There's a pair of shoes too," John said quickly, handing over a paper grocery bag. "Tennis shoes. I found them at the same time. They were with the purse."

"Where did you find all this treasure?" Gil asked.

Will Connor answered before his son had a chance to reply. "John and some friends were up by Scotts Flat Reservoir earlier tonight. That's where they found them. He and his buddies were just hanging out . . ."

Will was talking quickly, trying to gloss over the where, when, and why. And Gil got it. He understood. He recognized John Connor because he had seen his photo before in the sports section of the *Daily Dispatch*. The kid had a great record, and a whole lot of his future would be riding on what happened tonight.

Gil remembered how, as a kid, he had walked on the wild

side—gone to wild keggers and hung out with the wrong crowd. For a while during his senior year, it looked like he wasn't going to graduate with his class, but he managed to pull his GPA out of the fire at the last minute. Gil knew that no one would have been more surprised than his high school principal, Mr. Dortman, to learn that Gilbert Morris had grown up to be not only a cop but a well-respected homicide detective.

So Gil didn't need to ask what John Connor and his pals had been doing on a Sunday afternoon and evening at the Scotts Flat Reservoir in the middle of the winter. He already knew. They had definitely been up to no good, probably with booze or girls or both.

"Who else was there?" Gil asked.

John sighed. "Me and Tony Alvarez, Pete Bishop, and Jack Whitney."

Gil recognized those names as well. All four of the kids were starters on the Grass Valley varsity basketball team. If they got booted off the team, it was the end of what was starting to look like a championship season. Even so—even with all that at risk— John Connor had nonetheless done the right thing. He had picked up the purse and the shoes and had brought them to Gil.

"Tell me about the shoes," Gil said. He held them up to the outside light. They were Keds, white Keds. Considering what had gone on at Richard Lowensdale's house, they should have been speckled with blood. They weren't, and they weren't especially dirty either.

That struck Gil as odd. If someone had been out tramping around in the woods in them, they should have been a lot dirtier.

"They were right there on the edge of the lake," John Connor was saying. "Like somebody walked up to the water, kicked off their shoes, and went for a swim. I looked around. It's real sandy there. There could have been footprints coming and going, but I couldn't see them in the dark."

"Any sign of a struggle?"

John shook his head. "It was like she just took off her shoes and walked into the water on her own."

Gil nodded. "We'll need to check that out."

There was a problem with that. The Scotts Flat Reservoir was out in the country. That made for a whole other set of complications.

"Let's get your statement first," Gil said. "Then we'll need you to go back up to the lake so you can show us where all this went down."

Gil picked up the box and the bag. "I'll take these inside so we can maintain the chain of evidence," he said. "Then we need to go to an interview room so I can ask you some questions."

John nodded.

"I'll be recording the interview," he said. "It's important that you tell the truth. You know it's against the law to lie to a police officer."

John looked briefly at his father for guidance and then nodded again. The hopeless slump of his shoulders told Gil that the kid knew he was screwed, that he understood his hope of going to West Point was all over.

"All right," he said, sounding resigned. "Let's get this done and over with."

"Just to be clear," Gil added, "I have no particular interest in knowing what you and your friends were doing up at the reservoir tonight. You weren't drinking, were you?"

John Connor's eyes shot up and met Gil's questioning gaze. His shoulders straightened. "No, sir," he said. "I was not."

It was clearly an honest answer. John Connor had not been drinking, but that didn't mean the others hadn't been.

"Who else saw the shoes and the purse at the lake?" Gil asked.

"No one else. I was the only one."

"All right, then," Gil said, leading the way back inside. "We'll do the interview first. That shouldn't take long, and then we'll go back out to the lake so you can show me what you found where. Then we'll get you home to bed. Wouldn't want you to miss school tomorrow."

"No school tomorrow, sir," John Connor said. "Martin Luther King's birthday."

John didn't mean anything by that remark. It was informational only. Still it hit Gil like a blow to the gut. If his own kids were still here, he would have known that tomorrow was a school holiday.

"Come on," he said gruffly. "Let's get going."

During the interview, Gil asked only a few cursory questions about what John and his friends had been doing at the reservoir in the middle of the night. He let the answer "Hanging out" pass without demanding any more details. Gil focused instead on what had happened after John and his unnamed friends came back to town. How John had gone off on his own to open the purse, what he had found there, and his phone call to Camilla Gastellum.

When the interview was over, Gil picked up his phone and called one of the county detectives, Frank Escobar. He and Frank had worked together before on occasion, but they also went back a long way—back to some of those same wild high school keg parties. Gil wouldn't have to explain the situation with John Connor and his friends to Frank in any great detail.

"I've got a problem," Gil said, once Frank came on the phone. "A kid from Grass Valley was out at the Scotts Flat Reservoir tonight, hanging with a couple of his buddies. They found an abandoned purse and a pair of women's tennis shoes beside the lake. I'm thinking this could be a suicide, but according to the kid there's no sign of a body."

"Wait a minute," Frank said. "If I've got a possible suicide out in the country, what does it have to do with you?"

"It has to do with a homicide I'm working here in Grass Valley," Gil said. "The perp whacked off a few of the victim's fingers. Guess what the kid found inside the purse?"

"A finger?"

"Yes, and puked his guts out too."

"Okay," Frank said. "So my possible suicide turns out to be your possible prime suspect."

"That's it in a nutshell," Gil agreed. "So if you don't mind, once I inventory all this stuff, I'll turn it over to the crime lab for analysis. Later on, if your potential suicide turns into an actual suicide, we'll trade evidence as needed."

"Can you tell me where on the Scotts Flat Reservoir?" Frank asked.

"Somewhere close to the dam," Gil said. "I'm sure the kid can show us, but we're going to need to give him some cover on this."

"What kind of cover?"

"You tell me," Gil said. "Middle of winter, middle of the night, middle of basketball season."

"Gotcha," Frank Escobar said. "How about if you bring your confidential informant and I bring my crime scene tech and we all have a middle of the night powwow at the Scotts Flat Reservoir?"

"Sounds good to me," Gil said. "See you there."

Not wanting to have someone locked in the back seat of his unmarked vehicle, Gil let John Connor ride out to the lake in the front seat of Gil's Crown Vic with his father caravanning behind. On the way Gil couldn't help thinking both those guys were incredibly lucky: John had a great father and Will had a great son. For a change, this was a father and son duo who actually seemed to deserve one another.

At the lake, things were exactly the way John had described them. There was no sign of a struggle—and no sign of a body either. If Brenda Riley had walked into the lake and drowned herself, as cold as the water was this time of year, it could be weeks or even months before she floated back to the surface.

In the meantime, though, Gilbert Morris was hot on the trail of clearing his third case in three days. In the annals of homicide investigations, that had to be some kind of record.

37

Laguna Beach, California

While the three dogs—two big and one tiny—gamboled on the beach and darted in and out of the water, Ali walked beside Maddy Watkins.

"They make quite a pack, don't they?" Maddy observed. "I've never cared much for little dogs, but I promised Velma that I'll take Candy back to Washington with me when the time comes, which will probably be sooner than later."

"Her color's bad," Ali said.

"Yes," Maddy said. "I know."

As they walked, it had occurred to Ali that she had an odd collection of friends. Sister Anselm, Velma, and Maddy were all decades older than she was, yet she felt at ease with them in a way she couldn't understand. She remembered Aunt Evie telling her once that she, Ali, was "an old soul." Maybe being widowed in her early twenties had propelled her into a version of adulthood that usually came to people much later in life.

"Losing a friend is always hard," Ali said.

Maddy stopped walking abruptly and looked up at her.

"No," she said, shaking her head. "Not *having* a friend is what's hard. When Velma and I hooked up by accident on that round-the-world-cruise, it was a stroke of good fortune for both of us. We were by far the oldest people on the trip. There were some things we physically couldn't do, but we didn't do those things together. These past few years our friendship has been a huge blessing. I'll miss her terribly when she's gone, but I wouldn't have missed out on knowing her for the world."

Candy was the first to give up playing. She was small enough that she had to take three steps to each of the big dogs' one. She came back to Maddy and asked to be picked up and dried off. Ali did that while Maddy spent the next fifteen minutes expertly hurling a Frisbee for Aggie and Daphne to chase and fetch.

When the dogs finally tired of the game, the group walked sedately back to the condo building. Near the outdoor pool was a shower with a hose attachment. Maddy used that to remove lingering sand from the dogs' paws, then they made their way into the building through the basement garage.

By the time they got back to the apartment, the night nurse had helped move Velma from the chair to the hospital bed, but she was awake again. Maddy toweled off Candy's wet fur once more, then deposited the dog on Velma's bed.

"You keep her while I get the dog food dished up," Maddy said. "Once the dogs are fed, I'll see about rustling up some food for the humans."

Supper—a collection of cheeses, crackers, fresh grapes, and tangerines—was accompanied by glasses of chardonnay and eaten on trays in the living room. Velma barely touched her food or her wine, but at least it was offered. It was there if she wanted it. That was what Maddy offered her—the dignity of making her own choices.

They were still sitting over glasses of wine when there was a knock on the door and the dogs went into full-throated barking. Maddy gave Ali a wink.

"That will be Mr. Killjoy come to call. He doesn't like the dogs, and the feeling is entirely mutual. They don't like him either."

"Just a minute," she called. Maddy swiftly gathered glasses and trays and carried them into the kitchen. Then, before opening the door, she silenced the dogs and ordered them onto their rugs.

Ten minutes with Carson Trimble was enough to make Ali incredibly grateful for her son, Chris. Carson was arrogant and opinionated. To her misfortune, his hireling nurse had been outside smoking a cigarette when her boss arrived. He spoke mainly to her, asking the nurse pointed questions about Velma's condition rather than addressing his queries to the patient herself. He made it plain that he regarded both Maddy and Ali as unwelcome guests who should have had brains enough to go away and let his mother die in peace.

When Maddy announced that she was going to go clean up the kitchen, Ali followed.

"What a jerk!" Ali muttered.

Maddy smiled. "I told you so. He has a whole set of rules about how he expects his mother's death to play out, and it annoys him that she's doing things her way instead of his. As I said, you ever met my son, you'd think he and Carson Trimble were twins."

The mention of twins, real or not, reminded Ali that she needed to go down to her room and make some phone calls. By the time she returned to the guest suite, it was well after dark. Considering the time difference and her mother's early bedtime, she decided not to call her parents. Instead she called Chris and Athena.

"How are things?" Ali asked her son.

"Athena is already in bed but probably not asleep," he said.

"We went to Grandma and Grandpa's for dinner. That way I didn't make a mess in the kitchen. The laundry is done to the best of my ability. Athena's hospital suitcase is packed and waiting in the entryway closet."

Ali could have asked if "the best of my ability" meant that the colored clothing was improperly sorted, but she didn't. Chris had kept his color blindness a secret from her for a long time, and she decided to let that bit of family fiction go unchallenged.

"In other words, she's still a little grumpy."

"Do you think?"

"She's pregnant," Ali counseled. "If you were growing twins in your body, you'd probably be grumpy too."

"We see Dr. Dixon again on Wednesday," Chris said. "I'm hoping she'll say it's time to induce labor."

Ali heard the unreasonable assumption in what Chris said. He was hoping that once the babies were born, he'd be getting his wife back. Ali understood the reality of that particular pipe dream. Chris and Athena wouldn't be getting their previous lives back for the next eighteen or so years if ever.

"Get some sleep then," she told her son. "You're going to need it."

She spent half an hour IMing back and forth to B. He had moved from his conference hotel to a different one in downtown D.C. She brought him up to date on the day's happenings and about what she had learned from James Laughlin about Ermina Cunningham Blaylock.

She was in bed and sleeping soundly when her cell phone rang at one o'clock in the morning. Ali had left the cell plugged in and charging on the bathroom counter, so it took a few moments for her to stagger through the unfamiliar apartment to find it. She recognized the number. The call had originated at Camilla Gastellum's house, but it wasn't Camilla on the phone.

"Ali Reynolds?" the caller asked.

"Yes."

"I'm sorry to call in the middle of the night like this, but my mother insisted. I'm Valerie Sandoz, Brenda Riley's sister."

The estranged sister, Ali thought in relief. *Camilla must have called her after all.*

"Richard Lowensdale is dead," Valerie announced without further preamble.

"He's dead?" Ali asked. "When?"

"As far as I can tell, the detective didn't say when exactly. It must have happened sometime over the weekend."

"How did he die?" Ali asked.

"Somebody, Brenda most likely, put a plastic bag over his head. He suffocated."

There was a pause on the other end of the line. Ali heard Camilla's forceful objection to that conclusion rumble through the phone, but Ali was busy trying to sort out what she had just been told.

"Say again," she said.

Valerie sighed. "Somebody put a plastic bag over his head," she repeated impatiently. "The cops must think Brenda did it, since a homicide detective came here to the house looking for her. I don't think it was a social call. Naturally, Mom didn't get around to calling me until after the detective left. Brenda's been missing since Friday afternoon, and I didn't know a thing about it until Mom called me this evening.

"Then tonight, while Les and I were driving over from the Bay Area, some kid from Grass Valley called Mom too. It seems he spent this afternoon up in the mountains with some friends. According to him, he came across Brenda's shoes and purse abandoned by some lake or other. The kid found Brenda's cell phone in the purse and called Mom's number. She told him he should take it to the cops. I'm guessing Brenda knocked off Richard and then committed suicide."

Ali was trying to pay attention, but her ability to listen was hampered by what Valerie had said earlier about Richard Lowensdale's manner of death. A plastic bag over the head as a murder weapon? To Ali's way of thinking, it sounded a lot like Ermina Blaylock's dead father. In fact, it sounded *exactly* like Ermina's dead father. And if Ermina had gotten away with murder once, maybe she had decided to do so again.

Valerie was still talking when Ali started listening again.

"I tried to tell Mom we shouldn't bother you in the middle of the night this way, but she insisted. She said you were Brenda's friend—that you'd want to know."

"Your mother is right," Ali said. "I do want to know. Now about that detective who came to see your mother. Does he have a name?"

"Just a sec," Valerie said. She was off the phone for a moment, then she returned. "He left his business card. His name is Gilbert Morris. Detective Gilbert Morris. Do you want his numbers?"

Ali had gone out to the front room, where she hunted through her purse and found a pen. She jotted the name and phone number onto the back of Mina Blaylock's background check.

"All right," Ali said when she finished. "Please tell your mother thank you for having you call me. And tell her I'm sorry things are looking so bad for her, and for you too," she added.

Up to that moment, Valerie Sandoz had been all business—just the facts, ma'am, and nothing more. But those few words of sympathy from Ali were enough to crack the facade.

"Thank you," she muttered over what sounded like a sob. "Thank you very much."

Then the line went dead.

There was no question about what Ali needed to do. Checking the numbers Valerie had given her, she called the office number first and then the cell phone. In both cases she ended up reaching voice mail and left the same message. "My name is Ali Reynolds. I'm a friend of Brenda Riley. Her mother gave me this number. I understand you're investigating Richard Lowensdale's death. I may have some pertinent information. Please give me a call. Here's my number."

After leaving the messages, Ali sat on the sofa for a long time, watching a tiny silver of moon appear in the section of midnight sky that was visible beneath the overhang of the balcony above her unit. The slender sickle of light gradually disappeared into an equally blackened sea.

I shouldn't have told Morris that I was Brenda's friend, she thought. *He probably won't even bother to call me back.*

Ali should have gone back to bed, but she didn't. She sat there for a very long time, thinking, turning over one mystifying question after another, and looking for answers. Her "gut instinct," as her friend Detective Dave Holman liked to call it, told Ali that Ermina Blaylock, not Brenda, had murdered Richard Lowensdale. But why? Had she too been duped by Richard and taken vengeance on him for playing her for a fool? And what about Brenda? Had she somehow put together the connection between Richard and Ermina? Was that what had prompted the background check request she had e-mailed to Ali shortly before her disappearance?

And what about Brenda? Ali wondered. *Did Ermina murder her too? Then again, is Brenda really dead, or is that what Ermina wants us to think?*

Ali switched on a table lamp and read through the background check one more time. There was nothing there in the written report that was the least bit damning. If it hadn't been for Stuart Ramey's going the extra mile, no one would have put two and two together. No one would have connected what happened years earlier in Missouri to what happened to Richard Lowensdale this weekend.

Which means Ermina probably has no idea anyone is on to her.

Ali studied the background check some more and found the address on Heron Ridge Drive in Salton City. That way, if and when Detective Morris called her back, she'd be able to tell him what she had learned and give him an exact physical location to search.

And then Ali remembered something else—a snippet of something Sister Anselm had told her that day when they'd had tea together. Ali couldn't remember the exact words, but it had something to do with stepping out with faith that you would be in the right place at the right time. Ali had come to California thinking she was being guided to do something for Velma Trimble, but maybe she was wrong. Maybe the real intended purpose was for her to do something about Ermina Blaylock.

If not me, Ali asked herself, *then who?*

By a quarter to five in the morning, she was dressed and ready to head out. It had been a pain in the neck, going through the process of putting her Glock in the lockbox and having a TSA agent supervise her locking it, just so she could bring it along in her checked luggage. And it had been a pain retrieving it from baggage claim at the end of the flight, but as Ali put on her small-of-back holster, she was glad to have it. Not that she intended to get into any kind of armed confrontation with Ermina Blaylock. Going after a suspect without backup was one of the dumbest things any cop could do. Still, she was glad to be prepared, just in case. As for her pal, the Count of Monte Cristo? He remained untouched in the suitcase and was likely to remain so.

After leaving the apartment, she rode up in the elevator and slid a note under the door of Velma's unit. In the note, Ali explained that she had been unexpectedly called away and would be returning later in the day. In the lobby she encountered a sleepy doorman who was able to check the schedule of the guest unit. No, it was not booked for tonight, and yes, she could stay in it for the remainder of the week if she wanted. It wasn't booked again until the following Friday.

Driving north to the ten, she remembered that she had never returned her mother's previous phone call. By now, Edie would have taken the first batches of sweet rolls out of the Sugarloaf's ovens and would be getting ready to open the doors.

With her Bluetooth in her ear, Ali speed-dialed her mother's cell phone.

"Is this about the babies?" Edie asked anxiously. "Is Athena in labor?"

"It's not about Athena," Ali said with a laugh. "I'm just now getting around to returning your call."

"Oh," Edie said. "It's about time. I thought you had fallen off the edge of the earth."

"Close to it," Ali said. "I'm on my way to Salton City. You'll never guess what happened. Do you remember Velma Trimble?"

"One of the two old ladies who came to the wedding? Was she the one with the dogs?"

"No," Ali said. "Velma's the other one. She's had a recurrence of cancer, and she's in hospice care at home. Mom, she gave me a two-hundred-fifty-thousand-dollar donation for the Askins Scholarship Fund."

"I'm sorry to hear she's so bad off, but bless her heart," Edie said. "What a wonderfully generous thing to do. But why are you going to Salton City? I was there once, years ago with your father. Back then it seemed like the end of the earth."

I'm pretty sure it still is, Ali thought.

"Do you remember last summer when my friend Brenda Riley showed up down in Phoenix?" she asked.

"The one with the boyfriend troubles and the drinking problem?"

"The very one," Ali replied. "Now her former boyfriend, Richard Lowensdale, has been murdered. Brenda is high on the list of suspects, but I may have come up with another possible suspect who lives in Salton City. I'm just going over to have a look."

"Do you have your Taser along?" Edie asked. "And have you done a spark check recently? You know what they say, 'No spark, no zap.'"

"Yes," Ali said, smiling. "I've got plenty of spark."

"Oops," Edie said. "Customers at the door. Gotta go. You take care."

38

Grass Valley, California

After coming back from the reservoir at five a.m., Gil managed to grab three hours of sleep. Once he was up, he found he was out of cereal and milk, so he made do with a bologna sandwich and a cup of coffee.

Sitting at the breakfast counter, he listened to a message that had come in to his cell phone overnight. He hadn't heard it because the phone had been in the other room on the charger. The caller, someone named Ali Reynolds, claimed to be a friend of Brenda Riley's.

Just what I need right now, Gil thought. *Somebody else telling me that poor, sweet Brenda would never do such a terrible thing.*

Yes, Gil would call Ali Reynolds back—eventually. When he was good and ready. Right now, though, it took all his flagging energy to drag himself to the Nevada County Crime Lab.

"So what's the deal with the amputated finger from Scotts Flat Reservoir?" he asked Mona Hendricks, the chief criminalist in charge of the lab.

"It's a thumb, not a finger," Mona corrected, studying Gil over the top of a chipped coffee cup.

"Well, excuse me all to hell," Gil said. "It looked like a finger to me."

Mona ignored his sarcasm and added some of her own. "Anybody ever mention that you look like crap this morning?"

Gibes from Mona went with the territory.

"Thank you so much for the update. Let's just say I'm overworked, underpaid, and missing a lot of sleep at the moment."

Mona grinned back at him. "I don't think the underpaid part is going to wash. If you've got as much overtime in as I think you do, Randy Jackman is going to have a cow."

Randolph Jackman was the Grass Valley chief of police and Gilbert Morris's boss. Jackman was nothing if not a political animal. He had moved up in the world of law enforcement not on the patrol side as a cop on the streets but on the administrative side. His view of the world was firmly aligned with the bean counters of the world; he was more a city manager type than a Sergeant Joe Friday. Gil already knew that the overtime he had logged that weekend was going to be a headache, but when you stacked the OT up against three solved homicides, he figured he was all to the good.

"Let me worry about Jackman," Gil said. "Tell me about the thumb. Does it belong to Richard Lowensdale?"

"I believe so," Mona told him. "I had my people dust the wall next to the toilet in Lowensdale's bathroom. That's always a good place to pick up usable prints. On the wall we found prints that match the two fingers that were found at the crime scene, and there are prints that match the thumb print too. So, yes, that would mean this thumb also belongs to Lowensdale unless there were two people using the facilities at that address who are both going around getting fingers whacked off."

"Let's hope not," Gil said sincerely.

Mona rolled her eyes. "That was a joke, Gilly! Get yourself

some coffee and get on the beam. Of course it's Lowensdale's thumb. There aren't any other damned prints in the whole house. Lowensdale was the only person living there, and whoever killed him was wearing gloves."

"I've got two women who claim their missing fiancées lived at that same address— Richard Lydecker and Richard Loomis."

"They're mistaken," Mona said decisively. "I'm telling you Richard Lowensdale was the only resident. We didn't find anyone else's prints anywhere in that house."

It annoyed Gil to think he was so tired that he'd totally misread Mona's black humor remark.

"But here's what I don't understand," Mona said. "Why would someone do that?"

"Do what?"

"Leave a bloody thumb to rot inside a perfectly good purse?"

"I don't know the answer to that either," Gil admitted. "But I'm going to find out. Having the thumb match my homicide victim gives me enough probable cause to ask for a search warrant. So that's my next step—getting a warrant to search Brenda Riley's residence."

"Today," Mona said, smiling.

"Of course today. First thing."

"Good luck with that," Mona said. "You do know it's a holiday, right? If it hadn't been for your damned thumb, I wouldn't be here either. I don't think you're going to find many judges at your beck and call at the moment. Do yourself a big favor, Gilly. Take the rest of the day off. Get your search warrant tomorrow; execute it tomorrow."

"No," Gil said. "I'll get it today." He started to leave, then turned back to her. "What about the computer? Did you find anything on that?"

Mona shook her head. "Nope. Not a thing. Someone reformatted the hard drive about four o'clock on Friday afternoon. There's nothing left on it at all. Since he was a Mac user, your victim might have used iDisk or some other kind of web-based backup system, but to gain access to that, you'll need his passwords."

Good luck with that, Gil told himself.

"That reformatting timetable is within an hour or two of what Millhouse estimates the time of death. That also means there probably was something on the computer," Gil said. "Something incriminating that the killer didn't want us to see. What about the vacuum cleaner?"

"No prints. We opened up the bag. Didn't find much in it. Looks like it hadn't been used in a very long time."

Remembering the mess inside Richard's house, that seemed more than likely.

"But the motor's burned up," Mona added. "Like somebody turned it on and left it standing in one place in the living room until it overheated. It's a wonder it didn't burn the place down."

"If they weren't cleaning, what were they doing?"

"Have you ever used a vacuum cleaner, Gilly?"

"Not that I remember."

"Kirbys are supposed to be excellent for cleaning but they're very high on the noise scale. I think maybe the killer was using the vacuum for noise cover."

Remembering what Ted Frost, the real UPS driver, had told him, Gil nodded. "I'll bet you're right," he said.

Gil left the lab and went straight back to the department to draw up his request for a search warrant. Yes, he knew it was a holiday, and no, he didn't care. That had always been one of Linda's major complaints about him. She claimed he was too stubborn, too bullheaded. That once he got an idea in his head, he wouldn't let it go. This was probably more of the same. Gil was determined to find a judge who would sign off on his request for a warrant, and he would, holiday or not.

At ten a.m. Gil had his warrant request in hand and was on his way to track down District Court Judge William Osborne when Sergeant Kathleen Andersson, the Sunday day shift desk sergeant, stopped him on his way out the door.

"Chief Jackman wants to see you," Kathleen said.

"But I'm on my way to pick up a search warrant," Gil argued.

"Take my advice," Kathleen told him. "This didn't sound like an invitation—more like an order. ASAP."

More like a summons to the principal's office, Gil thought. Reluctantly, he reversed course and headed for the chief's office.

"I hear you've been a very busy boy this weekend," Chief Jackman said when Gil entered his office. "From what I see on the time clock, you worked damned near around the clock for three days."

"Three homicides in three days means working round the clock, and since I'm the only guy on the Investigations Unit who's in right now—"

"Good work on the first two," Jackman interrupted, "but I've got to tell you, we can't handle this kind of expense. It's unfortunate that Investigations is so shorthanded at the moment, but while your team members are legitimately off work for one reason or another, they're still on my payroll. In the meantime, you're running up enough overtime that it's turning into a budget disaster."

It seemed to Gil that the chief would have been better off mentioning that to the killers who made the messes rather than to the cop charged with cleaning them up. That's what he thought, but he didn't mention it aloud, because Jackman didn't leave room in his rant for any kind of reply.

"And don't you go tracking Judge Osborne down at home

today either," Jackman continued. "He just called to tell me you were on your way. He read me the riot act about it. He and his wife are trying to have a relaxing day off. The last thing they need is you turning up on their front porch."

"I need a search warrant," Gil explained, "for a person of interest in the Richard Lowensdale homicide."

"Yes," Jackman said. "By all means, let's talk about that." He clicked a few buttons on his computer. "That would be for the residence of one Brenda Arlene Riley on P Street in Sacramento, correct?"

Gil nodded.

"And your person of interest would be the same person who apparently went for a one-way swim in the Scotts Flat Reservoir over the weekend."

"We don't know for sure that it's a case of suicide," Gil began. "Yes, Brenda Riley's personal effects—her purse and her shoes—were found next to the lake, but as far as her committing suicide—"

"Do you personally know of a single woman who would just walk away from her shoes and purse for no reason? Here's some news from the front, Detective Morris. Your prime suspect offed herself. She left her shoes and purse there as a message, and not a message for you either. It's just a fluke that the Connor kid brought the purse to you, but if she did commit suicide, that's the county's problem and not ours. Your pal, Detective Escobar, can be the guy who pisses off Judge Osborne. We don't have to. Let him be the one who goes to Sacramento to search her house. That way it's on the county's budget, not the city's."

In other words, this was a budgetary issue that had nothing to do with the real world of justice, crime, or punishment.

"So here's what I'm thinking," Jackman continued. "I want you to stand down, Detective Morris. Take the rest of the day off. Get some sleep. In other words, no more damned overtime! And before you start writing checks on all this accumulated OT, you might want to think twice. Once your unit members get their butts back on the job, you can take it out in comp time. Fair enough?"

It wasn't fair, but this was a rhetorical question that came with an obligatory answer. Right or wrong had nothing to do with it. "Yes, sir," Gil said.

"Very well then," Jackman said. "Do us all a favor and head home."

Still steaming, Detective Gilbert Morris did exactly that.

39

Salton City, California

In the old days, Ali had sped around on L.A. area freeways with wild abandon. Today, as she made her way north to the ten and then east toward Salton City, she was glad to have the rental's GPS giving her play-by-play directions. It was early enough on a holiday morning that people weren't yet creating their own day-off rush hour traffic jams. The only downside was that she did much of the three-hour-plus drive heading straight into the rising sun—a blinding rising sun.

Not sure what kind of food she would find available in Salton City, Ali stopped off in Palm Springs for close to an hour to have breakfast and take on a load of coffee. By the time she turned onto Heron Ridge Drive, it was verging on nine thirty. Heron Ridge Drive was far longer than she expected, winding north along the edge of the Salton Sea. The name had a grand sound to it. The reality was nothing short of grim. Yes, there were clusters of motor homes parked here and there, but most of the few permanent structures looked as though they weren't long for the world.

At least, that seemed to be the case until Ali caught sight

of the Blaylock place, which looked more like a fortress than a house. The windows and doors of the structure were covered with closed roll-down shutters—metal roll-down shutters. It occurred to Ali that although they weren't exactly aesthetically pleasing, they were probably downright impervious. A silver sedan of some kind was parked in the driveway. Other than that, the place looked deserted. Abandoned. It didn't seem likely that anyone would be inside the structure with all the shutters rolled down and buttoned up. Too dark. Too hot. Too claustrophobic.

Ali drove past once. Then she turned around in another driveway about half a mile farther on. As she drove past the Blaylock driveway a second time, she was startled to see a beefy woman standing in the middle of the street with her hands planted on her hips. When Ali started to drive past, the woman flagged her down.

Ali pulled up next to her, stopped, and rolled down her window.

"Can I help you?" the woman asked.

"I was looking for the Blaylocks," Ali lied. "Mark and Ermina."

"That's their place over there," the woman said, pointing toward the roll-down shutter marvel. "Nobody's home. I saw her leave first thing this morning. She was all alone in that big old Lincoln of hers. I don't know where Mark is. His car is here, which usually means that he's here too, but I can't imagine he'd be inside the house with all those shutters down all the way. One thing for sure, he wasn't in the Lincoln with that battle-axe of his when she left. Who are you?"

The woman went from volunteering information to demanding it in one easy segue.

Ali didn't want to make the mistake of impersonating a police officer. With all the Blaylocks' burgeoning financial difficulties, it wasn't too much of a stretch to pretend to be the minion of a circling creditor. And the way the woman referred to Ermina implied there was no love lost between this frowsy neighbor in her faded tracksuit and Ermina Blaylock.

"It's actually about her Lincoln," Ali said confidentially. "There's a lien on it. I'm doing some scouting for the repo company."

"You mean to tell me Miss High and Mighty is about to lose that fancy car of hers?" the woman said with a wide-faced grin. "Don't that just beat all! And it would serve her right too. Care for a cup of coffee? I just made a new pot."

Ali could hardly believe her luck. She held out her hand. "Coffee would be nice," she said. "My name is Ali Reynolds, by the way."

"Like that old baseball player from Oklahoma?"

"No," Ali said. "I'm Ali with one *L* not two. And you?"

"Florence Haywood," the woman said. "Most people call me Flossie. Just pull right in and park in the driveway. Jimmy went off to play keno at the casino. He won't be back for hours."

All her life Ali had marveled at her mother's ability to know everything that went on in town and outside it. From Edie Larson's station behind the lunch counter at the Sugarloaf Café, she managed to keep her finger on the pulse of everything that went on in and around the Verde Valley. At the police academy down in Peoria, Ali had sat through several classes on the ins and outs of conducting interrogations, but nothing she had been taught there could hold a candle to what she had learned at her mother's knee.

Ali knew at once that Flossie was golden. She was nosy, she was lonely, and she hated Ermina Blaylock's guts. From Ali's point of view, that was definitely a win-win-win situation.

40

Grass Valley, California

Chief Jackman had ordered Gil to go home for the day in no uncertain terms. When Gil did so, he left his city-owned Crown Vic in the departmental parking lot and headed home in his bedraggled five-year-old Camry, which had been sitting forlorn and abandoned in the city parking lot since Gil been called out to the Herrera brothers crime scene on Friday afternoon.

On the way, Gil drove past Target. A few blocks beyond that, he made up his mind. Pulling a quick U-turn, he went back and parked in front of the store. He wasn't sure how much room was left on his Visa card, but he was about to find out.

Pushing a shopping cart, Gil marched through the homemaking aisles on the first genuine shopping spree of his entire life. He bought a set of dishes—four place settings of all blue dishes because blue was his favorite color and a set of silverware for four, stainless not silver of course. He picked up a set of twelve glasses—four each of three different sizes. He bought a toaster—$29.95—a dish drainer, a nonstick set of fry pans, a couple of spatulas, and a laundry basket. He bought two bath towels, two hand towels, and two washcloths as well as a new shower curtain to replace the moldy one with several missing rivets that currently hung in his bathroom.

Gil bought himself a new set of plain white sheets, a fitted sheet and a flat one that came with a pair of matching pillowcases. Then, just for good measure, he bought one of those bed-in-a-bag things that came with a blue plaid comforter and a couple of decorative pillows. At least from now on his damned AeroBed would look like a real bed. He also bought a four-drawer dresser that came in a box, some assembly required.

When he got to the checkout stand, he held back on the dresser just in case he ran out of room on his credit card. Fortunately, the charge went through without a hitch. Now, thank God and Visa, the time for Gil Morris to keep his clothing in one of Linda's discarded suitcases was finally a thing of the past.

He was alone now. It was high time he started living his own alone life.

Leaving Target, just for good measure and just because he could, Gil made two more stops on the way home. He went to the grocery store and replenished his supply of bread, cereal, milk, and cleaning supplies. Then he stopped by the liquor store and picked up a box of fifty Antonio y Cleopatra cigars. He was determined that the next time he had to show up at a crime scene, he would be the one handing out the smokes.

Before Linda took off, one of the things that had always mystified Gil about the woman was that whenever she was pissed at him, she turned into a housecleaning demon. In the past Gil had dreaded those cleaning marathons because he understood that the cleaner the house got, the more trouble he was usually in.

That Monday morning Gilbert Morris finally started to understand it. Huffing on one of the previously prohibited cigars and using his old cracked dinner plate as an ashtray, Gil went to work. He swept; he mopped; he dusted; he scrubbed. He decided that once he paid off his credit card purchases, he was going to buy himself a new television set, maybe even a baby flat-screen. He had seen some of those on sale at Target too and was surprised by how little they cost.

He unwrapped the dishes as well as the glasses and the silver-ware and ran them all through the dishwasher. He put his dirty clothes into the laundry basket along with his dirty sheets. He threw away his musty bath towel, the dead shower curtain, and his ragged, much-used sheets. He knew that Linda would never have considered putting new sheets and pillowcases on the bed without laundering them first, but Linda had taken the washer and dryer. Gil would be damned if he'd go to the laundromat and spend good money washing and drying brand-new sheets and pil-lowcases. He would sleep on them as is.

Linda had left the toilet bowl brush behind, but no toilet bowl cleaner. Fortunately he had picked up some of that at the grocery store. He didn't want his toilet bowel to resemble the ones he had seen in Richard Lowensdale's house. It took several tries and lots of scrubbing before, to his immense satisfaction, the stub-born stains finally disappeared.

He cleaned the bathroom sink until it gleamed and did the same thing to the porcelain sink in the kitchen. By then the dish-washer had run through its cycle. With the dishes still almost too hot to handle, Gil took them out and arranged them in the cup-board the way that suited him best, with the plates on the upper shelf and the glasses and cups on the lower one. This was his kitchen now; Gil would do things his way, not Linda's way.

The relatively mindless work of cleaning and scrubbing al-lowed plenty of time for thinking. Maybe that was what Linda had always known—the link between cleaning and thinking.

Gil let his mind wander back through the intricacies of those two somehow intertwined cases—Richard Lowensdale's murder and Brenda Riley's apparent suicide. Some of the puzzle pieces didn't make sense. For one thing, a luminol test of the shoes from the Scotts Flat Reservoir showed no sign of blood spatter of any kind. The booties might have accounted for that. Still, with as much blood as Gil had found on the scene, it surprised him that there were no traces at all. And for shoes that had evidently walked through the woods, the soles had been pristinely clean, with no dirt or gravel caught in the tread.

Since John Connor had handled the purse, Gil had been obliged to take a set of elimination fingerprints on the boy, but he was relatively sure that his manner of questioning John had left the kid—a good kid, evidently—plenty of wiggle room. There had been no questions about John's friends in the interview, and no mention of them in Gil's written report either. There was no reason to suspect that John and his friends were in any way responsible for what had happened to Brenda.

What mystified Gil most, however, were the contents of the purse, all of which he had carefully inventoried. It was the usual women's purse junk—a compact, several tubes of lipsticks, all the same color, two packages of new tissues as well as a loose collection of old ones, a change purse along with some loose change, a package of dental floss, some aspirin, several pens, a tampon container, and a wallet. The wallet contained four twenty-dollar bills, one credit card in Brenda's mother's name, and three crumbling photos—one of a man and a woman and a twenty-fifth wedding anniversary cake, and two high school senior photos of two women who looked very much alike. From the hairstyles Gil estimated that the photos were most likely of Brenda herself and maybe a female relative. A sister, maybe?

But what didn't fit in with all that was the bloodied thumb.

Why had Brenda taken it along to begin with? Without the thumb, it seemed likely that she would have gotten away with killing Richard Lowensdale. After all, as far as Gil had been able to discover, there was no physical evidence linking Brenda to the crime.

So what was the point of taking that one piece of incriminating evidence with her? Yes, killers often collected trophies, but collecting trophies and then committing suicide seemed illogical. After all, if Brenda was going to kill herself, why would she torture her poor mother by leaving behind the unmistakable message that her beloved daughter was also a murderer? That made no sense.

And then there was the purse itself. Gilbert was hardly a connoisseur of such things, but he knew that purses—even cheap ones—weren't free. Why would Brenda have decided to wreck hers? To Gil's unpracticed eye, the soft leather purse seemed expensive, but it was wrecked now. Because of the bloodied thumb, it now stank to the high heavens.

While returning all the separate inventoried items to the evidence box, Gil had picked up the tampon holder. On a whim, he pulled it open. Yes, there were two paper-wrapped tampons inside the plastic container, but there was also something else. A key of some kind, a key that could have been to a locker, perhaps, or maybe even a desk.

Gil had planned on taking the key to the crime lab later in the day to see if Mona and her crime techs could track down where it came from or what it opened. That, of course, was before Chief Jackman had sent Gil home, so chasing after the key was something that would have to wait for another day.

When it came time to tackle the dresser, Gil opened the box, fished out the directions, and determined what tools he would need—a Phillips screwdriver and an Allen wrench. With those in mind, Gil headed for the garage.

Had Linda made off with her husband's bright red rolling tool chest or if she had emptied it, there would have been all-out war. With two cars in the garage there had been barely enough room for both vehicles to park side by side. That had left the tool chest virtually inaccessible and had rendered the workbench under the window completely useless. Rather than a haven, the garage had become a passageway, good only for coming and going.

With Linda and the kids gone, Gil could have worked in the garage, but he hadn't. What had once been Linda's parking place was still stacked with a collection of stuff—items both loose and in boxes—that she had intended to take to Goodwill right up until she ran out of time. Other than that sad stack of discards, however, the garage was discouragingly neat—exhibiting the kind of cleanliness born of omission rather than effort, disuse rather than use.

As Gil opened the top drawer to retrieve his Phillips screwdriver, he had a sudden realization. Unlike Richard Lowensdale's house, the victim's garage had been clean—absolutely clean, utterly clean, with no trash on the floor and nothing out of place. For someone as messy as Richard, that could only mean that other than parking his car there, he never used it.

There had been no tools lying loose on his workbench, as in none at all—not a single one. Yes, there had been the smell of oil, but it was old oil, ancient oil. Still, Gil remembered clearly that there had been what appeared to be a whole case of motor oil—yellow plastic bottles of motor oil—on a shelf over that workbench. Why?

It seemed inconceivable that someone who left trash lying three inches deep on his living room floor and who dumped garbage down the stairs into his basement rather than hauling it out to the street would turn out to be a shade tree mechanic who did his own periodic automotive maintenance on the side. If Richard

Lowensdale couldn't be bothered with scrubbing out his filthy toilet, he sure as hell wasn't going to change his own oil.

With his heart beating hard in his chest, Gil left the Phillips screwdriver untouched in the drawer. On the surface this seemed like only the vaguest of hunches. It was hardly likely that Richard Lowensdale would have left anything of real value hiding in plain sight in his unlocked garage, but maybe he had. Gil was certain that the killer had searched for something all over the house without ever once venturing into that garage.

Chief Jackman's dressing down still echoed in Gil's consciousness. There was no way he was going to call in one of the uniformed officers to go check out his lead. If he was wrong and it came to nothing, then no one would be the wiser. If that happened, Gil would come straight home and finish assembling his dresser.

If he was right, though, and if there was something to be found in Richard Lowensdale's garage, Gil would see where that clue led him.

On the clock or off it, Detective Gilbert Morris was going back to work.

41

Salton City, California

On Sunday Mina sat at the kitchen table, drinking coffee, thinking about her life and listening to Mark's booze-fueled snores, which echoed from the bedroom and filled the whole cabin. She had no idea what time he had come home. She had awakened only when he finally came into the bedroom and crawled into bed beside her. That's when she had gotten up, gone outside, lit the fire in his precious barbecue grill, and burned up everything she had brought home from Grass Valley— the surgical booties, the blood-spattered clothing, and the Time Capsule. It was gone. By now the ashes should be almost cool enough to dump them out and bury in the beach's fine loose sand.

She sat at the remains of their once-grand dining room table. In the past the table had graced the immense dining room in their home in La Jolla. Polished to a high gloss and with all its leaves extended, the table with its inlaid mother-of-pearl trim had easily accommodated a dozen guests under a magnificent chandelier. Now, without the leaves, it was hardly larger than a card table. It sat in this grim excuse for a kitchen with its once-fine finish marred by scars left behind by the occasional cup of hot coffee or even a cigarette burn or two.

Mina had always hated the cabin. When she and Mark had lived in La Jolla, she'd never wanted to join him on his monthly outings to this desolate place. It was too rustic, too remote, too much like the childhood home she remembered from long ago. She had always been happy to let Mark go off on his weekends of "roughing it," because Mina knew too much about real roughing it. She didn't need to pretend. Besides, between having some time alone in the luxury of her water-view La Jolla home or making do in the gritty rusticity of the Salton City cabin, there had been no contest, not for her now and certainly not back then when there had been a choice in the matter.

At the moment, however, the choice part had been removed from the equation. In the face of forced bankruptcy, the cabin was all they had left—at least on paper, at least as far as Mark knew, as far as their creditors knew. The bank had taken the house back and most of the furnishings had been sold on consignment. They had been allowed to bring along a few pieces of decent furniture to replace the cabin's oddball collection of outdoor plastic.

Along with the humbled and shrunken table, they had brought with them a brown leather couch and matching easy chair that hadn't seemed all that large in their old living room but now seemed huge and occupied far too much of their diminished floor space. There was room enough for only two side tables, one at one end of the couch and one next to the chair. That one held Mina's precious laptop. The other served as Mark's drinks table as well as the spot for his collection of remote controls. He had installed a flat-screen TV on the living room wall. They had planned on keeping their king-sized bed, but it wouldn't fit inside the cabin's tiny bedroom. They'd had to settle for a queen-sized bed from one of their old guest rooms.

Mark was stuck in the past, grieving for everything they had lost. Mina was moving forward.

His snoring stopped abruptly, and she heard him stumble out of bed. Soon he appeared in the doorway of the bedroom, with his hair standing on end and his clothing rumpled. He had come to bed without bothering to undress.

He went over to the fridge, pulled out a beer, and opened it, spraying foam on the wall and floor, which he didn't feel obliged to clean up.

"Hair of the dog," he said unnecessarily.

"Where were you?" she asked.

"Busy," he said with a shrug. "You know how it is. Reprogramming the UAVs took longer than I expected."

"Right," she said. "I'll just bet it did."

Mark was hopeless when it came to lying. As he hurried over to the couch and reached for the television remote, Mina saw the deep flush that spread up his neck. She knew that she had nailed him, but she left him alone long enough for him to go surfing through the channels until he happened upon a golf tournament.

"Does that mean the UAVs are all reprogrammed?" she asked.

"Yes. All of them."

She was gratified that Mark didn't bother trying to explain what he'd been doing since then. Mina was convinced she already knew. He had been screwing his brains out with some bimbo or another. Besides, she had already seen the packaged UAVs with her own eyes, even though she'd had to move them herself. She hadn't dared leave them in the cage with Brenda there as well. Mina didn't believe Brenda would manage to get loose and damage them, but she didn't want to run the risk either.

"Good," she said. "About the UAVs, I mean. I figured you would have called me if there was a problem. And I already talked to Enrique. I told him we'd have them ready for pickup on Tuesday evening."

Mark nodded. "Good," he said. "It'll be good to finally have them out of our hair." Then, in a limp effort to keep Mina from questioning his absence, he tried changing the subject. "How did it go with Richard?" he asked.

Mina shrugged. "It could have gone better," she said.

"Why?" Mark asked, sounding worried. "What happened?"

"Richard Lowensdale is dead."

Mark sucked in his breath. "Dead? How can that be? Who killed him?"

"Who do you think killed him," Mina replied, "the Tooth Fairy? I asked him to give back the money we'd paid him. I asked him very nicely, but he wouldn't do it, so I killed him. I put a bag over his head, taped it shut, and waited until he stopped breathing."

Mina knew better than to tell Mark about the kitchen shears and the fingers. She hadn't a doubt in the world that hearing those ugly details would make the man puke.

As it was, Mark looked as though he was ready to cry. "Why did you do that? Are you crazy?"

"Hardly," Mina said. "You said yourself that you were worried we couldn't trust him, and I decided you were right. We couldn't. I also decided that once he was dead, he wouldn't have any use for our money. I looked all over his house, trying to find where he might have hidden it, but I couldn't find it." Mina shrugged. "No biggie, though. It's only fifty thou."

Mark was almost hyperventilating. His breath came in short, sharp gasps. She hoped he wouldn't have a heart attack and die. That would spoil Mina's fun.

"But what if the cops make the connection and come looking for us?" Mark objected. "What if Richard tried to double-cross us? What if he kept backups of the work he did for us that will lead investigators straight here? What then?"

"Do you think I'm stupid? Of course Richard kept backups," Mina replied. "He was that kind of guy, but I reformatted his hard drive. I also stole his Time Capsule. Had a big bonfire right here on the beach early this morning while you were sleeping the sleep of the dead. I burned up the capsule and I burned up the clothing I was wearing when I killed him. The ashes should be cool by now. I want you to go outside and bury them."

"Where?"

"Where do you think? Over on the beach. No one will pay any attention. People bury bonfire ashes there all the time."

Mark studied his wife. He seemed confused, as though he wasn't sure if she was telling him the truth.

"I don't believe any of this," he said at last. "You're kidding, right? Running me up the flagpole because I stayed out late?"

"I'm not kidding," she said. "Not kidding at all. But don't worry. They won't come after us. I've got the perfect fall guy for us—a fall woman, for that matter."

"Who?"

"Brenda Riley, Richard's old girlfriend."

"The one who came to the office looking for him a year or so after we let him go?"

"One and the same."

"You think you can pin this on her?"

"I don't just think we can pin it on her," Mina said. "I know we can. In fact, we already have."

She was careful to underscore the word "we." She wanted to let that one sink in. She wanted Mark to get the message. She wasn't going to let him get off easy simply by burying the ashes from her bonfire. She wanted to force Mark to accept the fact that he was an active player in all this, that he too was culpable.

"I don't understand," he said. "How do we frame her?"

"By providing blood evidence, which I've already done. There's only one tiny problem."

"What's that?"

"Right this minute, Brenda Riley is still alive. At least she's probably still alive. Somebody needs to kill her and ditch the body in some spot out here in the middle of the desert where no one will think to go looking."

"Who would do such a thing?" Mark asked. He sounded horrified.

Mina laughed outright. "Kill her and bury her? Oh, you poor baby," she said. "Who do you think? Do you think I'm going to do all the dirty work for you? I killed Richard Lowensdale. Now it's your turn. You kill Brenda Riley and get rid of her body, then we're even, fifty-fifty. And Tuesday night, once Enrique gives us our new IDs, we're gone. Out of here. Both of us together. Otherwise, somebody might be left holding the bag."

"I can't do that," Mark croaked. "I've never killed anyone in my life."

"It's not that difficult," Mina said. "I'm sure you can figure it out."

"Where is she?"

"In San Diego in the assembly room. I locked her inside the parts cage. She hasn't had food or water since Friday, so she's probably pretty thirsty right about now. And cold. I doubt she'll be in any condition to put up much of a fight."

Mark stared at Mina in apparent disbelief. "You can't be serious," Mark said. "You can't possibly mean this."

"Oh, but I do," Mina told him. "I mean every word."

He stared at her for the better part of a minute, then he raced for the bathroom. Mina listened while he puked his guts out. It did her heart good to hear it.

Richard Lowensdale hadn't had a clue about the dangers of messing around with Mina Blaylock. Neither did Mark. Sadly, Richard had already learned his very important lesson on that score, and Mark was about to do the same. Even if Richard had given up the money, Mina would have killed him anyway. The same thing was true for Mark as well, but he had yet to figure it out.

He had been a dead man walking long before he decided to screw around on her Friday night, but now there was more to it. Of course she would kill him, but before that happened she intended to toy with him a little.

He came back out of the bathroom still looking green—green and haunted. Mina knew he was a beaten man. So did he.

"Where are you going?" she asked as he headed for the outside door.

"To get my wheelbarrow," he said. "The wheelbarrow and a shovel."

42

Borrego Springs, California

Just after six on Monday morning, Mina closed the shutters on the Salton City cabin for the last time. She had every expectation that no one would go looking inside the place for a very long time. She left the house wearing a track suit and taking nothing but her purse and a single briefcase. Not that there was anything of value in the briefcase—only Lola Cunningham's cookbook. Mina had long since smuggled the contents of her safe out of the house. Everything that could be converted to cash had been, and all the cash, in turn, had been sent along to her numbered account.

She took Highway 78 west toward Julian and Escondido. Along the way, she looked for likely places to dump a body. Mina's original plan had been to fake Brenda's suicide by dumping the unconscious woman into the Scotts Flat Reservoir beyond Grass Valley on Friday evening. She had managed to unload both Brenda's purse and her shoes and was about to wrestle Brenda herself out of the trunk when everything had gone to hell. Some people—kids most likely—had turned up at a most inopportune time, leaving Mina no choice but to slam the trunk shut and drive off.

Mina prided herself on coping under pressure. With no other dumping places scoped out in advance, she'd felt she had no choice but to bring Brenda with her on the long drive back to San Diego. On the way Mina rationalized that things would probably work out for the best after all. It seemed likely that the abandoned shoes and purse would lead the local hick authorities to conclude that Brenda Riley, Richard Lowensdale's presumed murderer, had committed suicide. That assumption would hold regardless of whether her body ever surfaced.

Mina had gotten a kick out of tormenting Mark with the idea that she expected him to do the dirty work for her, but that had never been in the cards. She had known all along that he didn't have the stomach for it. She did.

It was a shame that Mina hadn't hooked up with someone like Enrique Gallegos to begin with. Compared to Mark, Enrique was a far more suitable partner, someone who did what he said he would do when he said he would do it. Mina had enjoyed doing business with him.

In exchange for the UAVs, Enrique had given her money. As a side deal, he had agreed to supply her with a specific set of illicit drugs without making any inquiries as to how she intended to use them. Finally, and for a steep price, he had delivered a set of impressively well-forged documents.

Mina's new passport, dog-eared and thoroughly worn, contained Mina's photograph, but the bearer of same was identified as one Sophia Stanhope, the divorced former wife of a British diplomat. Sophia herself hailed from Bosnia, with a home address in Sarajevo. Mina had no idea how Enrique had managed all those little details, and she didn't want to know, but according to the official-looking immigration stamps in the passport, Sophia had arrived in the United States via Gabo San Lucas two weeks earlier and was scheduled to depart for home on board an Air France transatlantic flight on Tuesday evening.

This evening she would have her final meeting with Enrique. He would give her receipts for the last transfers of money while she, in turn, would hand over a key to the warehouse and the alarm code. Tomorrow evening, about the time Mina was boarding her flight for Paris, Enrique would send a crew to Engineer Road to pick up the UAVs.

And sometime much later tonight, long after her meeting with Enrique ended, Mina would go to the warehouse, drag Brenda out of it dead or alive, and dump her somewhere in the Anza-Borrego wilderness where no one was likely to find the body.

Tomorrow, with all of Mina's hard work finished, Sophia Stanhope would go shopping and field-test her brand-new credit cards and ID. Mina had left the cabin in Salton City with nothing. Had she carried loads of luggage out of the house and into the car, she might have raised suspicion. On Tuesday she would do some serious shopping, probably at South Coast Plaza, where she would know no one. It pleased her to realize that she needed everything and she could afford everything: new underwear, new lingerie, new shoes, new makeup, new perfume, new clothes. And she'd also need some new luggage to transport all her purchases.

Mina was looking forward to that leisurely shopping spree. She'd be able to take her time, without Mark rolling his eyes at the expense or pointing at his watch to move her along. When Mina and Mark were first together, he had enjoyed spoiling her. He had given her carte blanche to buy whatever she had wanted. She, in turn, had loved every minute of it. Once money got scarce, though, and Mark started pinching pennies, it wasn't nearly as much fun. Too bad, Marky. Bye-bye.

Bottom line, most men were probably pretty much like Mark, she realized—fine to begin with, maybe even pleasant, but eventually troublesome, boring, and ultimately inconvenient. If you were lucky enough to be a woman with money of your own, why bother?

A few miles beyond the turnoff to Borrego Springs, Mina noticed a spot where the road had been straightened, leaving behind a generous pullout. She stopped there and walked over to the edge. Beyond the shoulder of the road was a steep drop-off that ended in a rock-strewn desert wash some fifty yards below. She was looking out at a stark landscape that remained largely unchanged since the days of a Spanish explorer, Juan Bautista de Anza.

Mina realized then that she would need something to contain the body. A bedroll might work, preferably a brown bedroll that would blend in with the desert surroundings. And she'd also need a way of making sure the body stayed inside the bedroll as it tumbled down the embankment.

Back in the Lincoln, Mina marked the location as a destination on her portable GPS. She'd be coming back here late tonight. This was the perfect spot, and she didn't want to miss it in the dark.

43

San Diego, California

When Brenda awakened again she was wet. Or at least slightly damp. And she had befouled herself as well. She could smell it, but there was nothing she could do. That was the thing about being in the dark. Sometimes she was awake, but mostly she slept or maybe it just seemed like she slept. It was hard to tell the difference.

She tried not to think about her kidneys shutting down, but they would. Eventually she would lapse into unconsciousness. At this point, that seemed like a welcome idea. At least she wouldn't feel the torture of hunger and thirst.

The temperature in the room hadn't changed, but she was hot now. Burning. So she was probably running a fever. Whenever she thought about it, she tried to flex her ankles. Wasn't that what people did on long plane trips so they didn't develop blood clots in their legs that could go to their hearts and lungs and kill them? But again, dying didn't seem like such a bad idea. At least it would be over.

Sometime long ago she had talked to . . . no, she had interviewed—there had been lights and cameras—a man who had spent days lost in the snowy Sierras. He had talked movingly about how hard it had been to resist the temptation to simply lie down in the snow and let the cold have its way with him.

This was the same thing even though it was just the opposite. She had loved Uncle Joe with all her heart, but she could never live up to the standard of courage he had set. She was no longer willing to choose to live that one more day. She was done. All she wanted was one thing—for it to be over.

Salton City, California

Once Flossie Haywood started talking, there was no stopping her.

"We've been coming here for years, and we've known Mark Blaylock all along since before his first wife died. His missus is Miss Johnny-come-lately around here. She couldn't be bothered slumming it, and we never saw hide nor hair of her until about three months ago, when she showed up with a U-Haul truck full of furniture from their other house."

"From the one they lost in La Jolla?" Ali asked.

It was important to put in bits and pieces of the story herself from time to time, so Flossie would feel like this was a conversation rather than a question-and-answer session.

Flossie nodded. "All kinds of fancy-schmancy stuff. And what did she do with the old stuff Mark had used for years? Tossed it out on the side of the street. Some Mexicans came by in pickup trucks and gathered it all up. Probably took it down to El Centro or Brawley and sold it at the swap meet. It was good enough to use, of course. Jimmy was going to go over and rescue some of the plastic chairs and the like. I told him if he did that, I wouldn't speak to him for a week. I wouldn't give a woman like that any more reason to look down her nose at us than she already had. I'll be damned if I'd be seen picking up her leavings. More coffee?"

Ali nodded and pushed her cup in Flossie's direction. "Please," she said. "Great coffee."

Flossie nodded. "Folgers," she said. "I can't stand all that Starbucks rigamarole. Five bucks for a cup of coffee? No way! So where was I?"

"She was moving her furniture into the house."

"Oh, yes. Her furniture. And that's it. Furniture, but no appliances. No washer or dryer. I'm good friends with Selma Thurgood, who runs the laundromat. It's one of those wash-it-and-fold-it kinds of places. I like to go there to save on water. That way we don't have to go into town to empty our tanks as often. And it's fun sitting around the laundromat jawing with people from all over the country while you wait for your clothes to finish up.

"Selma has a dry-cleaning service that comes over from Indio twice a week, to pick up and drop off. She told me she never did a lick of business with Mina Blaylock. She must take hers somewhere else. She sure as hell doesn't do her own washing and ironing at home."

"You call her Mina?" Ali asked.

"That's what Mark calls her. Short for Ermina. I mostly don't talk to her one way or the other. For one thing, she treats that poor husband of hers like he's so much crap. Jimmy Haywood may not be the brightest match in the box, but he married me and stuck by me, and he gets my respect, every day of the year. You don't see me taking off for days at a time a couple of times a month and leaving him out here batching it. That just ain't right.

"And if you ask me, Mark Blaylock is just a regular sort of guy. His first wife died, you know, and he married Mina on the rebound. Wouldn't be surprised if he's lived to regret it. He used to invite us over for a beer now and then, or a barbecue, but not since she rode in on her broom."

"What's the deal with the shutters?" Ali asked.

"There was a big fish die-off a few years back. This whole place stunk to the high heaven. People just had to walk away and leave their places for a while 'cause they couldn't stand to live in 'em. Of course, it wasn't enough to keep the damned looters out. They came through and stole everything that wasn't nailed down. After that a lot of people just gave up and didn't bother comin' back. Not Mark. He said he'd be damned if he was going to let the bad guys chase him away. That's when he installed the shutters. You ever seen things like that?"

"On shops in some places," Ali said. "Never on houses."

"It's the neatest thing. It works on something like a TV clicker, but it's even smaller. All you have to do is push the up and down buttons and them shutters just slide up and down as smooth as you please. I tried it once too," Flossie confided. "But don't tell Jimmy. He'd be mad enough to chew nails."

"You tried it?" Ali asked.

"Sure. Mark drinks some. He came home one night and had misplaced his clicker—not his television clicker, his shutter clicker. And there he was, stuck. Had to sleep the rest of the night in his car. He was pissed as hell about it. So he went out the next day and got himself a replacement—two replacements, actually. One to keep in his car and one to keep in a fake light fixture out in his carport. He told Jimmy about the extra, in case something went wrong with his house—like an electrical fire or something—so Jimmy and I could let the firemen inside to put it out.

"So one day, when Mark wasn't here and when Jimmy wasn't here either, I went over and tried it for myself. Works like a charm. They go up and down as smooth as glass with just the touch of a button. If I ever have another house that isn't a motor home, I'm going to get me a set of shutters just like 'em."

"My company is worried that Mina is trying to pull a fast one," Ali said.

"You mean like take the car and make a run for it?"

Ali nodded.

Flossie shook her head. "I saw her leave. She didn't have no luggage with her. Just her purse and a briefcase and what she was wearing. That was it."

Ali let her breath out. "That's good news then," she said. "And you haven't noticed anything unusual the past few days?"

"Well, let's see," Flossie said. "Mark was gone overnight this week. Friday night, I think it was. That's unusual for him. He's pretty much a stay-at-home. And then, there was the fire."

"Fire?"

"Middle of the night, Sunday morning, a little after three, I wake up smelling smoke. Believe me, you can't buy smoke detectors better than I am. Anyway, I look out the window, and there Little Miss Hissy Fit is tossing stuff into Mark's barbecue grill and it's burning like crazy."

"You could see all this from here?" Ali asked.

"Since I got my cataracts fixed, my eyesight is downright amazing. So I look out there, and she's got this roaring fire going in the grill. Like a bonfire. Only it stank to the high heavens. Mark only burns mesquite in his grill. He's like a purist or something. But she must have put some kind of plastic crap in there. That's what it smelled like. Burning plastic. I wanted to turn her in to somebody for burning garbage like that. We have waste management here. There's no excuse, but Jimmy told me to be a good neighbor and keep quiet, so I did.

"But then yesterday afternoon, what do I see? Poor Mark is out there in the yard wrestling with that Weber grill of his.

He loaded all the ashes in a wheelbarrow. Took 'em over to the beach, dug a hole, and buried 'em. We could go take a look if you want."

"What do you mean?"

"I was curious. So after Jimmy went off to the casino, I went over there with his metal detector. Screamed like a banshee, so there must be metal of some kind down there. I was going to wait for Jimmy to come home to check it out, but I know how to work the business end of a shovel. Want to go take a look?"

"Absolutely," Ali said. "Sounds like a great idea."

44

Grass Valley, California

There was yellow crime scene tape plastered across the front porch of Richard Lowensdale's house. There was crime scene tape strung across the broken front gate. There was no crime scene tape on the driveway or on the side entrance into the garage.

Donning yet another pair of latex gloves—he would need to go to the supply room for a set of refills soon—Gil let himself into the musty garage. The ten-year-old Catera was still in the same spot. Gil couldn't help wondering who would take the car, or would it be left here to molder away?

The oil was exactly where Gil remembered seeing it—on a wooden shelf over the workbench. It was in a cardboard box that had been cut off so that the bottles stood half exposed above their cardboard container. Reaching up, Gil pulled the first one out of its corner spot. The heft of it, the play of the heavy liquid inside the plastic, told Gil that he was wrong. What was in his hand was, as advertised, a bottle of premium motor oil with, according to the buzz on the bottle, an engine-cleaning chemical additive.

There were a dozen bottles in the box—four wide and three

deep. And all of the bottles in the front row clearly contained oil. The same held true for three of the bottles in the second row. When he picked up the fourth one, however, it seemed lighter than air, and instead of ponderous liquid, there was something or maybe two somethings inside the bottle that rattled when Gil shook the container. At first glance, the bottle appeared to be unopened. There was still a manufacturer's seal over the cap, but the bottle had clearly been tampered with.

Gil returned that bottle to its place and tried the first bottle in the back now. Like the one with the rattle, this one weighed considerably less than the bottles filled with oil, and whatever was inside this one wasn't liquid. It rustled when Gil shook it. Something inside went up and down with a kind of thump, but the noise didn't resemble the rattle in the other bottle. Whatever was inside this one took up far more space.

The second bottle in the back row was similarly loaded. The last two were entirely empty. No rattle, no thump.

Gil returned all the bottles to the cardboard container, then he lifted it down from the shelf. Because the load wasn't evenly distributed, he almost spilled it out onto the workbench. Then he lugged it out the door and down the driveway to his Camry, where he loaded it into the trunk.

He drove straight home and carried the box of bottles into the garage, where he placed them on his own workbench. After switching on his overhead work light, he examined the bottles from the back two rows. Under the rays of the lamp, it was easy to see that the bottoms of some of the bottles had been tampered with—cut through with something sharp and then glued back together.

Gil started with the one that had rattled. The glue, probably some of Richard's model airplane building epoxy, had created a bond, but not enough of one that it was impervious. Gil fastened the bottle upside down in a vise. Then, using a well sharpened wood chisel and an ordinary hammer, he gave the glued surface a sharp whack. The bottom gave way and disappeared into the bottle. Reaching inside, Gil pulled out the plastic bottom as well as two small items. Gil didn't regard himself as any kind of technical genius, but he recognized a pair of computer thumb drives when he saw them.

Setting those aside, Gil performed the same operation with one of the two thumper bottles. When the bottom gave way, it fell into the bottle, but only an inch or two, not nearly as far as the one with the thumb drives. It took some effort on Gil's part to coax the bottom piece back out of the bottle. Then, removing the bottle from the vise, Gil whacked the open end several times on the top surface of his workbench. On the third try, a sheaf of money came shooting out through the opening—a stack of hundred-dollar bills.

For a moment all Gil could do was stare. The pile of money lying there on his workbench was more cash in one place than he had ever seen before. He performed the same operation on the next bottle with similar results, and with a stack of money that was almost equal in size to the first one. Of the two remaining bottles, both empty, both had been cut open but not glued back together.

Standing and looking at the cash as well as the empty bottles, Detective Morris was able to draw several interesting conclusions. Richard Lowensdale had been involved in some kind of illicit behavior for which he was being paid in cash. His killer had come to the house expecting to find it and had, presumably, gone away empty-handed. That was what the missing fingers were all about. The killer had tortured Lowensdale expecting him to reveal his hiding place, and he had not.

So what was Brenda Riley's role in all this? Was she an active participant in what Richard had been doing? Had they been partners of some kind, and Brenda had betrayed him? Or had Brenda somehow stumbled upon what was going on and ended up in jeopardy right along with Richard? And did Brenda's part in this whole puzzle have anything to do with the key that she had kept hidden in her tampon container?

Thoughtfully, Gil put the two thumb drives in the front pocket of his jeans. He didn't have a computer at home. The family desktop had decamped to Mt. Shasta City with Linda and the kids. As for the money? Gil returned that to the applicable bottles and put the bottles back in the box. Then, he hefted the loaded box of oil up to the top shelf over his own workbench.

From where Gil was standing, it looked for the world like a perfectly innocent case of oil. He really was the kind of guy who still did his own oil changes.

45

Salton City, California

Curious, Ali followed Flossie Haywood as she trudged across the road and through the rock strewn sandy shoreline. Flossie carried the shovel. Ali lugged the metal detector, which she found to be surprisingly heavy.

But the walk gave her some time to consider. Richard Lowensdale's murder had taken place on Friday. Mina had lit her middle-of-the-night bonfire sometime overnight between Saturday and Sunday. What if she was burning evidence? Or trying to burn evidence? If Ali encouraged Flossie to dig up the leavings—or if she even allowed it—there was a good possibility they would both be tampering with possible evidence in a criminal proceeding. Ali wanted to know what Ermina Blaylock had been burning in the worst way. That was Ali—plain Ali. But the one who was almost a cop—almost a sworn officer—didn't want to do anything that might make it easier for Mina to get away with what she had done and whatever she was hiding, regardless of what it was.

"Here, I think," Flossie said. "Hand me the metal detector."

For several long seconds she ran it a few inches above the fine sand. Eventually it started alarming. "See there?" Flossie said. "I told you so."

She reached for the shovel, but Ali held it out of reach. "We can't do this," she said.

"Yes, we can," Flossie said. "I was raised on a farm. I was shoveling manure before I learned how to read and write."

"It's not the digging," Ali said. "It's possible that this may be important evidence. If we disturb it in any way, and if Ermina Blaylock has committed a crime, our messing with the evidence might make it impossible for a district attorney to convict her."

Flossie stood stock-still. "Are you saying you think she's done something wrong? I mean something really wrong, not just disrespecting her husband. You mean like something against the law?"

"Yes," Ali said, "that's exactly what I mean, and I don't want to be responsible for letting her get away with it."

"Neither do I," Flossie said. "So what do we do?"

"Get a rock," Ali said. "A big rock that you can use to mark the spot so we can find it again."

Flossie nodded. "Okay," she said, but she seemed disappointed.

It took some time for her to find a suitable rock. Then Ali helped carry the equipment back across the road.

"So what am I supposed to do now?" Flossie asked. "Just forget about it?"

"No," Ali said. "Not at all. It may take some time, but I'll call it in."

"Are you some kind of a cop?"

There were times when telling the truth was the only option.

"No," Ali said thoughtfully. "I'm no kind of a cop at all. I have a friend named Brenda Riley, at least I had a friend named Brenda. She may be dead, and I have reason to believe that Ermina is responsible for what happened to her. If that turns out to be the case, I want her caught and convicted."

"All right," Flossie said in grudging agreement.

"But there is something you can do," Ali offered.

"What?"

"If I can make this work, a little later on tonight, a bunch of cops are going to show up here with a search warrant, and you can do them a big favor."

"What's that?"

"Show them where to find that clicker. It'll be a lot easier for them to get inside the Blaylocks' house if they can raise or lower the shutters."

"You think there's a chance that bitch will go to jail?"

"Yes," Ali said. "I certainly do."

"Then you can count on me," declared Flossie Haywood. "I will not let you down."

Ali waited only long enough to drive out of Flossie's sight before she was on her Bluetooth and dialing Stuart Ramey. Yes, it was a holiday, but she had every confidence that Stuart would answer—which he did, once she managed to outwit the series of voice mail prompts.

"Hey, Stuart," she said. "I want you to look up a telephone number for me. The name is Gilbert Morris, Grass Valley, California. I have his cell phone and his work number. I'm looking for a home number."

"Have you tried information?"

"He's a cop," Ali said. "I'm guessing it's unlisted."

"That may take a little longer."

It turned out the number was unlisted and getting it did take a little longer. Wanting to be able to write down the number, Ali pulled over and parked in a small business park bustling with weekend campers on their way back to their respective cities at the end of the three-day weekend.

"Okay," Stuart said, "you called that shot. Here it is."

Ali jotted the home number down on the back of Ermina's background check, right along with Gilbert's office and cell phone numbers. When the phone started to ring, she held her breath.

Answer, damn it! she thought. *I don't want to give you another chance not to call me back.*

"Hello." He sounded tentative, uncertain. Before dialing his number, she had put in the code that would block her caller ID.

"Is this Detective Gilbert Morris?" Ali asked. Her tone was brisk, businesslike.

"Yes, it is," he said. "But who's calling, please?"

"My name is Alison Reynolds," she said. "I called earlier and left you two messages. You didn't call me back."

"This is an unlisted number. How did you—"

"Listen very carefully," she said. "I have important information, but since you probably won't believe me, I want you to call a third party. Do you have a pencil handy?"

"I have a pen," he said.

"Good. The guy's name is Laughlin. Detective James Laughlin. He's a retired homicide cop from Jefferson City, Missouri. I want you to call him. Ask him about Ermina Vlasic Cunningham. Once you do, I believe you'll be interested in calling me back. Here's his number."

After reading off James Laughlin's number, Ali hung up, without leaving her own number or answering any questions. When Gil Morris got around to calling her back—as she was certain he would—he could damned well go looking for her number. After all, she had already given it to him. Twice.

46

Grass Valley, California

Gilbert Morris was pissed. He had no idea who had given this pushy broad his number but he intended to find out and then there would be hell to pay. This was exactly why cops had unlisted numbers—so every crazy in the universe couldn't pick up the phone and give them pieces of their ringy-dingy minds just because they felt like it.

His first instinct was to ignore it. She'd already told him that she was a friend of Brenda Riley. Yes, he probably should have picked up the phone and called her earlier today, but he hadn't, primarily to get back at Chief Jackman more than anything else. He had told himself he'd make the call tomorrow. But now she'd had nerve enough to call him at home. On his unlisted number.

But still, something about the call rang true. Who the hell was Ermina Cunningham anyway? And who was Detective James Laughlin? And what did any of it have to do with the price of tea in China?

Finally curiosity got the better of him. He called the number. It was two o'clock in California. Four o'clock in Jefferson City,

Missouri. A woman answered with an accent so southern that it sounded like verbal honey.

"Yes, of course," she said. "He'll be right here."

"Jim here," a male voice said a minute or so later. "Who's this?"

"My name is Gilbert Morris," Gil said, feeling stupid. "I'm a homicide detective with the Grass Valley Police Department in Grass Valley, California. Someone suggested that I should give you a call and ask you about someone named Ermina Vlasic Cunningham. I'm not sure why."

"That's odd," Laughlin said. "That's the second request I've had for information about her in as many days. Someone else was asking about her six months or so ago. Long story short, Ermina lived here for a few years with her adoptive parents, Lola and Sam Cunningham. Lola died. Sam supposedly committed suicide. I didn't buy it then, and I'm not buying it now. I know, as sure as you're born, that Ermina killed her dad but I've got no way to prove it. The inquest ruled Sam's death a suicide. The daughter was never charged."

Gil knew what was coming before he ever asked the question. "How did he die?"

"He was drunk," Tom said. "Somebody put a plastic bag over his head and taped it shut."

"Holy crap!" Gil said. "And now she may have done it again!"

He ended the call, opened the earlier message—the one he had ignored—and jotted down Ali's name and phone number before calling her back.

"Okay," he said, "I talked to Laughlin. Where are you? What have you got? How did you make the connection, and are you a cop?"

Disregarding all Gil's questions, Ali asked, "Do you have a fax machine?"

Gil glanced around his clean but bare-bones living room. "Are you kidding? I'm at home. I barely have a microwave. Why?"

"An iPhone maybe?"

"Lady, look, if you're looking for high tech, I'm not your guy. There's a fax machine at the office. What do you want to send me?"

"As I told you in my earlier message, Brenda was my friend. On Friday, just before she disappeared, she sent me an e-mail, requesting that I order a background check on Ermina Blaylock. That's what led me to Detective Laughlin."

"You're not a cop?"

"No. Not for lack of trying. I made it through the academy but my department furloughed me due to budgetary considerations."

Great, Gil thought. *An unemployed almost cop.*

"So what are you, then, a glorified PI?"

"I'm not a PI, and I'm currently in Salton City, east of Palm Springs. I've just come from the home of one of Mark and Mina Blaylock's neighbors. The woman, Florence Haywood, witnessed Ermina burning something in a barbecue grill bonfire in the early hours of Sunday morning. Later on, that same woman—sort of a neighborhood busybody—saw Mark Blaylock dump the ashes into a wheelbarrow and bury them. We used a metal detector to locate the site. It's marked so we can find it again. Florence was all set to dig it up. I cautioned her that since this might be critical evidence, she needed to leave it as is."

Gil thought about that for a minute. "Salton City. What county is that, Riverside?"

"Imperial," Ali replied.

"I'm a city cop. A Grass Valley cop investigating a crime that happened inside my city limits. There's no way a judge is going to grant me a request for a search warrant in a county that's half a state away from here so I can try to figure out who killed Richard Lowensdale."

"I don't give a damn about Richard Lowensdale," Ali told him. "I want to know what happened to Brenda Riley. As far as I'm concerned, those two cases are bound together, but whatever Mark Blaylock was seen burying, it isn't on private property," Ali replied.

"It's public property?"

"Yes. It's out on the beach. No one is going to require a search warrant to dig it up, but in order to maintain the chain of evidence, I need a sworn officer in attendance. You're my first choice."

"Look," Gil said. "I appreciate the tip, I really do. And I'd like to be there, but it's not going to happen. I already got hauled into my chief's office earlier today and bitched out for all the OT I put in this weekend. I was given a direct order to stand down. Based on that, I can't very well go back to him now and say, 'By the way, I need to take a four-hundred-mile side trip in hopes of picking up some evidence.' Besides, even if he said yes, that's at least a ten-hour trip, most likely longer today. There'll be lots of people heading home after the three-day weekend."

"I'm friends with a Nevada County detective named Frank Escobar. Since Brenda Riley's effects were found in the county, he's the one assigned to her possible suicide. Maybe he has some connections down where you are."

"The more people we involve, the more cumbersome it's going to be," Ali told him. "Did I understand you to say you're off work today? That your chief sent you home?"

"Yes."

"So do me a favor," she said. "Give me the fax number for your department. There's a general store here. I already checked. They happen to have a working fax machine. I'll send you a copy of this report so you'll have it in hand. I'll also send you what I have on Richard Lowensdale. Once you read the fax, give me another call. By then maybe I'll be able to figure out what our next move should be."

Our move, he thought. *Right.*

But still, Gil had to admit he was intrigued. He had to look at one of his own business cards to come up with the fax number.

"I need to shower," he said, after giving it to her. "It'll take me half an hour or so."

"All right," she said. "Bye."

47

Salton City, California

The Salton City Pay and Tote was jammed with customers buying drinks, sandwiches, chips, snacks, and gas for their journeys home. Ali waited in line. When she turned over her stack of documents to be faxed, the harassed clerk shook her head.

"All of these? Can't you see I'm busy? This is going to take time."

Ali took a twenty from her purse and laid it on the counter. "That's for you," she said. "I'll pay for the faxes separately."

"Okay," the clerk said. "Just a minute."

It took more than a minute—lots more. The machine was balky. The first three attempts, it cut off after sending only three pages, and each time the clerk started it, she came back to the cash register to help the next person in line.

While Ali waited, she used her iPhone to scroll through her e-mail account.

During Ali's years in California, as the wife of network executive Paul Grayson in a spare-no-expense era, she had made use of his company's corporate jet connections on numerous occasions. Once the network started cutting costs and shedding "nonessential" personnel, the corporate jets as well as their pilots had been jettisoned at about the same time Ali had been kicked off the air.

The pilots, most of them former military, were a good bunch of guys. Somehow a few of them had banded together with some other pilots, pooled their resources, and purchased a couple of the network's stable of secondhand jets. They had used those aircraft to start their own charter service. In turbulent financial times and against all odds, they had started You-Go Aviation and were somehow succeeding at being the low-priced spread in California's once-thriving private jet business.

Ali wasn't sure how her e-mail address had been added to You-Go's customer mailing list, but she received frequent updates advertising their various specials, one of which was $1,995 an hour all in for charters flying anywhere in California, Arizona, and Nevada. Ali remembered from reading their corporate literature that from You-Go's home base in Fresno, most flights could be done with a mere six hours' notice where most other companies required a full twenty-four. When Ali dialed their operations center, she was hoping to take a big chunk out of the six.

The young woman who took Ali's call sounded dubious when she asked to be put through to Allen Knox, one of You-Go's cofounders and a pilot Ali had known well back in the old days.

"I'm sorry," the call center clerk named Amelia told Ali. "Mr. Knox is our CEO. He doesn't involve himself in day-to-day flight arrangements."

"This is urgent," Ali said. "My name is Ali Reynolds. Please give him this number."

"Today's a holiday. I may not be able to reach him, and even if I do, I can't guarantee he'll call you back."

"Just give him the number," Ali said. "He'll call."

And he did, less than five minutes later—just as Ali was paying off the faxing bill and reassembling her stack of paper.

"Hey, Ali," Allen said. "Good to hear from you after all this time What's going on?"

"I'm involved in a possible kidnapping situation," she said, fudging a little. "In order to maintain the chain of evidence, I need to get a homicide cop from Grass Valley to Palm Springs ASAP. How fast can you get someone from there to Jackie Cochran?"

"Today?"

"Yes, today."

"How many passengers?"

"One."

"Luggage?"

"He'll most likely be traveling light."

"All right, Nevada County Air Park is a pretty short runway. Hold on. Let me see if we have a CJ1 available."

He put her on hold and was gone for some time. While she waited, Ali finished sorting and clipping her papers and bought herself a bag of chips. She needed something to soak up those many cups of Flossie Haywood's Folgers.

"You're in luck," Allen said brightly. "Our new CJ1+ just put down here in Fresno. The pilot's still here, so we don't even have to call him out. He can refuel, file a flight plan, and be in Grass Valley in about an hour and a half. With ten minutes or so on the ground in Grass Valley, we should be able to have your guy on the ground in Palm Springs, about an hour and a half after that. So we're talking three hours give or take. Will that work for you?"

"That works."

"Let me put you back on the line with Amelia, then. She can take the passenger information and your credit card, give you the tail number and the address of Airpark Aviation, the FBO we use in Grass Valley. You haven't flown with us since we became You-Go, have you?"

"Nope," Ali said. "This is a first."

"Well, I certainly hope it's not the last," Allen said. "Welcome aboard."

Amelia worked her way through the details in a no-nonsense fashion. Once they were ironed out, Ali called Gil back, on his cell phone.

"Are you at your office yet?" she asked.

"No, I'm still at the house. I just got out of the shower. I'll be heading out in a few minutes."

"You might want to pack a bag," Ali said. "You need to be at Airpark Aviation at the Grass Valley airport in about an hour. I'm sending a plane to pick you up."

"A plane?" Gil asked. "You mean like a Cherokee or a Piper or something—one of those little outfits?"

"It'll be a CJ1," she told him. "A jet—definitely not a Piper."

"Do you mind telling me where I'm going?"

"Jackie Cochran Airport outside of Palm Springs, I'll pick you up there. Once you read the background material, you'll understand."

"Great."

"One more thing," Ali added.

"What's that?"

"I'm assuming you're armed. Don't worry. Flying private, you'll be able to wear your weapon on board with no problem. Just be sure you show up with government-issued photo ID. And if you happen to have a couple of Kevlar vests lying around, you might want to bring them along. One for you and one for me. I wear a size large."

"You want me to bring vests?" Gil asked. "I thought the purpose of this trip was to dig up evidence with shovels. You think someone is going to be taking potshots at us?"

"You never can tell," Ali said. "Better to have vests and not need them than the other way around."

She hung up on Gil before he could say anything more, then she redialed High Noon. "What now?" Stuart Ramey asked when he picked up.

"Don't you ever take any time off?"

"Not so you'd notice."

"I need more phone info," she said.

Stuart laughed. "I guess it pays to be the boss's girlfriend. I was just talking to B. He said I should give you whatever you want."

"Cell phone numbers," she said. "For people named Mark and Ermina Blaylock."

"The people who used to live in La Jolla but who now live in Salton City."

"The very ones," Ali said.

"Okay. I'll call you back when I get something."

Ali looked at her watch. Given the holiday traffic, she estimated it would take an hour to make it from Salton City to the airport. She had flown in and out of Jackie Cochran on occasion. The general aviation terminal there would have a place where she could work while she waited for Detective Morris to arrive.

The terminal had something else that was high on Ali's current list of priorities—decent restrooms. After swilling down all those cups of coffee, restrooms were more than a priority, they were an absolute necessity.

48

Grass Valley, California

Gil got off the phone, shaking his head, convinced that this Ali Reynolds character was one pushy broad. She wanted him to "pack a bag"? Really. It wasn't like he didn't have a suitcase or two. Since the chest of drawers from Target was still in the box, his clean clothes were still in the battered old suitcases on the floor of his bedroom. He picked up the one filled with his underwear and dumped the contents of that into what he thought of as his "sock suitcase."

He gathered up a pair of socks, clean underwear, and the last of his clean shirts from the laundry and stuck those in the now-empty suitcase. He added in his shaving kit, his own Kevlar vest, and a stack of spare note cards. He put his bottle of ink in a Ziploc bag, cushioned it with some of his new paper towels, and hoped the bottle didn't leak. He put that in a side pocket so it wouldn't rattle around, but when he closed it, the suitcase was still more empty than it was full. Even adding in a second vest wouldn't make much difference. This was traveling light in the extreme.

Then he remembered he'd barely eaten all day. When he'd

first come home from shopping, he'd had a bowl of cereal from his new box and made a pot of coffee. Now though, thinking it might be a long time before he saw another square meal, he made himself another bologna sandwich with bread from the new loaf. He packed the sandwich in his suitcase as well—in yet another Ziploc bag in another side pocket.

He closed the suitcase, hefted it, and laughed when he heard things rattling around inside.

"Gilbert, Gilbert, Gilbert," he laughed to himself. "You are certainly one sophisticated son of a bitch!"

He was relieved that the parking spot reserved for the chief of police was empty when he pulled into the departmental parking lot. Leaving his suitcase in the car, he hurried inside. Sergeant Andersson looked up in surprise.

"I thought you were gone for the day."

"I am," he said. "I just stopped by to pick something up. Do you happen to have a fax for me?"

Sergeant Andersson turned her chair around and plucked a stack of papers off her credenza. "More like *War and Peace* than a fax," she said. "It came in a while ago. I hadn't gotten around to putting it in your box."

Taking the fax with him, Gil used a key to let himself into the armory, where he signed out one of the spare vests. Sergeant Andersson was talking on the phone when he headed back out. He waited in the doorway until she hung up.

"You might want to let Chief Jackman know that I won't be in tomorrow," he told her. "I've been called out of town. You can mark it down as a comp day. I understand I have several of those coming."

She was making a note of it as he hurried out the door. He doubted she noticed the extra vest. Better to explain later than to ask permission.

He drove to the Nevada County Air Park and went looking for Airpark Aviation. He found a place to park and went inside, carrying his still-rattling suitcase. A young woman seated behind a counter looked up at him and smiled.

"Flying today?" she asked.

Gil nodded.

"What's your tail number?"

"I have no idea."

"The only aircraft we have coming in in the next little while is a You-Go Aviation CJ1, flying from here to Palm Springs."

"That must be it, then."

"Do you need help with luggage?"

He held up his single suitcase. "Got it. Where do I park?"

"Wherever," she said. "Don't worry about parking. Do you want some coffee? Popcorn?"

"No, thanks," he said. "I'm fine."

I've got my very own bologna sandwich.

Gil took a seat by a window, opened his suitcase, and pulled out the stack of faxes. He was interested to see that two sections of material were devoted to Richard Lowensdale. For right now, though, he needed to know everything there was to know about Ermina Cunningham Blaylock.

He made his way through the material. Without the call to Detective Laughlin in Missouri, Ermina would have seemed entirely harmless. And understandable. Mina and her husband had overextended in order to buy Rutherford International, but they had bet on a losing horse and now they were busted. They had lost their house in La Jolla, lost their fancy cars, lost their golf course membership. They ended up living in a house in Salton City that the county tax assessor said was worth $45,000. That was a big comedown, but nothing he read did anything to explain the relationship between Richard Lowensdale and Ermina.

The only connection Gil could see had to do with the money he had found squirreled away in Richard's pristine garage. If that was what the killer was looking for—and Gil thought it was—where had it come from? Was it possible Richard had been blackmailing Ermina? Given the situation in Missouri, that wasn't such an oddball idea. Maybe Mark Blaylock didn't know about his wife's somewhat questionable past. But if Richard was blackmailing Ermina, where was she getting the money to pay him?

Gilbert wasn't long on forensic accounting, but from what he could see of the Blaylocks' financial records, it seemed unlikely that there would be fifty thousand dollars just lying around loose. It also occurred to him that there was a lot more information included in the report than he would have expected. He was so engrossed in what he was reading that he lost track of time.

"Mr. Morris?"

Gil looked up. A plane had pulled up and stopped on the tarmac just outside the door. Standing in front of him was a man in a pair of chinos and a black golf shirt with the words You-Go Aviation emblazoned in gold on the pocket.

Gil stuffed his paperwork into his suitcase and zipped it. "That's me," he said.

"I'm Phil Canby, your pilot. I understand we're on the way to Palm Springs?"

Gil nodded.

"We don't need fuel, so we'll only be on the ground here for ten minutes or so," Phil said. "It's not a long trip, an hour and a half. The weather's good except for some tailwinds going into Palm Springs. That part of the trip could be a little bumpy. Now, if you'll show me your ID, I'll take you out to the aircraft and get you settled in. I didn't see any catering order. Did you order food?"

"No," Gil said, pulling out his ID. "No food. I'm fine."

He didn't say a word about the bologna sandwich lurking in his suitcase. He settled into the soft leather seat—a leather seat with plenty of leg room.

So this is how the other half lives, he thought as he fastened his seat belt.

The pilot came on board and pulled the steps and door shut after him. "You flown the CJ before?"

Gil shook his head.

"Okay, so let me give you the full safety briefing."

Gil listened, but only partially, to information about emergency exits, oxygen masks, etc. "Any questions?" Phil Canby asked when the briefing ended.

"How much does all this cost?"

"Our company is unusual in that we have an all-in cost of just under two thousand dollars."

"Get out. Two thousand bucks to fly from here to Palm Springs?"

Phil Canby looked at him, grinned, and shook his head. "That's two thousand an hour. So it's over three thousand, to get from here to Palm Springs plus the forty minutes it took to get from Fresno to here. I take it you're not paying the freight, then?"

Gil shook his head.

"Then I suggest you sit back and enjoy it," Phil said.

The pilot disappeared into the cockpit. The irony wasn't lost on Gilbert Morris. He had just maxed out his Visa card shopping at Target. He had no idea of who or what Ali Reynolds really was, but one thing was clear. If she could afford to blow that much money on bringing him along for no other purpose than to "maintain the chain of evidence," then the lady had to be loaded.

As his mother would have said, "More money than sense."

That reminded him, of course, of that other "chain of evidence" problem. The phony oil containers that he had removed from Richard Lowensdale's garage were still in his garage. In a court proceeding against Ermina Blaylock, that could turn into a big problem for Gil. Which reminded him of something else his mother always said: "I'll cross that bridge when I come to it."

49

Palm Springs, California

Ali spent most of her two-hour wait in the Jackie Cochran terminal talking on the phone to Stuart. Locating the needed cell phone numbers was proving more difficult than expected because they had no idea who the provider was. It was only after some unauthorized snooping through the Blaylocks' none too secure bill pay program that Stuart had managed to get on track with that. Ali had given Flossie Haywood her cell phone number and asked her to call if either Ermina or Mark Blaylock returned to the cabin. So far her phone had remained silent.

Despite the fact that Mina had left home with no luggage, Ali was convinced that she was about to make a run for it. So far, the only other possible address they had for her was in San Diego. Rutherford International may have ceased operations, but according to the bill pay records, they were still paying utility bills on two separate addresses in the Clairemont Mesa Business Park. That wasn't an especially promising lead, but as far as Ali knew, that was the only one they had.

When she saw the You-Go Aviation CJ touch down, Ali gathered up her paperwork, stuffed it into her purse, and went to the terminal door.

Ali recognized Phil Canby as one of the pilots she knew. He sauntered toward the terminal accompanied by a man Ali assumed to be Gil Morris. The detective looked a little older than Ali and about Ali's height, although there was a lot more muscle on his frame than there was on Ali's. His crew cut was definitely turning gray. Carrying a single battered suitcase as though it weighed nothing, he looked distinctly lowbrow. Ali liked the fact that he wasn't particularly good-looking. She'd had more than one unpleasant encounter with detectives who had very high opinions about their own special appeal and who came equipped with egos to match.

If Gil Morris considered himself a hunk, it wasn't apparent in the way he was dressed or the luggage he carried. His jeans were faded thanks to numerous washings rather than having been purchased that way. His navy blue golf shirt had a spot on it where something like olive oil hadn't quite come out in the wash, and the end of the zipper on the suitcase was held in place by a strategically located piece of duct tape.

When Ali stepped outside to greet them, she found a steady wind blowing west to east across the tarmac, leaving trails of sifting sand drifting across the runway.

"Good to see you again, Ms. Reynolds," Phil Canby said, shaking her hand. "Here's Mr. Morris, safe and sound."

"And a hell of a lot faster than I would have been here if I had driven," Gil Morris said with a grin.

Ali greeted Gil with a smile of her own as well as a handshake, then she turned back to the pilot. "It's good to see you too, Phil. Do you know if you're booked on another trip right now?"

"Not that I'm aware of," Phil said. "Why?"

"Detective Morris and I have to go back to Salton City for a while, but we may need to fly somewhere else later on today. If you could stand by until I know for sure . . ."

"No problem," Phil said. "I'll let operations know. Then I'll refuel. That way, once you say yea or nay, we can get off the ground immediately."

Ali nodded to Phil and then looked at the detective. "Is that all your luggage?"

"What you see is what you get."

"Come on then."

50

Salton City, California

Gil followed Ali Reynolds outside and clambered into her rented Infiniti SUV. He fastened his seat belt before he said anything. "Okay," he said, "I'm suitably impressed. Obviously you've got more money than God, but I'd like to know what the hell is going on and why the big hurry."

Ali put the SUV in gear and backed out of the parking space. "Right this minute, Ermina Blaylock probably still believes she's in the clear. As long as that doesn't change, we have a better chance of finding her."

She handed Gil a piece of paper. "There's the license information on her vehicle, a silver Lincoln Town Car. I believe she's a person of interest in your homicide. Since I'm not a sworn police officer, I can't put out a BOLO on her. You can. Do it."

Rich and pushy and issuing orders, Gil thought, *but she's also right.*

He took out his cell phone and called Grass Valley. There had been a shift change. Kathleen Andersson was now off duty. Sergeant Frieda Lawson had taken her place. The two desk sergeants were sometimes referred to as the Valkyries, but that moniker was only used behind their backs. Gil was relieved. Frieda Lawson had no way of knowing that Chief Jackman had ordered him to go home. It was nice not having to explain to her why somebody who was off duty needed a BOLO.

"So what's the situation here?" he asked, once he was off the phone. By then they were already headed south on California Highway 86, where rivulets of moving sand slithered across the asphalt in front of them. "And are we really going to get out and dig around in the sand in the middle of a windstorm?"

"Yes, we are," Ali said, "unless drifting sand has covered over our marker. According to the Blaylocks' nearest neighbor, Ermina left home bright and early this morning on her own. Mark's car is at the house, but since the shutters are closed, it's likely he isn't there. I want to do our big dig before either one of them returns."

"If they return," Gil offered.

"Exactly," Ali said.

"And how are we going to do this dig, with our bare hands?"

"I'm sure Flossie will lend us a shovel, if she hasn't already done the digging herself."

"Flossie?" Gil asked.

"Florence Haywood. The neighbor. That's what she calls herself, Flossie. She was all hot to trot to dig before I left. The only way I could dissuade her was by telling her that disturbing the evidence might result in Ermina's getting off. There's apparently not a lot of love lost between Flossie and Ermina."

"You told this woman that Ermina's a suspect in a homicide?"

Ali gave him a scathing look. "As far as Florence Haywood knows, I'm working for a creditor who's trying to repossess Ermina's Town Car. Yes, I know. It was a lie, but it would probably be in both our best interests to stick to that story."

Gil nodded. He was a visiting cop who was a long way out of his own jurisdiction. Ali Reynolds didn't have one.

In other words, he thought, *we're a match made in heaven.*

Ali turned off the highway and onto a series of meandering roads that ran along beside the lake. Gil had spent his whole life in the foothills of the Sierras. He loved the trees and the mountains and the surprising lakes and reservoirs that lay hidden in the mountain valleys. The Salton Sea, surrounded by flat, forbidding desert and distant mountain ranges, seemed like a page taken from some other planet.

The road they were on curved and changed names, becoming Heron Ridge Drive, although as far as Gil could see, there were no ridges anywhere around, and no herons either.

"That's their place," Ali said, nodding toward a small house that was totally encased in what looked like sturdy metal shutters. "And this is Flossie's."

She turned into a driveway that ended at a parked motor home. "I'll tell her we're here and see if she'll let us use her shovel."

Ali didn't come right out and say, "Wait in the car," but Gil got the message. And he didn't argue. He had napped some on the plane, but he hadn't had nearly enough sleep. He was tired, and he knew it.

Ali returned to the car a few minutes later, followed by an immense woman carrying both a shovel and a stack of boxes that were evidently discards from the local liquor store.

"She says we can park here," Ali said, leaning into the car. "Where we're going is on the beach on the other side of the road."

Gil piled out of the SUV and followed the two women across the road and onto a beach covered with treacherous powdery sand punctuated by boulders.

"I was worried about losing the rock," Flossie was saying. "I came out and dusted it off a couple of times, just in case. And here it is."

Flossie moved the rock out of the way, and Gil took charge of wielding the shovel. He had turned over only a few spadefuls of sand when the blade of the shovel struck something hard. The next time Gil raised the shovel, a squarish piece of what appeared to be melted plastic sat in the bowl of the shovel. Ali examined it as he lowered the load into one of the cardboard boxes.

"See the white plastic?" Ali asked. Gil nodded.

"I'll bet I know what that is," she said. "A Time Capsule, for a Mac."

Gil remembered all the apparently undisturbed computer gear on Richard Lowensdale's desk. He had assumed it was all there. Evidently that assumption was wrong. Without another word, Gil resumed digging. The next load of sandy dirt came up with something that was only partially burned, something light blue. It took a moment for him to realize what it was—the remains of a Tyvek surgical bootie like the ones that had left bloodied tracks all through his murder victim's house.

Yes, he decided, *Ali made the right call. We really do need to maintain a chain of evidence.*

He kept digging and found a few more bits and pieces. Finally though, when his shovel loads were yielding nothing but sand, a cell phone rang—Ali's cell phone.

She answered it, listened, and then gave the house across the street a long, appraising look. "Right," she said, finally. "Got it."

Without saying anything to Gil or Flossie, she immediately dialed a number—the pilot's, presumably. "We're flying to San Diego. Wheels up in an hour," she said. She paused and listened again. "I'm not sure which airport," she said. "Whatever's closest to the Clairemont Mesa Business Park. When you figure out what airport, call Hertz and give them my profile number. Tell them we'll need a car wherever you're taking us."

She turned to Flossie. "We need to leave now," Ali said urgently, "just as soon as we get these boxes loaded in my car. I appreciate all your help, but I'm worried about Mr. Blaylock. Do you think there's a chance he's inside the house? I know you said he wouldn't be with the shutters down that way, but after we're gone, you might want to check. You did say he gave you access to a remote, didn't you?"

"Sure," Flossie said. "I'll be glad to go check on him. It won't take but a minute, if you want to wait."

"No," Ali insisted. "We need to go. We've got a plane to catch."

Gil figured that was a fib on Ali's part because he was pretty sure the plane wouldn't go anywhere without them.

As soon as the boxes were loaded, Ali headed for the driver's side, jumped in, turned the key, and gunned the engine. Gil clambered into the passenger seat, slammed the door, and fastened his seat belt. The whole vehicle reeked of wood smoke and burned plastic.

"What's the big hurry now?" he asked as she pulled out of the driveway and then accelerated down Heron Ridge Drive.

"My phone guy just called," she said. "Stuart got a hit on Mina's phone. According to cell phone towers, she's somewhere in downtown San Diego. Since there's been no activity on Blaylock's phone, Stuart tried calling that one."

"How can your guy be doing all this tracing without a court order?"

"Don't ask," she said.

"And?"

"Nobody answered Mark Blaylock's phone, but it looks like it's right here in Salton City, most likely in the Blaylocks' shuttered house. I'm willing to bet Mark Blaylock is inside there too."

"And in no condition to answer the phone," Gil concluded.

Ali nodded.

"How come Flossie would have access to the shutter controls?"

"I'm not sure they were actually given to her. Let's just say she knows where the controller is located, but if she walks in and finds what I think she's going to find, we don't want to be anywhere around. If we were to get caught up in another homicide investigation right now, it would really slow us down. We need to be in San Diego."

They weren't even on the highway yet when a set of flashing red lights appeared in front of them. Ali pulled over and stopped. Moments later a speeding Imperial County Sheriff's Department patrol car swept past them and sped toward Heron Ridge Drive, the way they had come.

Gil looked at Ali. "Guess you called that shot," he said.

Nodding, she pulled back into traffic, leaving Gil to reconsider his initial impression of her.

Yes, he thought, *rich and pushy, but also smart—very, very smart.*

"Of course, the fact that we put out a BOLO on the wife's car before Flossie called nine-one-one is probably going to raise a few eyebrows."

Ali looked at him and grinned. "They'll have to catch us first," she said.

Gil was starting to like this girl.

"And what about your phone meister?"

"Don't worry," Ali said. "Stuart knows how to cover his tracks. Let's just hope he can keep on working his telephone tracing magic with Ermina."

"You realize I'm out of my jurisdiction and I don't have an arrest warrant."

"Don't worry," Ali said. "If we can catch her, I'm sure we'll be able to come up with something that will work."

51

Escondido, California

Although Mina's major shopping excursion would be tomorrow, she needed to do some shopping today. First up was a lightweight mummy sleeping bag, one that zipped up completely and came in Mina's preferred design and color—desert camouflage. She purchased that for cash at an army surplus store in Escondido. Next on Mina's list for today was solving the problem of what to wear for tonight's meeting with Enrique.

Mina had left Salton City in a tracksuit that would do fine for dealing with Brenda, later in the evening, but it wouldn't do at all for her meeting at Enrique's penthouse unit in a newly opened high-rise condo tower in downtown San Diego.

In Escondido she spent some time looking before she located a small wedding boutique where, hidden in among all the pastel bridesmaid garb, she found a surprisingly suitable little black dress and a pair of pumps. Across the street Milady's Day Spa encouraged walk-ins. She opted for a relatively inexpensive mani-cure and pedicure, followed by a facial, a deep-tissue massage, a steam bath, and a shampoo/blow-dry. In the spa dressing room, she reapplied her makeup from the ground up. When she left the spa four hours after entering it, she was transformed. She returned to her Town Car in the tight-fitting little black dress with the tracksuit safely stowed in a shopping bag.

Mina was glad Enrique had invited her to dinner at his new San Diego condo rather than their usual haunt at the casino near Palm Springs. San Diego was far too close to La Jolla for Mina to be comfortable visiting one of the city's hip restaurants. Once she and Mark had been part of the social scene in town here, and she didn't want to run into any of the folks from those old days. The last thing Mina needed tonight was for some former acquaintance to rush up to her, gush over Mina, lie about how much everyone missed seeing them, and ask where was her wonderful husband, Mark. They'd all know about Mark soon enough, but not now, not tonight.

She drove to McClintock Plaza and parked her Lincoln in a compact parking place that was several inches too small. It was a source of annoyance to Mina that there were far more parking places for little cars these days than there were for big ones. Leaving the car behind, she collected several shopping bags. One contained the bedroll, one held her track suit and running shoes, while a third contained her portable GPS. Then she meandered through the mall and had coffee in Starbucks before summoning a cab to take her to the airport. Once there, she made her way to the car rental desks, where Sophia Stanhope rented a Cadillac sedan, which she would return to LAX the next afternoon, prior to her scheduled Air France flight.

In her rented Cadillac, Mina drove to Kettner Boulevard in downtown San Diego and parked in a pay lot just across the street from the condominium tower. There were precious few lit windows showing in the lower floors of the building, but the penthouse blazed with light. Other people might not have money enough to close on their new condo units, but apparently drug dealers were still doing fine financially, thank you very much.

Inside the lobby, Mina gave the concierge her name—her new name.

He checked a list on his computer. "Welcome, Ms. Stanhope. Mr. Gallegos is expecting you. Right this way, please."

The concierge led Mina to a private elevator, one with no buttons, where he used a key card to send her zooming nonstop to the penthouse floor, thirty-five stories up. When the elevator door opened in a secured lobby, Enrique was standing there waiting for her.

"Welcome, my dear," he said, brushing her cheek with his lips. "You're looking lovely this evening. Do come in."

He took Mina's elbow and ushered her inside—into a lush, glass-walled unit with the whole of San Diego's nighttime skyline gleaming in front of her. The view was enchanting. Walking over to look out the windows, Mina was filled with the sense that she was finally putting gritty Salton City behind her.

Moments later, Enrique returned to her side and handed her a chilled crystal flute filled with bubbling champagne. With everything else she needed to do later that night, Mina knew she couldn't afford to drink very much, but a champagne toast was definitely in order.

"To us," she murmured, clinking glasses. "And to making this deal happen."

San Diego, California

Brenda was awakened by the noisy rumble of another plane. She did not want to awaken. Unlike Uncle Joe, she had given up. She was choosing to die rather than choosing to live, but evidently choosing had nothing to do with it. If wishing to die worked, she would have been gone a long time ago.

Feverish and drifting in and out of consciousness, she no longer wondered where she was. That didn't matter. She no longer cared that some poor someone was bound to find her stinking, filthy body. Her condition didn't matter either. Once she was dead, she would no longer have to be embarrassed about that.

Brenda wished she could see her mother one more time and tell her that she loved her. And Valerie too. They had fought like crazy for as long as Brenda could remember, but Valerie Sandoz was her sister—her only sister. That was Brenda's only regret, that she wouldn't be able to tell her mother and sister how sorry she was. For everything.

And as for those other people—the woman who had put her here, and that man, what was his name again? Oh, yes, Richard. They were fading away. She could barely remember them, but she forgave them too. Why not? Sitting here dying, forgiveness was the only thing Brenda Riley had left to give.

52

Palm Springs, California

They were halfway back to the airport when Ali's phone rang. A glance at the caller ID window showed a number she recognized as Flossie Haywood's, but the voice on the phone wasn't Flossie's.

"My name's Jim Haywood. Are you the lady who was just here talking to my wife?" he demanded.

"Yes," Ali said.

"Flossie wanted me to call you. After you left, she went ahead and let herself into the house just up the road. You won't believe what she found!"

"Tell me."

"Poor Mr. Blaylock, dead as a doornail and lying in his bed. Flossie was so upset, she about had a heart attack. They're taking her into Indio to the hospital to be checked out, but she wanted me to let you know about it."

"Could she tell what happened to him?" Ali asked.

"Looked like he was just sleeping, until she tried waking him up. She called nine-one-one. There's a deputy there now. He went inside and said it may have been a suicide. There's a homicide detective on his way to the house from El Centro. The whole thing upset Flossie so much that she started having chest pains."

"Chest pains?" Ali asked. "Is she going to be all right?"

"I hope so. Like I said, they hauled her away in an ambulance. I'm on my way there right now too, but before they took her away, she gave me her phone and asked me to call you. I'm not sure what this is all about. She said something about digging up evidence from over across the road, which didn't make any sense to me. She said the detective will probably want to talk to you."

"I'm sure he will, Mr. Haywood," Ali said. "Feel free to give him this number."

"Blaylock?" Gil asked.

Ali nodded. "Dead in his bed, and thanks to my phone guy the body was found a whole lot sooner than Mina Blaylock wanted him to be found. According to Jim Haywood, there's a homicide detective on his way to Salton City right now."

"The local cops are going to want to talk to us."

"I know," Ali said, "and we will talk to them. We'll tell them everything we know, but after we get to San Diego, not before."

They drove for a while in silence while Gil considered how Chief Jackman was going to react to all this news once it got back to him. It wouldn't be pretty.

"How did Blaylock die?" Gil asked as Ali turned onto the airport drive. "Don't tell me she pulled another plastic bag stunt."

"Mr. Haywood didn't say—just that he was dead."

"How long will it take to get to San Diego?"

"Once we take off, only about half an hour."

"I'll call El Centro once we land," he said.

Ali nodded. "Good."

It was dark by the time they pulled into the terminal driveway. When the pilot saw them unloading several cardboard boxes, he came out with a rolling luggage cart. "Should these be in front or in back?" he asked, sniffing with distaste when he caught a whiff of the odor.

"In front and belted in," Ali said. "But in order to maintain the chain of evidence, Gil needs to sign them. Then we'll need some transparent packing tape to put over his signature and seal the boxes shut. That should help some with the smell."

After all, that was the whole point—maintaining the chain of evidence.

Once on the plane, they skipped the safety briefing because Ali's phone was ringing. It was B. "You realize that what Stuart has been doing is right on the edge," he said. "It's actually over the edge. In tracking down the Blaylocks' phone information, we've violated a whole bunch of privacy rules."

"Yes, I know," she said. "I'm sorry. But we've just uncovered another of Ermina Blaylock's victims. That makes three in all—her father in Missouri, Richard Lowensdale in Grass Valley, and now, if I'm not mistaken, Mark Blaylock too, in Salton City. Not to mention Brenda Riley. Ermina is a maniac, B. We need to catch her before she gets away or has a chance to kill anyone else."

B. sighed. "Where are you now?"

"On the plane, getting ready to fly to San Diego. I know, it's a long shot, but that's the only other address we have for her—the business park at Clairemont Mesa. Even though Rutherford International went out of business months ago, the utilities on two of their three office park units are still current. As broke as they are, there must be a reason those bills are being paid. We're hoping she'll show up there. Otherwise, we've got nowhere else to look."

B. was quiet long enough that Ali worried he might have hung up on her. She didn't blame him for being angry. When she had enlisted Stuart's help, she had been so preoccupied with her own concerns that she hadn't thought about the long-term ramifications for High Noon Enterprises if any of this came to light.

"I'm sorry, B.," she began, but he cut her off.

"I just had a thought," he said. "I don't know if it'll work or not, but call me again once you land."

"Who was that?" Gil asked, once she put her phone away.

"My boyfriend," Ali said. "He's also the technically savvy genius who's behind the guy you call my phone meister. He seemed to think that he had come up with an idea that might help us find Ermina."

"I hope so," Gil said. "I've only been to San Diego a couple of times, one of which was to take the kids to the zoo. It's a pretty big haystack, and Ermina Blaylock is a mighty small needle."

The CJ rose precipitously through the cold night air. Soon Palm Springs and the surrounding cities were narrow strings of lights crisscrossing the darkened desert. Leaning back in her seat, Ali was thinking about B. and regretting the untenable position her actions had created for him and for his company.

"I don't think they're broke," Gil said from across the aisle, interrupting her chain of self-recrimination.

"What?"

"I don't think the Blaylocks were broke," Gil said again. "At least not as broke as they led everyone to believe. First Ermina killed Richard Lowensdale. Then she went searching for something but didn't find it."

"How do you know she didn't find it?"

"Because I did. There was a stash of empty motor oil bottles out in Richard's garage. Hidden inside I found fifty thousand dollars in cash and these."

Gil reached into the pocket of his jeans and pulled out the two thumb drives and handed them over to her. "I don't have a computer at home, so I didn't try to look at them, but between these and the cash, I figure we're dealing with one of two things. Either Lowensdale had found out about Ermina's background and was trying to blackmail her, or else he was still working for her. My guess, it's the latter rather than the former. Once the guy outlived his usefulness, Ermina got rid of him. She got rid of your friend Brenda too, after planting evidence that would make us believe Brenda was responsible for Richard Lowensdale's death."

"What evidence?" Ali asked.

"Three of Richard Lowensdale's fingers were hacked off with a kitchen shears before he died," Gil said quietly. "We found his thumb in Brenda's purse, which was left at the Scotts Flat Reservoir. I have no doubt that Brenda's body is there too. It's just going to take time for it to float to the surface. I know they have underwater equipment that could expedite a search, but I doubt the county can afford it."

"Brenda was a friend of mine," Ali said. "I kept hoping we'd find her alive."

"I know," Gil said. "I'm sorry. What do you think about the thumb drives?"

"I left my computer in Laguna Beach," she said. "When we get to the terminal in San Diego, I'll handle the car rental. Then while you load the car, I'll see if I can log on to one of the computers and send B. whatever's on the thumb drives. Then you can have them back."

"What's his name?" Gil asked.

"B.," Ali said. "B. Simpson. He was born Bartholomew Simpson; people used to call him Bart. He got tired of being teased about that. He changed his name to B. Period."

"I don't blame him," Gil said. "I think I would have done the same thing."

When the plane parked next to the terminal at Montgomery Field, Phil Canby came to open the door. "Clairemont Mesa's just to the right of us," he said, motioning. "Your car is here on the tarmac."

"Do you think I could use a computer in the FBO?" Ali asked.

"I don't see why not," Phil said. "It doesn't hurt to ask."

Ali hurried into the terminal, where the receptionist took her back into a computer-stocked room that was usually reserved for pilot use only. As she plugged the first of the thumb drives into the computer's USB port, she worried that Richard Lowensdale might have booby-trapped the drive so it would self-destruct if anyone else tried to open it. Rather than opening it, she simply copied the data as an attachment into an e-mail and sent it both to B. and to Stuart. She was in the process of uploading the second drive when her phone rang.

"Since you just sent me an e-mail, I'm assuming you're on the ground," B. said.

"Sorry," Ali told him. "I wanted to send these first."

"I know. Stuart and I will both take a look at them in a minute, but right now, I have some good news. That phone call Ermina made went to the local Hertz rental line. I went into their computer system. Two minutes after that call, a San Diego car rental reservation record shows up in the Hertz database in the name of Sophia Stanhope. She picked it up an hour later. A silver Cadillac DTS. She's supposed to drop it off at the rental return at LAX tomorrow."

"Who's Sophia Stanhope?"

"She's supposedly a divorcée from Sarajevo," B. said. "I'd be willing to bet she's really Ermina Blaylock, traveling with some kind of forged documents."

"Do you happen to have the tab number on that rented Caddy?" Ali asked.

B. laughed. "What do you think? Am I a full-service hacker or not?"

"Definitely full-service," Ali replied.

By the time she finished writing down the license information, Gil was standing looking over her shoulder.

"What's that?"

She gave him the note. "It's the plate number for a silver Cadillac DTS someone named Sophia Stanhope rented from a local Hertz agency earlier this evening," Ali told him. "Sophia and Ermina are most likely one and the same, and you may want to revise that BOLO to have information on both this vehicle and the other one. And you should probably expand it to include both the L.A. and San Diego metropolitan areas."

After sending the second e-mail, she removed the second thumb drive and handed both drives over to Gil. "Copied only," she assured him. "Did nothing with the data."

Nodding, he returned the two drives to his pocket. "Okay," he said. "You finish signing for the car. I'm going to call El Centro and see if they'll put me through to the detective."

Gil had pulled the rental car—a Mercury Marquis—through the airport gate and parked it in front of the terminal. When Ali opened the door, she was grateful that the cardboard boxes had been banished to the trunk. She found a Kevlar vest, size L, hanging on the steering wheel. She put it on.

There was no way to tell if Ermina Blaylock would be armed. If she was planning on traveling by air, she most likely wouldn't try to carry a weapon on board an international flight, but between then and now, all bets were off.

While Ali waited for Gil to emerge from the terminal, she called Stuart back.

"You're certainly keeping the phone lines humming today," he said. "I thought B. was going to hand me my walking papers when he found out what we'd been up to."

"He didn't, did he?" Ali asked guiltily.

"No. In fact, I think he'll be getting back to Hertz very soon to let them know that their secure rental database isn't especially secure. So what can I do for you now?"

"I need the addresses of those two locations in San Diego where Mark and Mina Blaylock are still paying the utilities."

"Easy," Stuart said. "Here you go."

By the time Gil got into the car, Ali had already loaded the address on Engineer Road into the rental's NeverLost GPS system. It turned out the two addresses in question were less than two miles from where they were currently parked.

"I thought it was something when I got on the plane in Grass Valley, but this is amazing," he said, as he picked up his own Kevlar vest and pulled it on over his golf shirt. "You fly up in your sweet little corporate jet and the car is parked right there on the tarmac waiting for you. No security lines. No baggage check. No car rental lines."

"It's fast," she said. "It's convenient."

"And expensive," he put in.

"That too."

"So what's your connection to all of this?" he asked.

"To Lowensdale's case?"

Gil nodded.

"Guilt," she said. "I'm the one who blew the whistle on Richard Lowensdale in the first place. Until I came up with that first background check, Brenda didn't even know what the man's name was, much less anything about the other women . . ."

Gil looked at his watch. "Crap," he said.

"What's wrong?"

"Janet Silvie, one of Richard's many girlfriends, is probably on her way into Grass Valley right this minute. She was flying into Sacramento today, and I'm not there to talk to her."

"What are you going to do?" Ali asked.

"Call the desk sergeant, Frieda Lawson," he said. "If anyone can pull my fat out of the fire, she's the one."

While Gil dialed a number on his cell phone, Ali added a new waypoint to the GPS and drove to the nearest Carl's Jr. It had been a very long time since breakfast. If she and Gilbert Morris were going to be stuck in a car on a long stakeout, Ali was determined not to starve in the process.

San Diego, California

While Ali pulled the Mercury into the drive-up line at Carl's Jr., Gil was busy having his ass chewed. Over strongly voiced protests, his call to the desk sergeant had been put through to the chief's office. Unfortunately Chief Jackman was in.

"Do you realize I have not just one but two hysterical women here in the department, both of them raising hell?" Jackman demanded.

"Two," Gil echoed.

"Yes, two. Someone named Dawn Carras showed up an hour or so ago with a worthless little dog that seems to want to take a piss on every chair leg in the waiting room. When Sergeant Lawson couldn't reach you, she called me instead. Thanks a lot. So I was here handling that crisis when Janet Silvie shows up. Now they're out in the lobby having a screaming match. You need to get your butt in here right now and take care of it."

"I can't," Gil said.

"Why the hell not?"

"Because I'm in San Diego."

"San Diego?" Jackman roared. "I told you to take the day off. I didn't say you could go to San Diego."

"You didn't say I couldn't," Gil said. "And if you'll look on the roster, you'll see I won't be in tomorrow either. It's a comp day. I worked eight days straight."

"Detective Morris, that sounds a lot like insubordination."

"It's sounds like time to file a grievance to me," Gil returned, and ended the call.

Pulling out of the drive-up, Ali handed him a bag with a burger, fries, and a soda. "I guess it's safe to assume that didn't go too well."

"Actually, I think it's fine," Gil said. "Leaving Randy Jackman to deal with two hysterical women and a pissy little dog is exactly what the man deserves. Now where are we?"

"That's Engineer Road right up ahead," she said, driving into a maze of streets lined with similarly constructed office buildings and warehouses. "We're going to drive around and see if we can see any sign of either the Cadillac or the Lincoln. If she traded that Lincoln of hers for a rented Cadillac, she might have left the Lincoln parked somewhere nearby."

When Gil's phone rang again a few minutes later, he expected it would be Jackman again. It wasn't.

"Detective Manuel Moreno with the Imperial County Sheriff's Department. I understand you called my department to say you might have some information in regard to my Salton City homicide. So I have two questions. Who are you and what kind of information?"

"I'm Gilbert Morris, a homicide dick with the Grass Valley Police Department. I'm investigating a homicide too, one that happened on Friday of last week. I have reason to believe you and I share a suspect. So let me ask you about Mark Blaylock. You know his death is a homicide rather than a suicide?"

There was a pause. Gil could imagine Detective Moreno staring at the cubicle wall in front of his desk, wondering if he should answer the question or tell Gil to go to hell.

"It could be suicide," Moreno said. "We found an empty bottle of Ambien in the trash and took it into evidence. What we didn't find was any kind of suicide note. At all. The coroner says the victim died sometime overnight last night, probably right around midnight. This morning his wife gets up bright and early, locks up the house, and then takes off for parts unknown without bothering to dial nine-one-one and without mentioning that her beloved husband is dead in their bed. And if it hadn't been for someone encouraging a nosy neighbor to go check on Mr. Blaylock's welfare, it could have been days or weeks before anyone found him. So what do you think, homicide or suicide?"

"I think the same thing you do," Gil said. "Only for a lot more reasons."

While Gil laid out to the Imperial County detective what they knew, what they thought they knew, and when they knew it, Ali did her best to ignore the telephone conversation and concentrate on driving.

The streets of the once-thriving business park wound around and around in seemingly never-ending circles. A lot of the buildings were tagged with graffiti. Many of the lights that should have illuminated the street addresses printed on the buildings were broken or had burned out. There were weeds in the grassy medians and trash blowing around in the gutters and up beside the buildings. The parking lots beside the buildings were mostly empty. That could have been because it was night, or it could have been because the business park was close to being a ghost town. There was no way to tell.

Driving past the two Rutherford units, Ali saw that one of them had a loading bay as well as a regular walk-in entrance. The other unit had only a single door. She drove to the end of the street, counting doors and units as she went, then she traveled up an alley on the far side of the building, counting in reverse. Both Rutherford units had back doors, which meant that both front and back entrances needed to be watched.

Before Gil finished talking to Moreno, however, Ali's phone rang. "UAVs," B. said. "I've had one of my friends take a look at the schematics. Stuart tells me that according to the background check, Rutherford International was hired to dismantle a bunch of UAVs."

"Yes," Ali said. "I remember seeing something like that. A statement, signed and sworn by some government inspector, saying that the UAVs had been properly disposed of."

"Then it's likely the inspector lied," B. returned. "According to the files on the thumb drives, someone—Richard Lowensdale, most likely—was tinkering with the guidance system files and making changes in their code as recently as two weeks ago."

"Who would want to buy UAVs?" Ali asked.

"Who wouldn't want to buy UAVs?" B. responded. "Anyone with a beef against the United States could be in the market for UAVs."

Ali had pulled over and stopped in a parking place that allowed her to see both Rutherford doors. Suddenly there was a sharp rap on the window near her head. Outside stood a uniformed rent-a-cop who had arrived silently on a bicycle.

"This is private property," he said. "You need to move along."

Gil started to respond, but Ali stopped him. "We're waiting to meet with a leasing agent," she said, glancing at her watch. "She's running late, but she's supposed to be here any minute."

"What was that all about?" B. asked into her ear.

"A security guard just paid us a visit," she said. "Trying to give us the bum's rush."

"Where are you?"

"Outside the front door of the two remaining Rutherford facilities in San Diego."

"Who's there with you?"

"The security guard is here, but he's not really with me. The other guy is Gil Morris, a homicide cop from Grass Valley," Ali answered.

"Shouldn't you have some local backup?"

"So far we don't have any grounds for backup," Ali said. "Nothing that would stand up in court."

"You can tell your friend that we don't have an arrest warrant at this point," Gil said, "but Detective Moreno from El Centro is currently en route. He says that if we can locate Ermina, he'll be able to question her as a person of interest in her husband's death. That's not an arrest as such, but if she's planning on leaving the country, that should at least slow her down, maybe long enough for arrest warrants to be forthcoming."

"All right," B. said. "I suppose that, as usual, you're armed?"

"And dangerous," Ali said with a smile. "So is Gil for that matter—armed and dangerous—and we're both wearing vests."

"Somehow that doesn't make me feel any better," B. said, "especially since you're on one side of the country and I'm on the other."

Ali could hear a lecture coming about her putting herself in harm's way. Even if it was true, Ali didn't want to hear it.

"I'm going to have to hang up now," she said. "My Carl's Junior burger is getting cold."

She ended the call and rustled open the bag, but for some reason, she discovered, she was no longer hungry. Even without the lecture, B.'s question had gotten to her. She and Gil were armed, but there was no telling if their opponent, who might or might not show up, would be armed as well.

"Do you think Ermina's carrying?" Ali asked.

Gil thought about it for a moment before he answered. "Present company excluded," he said, "most women I know don't carry weapons. Yes, Ermina was willing to get up close and personal with Richard, but only when he was hogtied, hand and foot. Someone who would stoop to using plastic bags or poison isn't going to have guts enough to use a gun." There was a pause and then he added a somewhat plaintive, "At least I hope she doesn't."

They both laughed aloud at that, and the laughter noticeably reduced the tension. It seemed odd for Ali to realize that although they had known each another for less than twelve hours, they were both operating on the same page. How was that possible?

She worried that the bike-riding security guard would come around again, but he didn't. Then, just when Ali was beginning to think she might need to go find a bush somewhere, the headlights of a vehicle came sliding slowly down the street. First the turn lights came on. Then, activated by a remote control, the rolling door in the loading bay part of the building went up. A silver Cadillac drove inside and stopped, then the door came back down behind it, closing it from sight.

"Okay," Gil said. "Here's the way I see it. There are two of us and, from what I can see, only one of her; two vehicles; and five doors altogether. I'll take the back two, you take these. If she tries to come out . . ."

Without a word, Ali restarted the Mercury's engine and put it in gear. "You need to get out," she said.

"Why?" Gil asked. "What are you doing?"

"I'm going to block the driveway," Ali said, jarring the Marquis's wheels up over the sidewalk. She waited long enough for Gil to scramble out the passenger door, then she parked so his side of the vehicle was within inches of the rolling door.

She rolled down her window as he came around to the driver's side.

"Looks like that'll work," he said.

Ali nodded. "I call it athwart parking rather than parallel parking. My Hertz profile says I take every insurance they offer. If Ermina tries to drive out of the garage, she'll have to go through this thing or over it."

"Good thinking," Gil said. "By my count that leaves only four doors to cover, and we outnumber her two to one."

"Do we wait for her to come out on her own?" Ali asked. "Or do we try to bring her out?"

"Let's try to maintain the element of surprise," Gil said. "I'll call you once I'm in position in the alley. Then as far as I'm concerned, I think we should sit tight. Ermina came here for one of two reasons—to pick something up or to drop something off. I doubt she's planning on staying here all night."

Gil had just disappeared from sight behind the end of the building when the security guard reappeared. Knowing he would most likely demand that she leave, Ali grabbed the car keys and shoved them out of sight into the crack between the two front seats. Then she punched her cell phone so it would dial Gil's number.

"Where's your friend?" the rent-a-cop asked.

"A call of nature," Ali said, nodding in the opposite direction from the one where Gil had disappeared.

"He can't do that. This is private property. You need to move your vehicle now. It's blocking the driveway."

"I'm sorry," Ali said. "He took the keys. He'll be back in a minute."

"You don't have a minute," the guard said. "Your presence here is impeding a federal investigation." He leaned toward the window holding an ID wallet. The badge inside said, very clearly, FBI. "Either you leave right now, or I'm placing you under arrest."

"I guess you'll have to arrest me then," Ali told him. "Because I'm not leaving."

"Step out of the vehicle," he said. "Place your hands on your head."

53

After endless hours of utter darkness, when the lights came on overhead, their brilliance exploded in Brenda's head, temporarily blinding her. She heard rather than saw the key turn in the lock. When she could see again, a woman—the woman Brenda knew as Ermina Blaylock—was approaching the chair where Brenda was imprisoned. Her face was screwed up in a strange grimace, as though the stench of the place was beyond bearing.

Brenda had moved far beyond that. She had become so accustomed to the foul odors lingering around her that she could no longer smell anything at all. But then Brenda saw the bottle. Ermina was carrying a bottle of water—a large bottle of water.

"I'll bet you're thirsty," she said, forcing a smile. "I brought you something to drink."

Brenda stared at the bottle. She wanted the water inside it more than she had ever wanted anything in her life. But then she remembered Friday. Or, at least, she remembered parts of Friday, how during lunch she had suddenly begun losing track of who she was and what she was doing.

She wanted the water, yes. But what if Ermina had slipped something into it? In her terribly weakened condition, even a little bit of something extra might be too much. Something that might have induced unconsciousness on Friday might well prove fatal now.

Ermina twisted the cap off the bottle and held it up to Brenda's lips. "Here," she said. "Have a drink."

Brenda leaned back in the chair and closed her eyes. Once again, through the trailing ethers of memory, she heard Uncle Joe's voice. "Choose to live."

Yes, she would die of thirst, but she would not willingly swallow whatever poison Ermina was offering her. She waited. Only when the open end of the bottle touched her lips did she bring her head forward, swinging it from side to side. Ermina had expected compliance, and she was caught unawares. Brenda smacked the bottle with the side of her cheek and sent it flying out of Ermina's hand. It rolled across the floor, spilling precious water as it went. Finally it came to rest against the bottom of a chain-link fence.

"You stupid bitch!" Ermina exclaimed. "Why did you do that?"

She reached out and slapped Brenda's face with an open-handed blow that left Brenda seeing stars, but the pain of it was enough to jar Brenda fully out of her stupor. And even as Ermina readied another blow, Brenda realized that Uncle Joe would have been proud of her. For once in her life Brenda Riley had measured up.

Then suddenly the chair she was imprisoned in was moving. With Brenda still in it, the chair rolled out through the open gate in the chain-link fence, across the tiled floor to yet another door. She sped through the second door and into another interconnected section of the building. There was a car inside. Ermina wheeled Brenda past a tall stack of cardboard boxes and stopped next to the trunk of the car.

Without a word, Ermina opened the trunk. Then, after donning a pair of latex gloves, she reached inside and pulled out a plastic-wrapped package. Using a box cutter, she tore though the packaging and then shook out the contents. Brenda watched as a narrow bedroll unrolled. For some reason it reminded her of an uncoiling snake.

Ermina unzipped the bedroll and then she cut through the tape that had bound Brenda's legs. "Stand up," she said.

Brenda looked down at her feet. After being forced to sit for days on end, her limbs were severely swollen, distended. She understood without being told that if she ever got inside that bedroll, there would be no coming out. And she also understood that there was no point in screaming. She had already tried that once, to no avail. Besides, she didn't have the strength.

"I can't," she said.

"You can and you will," Ermina replied.

She held the opening of the bedroll over Brenda's head and slipped it down. As the thick material shut out the light—as darkness descended again—Brenda tried to struggle against it, but it was no use. She felt herself propelled up and out of the chair, which skittered away from her and banged up against a wall somewhere behind her. She landed hard inside the trunk as her head came to rest against the upright wall at the far end of the trunk. And then, although she struggled hard against it, she heard the zipper closing inevitably, shutting her in.

Brenda tried shouting then, one last time, in the vain hope that someone would hear her, but the down-filling of the bedroll muffled her cries.

She heard the car's motor start. She heard a racket of some kind, like a garage door opening. She felt the car start to move, and then she heard a crash as it stopped moving. Her head smashed hard against something she couldn't see, and then another kind of blackness descended around her and carried her away.

54

Clairemont Mesa Business Park, San Diego, California

Gil heard the guy talking in the background on Ali's phone. For a moment he was torn. Did he abandon his post and go give Ali backup, or did he stay where he was in case Ermina heard the racket out front and made a break for it? Then Gil heard another sound in the background—a garage door rolling open. He turned and sprinted back the way he had come, but he was the better part of a block away.

The grinding sound of a crash—of crunching metal and breaking glass—was immediately followed by a shout of surprise that could have been from someone being hit or hurt.

A car engine revved. More than revved, it roared. There was another horrendous grinding and scraping of metal on metal. Gil made it around the corner in time to see the back of a Cadillac DTS T-boned into the side of the Marquis. The security guard's bicycle had been flung across the street. With its front wheel still spinning, it lay at an odd angle next to the gutter. In the middle of the street, next to the Marquis, lay the fallen security guard.

Gil took it all in as he ran. Then a woman in what looked like a tan tracksuit erupted out of the open garage door. She sped away from Gil with so much distance between them that he knew he'd never catch her. Just then, Ali sprang out of her car. She had to dodge around to keep from stepping on the fallen security guard, but then she caught her balance and ran too. She ran with her head down and her arms pumping; she ran like she meant it.

Gil paused briefly when he reached the security guard. He seemed to be coming around. Leaving the fallen man where he was, Gil pounded after the two fleeing women, who by then had disappeared around the far end of that same set of buildings.

As Gil rounded the corner, they were still far ahead of him, but he could see that Ali was closing the distance. She was a runner who worked at it chasing someone who didn't. Ali didn't shout out a warning that she was a police officer, because she wasn't, so Gil did it for her.

"Stop," he yelled. "Police."

Sirens sounded in the background. Pulsing lights showed that slowing police cars were converging on the area. Gil couldn't be sure if it was the shout or the sirens or neither one, but Ermina seemed to lose heart. She paused for a moment, and that moment was enough. Ali caught up with her.

"On the ground!" she shouted. "Now."

For a few seconds, the two women stood facing one another panting, out of breath, glaring at one another in animal fury. Then, as Gil watched in amazement, Ali Reynolds grabbed Ermina Blaylock by the arm and executed a flawless hip toss.

He caught up with them just then, stumbling to a stop in time to see Ermina land hard on the sidewalk. Her face was bloodied. Ali was astraddle her with one knee in the small of her back.

"I tried to warn you," Ali gasped breathlessly. "I told you to get on the ground!"

Moments later the business park was alive with men and women in windbreakers emblazoned with the letters FBI. Two agents stepped forward. One of them took charge of Ermina. The other one reached for Ali. Exhibiting his own badge, Gil waved him off.

"She's okay," he said. "She's with me, but you'd better go check on your undercover guy. He's down back there in the street. When I came by him, he seemed to be coming around. He's probably wearing a vest, but those are better for stopping bullets than cars, so he might have internal injuries."

One agent led Ermina away, while the other jogged off in the direction Gil had indicated. Once they were gone, Gil helped Ali to her feet.

"I couldn't believe it," Ali said. "The security guard was standing by the window hassling me when Ermina came screaming out of the garage without even glancing in her rearview mirror. I don't know how fast she was going when she hit my car, but it was with enough force that it slammed the driver's side of the Marquis into the guy on the bicycle. I saw him go down and the bicycle go flying, but I didn't stop to check on him. She was getting away."

"I think the guy on the ground is probably okay," Gil said. "But what about you? Are you all right?"

"Still out of breath," she managed. "But okay."

"You're fast," he said admiringly. "It's a good thing you were the one chasing her. She would have left me in the dust. Let's go check on that guard. And I hope you're right about your insurance, because that Mercury you rented is toast!"

The fallen FBI agent still lay on the ground with a group of fellow officers clustered around him. Somewhere in the distance came the shrill wail of an arriving ambulance. As Ali walked toward her car, one of the FBI agents broke away from the group around the injured officer.

"Okay," he said. "Now I want to know who you are and what you're doing here besides screwing up a major bust."

As Gil reached again for his ID packet, Ali leaned inside the open window on the driver's side of her wrecked car, looking for the rental agreement and her purse. Ali, Gil, and the agent all heard the noise at the same time—a muffled thump coming from the trunk of the wrecked Cadillac.

"What the hell is that?" the FBI agent demanded.

Ali was closest to the conjoined vehicles. She darted around the front of her car and arrived at the smashed rear end of the Cadillac just as another thump sounded from inside the crumpled trunk. The rear bumper had been smashed into the body of the vehicle, leaving the trunk lid jammed in place.

Wrenching open the driver's door, Ali reached for the trunk release. She found it at last and pulled it, but nothing happened.

"Hey," the agent called out, "somebody bring me a tire iron or a crowbar. We need to open this thing up."

Thirty seconds of prying later, the trunk lid gave way and opened. While the agents worked to open the trunk, Gil stayed front and center. Once the trunk lid finally sprang open, Gil peered inside at what appeared to be a squirming mass of bedroll—a smelly squirming mass of bedroll. Gil lifted the slithering mass of bedroll out of the trunk and placed it gently on the weedy grass next to the driveway. One of the agents dropped his crowbar and unzipped the zipper, letting a terrible stench loose into the air.

"Thank you," whispered a cracked voice that barely sounded human. "Water, please."

Ali was the one who recognized her.

"Oh, my God!" she exclaimed, falling on her knees beside the badly injured woman. "It's Brenda Riley. I don't believe it. She's alive!"

"Hey," the agent shouted. "Send those medics over here. Order another ambulance for Sinclair. Looks like this one is hurt a lot worse than he is."

55

Sharp Mary Birch Hospital, San Diego, California

A squawking ambulance whisked Brenda Riley away from the scene and took her to the Sharp Mary Birch Hospital ER, which was only minutes away. Ali and Gil rode there in a black Suburban with San Diego FBI Agent in Charge Sam Hollingshead at the wheel. They had transferred the luggage to the Suburban—Gil's single suitcase as well as the three cardboard boxes that still reeked of smoke and leaked trailing bits of sand.

While ER personnel attended to Brenda, Hollingshead commandeered a conference room and herded Ali and Gil inside.

"I don't know if I should thank you or throw the book at you," he said. "You caught Ermina, and from what she did to that poor woman in there, she surely needed catching, but you may have blown the cover off an operation we've been working on for months. The problem is, this is a white-collar crime case with overriding national security issues. Without a proper security clearance, I can't even discuss it with you."

"We know about the UAVs, if that's what you mean," Ali said.

Hollingshead looked at her sharply. "How would you know anything about that?"

Gil reached into his jeans and pulled out the two thumb drives. "From these," he said, placing the drives on the table in front of Hollingshead. "My homicide victim in Grass Valley, Richard Lowensdale, had these hidden in his garage. Ali was able to run the files past one of her computer people. They're the ones who came up with the drone angle."

Ali appreciated that creative bit of understatement. There was no mention of High Noon Enterprises in anything that had been said, and she doubted Sam Hollingshead would be terribly interested or motivated to track down the details. He seemed to be preoccupied with his own concerns.

"All right, then," Hollingshead said, "so you know about that too. We figured Richard was involved in the Blaylocks' drone project. We had court-ordered access to his computers, and we used his own CCTV to maintain surveillance on his house."

"So you know about the cyberstalking?" Ali asked.

"Yes," Hollingshead said, with a dismissive shrug. "As far as I could tell, it was just a harmless hobby. He didn't appear to be doing anything wrong."

Ali did a slow burn at that statement, which said more about SAC Hollingshead than it did about Richard Lowensdale.

"What he did to those poor women may have been legal, but it was most definitely wrong," Ali said.

"Yes," Hollingshead agreed, "I suppose it was, but that didn't concern us. It wasn't part of our investigation. We were convinced that Richard was working for Ermina, but since we haven't been able to find any record of payments, I surmised that perhaps they had some other involvement that overrode any monetary considerations."

"You mean you thought Richard and Mina were involved sexually?" Gil asked.

Hollingshead didn't bother denying it. "Look," he said, "she drove up there last weekend like she usually did every month or so. She went into Lowensdale's house in Grass Valley. She went inside for a while and then she came back out again. Maybe she stayed inside a little longer than she usually did, but we had no idea that she had killed the guy while she was there."

"So you had surveillance in place, but you didn't actually follow her?"

"The CCTV at Lowensdale's house went on the fritz while she was there."

"The video feed ended," Gil offered.

"Correct."

"What about her car? Did you attempt to follow it?" Ali asked.

"We didn't need to," Hollingshead said. "We had a GPS bug on her car. We know where she went and when right up until tonight when she ditched the car and gave us the slip."

"So you didn't know she had picked up Brenda Riley?" Ali asked.

"From what we can tell, Ermina drove to Brenda's mother's place on P Street in Sacramento. We're assuming that's when she met up with Brenda, but we don't know positively."

"But you knew she drove to the Scotts Flat Reservoir?" Gil asked.

"Yes, and we wondered about it after the fact, but she was only there for a few minutes, then she headed home. Since the spot didn't appear to have any bearing on our case, we just let it go."

"What about Ermina's background?" Ali asked. "Did you have any idea about what she's suspected of doing to her adoptive father in Missouri?"

Hollingshead paused for a moment, then he nodded. "Yes," he said. "One of our agents spoke to Detective Laughlin months ago. He sounded like an old guy all hung up on a long closed case. We learned about Lowensdale's death sometime yesterday, but you need to understand, there was nothing we could do about it. Our hands were tied. If we had acted on any of that information prematurely, we might have risked jeopardizing the mission."

"Yes," Ali said, "but if you had, maybe Mark Blaylock wouldn't be dead right now."

"He was part of this too, you know," Hollingshead said. "Ermina didn't do all of it on her own."

"You *think* he was part of it," Ali pointed out. "It's also possible that he was innocent—innocent and dead, an outcome you might have prevented."

"I agree," Hollingshead said. "It's an unfortunate outcome."

"Especially unfortunate for Mr. Blaylock," Ali insisted.

Hollingshead seemed to be running out of patience. "Look, Ms. Reynolds," he said placatingly, "I understand that you're angry. You have every right to be. At least two people are dead who probably shouldn't be, and your friend Brenda has suffered grievous harm, but we need to keep a lid on this. We *must* keep a lid on it.

"Our intelligence tells us that the drone shipment is due to be picked up sometime tomorrow. We're attaching bugs to each of those individual boxes. We're going to let them be picked up and delivered and delivered without incident. We already know that the middleman is a guy named Enrique Gallegos who has been on the FBI's watch list and also the DEA's for a very long time. Our intention is to take down the end users—whoever they are and wherever they might be.

"So don't expect to read about this in the paper tomorrow morning, because it turns out nothing at all happened at the business park tonight, understand? Your damaged car has been hauled away, and so has hers. The Rutherford garage bay has been cleaned up and buttoned up. Hertz is in the process of delivering a replacement vehicle to you here, no questions asked."

"Wait a minute," Gil said. "You're whitewashing this?"

"For the time being."

"You can't do that. I'm investigating a homicide that happened on my watch in Grass Valley. Detective Moreno down in Imperial County has one too. In both of those cases, the presumed doer is Ermina Blaylock, and I can assure you that we aren't going to shut up and go away just because you said so."

"And what about Brenda?" Ali demanded. "She came within inches of dying at Ermina Blaylock's hands. And then there's your own officer. She assaulted him with a moving vehicle, which counts as a deadly weapon in my book. You expect us to keep a lid on all that? Are you nuts?"

"Not nuts," Hollingshead countered, "but I am in charge. For right now, we've taken Ermina into custody. We intend to hold her at least until the drone delivery takes place. Longer if possible."

"Charged with what?" Gil asked.

"Falsifying a federal document. She may lawyer up, but there's also a chance she'll talk to us."

"This isn't my first day of being a cop," Gil said. "What talking to you really means is that you're going to try to make a deal with her, and your best bargaining chips will be reducing the charges against her—our charges, my charges."

"I'm not saying yes, and I'm not saying no," Hollingshead said.

"Which turn out to be standard weasel words for yes," Ali said.

Hollingshead said nothing in reply.

"And what will happen to the UAVs?"

"We'll be following the shipment. We'll also be following the money."

"With the same kind of GPS efficiency you demonstrated in following Ermina's car?" Ali asked without trying to disguise her sarcasm.

"Look, if we had known how dangerous she was—"

"I'm not buying that," Ali said. "You did know. Someone from your agency had already spoken to Detective Laughlin. You endangered any number of lives in order to protect your 'mission,' and now you're going to try to cover it up. Good luck with that. You underestimated Ermina Blaylock, and I suspect you're underestimating Gil and me too. When this is all over, I suggest you send yourself back to the academy for some remedial classes in fatal errors—you know, those ten mistakes cops make that end up getting them killed? Failure to call for backup is one of the biggies, but what if the agent in charge fails to call for backup? What then?

"You're all focused on your fancy electronic gizmos. Great, but what about your people? What about leaving Agent Sinclair on the street without any kind of backup? The only backup he had was Gil Morris and Ali Reynolds. If it hadn't been for us, Ermina might have gotten away and claimed another victim in the process."

With that, Ali pushed back her chair and stood up. "Now, if you'll excuse me, I have a phone call to make. There's a woman in Sacramento who needs to know that her supposedly dead daughter isn't dead!"

Ali stalked out of the conference room with Gil on her heels. "Remind me not to make you mad," he said.

"He deserved it," Ali replied.

Out in the lobby, a guy wearing a yellow Hertz shirt flagged Ali down and handed her a new rental agreement and a new set of keys.

"It's just like the one you had before," he said. "Another Marquis. It's parked in a loading zone just outside the hospital entrance. There's an FBI agent waiting beside the door. He told me to tell you your property has already been loaded."

"In other words, here's our hat, what's our hurry," Ali said.

Taking the keys, she walked back to the ER admitting desk. "Can you tell me anything about Ms. Riley?" Ali asked. "I'm about to call her mother."

"You're not a relative?"

"No. I'm a friend."

"Then I'm not authorized . . ."

Ali walked away without waiting for the usual speech about patient confidentiality. The whole thing seemed wrong somehow. It was due to Ali and Gil's efforts that Brenda Riley was even alive, not to mention in a hospital with a possibility of surviving. Still, by federal mandate, her rescuers weren't allowed to know anything about her condition.

"Let's go," she said.

"Where?" Gil asked. "It's almost midnight."

"I don't care how late it is," Ali said. "I've got a two-bedroom apartment waiting for me in Laguna Beach and I'm going there. I'll make my phone calls along the way. Now, are you coming along or are you staying here?"

"Oh, I'm coming along all right," Gil said, dropping into step beside her. "I just used up all my available credit buying household goods at Target. You dragged me down here where I have no car, no place to stay, no money, and no way to get back home. In other words, if I don't go with you, I'm pretty much screwed."

"Not so much," Ali said. "You remember all that money Sam Hollingshead was just saying he couldn't find? Ermina couldn't find it either. You gave Hollingshead those two thumb drives, and he was ecstatic. He's not going to give a damn about that missing money. There's no one left to look for it."

"But—"

Ali stopped him with an upraised hand. "We've both just had a lesson in the FBI's high cost of doing business," she observed. "If somebody happens to die here and there along the way, so what?

Let's not 'endanger' the precious mission. And if Hollingshead has to make a plea deal in a homicide or two in order to nail their man or woman, that's no big deal either, right? What if Richard Lowensdale's missing money is part of the same thing—the high cost of their doing business? It's a lot like my wrecked car. Never happened. No questions asked. It would serve them right."

Gil didn't know her well enough to be able to tell if she was joking or not, but he assumed she was.

When they got outside, the agent they'd been told about was indeed keeping a discreet eye on Ali's newly rented Marquis. He moved away when they approached the vehicle and Ali used a button on the key fob to unlock the door.

They stopped on opposite sides of the car, looking at each other over the top of it. "Did anyone ever tell you you're a pushy broad?" Gil asked. "Smart but very pushy."

She grinned back at him. "Believe me, Detective Morris, you're not the first to tell me that, and you won't be the last."

"By the way," he added, "just for the record. That was one sweet hip toss."

"It's my specialty," she said. "Best thing I ever learned at the Arizona Police Academy."

56

Laguna Beach, California

When they arrived at Velma's condominium building at two o'clock in the morning, it seemed to Ali that the doorman leered at them a little as he let them into the building. She didn't bother explaining to him that their being together didn't mean they *were* together. If the doorman had a dirty mind, it was none of Ali's business.

Once in the unit, they took one cursory look at the nighttime ocean view from the balcony, then they disappeared into their separate bedrooms. Ali fell asleep immediately. The next morning she was up bright and early. She went for a morning stroll on the beach with Maddy Watkins and the three dogs. Two hours later, she was drinking coffee and typing an e-mail to B. when Gil finally made his tardy appearance.

He wandered over to the kitchen counter and poured himself a cup of coffee.

"There are bagels on the counter and cream cheese in the fridge," she said. "Help yourself."

Gil found what looked like a bread knife in a utility drawer.

When he sliced a sesame bagel in half, he was amazed at how much sharper the knife was than the sole remaining one in his knife block at home. Something else to put on the list for his next household goods extravaganza.

He put the sliced bagel in the toaster and pushed down the button. "How's your friend this morning?" he asked.

It had taken them close to an hour and a half to drive to Laguna Beach from the hospital in San Diego. They'd done a lot of talking on the way. In the process Ali had told Gil about her dying friend, Velma Trimble.

Ali shook her head. "Not well. I went for a walk on the beach this morning with Maddy and the dogs. She said Velma's not doing well at all, and she seems anxious about my getting the check she gave me deposited. She's evidently concerned that there might be some kind of blowback from her son about her making that donation. She wants to be certain all the t's are crossed and i's dotted."

"You'd better handle that today, then," he said. He sat down across from her and took a sip of his coffee. "Have you heard from Camilla Gastellum?"

Ali nodded. "Valerie, her other daughter, and her husband drove all night. The three of them got to the hospital in San Diego this morning about eight. Brenda is out of the ICU. Her condition has been upgraded from critical to serious. They're treating her for dehydration. There's some concern about blood clotting issues as well. She was evidently left sitting in that chair for so long that there's concern about her developing DVTs."

"What's that?"

"Deep vein thrombosis from sitting for long periods of time. Blood clots that form in your legs can break loose and travel to the heart or lung or brain."

"I'm glad her family is there," Gil said. "I'll need to talk to

Brenda once she gets back north. It sounds like the actual kidnapping took place in Sacramento, but that all needs to be sorted out. That was my chief on the phone, by the way, calling to give me hell."

Ali had heard Gil's cell phone ringing earlier. That was evidently what had propelled him out of bed.

He retrieved his toasted bagel, put it on a plate, and brought that, a butter knife, and a container of cream cheese to the table.

"Chief Jackman told me yesterday that he wanted me to take comp time to make up for all the overtime, but it turns out he didn't mean I should take it now. And the fact that you and I managed to track down Richard Lowensdale's killer on our own time and that we saved Brenda Riley's life in the process barely registers in his little bean-counting skull. I told him I'll be in tomorrow. With that in mind, I guess I'd better rent a car someplace and head north."

"No," Ali said.

"What do you mean no?"

"As you pointed out last night, I'm the one who got you down here and I'm prepared to get you back. I've called You-Go. They'll have yesterday's CJ at John Wayne Airport, KSNA as it's known in aviation circles, at one p.m. You should be back in Grass Valley, KGOO, by about two thirty."

"You can't do that," he said. "I can't *let* you do that. It's too expensive."

"You can't stop me because it's already done. Here's your tail number. They asked about catering. I told them to order you a chicken salad. Hope that's okay."

"But—"

"No buts," Ali said. "I owe you, Gil. Brenda's alive. If it hadn't been for you, she probably wouldn't be."

"All right," he said. After a moment's reflection he took the piece of paper with the tail number on it and slipped it into his pocket. "But I won't be able to pay you back anytime soon. I did a lot of thinking about the money situation last night," he said. "I'm not going to keep it."

Ali looked at him and smiled. "I never thought you would," she said. "You're not that kind of guy."

He raised his coffee cup. "You aren't either."

By noon, the kitchen was back in order. They were packed and ready to leave. "I need to stop by and see Velma one last time," Ali told him.

"You do that," Gil said. "I'll take the bags downstairs and wait for you in the lobby."

As soon as Ali rang the doorbell on the penthouse floor, there was the expected response—frantic barking from the three dogs, followed by a stern "Quiet," followed by "Get on your rug." When Maddy Watkins opened the door, the room was perfectly quiet.

"I'm not sure she's awake," Maddy said.

"Who is it?" Velma asked from her hospital bed by the window.

"It's Ali," Maddy replied. "Ali Reynolds."

"I'm awake," Velma said. "Send her over."

Ali was surprised by the difference even a single day had made. Maddy was right. Velma was losing ground, physically if not mentally.

"Have you been to the bank yet?" Velma wanted to know.

"Not yet," Ali said. "I'm on my way to the airport. I'll probably see a bank branch somewhere along the way."

"Good," Velma said. "I want you to have that money. Actually, I want your scholarship kids to have the money. If I put it as a bequest in my will, my son might figure out a way to keep it from happening. I love him, you see. I just don't trust him."

Ali went over to Velma's bed and gathered Velma's rail-thin

hand in her own. "I have to go now," Ali said, leaning over to kiss Velma's weathered cheek.

"I do too," Velma said with a slight smile. "Don't bother coming to the funeral," she added. "It's going to be what my son wants, not what I want, but it won't make a bit of difference to me. Having you here to drink Maddiccinos with Maddy and me was a lot more my speed. Goodbye, Ali. Thanks for everything."

Blinking back tears, Ali paused long enough to hug Maddy on her way out. "I'm glad you're here," she said.

Maddy nodded. "So am I," she said.

The day after a bank holiday was a busy one at the Bank of America branch Ali found on their way to the airport. Ali was halfway through the teller line waiting to deposit Velma's check when her cell phone rang. It was Chris.

"Hey, Grandma," her son said. "If you want to see your grandkids make their grand entrance, you'd better head home. We're on our way to the hospital in Flagstaff right now. Dr. Dixon said she'll meet us there."

"Did you say right now?" Ali asked.

"I said right now."

"Okay," Ali said. "I'll do my best."

Her next call was to operations at You-Go. "Do you have another CJ available this afternoon?"

"From where to where?"

"The first one is due to go from John Wayne to Grass Valley. I'd like to take that one for myself and fly from KSNA to Flagstaff, Arizona. When the second aircraft arrives, that one can take Detective Morris from KSNA back to KGOO in Grass Valley."

"The soonest I could have another aircraft at John Wayne is two thirty," the operations clerk said. "That's an hour and a half after Mr. Morris's scheduled departure. Are you sure that's all right with him?"

"It'll be fine," Ali said. "He doesn't care what time he gets home as long as it's today. My son and daughter-in-law are on their way to a hospital. They're about to have twins, and I want to be there."

"Your aircraft is about twenty minutes out," the young woman said. "I'll advise your pilot of the change in plans and that you need a very short turnaround. What about catering?"

"We'll both have chicken salad."

Gil was waiting patiently in the car when Ali emerged from the bank.

"It seems there's been a slight change in plans," Ali told him. "I'm going home to Arizona in your plane, and they're sending another one for you."

Gil looked at her anxiously. "I hope it's not some kind of emergency."

"It not an emergency of any kind. I'm about to become a grandmother," Ali said with a smile. "And I wouldn't miss it for the world."

J. A. Jance
Trial By Fire

When a brand-new housing estate goes up in flames,
everyone hopes that the unfinished, unoccupied homes
will yield no victims. But there is one. Barely alive and
disfigured beyond recognition, a woman is found amid
the wreckage.

When the victim eventually awakes from a medically-
induced coma, she has no idea who she is or where she
came from. Her only hope is to find the people who
saved her life - and the people who tried to kill her . . .

In her new role as media relations consultant with the
Yavapai County Police Department, Ali Reynolds is
called upon to grant the dying woman's final wishes. But
when she is diagnosed with a fast spreading terminal
cancer, the quest to discover the woman's identity takes
on an even greater urgency.

ISBN 978-1-84739-405-7

J. A. Jance
Cruel Intent

Ali Reynolds doesn't go looking for trouble - but trouble
comes looking for her when the battered, bloodstained
body of Morgan Forester is discovered by her twin
daughters. For the prime suspect, Morgan's husband, is
the contractor Ali has hired to help re-design her home.
Bryan Forester swears he had nothing to do with the
killing - but no one, including Ali's boyfriend, Detective
Dave Holman, believes him.

Was Morgan's death the result of a domestic dispute that
turned violent - or is her murder part of something far
more sinister? In her determination to prove Bryan's
innocence, Ali finds herself drawn into a terrifying web
of deceit that could cost her her life.

ISBN 978-1-84739-404-0

J. A. Jance
Hand of Evil

His hand trapped in the door of a speeding car, a man
struggles to remain upright as he's dragged along a
deserted stretch of mountain road. It's the perfect place
to drive a man to his grave - literally. Starting with a
crime so gruesome even prowling coyotes keep their
distance, a killer begins crisscrossing the southern states
on a spree of grisly murders.

A hundred miles away, Ali Reynolds is grieving. The
newscasting job she once delighted in is gone and so is
the philandering husband she loved and thought she
knew. When a member of the family who gave Ali a
generous scholarship for her education decades earlier
suddenly requests a meeting, Ali wonders what it can
mean. But before she can satisfy her curiosity, she
receives another startling call: a friend's teenage
daughter has disappeared. Ali offers to help but, in
doing so, she unknowingly begins a quest that will
reveal a deadly ring of secrets, at the centre of which
stand two undiscriminating killers.

ISBN 978-1-84739-048-6

This book and other **J.A. Jance** titles are available from your local bookshop or can be ordered direct from the publisher.

978-1-84739-405-7	Trial By Fire	£6.99
978-1-84739-404-0	Cruel Intent	£6.99
978-1-84739-048-6	Hand of Evil	£6.99
978-1-84739-047-9	Web of Evil	£6.99

Free post and packing within the UK
Overseas customers please add £2 per paperback
Telephone Simon & Schuster Cash Sales at Bookpost
on 01624 677237 with your credit or debit card number
or send a cheque payable to Simon & Schuster Cash Sales to
PO Box 29, Douglas Isle of Man, IM99 1BQ
Fax: 01624 670923
E-mail: bookshop@enterprise.net
www.bookpost.co.uk

Please allow 14 days for delivery. Prices and availability are subject to change without notice.